A DEATH IN TUSCANY

Michele Giuttari

Translated by Howard Curtis

WINDSOR

PARAGON

First published in UK 2008
by Abacus
This Large Print edition published 2008
by BBC Audiobooks Ltd
by arrangement with
Little, Brown Book Group

Hardcover ISBN: 978 1 405 64989 6
Softcover   ISBN: 978 1 405 64990 2

British Library Cataloguing in Publication Data available

Printed and bound in Great Britain by
CPI Antony Rowe, Chippenham, Wiltshire

To Christa

Friendship is preferable to honours.
It is better to be loved than honoured.

Aristotle

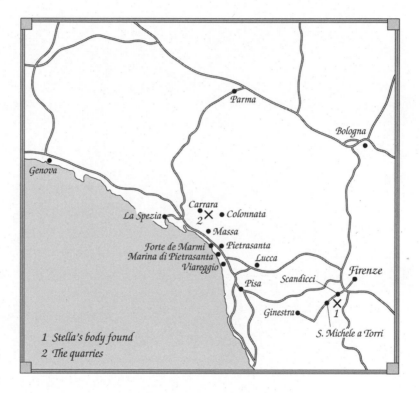

Parma

Bologna

Genova

Carrara
Colonnata
La Spezia
2
Massa
Forte de Marmi
Pietrasanta
Marina di Pietrasanta
Lucca
Viareggio
Firenze
Scandicci
Pisa
Ginestra
1
S. Michele a Torri

1 Stella's body found
2 The quarries

1

Florence, 2001

The girl, little more than a child, was found on the edge of a wood on the road above Scandicci, scantily dressed, without papers, and dying of an overdose, at dawn on Sunday 29 July, and was taken to the Ospedale Nuovo. But it wasn't until almost a week later that Chief Superintendent Michele Ferrara, head of the Florence *Squadra Mobile*, really became involved with the case.

Friday 3 August.

He was already in a bad mood when he set foot in the office. The weather was hot and muggy, even though it was only eight in the morning. Chief Inspector Violante's report on the girl's death was in his in-tray: one of the many documents that awaited his routine examination at the beginning of every day, arranged with almost maniacal care by his secretary, Sergeant Fanti, who always got in at least half an hour before he did.

It wasn't somewhere in the middle of the pile, though. It had been placed right on the top.

And Fanti wasn't the kind of person to be impressed by the death of yet another junkie.

Ferrara had picked up his pen as soon as he sat down: an automatic gesture after so many years of deskwork. Now he replaced it and took out a cigar. His morning cigar and coffee both helped to revive brain cells undermined by time and stress.

He lit his cigar without even looking at it as he

read Violante's report.

He didn't like what he read.

When, the previous Sunday, he had seen the first report from the officer on duty at the hospital, he had automatically pigeonholed the case as yet another tragedy after a night at the disco, almost a commonplace event on Saturdays in the global village. The city and the surrounding hills were awash with drugs and alcohol, like the River Arno in full spate, and like the River Arno they threatened to overflow, but with even more tragic consequences than those of the flood of 1966.

Ferrara had been feeling his age for some time. The world, it seemed to him, was getting worse rather than better, and he often found himself thinking that 'things weren't the way they used to be', just like his father and presumably his grandfather before him. He had delegated the investigation—a perfectly routine one—to Chief Inspector Violante and dismissed the case from his mind. Now it came back to hit him like a slap in the face, and he didn't really know why.

Because she was dead?

That happens to junkies.

Because her age was estimated as being between thirteen and sixteen and yet, despite being so young, she had managed to shoot a lethal dose of heroin into her body?

Perhaps.

Or because, after nearly a week, they still didn't know who she was? A small detail, a mere speck, which might turn out troublesome, like a mote in the eye of justice.

But when it came down to it, if there was anything wrong with the investigation, the fault

2

was his.

*   *   *

'Fanti!' he called.

Between his office and his secretary's, the door was always open.

Sergeant Fanti had just turned forty. He was more than six feet tall and terrifyingly thin, with hollow cheeks, blue eyes and short, wiry blond hair. He had lived in his home town of Trento until the day—almost twenty years ago—when he had joined the police. Florence had been his very first posting, and here he had stayed. He had immediately become noted for his meticulousness, his discretion, and his skill at research, whether in the records or on the internet.

Such was his passion for computers, he had even updated the office's facilities at his own expense. When Ferrara had taken up his post, he had found the new equipment already assigned by his predecessors to the secretary's office and he had okayed that, although he himself occasionally made use of it when he had some particularly sensitive information to track down.

'Yes, chief?' Fanti replied, materialising in front of Ferrara's desk almost instantaneously, as usual.

Ferrara often wondered if the man spent his time with his ear against the wall, ready to burst in as soon as he had any inkling that his chief was about to summon him. Of course if he'd been doing that, he wouldn't have had time to perform the thousand tasks around the office with the efficiency, the meticulous precision, of which he was so proud. It was by far the tidiest, best

3

functioning office in the whole of Florence Police Headquarters. In the end, Ferrara had come to the conclusion that Fanti had a sixth sense.

'Well?' he asked without preamble.

The sergeant shrugged. It wasn't his job to draw conclusions or make judgements. But it was clear from the look on his face that he'd been expecting exactly this reaction from his boss, and that it didn't surprise him that Ferrara hadn't even opened the other files. Or that the cigar had been left in the ashtray to go out by itself.

'A young girl, maybe no more than a child,' Ferrara said, lowering his voice as if he were thinking aloud rather than addressing his subordinate—although it was also useful to have him to think aloud to—'maybe no more than a child, right? It's hard to say these days, they grow up so quickly . . . They already have breasts when they're eleven or twelve, and go around with their navels showing. Are they trying to look like whores, or are the whores trying to look like schoolgirls? A paedophile culture, that's what we're living in, Fanti. And then everyone complains when . . . But what can you do? Children today want to look like adults, and adults want to stay children forever, no one wants to grow up, no one wants to grow old, they all think they can stay in an eternal kindergarten without rules or restrictions, and not worry about time passing. Maybe I'm angry because I feel the weight of my years, every single one of them and maybe a few more. But in my day, damn it, this girl would have been a child! She would have been playing with her dolls, not with syringes! What kind of world is this? What kind of shitty world? And isn't there anyone looking for her? In the whole of Florence, isn't there a mother with a missing daughter, an uncle who's lost his niece, a tourist desperate to find his child?'

'Right, chief,' Fanti said, not knowing how to respond to this outburst.

'And what about us? What have we done to identify her? What has Violante done? Has he been twiddling his thumbs? Taking his children to Rimini?'

'Chief Inspector Violante's children are grown up and can look after themselves. With all due respect, I don't think they need their father to take them to the seaside any more. And I'm sure the chief inspector hasn't been deliberately wasting time. We used to think he was a shirker, but he isn't. I think you yourself discovered that during the Ricciardi case, didn't you?'

Good old Sergeant Fanti—the voice of conscience.

Ferrara took a deep breath, then lowered his head and stared down at his desk. 'Send for him. But first bring me the complete file. Then, after Violante, I want Rizzo in here. I don't like this case at all. What are we supposed to do? Bury this girl without even finding out her name?'

'Superintendent Rizzo is on holiday, chief.'

Of course. He remembered now that at the beginning of the week Superintendent Rizzo, to all intents and purposes his deputy, had come to say goodbye before leaving for two weeks to visit his relatives in Sicily. Lucky him.

'Who's on duty?'

'Superintendent Ascalchi.'

A Roman, who knew Florence as well as Ferrara

knew Asia Minor!

'Oh, great! Well, what can we do? Send for him. Then find out from the Prosecutor's Department what time the autopsy is scheduled for and who it's been assigned to. Whoever that person is, I want to speak to him as soon as possible.'

'Of course, chief,' Fanti replied, and went back to his office.

*　　　*　　　*

Like Rizzo, Ferrara was a Sicilian. He had been planning a journey to Sicily for months, but each time he'd had to postpone it.

While he was waiting, he phoned his wife Petra, to tell her he wouldn't be home for lunch. He didn't tell her why, there was no need. It was always like this. Even in summer. Or rather, especially in summer, when Ferrara, short-staffed because of his men's holidays, was invariably forced to give up his own.

Not that he minded: he was used to it. But he felt sorry for his wife, who insisted on staying with him all through these stifling months when the sun beat down mercilessly on Florence, the city of excess. But whenever he told her they wouldn't be going away, she would greet the announcement with a smile as predictable as the infernal heat and say that she wouldn't have been able to leave home for long anyway, because there'd be no one to water her beloved plants. He would always agree with her. They both knew this was a convenient fiction, because the terrace was equipped with a state-of-the-art irrigation system to ensure that their beautiful roof garden was always

6

properly tended. But that was all right. It made them equal.

'All right, Michele, but whatever you do, don't go into the office tomorrow and make us miss our weekend at Massimo's, as usual. You promised him this time!'

'Don't worry, even if the sky falls, we'll be on that autostrada tomorrow morning before the tailbacks start.'

'I'll take your word for it, and I won't forgive you if—'

'So your dear Massimo takes precedence over everything, does he?'

'*Dein lieber* Massimo, you mean,' Petra replied. In spite of the many years she'd lived in Italy, she sometimes broke into a few words of her native language. It happened when she was tired, emotional or excited, but also when she wanted, however unconsciously, to underline the superiority of German precision over Italian vagueness.

'*Our* Massimo, shall we agree on that?' Ferrara said. 'See you later!' He had just seen Fanti coming in with the file on the girl.

*   *   *

Everything was in the file, starting with the record of the girl's admission to hospital, and the report by the paramedics who, alerted by an anonymous caller, had driven up the hill road leading from Scandicci to Montespertoli until they had found the girl, unconscious and barely able to breathe. They had tried to revive her, without success, and had then taken her to the nearest hospital.

7

The subsequent reports by Inspector Violante were detailed and irreproachable. He had examined all the missing persons reports from that period, but none of the descriptions matched. He had also checked the latest bulletin from the Ministry, but again without success. He had even gone on the internet and checked the website of a well-researched TV programme called *Has Anyone Seen Them?* which was often consulted by the police in relation to missing persons cases.

There followed copies of the telegrams, marked *Priority*, which Violante had sent to other police forces, with a summary of the case and a description of the girl, appealing for help in identifying her.

Attached to the report was a photo he had sent other forces by email. It had been taken in hospital using a digital camera, with the permission of the doctors. Given the conditions in which it was taken, the quality left something to be desired, but behind that pale, pained expression, it wasn't difficult to imagine the girl in all her radiant beauty. The features were regular, framed by soft ash-blonde hair, and the lips, even though bloodless in the photo, were full. The eyes were closed, but Ferrara—who for some reason thought they must be green—could imagine them full of life.

As was to be expected, Violante had followed the correct procedure to the letter. But the girl, who had clung on to life while they followed up various inconclusive leads, had died without either the comfort of relatives at her sickbed or the dignity of a record that at least restored her name to her.

8

Cardiac and circulatory failure following acute heroin poisoning was how the consultant in charge of the intensive care unit, Professor Ludovico d'Incisa, concluded his report.

RIP and amen.

*   *   *

'Come in!'

Nothing happened.

'COME IN!' Ferrara screamed a second time in response to the discreet knocks on his door. In the meantime, Fanti had run to open it, and Chief Inspector Violante, a grey man—grey hair, grey clothes, grey demeanour—who was deaf in one ear, came in and took up his position in front of Ferrara's desk.

Ferrara waved away the cloud of pale blue smoke from his second cigar, which he had just lit, and indicated the two armchairs for visitors.

'Choose whichever you want, but for God's sake sit down.'

Violante did as he was told, but perched on the edge of the seat, in an uncomfortable position. He was visibly nervous, as if expecting to be reprimanded.

'About this child . . . The one who died of a drug overdose . . . Where are we with that?'

'Nowhere really. Apart from the victim—did you say child, chief?'

'Why? Would you call her a woman?'

Violante's only response was to shrug his shoulders.

'I'm talking about the victim in the report I found on my desk. What has your investigation

9

come up with?'

'Nothing in particular, chief. Time to close the file, I think . . .'

'I'll decide that, if you don't mind,' Ferrara replied. He didn't like to hear that tone of fatalistic resignation from one of his men.

Violante seemed not to understand. 'Of course, chief. But did you read the whole file?' He could see that Ferrara had it in front of him.

'Obviously. I didn't send for it just to give it an airing.'

Why was Ferrara so irritable? Violante wondered. Why was he treating him like this? He'd done his job, and he'd done it well.

'You'll have seen that we did everything we possibly could. I dealt with it personally and didn't neglect anything. But in the meantime, the girl died . . .' He shrugged his shoulders by way of conclusion.

'And yet we don't even know who she is! After nearly a week!'

Violante still did not understand.

Considering everything they had on their plates at the moment, especially with a reduced workforce, the death of a junkie wasn't exactly a priority. His many years' experience had made him cynical, and he was convinced that a girl who wasn't even missed by her family didn't really matter that much to anyone, so he was surprised by Ferrara's sudden insistence. But he also had to admit that he respected it. It was as if there was still room for a glimmer of humanity in their work: something he'd stopped believing in since he'd started counting the days until his retirement.

10

'A week isn't so long, chief. In fact, it's quite normal. If no one comes forward and the subject has no papers or anything else that makes identification possible, you know as well as I do that it can take months, and sometimes we get nowhere.'

It was true, and Ferrara wondered again why it was that he had reacted so impulsively. He was usually cautious, usually thought long and hard before blowing up. This death might have its curious aspects, but it was hardly unusual in a modern city. And Florence was no different from any other modern city in this respect.

Something about the case, though, didn't feel right. What was it? Everything, he thought, fishing out the victim's photo and taking another look at it: the pale face, the closed eyes, the tense, tormented features, heartbreaking in their still-childlike beauty.

Everything and nothing, as often happens. But he was pigheaded. If his instinct told him something was wrong, then he had to see it through to the end. Without thinking too much, at least for the moment.

'You saw her,' he said. 'How old do you think she was?'

'I'm hoping the autopsy will tell us for certain. Not very old, I'd say.'

'Old enough to be a junkie?'

'Are you asking me, chief? What do I know about kids today? I didn't understand my own children twenty years ago . . . All I know is that she died from acute heroin poisoning. That's what's written on the medical certificate. A classic overdose—all too common, unfortunately.'

11

'Yes,' Ferrara admitted. 'You may be right. Maybe that's the way it was. Just one more statistic for the new millennium. But I don't like it. Do you remember how we used to feel when we went to school and we hadn't done our homework? That's how I feel now. I'm not criticising your work in any way. But you've been following the case from the start. What are your impressions?'

'For what it's worth, I think the girl was almost certainly an illegal immigrant, that's why no one has come forward.'

Ferrara nodded. Although it had taken Violante to say it openly, the thought had been lurking at the back of his mind.

An illegal immigrant without a family: he refused to believe that her parents hadn't come forward simply because they were afraid of being deported. Besides, a young immigrant doesn't have the time or the inclination or the money to buy drugs. It was much more likely that she was a victim of the international traffic in human beings, which was reaching staggering proportions: the number of children who disappeared each year throughout the world and ended up in the clutches of unscrupulous traffickers was horrifying.

'From Eastern Europe . . .' he said, looking at the photo again.

'That's what I thought.'

'Anything else?'

Violante hesitated.

'Well?'

'Nothing I can put my finger on. Just an impression . . . But, all things considered, it doesn't matter, believe me.'

'What do you mean, "all things considered"?'

'You know what I mean. An illegal immigrant
. . .' Violante replied with the air of resigned
indifference people use to talk about subjects
they'd prefer to sweep under the carpet.

Yes, he knew what Violante meant.

An unidentified illegal immigrant who'd died of
a drug overdose was like a rubbish bag ready to be
collected and placed in the appropriate pile: on
one side those who matter and are talked about in
the press and on TV, and on the other all the rest,
whose records no one will ever consult. In other
words, this was a case to be concluded without any
fuss and without causing the Commissioner any
needless worry—because, as everyone knew, he
had plenty of other things on his plate.

That was the explanation for Violante's
resigned attitude.

'No,' Ferrara replied, calmly, without jumping
down his throat again. 'This time I don't know.
Tell me your impressions and let me draw my own
conclusions, okay?'

'Okay, chief, but the thing is . . . well . . . I don't
really know. It's the hospital. There's something
strange going on there.'

'What do you mean?'

'It's as if . . . as if once they found out no one
was coming forward, they just dropped her. I
mean, as if they didn't really take care of her. And
now that she's dead, she's become a nuisance, and
they're in a hurry to have done with her . . . like
they wanted to get rid of her as quickly as possible,
you know what I mean?'

'Yes, I think I'm starting to . . .'

'Since she died, they've hurried everything up.
Yesterday my colleague on duty at the hospital

13

even phoned to ask me if I could finish my report as soon as possible. As if we had nothing else to do, as if I'm bone idle.'

'Did he tell you why?'

'He says the consultant asked him. But it seems as if even the Prosecutor's Department wants to close the case as soon as possible.'

Why, for God's sake? And why was the consultant in such a hurry?

'Do you think maybe they could have saved her but made a mistake?'

'Who knows? I'm not a medical expert. But I think something strange is going on. Maybe it's just because it's August, everyone wants to get off on holiday, they're overworked, they need the beds, the case was hopeless . . .'

'Especially if she was an illegal immigrant,' Ferrara said, and realised he was getting angry again. 'If there's the slightest suspicion of malpractice we're not going to let them get away with it, okay? Do you have the medical records?'

'No—I didn't think . . .'

'What?'

'I didn't think there was any point . . . and besides, we'd need a special warrant from the deputy prosecutor who's dealing with the investigation.'

'Which deputy prosecutor is that?'

'Anna Giulietti.'

Excellent, Ferrara thought. He'd developed a good professional relationship with her during the recent Ricciardi case, and they had come out of it firm friends. He'd have to have a chat with her as soon as he could.

'Put in a request for the warrant immediately,

14

Violante.'

'All right, chief.'

'We haven't finished with this case yet. I want you to carry on. How many men do you have on it?'

'What?'

Ferrara repeated the question, more loudly.

'Not many, chief. We're short-staffed.' Violante's tone was one of complaint, but there was a gleam of life in his eyes.

'Fanti!' Ferrara called. Before the sergeant had even come in, he asked, 'Is Sergi on holiday, too?'

'No, chief,' Fanti replied from the other room.

'I want him to work with Violante, as of now. And put as many men at their disposal as you can, okay?'

'Of course, chief,' Fanti replied as soon as he appeared, before vanishing again.

'Here,' Ferrara said, handing Violante the report. 'It needs changing.'

'How?'

'For cause of death, cross out "overdose". For the moment, assume it's homicide caused by persons unknown through the administration of narcotic substances, either of bad quality or in an excessive dose.'

'Okay, chief, I'll get on it straightaway.'

Violante left the room with a new spring in his step.

2

'And what about you? When are you going on holiday?'

'Already been,' Superintendent Ascalchi replied. He had come in immediately after Violante had gone out.

And indeed he had a handsome tan. Well, a tan at least, Ferrara corrected himself. Short, stocky, with a slightly crooked nose and an asymmetrical chin, he could hardly be described as handsome.

He had been on holiday in July, and Ferrara hadn't even noticed—that was how much he valued him! But maybe it wasn't his fault. He tended to rely on those of his men who were of proven experience, whereas Ascalchi, who had only been in Florence for just over a year, wasn't yet at ease here, however well he concealed it beneath his tough Roman exterior. He ought to use him more. Well, whether he liked it or not, now was his opportunity.

'At dawn last Sunday a girl was found dying in the hills not far from here. She'd been drugged. She died yesterday afternoon.'

'Yes, Violante told me. An overdose, wasn't it?'

'Apparently.'

'Maybe the drug was cut with some other crap, chief. Unfortunately it's easy to get ripped off where dope's concerned. People who do drugs always run that risk.'

'Those who "do drugs", yes, but it's possible this poor girl was only thirteen. Do you think a girl of thirteen is the kind of person who "does drugs"?'

Gianni Ascalchi looked at him uncertainly, not sure what he was getting at. All he said was, 'Don't know.'

The telephone rang.

'Dr Francesco Leone,' Fanti announced.

'Put him on.'

Leone came on the line. 'Hello, Chief Superintendent. I hear you've been looking for me.'

'If it's you they've asked to do the autopsy on the girl who died at the Ospedale Nuovo, then I have.'

'You mean the junkie?'

Even to Leone, that was all the poor girl was. One less thing for society to worry about, now that she was dead.

'I mean the child,' Ferrara replied, making clear the difference in their viewpoints.

Leone ignored Ferrara's argumentative tone: they had known each other and respected each other for too many years to start splitting hairs. 'You've caught me red-handed, my dear Ferrara. I'm just on my way to the Ospedale Nuovo now to do the autopsy.'

'So soon? It hasn't even been twenty-four hours yet . . .'

'Don't worry, she's not in suspended animation. Her heart failed and they couldn't revive her. She's no longer among us, we're sure of that. It was the deputy prosecutor who told me to hurry things up. It's August, Ferrara . . .'

Or maybe there was someone who was 'in a hurry to have done with her, to get rid of her as quickly as possible', Ferrara thought: wasn't that what Violante had said?

17

'May I ask,' Leone continued, 'why this case should be of such interest to the head of the *Squadra Mobile*? From what I gather, it's a simple overdose, which isn't exactly uncommon these days—or am I mistaken?'

'No, I don't think you're mistaken. The fact is, my men haven't managed to identify the girl yet, we don't even know how old she was, and I was wondering if . . .'

Leone laughed heartily. 'You've come to the wrong address, my dear Ferrara. I'm good, I admit—one of the best in the field. But unless the poor girl swallowed her identity card, without chewing it, I don't think I can help you. Names and dates of birth aren't written in the DNA.'

Why did everyone have to make jokes all the time? What was so funny about a life that had barely begun and had already ended in the morgue? Maybe it was the only way they could live with the most unbearable aspects of their respective professions, but Ferrara wasn't like that. Years spent fighting crime in its various forms had made him feel like an explorer of an underground world which increasingly disturbed the apparently tranquil surface of daily life; a world in which he, like everyone, could easily become trapped.

He remembered the words the then-Commissioner, Angelo Duranti, had used in welcoming him to Florence as the newly appointed head of the *Squadra Mobile*. They all used to call Duranti 'Mephisto', because of his gloomy character, but many now missed him. 'Be careful, Chief Superintendent. In this city, if you stick your finger in shit, you're likely to pull out shovelfuls of the stuff!'

18

He was still fond of Duranti, and visited him every now and then at his house in Liguria, where he was spending his retirement looking at the sea and the Palmaria Islands, Tino and Tonetto, growing fruit trees and writing his memoirs. He was still a great teacher, full of invaluable lessons, not only in how to apply the law, but also in how to negotiate the vagaries of police bureaucracy as well as, more importantly, those of the human heart.

'I know that,' Ferrara said, after Leone's laughter had subsided. 'I wouldn't ask that much even of you. But we suspect she may have been a foreigner, an illegal immigrant, and you might be able to confirm that. Anyway, it's your fault, Doctor. You've got me used to surprises, so I'm expecting you to tell me something I can really use.'

'If she ever had an operation, or had dental care, then it's just possible we could find out her nationality . . . But if you're so interested, why don't you honour us with your presence?' It was a provocative question: Leone knew how averse Ferrara had become to such things over the years.

It had been ages since he had last attended an autopsy, a thankless task which he preferred to leave to others. Usually it fell to Rizzo, the most trusted of his men. For a moment, Ferrara looked at Ascalchi, who was sitting right there in front of him, but he dropped the idea: he had something else for Ascalchi to do.

'You say you're on your way to the hospital now?'

'The autopsy room at the hospital morgue, to be precise. Why do you ask?'

'I'll be there. In half an hour, is that okay?'

Leone gave a long, incredulous whistle. 'I'll wait for you in intensive care, in the consultant's office. But please don't be late. I have a feeling this d'Incisa fellow isn't very patient. What's so special about this unknown foreigner anyway?'

'She was young,' Ferrara commented laconically, bringing the conversation to a close.

'Almost a child, don't you think so?' he said to Ascalchi, who had been patiently following the conversation to get a better idea of the case.

'At thirteen? What do you want me to say, chief? Some are still children, some hardly at all . . .'

'To me they're all still children, whether they like it or not. What can anyone understand at that age? What fault is it of theirs?'

'I blame the parents. They're the ones who should be thrown into prison.'

Yes, the parents. Perhaps this girl's parents had sold her, or perhaps they were still looking for her in some Eastern European country.

'As you heard, the likeliest hypothesis at the moment, given that no one has come forward, is that she was an illegal immigrant. She may have fallen into the clutches of the Albanians or the Romanians or God knows who.'

'Right, chief,' Ascalchi said. 'We can check out the pushers, but it's a jungle out there . . .'

'So buy a machete. But not yet. For the moment you don't have to venture any further than Narcotics Division. True, you might come across a few savages there, but don't be deceived, they're good people. See if there any current investigations into cases of heroin overdose, and ask them how they see the situation in the city and the surrounding areas. Oh, and also try and find out the minimum age at which minors have access to drugs.' Thinking that Ascalchi hadn't quite understood, he added as he stood up, 'What age they start, is that clear?'

'I did understand what you meant, chief,' Ascalchi protested, also standing.

*   *   *

Narcotics was one of the divisions of the *Squadra Mobile* and occupied the last four rooms in the corridor on the first floor of Police Headquarters, the area furthest from prying eyes.

Superintendent Ascalchi, who had never been there before, wondered if the choice of location had been deliberate. Certainly, the atmosphere was quite different from the rest of the Squad, and so were the officers, who were all very young and casually dressed. The men wore earrings, and the women had pierced navels, which they left proudly uncovered.

'Do you know where Ciuffi is?' he asked the first person he saw: a tall, well-built guy he wouldn't have liked to meet on a dark night in a street on the outskirts of town. Not even in the centre of town, come to think of it.

'Superintendent Ciuffi to you. Who the hell do you think you are?'

'Superintendent Ascalchi,' he replied coldly. 'Ferrara sent me.'

'I'm sorry, sir . . . Superintendent Ciuffi is in the last room on the left.'

'Thanks. Don't put yourself to any trouble, I can find the way.' He left the officer rooted to the spot, looking astonished and mortified.

The head of the section was a friendly, talkative thirty-two-year-old Neapolitan. Ferrara had met him in a canteen during a summer seminar organised by the American police, where he had been doing a course on anti-Mafia strategies in Italy and Ciuffi was on a refresher course given by the DEA. After talking for fifteen minutes over a dish of cold chicken that tasted of plastic and overboiled potatoes—everyone was overdosing on ketchup and mustard to make it palatable— Ferrara had realised that this man was a first-class officer and decided that if ever he had his own squad he wanted him in it at all costs.

Unlike his colleagues, Ciuffi dressed normally. Ascalchi had only seen him once before, when he had arrived at Florence Police Headquarters for the first time and Ferrara had introduced him to all his colleagues.

'Plenty of work, eh?'

'This isn't Rome or Naples, but we aren't lagging far behind, I can tell you. There are lots of drugs around, and it's hard to keep up. We do what we can, as you can see.' Ciuffi pointed at the walls, which were covered with posters and newspaper cuttings about the team's most recent operations: a proud record, which Ferrara had tolerated because it was an incentive to further improvement. 'But there aren't that many of us, so what can we do?'

'How many exactly?'

'Twenty in all, more men than women. Most of them prepared to go undercover among the dealers.'

'I noticed. I was thinking I should raid the

place.'

Luigi Ciuffi smiled. 'Real characters, eh? And you didn't see all of them. The best ones we keep in mothballs.'

Ascalchi didn't envy them. These were men who, when they went undercover, didn't come into the office and sometimes didn't even see their families for long periods. They were a select few, who ran the greatest risks and needed uncommon courage and a really cool head.

'So Ferrara has sent you to help me out, has he?' Ciuffi joked.

'Oh, no, not at all! Quite the opposite, you may be able to help us out . . .'

Ciuffi sighed. 'Don't worry, I got the idea. Okay, shoot.'

'A young girl died of an overdose yesterday.'

'The one in the Ospedale Nuovo?'

Obviously, as head of Narcotics, he had read the initial report from the hospital.

'Yes.'

'We don't know anything about her yet. What's your interest?'

'We need to know if you're investigating any cases of heroin overdose where the stuff is either too pure or it's been cut with something harmful.'

'Affirmative.'

'A lot of them?'

'Yes, we've had a sudden rash of them. Not that there weren't any before, of course there were. But they weren't so frequent and they were almost always relative overdoses. What we're getting now are a lot of absolute overdoses from heroin cut with starch, talcum powder, sometimes strychnine, the usual things, you know? There've been six

23

cases in the last two months alone. Deputy Prosecutor Erminia Cosenza is in overall charge of the investigation.'

'Hold on, I don't quite follow. What's all this about relative and absolute overdoses?'

Luigi Ciuffi seemed pleased to have a chance to show off his expertise to a colleague. 'An absolute overdose is caused by the consumption of a dose, pure or cut, that's above general tolerance levels. A relative overdose is caused by the consumption of a dose higher than the particular tolerance level of a specific individual, and that can depend on a number of factors.'

Ascalchi ignored his colleague's somewhat didactic tone. 'So in cases of absolute overdose the dose would be fatal for anyone, whereas in cases of relative overdose only for some and not for others?'

'Precisely. And what we're getting in Florence at the moment is a lot of absolute overdoses.'

'How do you explain that?'

'The likeliest explanation is that there's a gang war going on for control of the territory.'

'Between who?'

'As you know, the Albanians are trying to muscle in on various illegal activities in Florence—including drugs, of course. I don't mean soft drugs, hashish, marijuana, they've been in absolute control there for some time. I'm talking about heroin, cocaine, amphetamine, crack—the whole kit and caboodle.'

Even Ascalchi was aware that Albanian gangs were active in Florence. He knew that for some years now there had been a huge increase in the number of prostitutes from Eastern Europe. The

24

traditional figure of the pimp was on the way out, replaced by specialised groups who recruited women abroad, smuggled them into Italy, and once they had arrived, forced them into prostitution. The groups were well organised, efficient, highly feared, extremely violent and determined. They had made a lot of money from prostitution and now, if Ciuffi's hypothesis was correct, were investing heavily in drugs.

'One sign of this,' Ciuffi continued, 'is the number of fights and attempted murders involving North African pushers.'

'I don't follow you.'

'For years the North Africans have been the main, if not the exclusive suppliers to addicts in Florence and the province.'

'I know that, but where do the Albanians fit in?'

'Let me finish. They're the ones who supply the North Africans, but they're playing a double game.'

'What do you mean?'

'They're trying to lose them their customers. If the rumour starts spreading among addicts that the stuff the North Africans are selling isn't as good as it used to be and puts you in a coma, they've won. The addicts are going to look for other sources of supply, and the Albanians will be waiting for them with open arms.'

'So the bastards are supplying these stupid dealers with crap to make them lose face.'

'That's what we think. As I said, it's the likeliest explanation, and one we're actively working on. The Albanians are trying to monopolise the drug market, not just wholesale but retail too. We've had some tip-offs that bear this out, and we've got a few names . . . But you know what the Albanians are like! They never stay in one place for very long. Today they're in Florence, tomorrow in Milan, Naples, Turin . . . And the gangs do each other favours, swap members. With all these people working in different places, it's harder to identify and investigate them.'

Ascalchi nodded.

Extreme mobility was one of the characteristics of the Albanian underworld. The traditional methods of surveillance didn't work any more. Most of the time, no sooner had you located one of the criminals than you lost all trace of him, because the Albanians rarely used the same means of transport or the same telephones twice.

In addition, they frequently resorted to violence in their daily operations and as a means of resolving conflicts, had fingers in many different pies, used intimidation, and had a code of silence typical of Mafia-style organisations. Organised into clans, following the traditions of their home country, they used the same methods as the Mafia but with even greater determination and cruelty.

'I see what you're saying. If this girl who died yesterday was supplied by a North African who'd been screwed by an Albanian, we're fucked, right?'

'If you're thinking of nabbing the dealer who gave her the stuff, I'd say you were. Either we grab him in some other operation, or you forget about it.'

'Sorry, one more thing. At what age do the kids around here start taking drugs?'

'Why?'

'Because the girl in the Ospedale Nuovo may have been only thirteen, or even less.'

A grave expression appeared on Ciuffi's face. 'Really? We came across a boy of sixteen two months ago. Younger than that I find hard to believe. Though it's hard to know where the limits are these days. I don't know if there's anything that would surprise us any more.'

*   *   *

Ascalchi went back to Ferrara to report, but only Fanti was there.

'Involuntary manslaughter,' he said in answer to Fanti's questioning look. 'The culprit is a black bastard who doesn't know his arse from his elbow manipulated by a white bastard who strikes at random and doesn't give a damn who the victim is. Got that?'

'I'll pass it on.'

'Forget it,' Superintendent Ascalchi said, not sure if Fanti was serious or pulling his leg. 'Just tell him I was looking for him.'

'Join the queue, Superintendent. The Commissioner has been looking for him too.'

3

Because of the traffic, Ferrara had taken nearly half an hour to reach the area where the hospital was located. The car from the police pool was baking in the sun, and the defective air conditioning wasn't much use. He had had to open the window, so now in addition to the heat he had to put up with the nerve-racking cacophony of

27

horns, voices and the exhaust pipes of motorbikes and mopeds.

Fanti had called him on his mobile as they were nearing the hospital, to tell him that the Commissioner had phoned. As he was already late, Ferrara decided he wouldn't return the call yet: he had more than enough to worry about already. He smiled, pleased that he had never given the Commissioner the number of his private mobile, only the official one, which he always kept switched off when he was out on an investigation. That way, only Fanti could contact him if it was necessary.

His relations with Riccardo Lepri, who had succeeded Mephisto and was so different from him, had never gone beyond mutual tolerance, despite a few attempts on both sides which had soon come to nothing.

Built in the Sixties to replace the old hospital in the city centre, the Nuovo, as it soon came to be called, could house more than a thousand patients. Situated on the south-western edge of the city, it was still a relatively modern complex after all these years and had stayed in the forefront of scientific and technological advance. The only thing the original planners had not foreseen was the exponential increase in traffic on the roads leading to it. There were often jams close to the main entrance, making it hard even for ambulances to go in and out easily.

Today, Friday 3 August, was no exception.

They were held up a hundred yards from the gate. Ferrara didn't see any point in adding his own siren to that of the ambulance making its way out, with great difficulty, at that moment.

'Wait for me at the entrance of the emergency department,' he said to the driver. He got quickly out of the car and started walking towards the intensive care unit. This marathon left him in a state of dishevelment that was unusual for him: his tie loose, his shirt collar open, his silk shirt stained with sweat, his jacket hanging over his arm like an unwanted rag.

The patients, doctors and nurses moving around the forecourt or entering and leaving the various buildings paid no attention to him: many looked as dishevelled as he did. When, at last, he climbed the stairs to the first floor of a low glass and concrete building where the office of the consultant in charge of intensive care was situated, he tried to smarten himself up as best he could, wiping the sweat from his face and hurriedly putting his jacket back on. With little success, to judge by his image reflected in the glass wall that ran alongside the corridor, but he had no time to do anything more.

The air conditioning had been turned up to maximum. By the time he found the right door, it had frozen his damp clothes.

'Come in, come in!'

The voice from inside was forceful and impatient. Not unpleasant, but Ferrara shuddered and wasn't sure if it was because of the sudden cold or that not very cordial invitation.

Anyway, he couldn't complain: he hated latecomers, too.

Leone greeted him with a smile. 'Hot, isn't it, Chief Superintendent?' The allusion to his rumpled state could not have been more obvious, even though the pathologist clearly intended it as a friendly rather than a disapproving remark.

'A lot of traffic, too,' Ferrara replied, trying to spare himself further apologies.

'Doctor Leone also had to get here from the centre of town.' The comment came from the other man in the room, who was studying him closely. He said it calmly, as a statement of fact, rather than as if he were trying to provoke him.

Leone hastened to introduce them before Ferrara could respond in kind to the concealed rebuke. 'Chief Superintendent Michele Ferrara, Professor Ludovico d'Incisa.'

The contrast could not have been more striking.

D'Incisa was distinguished, elegant and tanned. Cool, Ferrara might have described him with a touch of envy. As cool as the vague smell of sandalwood perfume he gave off. A successful man, sure of himself, tall, nearly seventy but still robust, his apparently placid but clearly inquisitive blue eyes and the thick, well-groomed fair hair making him all the more authoritative. Everything about him seemed to command awe and respect, and Ferrara felt even more slovenly in comparison.

Glancing at his solid Franck Muller wristwatch—Ferrara was no connoisseur but he doubted it was a fake like the ones sold by Moroccans at the seaside—Professor d'Incisa rose from his armchair. 'Now we're all here *at last*, we can begin.'

He led them out of his office and along the corridor to a flight of stairs. The morgue was in the basement.

They walked across a room of hermetically sealed freezer cabinets to the autopsy room, which had a sign in Latin above the door: HIC MORS GAUDET SUCCURE VITAE. Memories of school Latin came to his rescue: 'Here death delights in helping life' or something like that—an epigraph illustrated by a reproduction of Rembrandt's *The Anatomy Lesson of Dr Nicolaes Tulp* on the wall of the autopsy room.

But what most struck Ferrara was the girl's corpse, lying on the metal table in the middle of the room.

Seen in the flesh, completely naked, she seemed even more beautiful and innocent. The undeveloped breasts with their small pink nipples, the mount of Venus with its sprinkling of dark hair, the delicate, tapering limbs: objectively, it was hard to say if she had been an undeveloped adolescent or a somewhat precocious child, although Ferrara still inclined to the latter.

In life, she must already have had her own undeniable sensuality, but her hands—the fingers still slightly chubby, the nails chewed and bearing traces of vermilion varnish, the kind used in children's games—were certainly a child's, and of aching tenderness.

A sacrificial victim, he thought, obscenely exposed to the avid curiosity of the doctors Rembrandt had portrayed so well. They would cut her up, extract every secret they could from her body, and then she would be laid in the ground and return to dust.

At least sixty years too early, Ferrara thought sadly.

There was a label tied to the big toe of her right foot. On it, someone had drawn a question mark with a black felt-tip pen where the name should have been. The same mark appeared on one of her legs.

Two people were waiting for them beside the corpse: the autopsy room technician from Leone's team—Ferrara had met him a couple of times before—and a young doctor.

In the meantime, d'Incisa and Leone had put on white paper aprons, latex gloves and masks. Ferrara did the same, although he left off the gloves.

Leone began the external examination. 'Female, Caucasian, indeterminate age, though at first sight I'd say about fourteen. Do you agree, Professor?'

He was speaking in a loud voice for the benefit of those present, but also so that his words could be captured by a small portable tape recorder. He was a short, thin man, his hair prematurely white in marked contrast to his thick black eyebrows. He wore big, round steel-rimmed glasses, which stood out on his long, hollow, perennially tanned face.

'I wouldn't like to hazard a guess,' Professor d'Incisa replied, cautiously.

'Well, it doesn't matter for the moment,' Leone said, as he opened the corpse's mouth to study the teeth. 'When we have the results of the bone density tests we'll be able to make a good stab at it, but the teeth suggest she's probably at least fourteen, but no older than sixteen. Which confirms the previous hypothesis that she was between thirteen and sixteen. The body measures 146 centimetres. There are no external signs of lesions, contusions or blows. The state of nutrition appears to be within the normal range for her height and weight.'

He looked carefully at both arms.

'There are no obvious marks to indicate the use of syringes, apart from those which can be

32

attributed to the drip she was on and the blood tests that were taken in the hospital. Can you confirm that?'

'Of course. I would add, though, that when she arrived here she did have one or two marks. That was why we did blood and urine tests which showed the presence of morphine, the fundamental metabolite of heroin.'

'Yes . . .' It seemed to Ferrara that Leone hesitated for a moment, lost in thought. 'I'd say it was very likely she died of an overdose, but I'd be curious to know if she was a habitual user. We should be able to ascertain that from an examination of her hair, liver and bile.'

The professor nodded in agreement. It was clear that he wasn't really interested: he had treated a case of overdose, and provided this was demonstrated, anything else was for others to speculate about.

Leone went on to examine the hands and feet.

'Nothing under the fingernails or toenails, no mould, no hard particles.'

'Isn't that strange, considering where she was found?' Ferrara asked.

Leone shrugged. 'Hard to say. We don't know how she got there or what she did there.'

D'Incisa agreed, throwing Ferrara a reproving glance, as if annoyed by this untimely interruption from a layman.

Francesco Leone moved to the genital organs. He looked closely at the labia majora, frowned, and thrust a finger into the vagina. 'The hymen is broken and, unless tests prove otherwise, already atrophied.'

'What does that mean?' Ferrara asked, at the

33

risk of further antagonising d'Incisa.

'That she hadn't been a virgin for some time,' Leone replied. 'Contrary to popular belief, the hymen doesn't disappear after the first act of sexual intercourse, or even after the succeeding ones. Adaptation to coitus is a gradual process. Eventually the hymen atrophies, as it has in this case, and loses its morphological features.'

While speaking, he had raised the corpse's pelvis slightly and was now inspecting the anal sphincter.

The professor was following his colleague's work with curiosity, although he continued to glance every now and then at his expensive watch.

'The folds around the anus present traces of discoloration, and despite the rigor mortis I note that there is a decided loss of tone in the sphincter and some relaxation which appears to be funnel-shaped.

'In other words,' he added for Ferrara's benefit, switching off the tape recorder for a moment, 'she was entered repeatedly from behind.'

'Does that mean she was raped before she went into a coma?'

'I can't tell you that. As I've already said, there are no signs of violence. Maybe that was the day she stopped being a little saint . . .'

'Had you noticed this?' Ferrara asked d'Incisa.

'That she was a whore?' the professor replied in a contemptuous tone that angered Ferrara: considering the girl's age, it was not a term he himself would have used. 'Why should that have concerned us? This unknown girl was brought in showing clear signs of an overdose. We administered Narcan—that's an antidote to opiate

34

poisoning,' he said to Ferrara, 'which confirmed our suspicions, as did all our subsequent tests, as I've already said. The death that occurred after the coma was clearly due to the overdose. I wrote that in the report and I repeat it now. The rest was none of our business.'

'Not even if she was drugged in order to be abused?' Ferrara retorted.

'Not even then,' d'Incisa said firmly. 'We're doctors, not policemen. Let's each of us do our job.' The scornful undertone was obvious.

Ferrara ignored him and turned to Leone. 'Is it still possible to find traces of sperm after so many days?' He thought he knew the answer but, lacking the technical knowledge, he preferred to make sure. 'I'm sorry, Professor, but as you yourself said I have to do my job.'

'I appreciate that. As a matter of fact, it's a sensible question. A patient in a coma is washed and catheterised, and you may well think that would affect any traces of sperm. But it isn't so, is it, Dr Leone?'

'No, it isn't. The sperm remains in the mucous membrane of the uterus for a long time, and laboratory tests should be able to find it, if the girl had complete intercourse, without precautions.'

'Does it remain for more than five days?'

'Sometimes more than double that, Chief Superintendent.'

'And given her profession,' d'Incisa said, dryly, 'I'd be surprised if there wasn't any, and from different men, too!'

Perhaps Ferrara was influenced by Violante's suspicions, but he definitely didn't like the man. He wasn't thinking of that, though—he was weighing up other possibilities: the girl had been someone's sex slave, a paedophile had shot her up with heroin to make her docile, she'd been gang raped, or she'd taken part in one of those parties involving adults and minors about which there had been persistent rumours in Florence, without there being any concrete evidence.

There were many possibilities. Including the possibility that the girl was just an underage prostitute who'd taken an overdose. D'Incisa was clearly convinced of that, and Leone might also be inclining that way. It was certainly the simplest explanation. But it was too simple. If they could confirm that she wasn't a habitual drug user, it would start to crumble.

Once he had finished the external examination, Leone nodded to the technician, a short, stocky man of about fifty, who until now had been standing by the instruments trolley, watching and listening with cool detachment. Now he walked over to the wash basin, picked up a plastic headrest, and fixed it beneath the girl's chin.

It was at this point that Ferrara realised he had no desire to be present at the slaughter that was about to begin: Leone would make a Y-shaped incision and open the thorax, then he would cut open the abdomen, and finally he would pull back the scalp and saw through the cranial vault.

Pathologists have a special relationship with death, but he didn't. It had been a while since he'd last been present at an autopsy and he had got out of the habit. He realised now that he preferred not to reacquire it.

'I have to go,' he said before Leone could proceed. 'If you have a minute, Professor, I'd like to ask you a few questions before you leave.'

For the umpteenth time, the consultant looked at his watch. 'I'm in a bit of a hurry, to tell the truth . . .' He glanced at Leone.

'Don't worry,' Leone said. 'I'll be quick.'

'It won't take long,' Ferrara said. 'Just a few questions.'

D'Incisa sighed. 'All right.'

'This is for you, to pass the time,' Leone said to Ferrara as he walked him to the door, and handed him a small plastic bag. 'The dead girl's personal effects.'

Once he was out in the corridor, Ferrara was assailed with doubts. What if he was barking up the wrong tree? What if this was nothing but the drug-related death of a young girl forced into prostitution, like millions of others her age all over the world?

He sat down on a bench, opened the bag, and took out a pair of dirty, faded blue jeans, without any label, a cheap lavender cotton T-shirt with a label he didn't recognise, a pair of tacky earrings—too flashy for a child—and a small imitation gold ring set with a piece of purple glass trying to imitate an amethyst.

That was all.

Apart from three sticks of mint chewing gum in the pockets of the jeans, that, sadly, was the sum total of the dead girl's personal effects.

He wondered if Leone had been trying to tell him something by giving him the bag. Had he, too, noticed the curious lack of shoes and underwear? There was no bra, though the girl could have done without it. But there were no knickers either, and it was harder to believe she didn't wear them,

37

whether she was a convent girl or a whore, someone with her papers in order or an illegal immigrant.

As he put the things back in the bag—he'd pass it on to Forensics—the ring fell to the ground. He watched it rolling, feeling strangely disturbed.

The personal effects of the dead are always disturbing. It is as if they have suddenly lost their value along with their owner. They appear as what they are, piles of objects more or less worn down by a use to which they will no longer be put. Some will find other owners and live again, acquire other meaning, other memories. Others—the majority—will fade.

Objects full of melancholy, in any case. But that wasn't what disturbed Ferrara as he bent to pick up the wretched market-stall ring. It was the image of the girl reaching out her little hand to choose it from among others, the childish illusions she may have had in her mind as she slipped it on her finger.

And there was something else, too, something he couldn't put his finger on, but which gave him the incentive he needed.

He phoned Headquarters and asked to speak to Ascalchi.

'I was just about to report to you . . .' Ascalchi began.

'Never mind, you can tell me later. Now listen. Check with the emergency services and find out the exact spot where they found the girl, let me know, then go out there with a few people from Forensics. Get Sergi to help you out, if he's not busy with Violante, and anyone else who's available. Cordon off the area and give it a thorough going over. I'll join you there as soon as I can.'

'Do you think it's murder?' Ascalchi asked in surprise.

'I don't know, but act as if it is.'

'Is this all above board?'

'Don't worry about that. I'll take responsibility.'

'Are we looking for anything in particular?'

'The usual things. But shoes, bra and knickers in particular. And condoms.'

'All right, chief,' Ascalchi said, unenthusiastically. He hadn't joined the police to be a street cleaner, and if those wooded hills were the way he imagined, the harvest of used condoms would be plentiful.

Disgustingly plentiful, he thought with horror.

Immediately after, Ferrara called Fanti.

'Yes, chief?'

'Find out everything you can about a make of T-shirt called "Steaua Rosie".' He spelled it for him. 'Have you written that down?'

'Yes, chief.'

He rang off and settled down to wait, wondering if he wasn't wasting precious time. But at this stage of an investigation, all leads were equally vague and equally important. Many would turn out to be inconclusive, but none could be ruled out.

*　　　*　　　*

The one interruption while he waited was a call that Fanti put through. It was Ascalchi, with details of the place where the body had been discovered.

Ferrara did not have to wait as long as he had anticipated. At the first opportunity, as if to prove that he really was in a hurry, Professor d'Incisa emerged from the autopsy room.

Ferrara leapt to his feet and joined him. 'As I promised, this won't take long.'

'Can we talk as we're walking? I have to meet my wife. We're off to Viareggio today and we're already late. We were hoping to leave early to avoid the traffic.'

'I understand,' Ferrara said, walking beside him. The doctor had a rapid, energetic gait. 'I also have to go somewhere. Marina di Pietrasanta. I'm leaving tomorrow. So I'm in a hurry, too, if I want to get through everything today. It's only for the weekend, though. Are you going on holiday?'

'If only! No, I'm taking my wife to our villa, but I'm coming back on Sunday. Our work here is never done . . .'

'Tell me about it.'

'What did you want to ask me?'

'Was the girl in a coma all the time she was here? Didn't she ever come to, even for a moment? Did she ever speak in her sleep? Did she moan?'

'After we administered Narcan, she started breathing again normally, but that was the only reaction I observed. As far as I know she never regained consciousness, and I never heard her moan.'

'Could a nurse have heard something?'

'It's possible. But you'd have to ask them.'

'Is there anyone in particular I can talk to?'

'The head nurse, Signora Finzi.'

Ferrara wrote the name in a notebook. 'One more thing.'

They had left the building and were descending

40

the steps which led to the reserved parking spaces.

'Go on.'

'The girl was in a coma for five days. Do you think she was given the care she needed during all that time?'

Professor d'Incisa stopped dead, but did not explode as Ferrara had feared he might. On the contrary, the inflexibility and hostility he had shown him from the start appeared suddenly to thaw—at least as much as a consultant in a large Florentine hospital could thaw. It was as if he'd been relieved of a burden.

'Now I understand . . .' He looked Ferrara straight in the eyes and after a moment's reflection, continued. 'I give you my word of honour that, while she was under my personal observation, she was treated with the greatest care and attention. Can I guarantee that no errors were committed, not even a small one? No. Obviously, I hope there weren't, but this is a large hospital and we have a lot of patients. And it is August, Chief Superintendent. You know what that means, you work in a public institution yourself. And you also know how important prestige and reputation are to such an institution. So I'll leave it to you to do as you see fit. For my part, I'll make sure there's an internal inquiry and let you know the results. Have a good weekend.'

And with that, he unlocked the door of his gunmetal grey Maserati coupé by remote control.

Ferrara once again wondered if there had been malpractice. Was that why d'Incisa had asked to attend the autopsy, despite being in a hurry to get away to the seaside? And was that why he had pressed for Violante's report to be completed

41

quickly?

He stood there, watching as the doctor pulled out of the parking space and drove away. With him went that sandalwood scent, to be replaced by a vague, pungent, evil odour.

Ferrara had put his finger in shit this morning.

He was sure of it now.

4

The road snaked its way around the flank of the hill, which bristled with beeches and brambles on either side. Occasionally, through gaps in the wild undergrowth, he caught a glimpse of the expanse of vineyards and olive groves, with their neat, man-made rows.

The officers were at work on a spur of beaten earth to the right of the road, which at that point veered sharply to the left, leaving an area of open ground where there was room for four or five cars. Their cars, though, were not parked there, but to the side, taking up part of the narrow provincial road, and two officers with signal paddles stood on either side of the bend, making sure that the local traffic got through safely.

Ferrara got out of his car and walked over to where Ascalchi and Sergi were giving rather tentative instructions to two forensic technicians equipped with cameras, both still and video.

'Found anything?' he asked.

'Nothing, chief,' Ascalchi replied. 'Just a few empty bottles of water, a lot of cigarette stubs, empty crisp packets, beer and coke cans. No knickers, shoes or bras. This isn't a place for couples, I can tell you that.'

'How about syringes?'

'Are you kidding, chief? We're at least half a mile from anywhere remotely civilised, and there are at least a hundred better places to shoot up between there and here.'

Ferrara looked at Sergi—known as Serpico because of his resemblance to the main character in the Al Pacino film—and found conformation in his eyes, as well as a certain puzzlement. He seemed to be wondering what he was doing here.

'Where was the body found?'

'Over there,' Ascalchi said, leading him to a point immediately beyond the edge of the open space, where the ground started to fall away. Here, an area of flattened vegetation marked the spot where the body had lain.

Ferrara stopped close enough to see, and stopped Ascalchi, too. 'Any sign of the body being dragged along the ground?'

Ascalchi hadn't thought of it, perhaps because he hadn't specifically ordered him to. With Rizzo it wouldn't have been necessary.

'But, chief, the paramedics were here . . . they took her on a stretcher to the ambulance, so . . .'

'So you didn't think of looking? Is that what you're trying to say?'

Sergi intervened. 'No, chief. The team have done their job well, they've been very careful, as always, but as you can see—'

'As I can see, the area needs to be checked thoroughly.'

'Yes, chief,' Sergi replied, obviously sceptical.

In his heart Ferrara couldn't really fault him.

This didn't look like a crime scene, if indeed there had been a crime.

There were many tyre tracks, some quite close to the place where the body had been found, and lots of shoe prints, often one on top of the other. Ferrara ordered the technicians to photograph both the tracks and the prints, and they obeyed so as not to contradict him and to keep themselves busy, even though they had already taken quite a lot, and as far as they were concerned they had already finished.

'The one thing we can be sure of is that the body wasn't dragged along the ground,' Ferrara said eventually. 'Do we agree on that?'

'Absolutely,' Sergi said.

'And that if kids come here they don't get out of their cars, not even to pee,' Ascalchi commented. 'In my opinion, these are all adult prints, chief.'

Perhaps it was only meant as a joke, but it showed that Ascalchi had good observational skills.

'I'll wait till I've seen the photos, but I'd say you were right. So if she was barefoot, and that's something we'll be able to check on, she certainly didn't walk anywhere around here. Leone didn't find any traces of mould or hard particles under the toenails.'

'Which would mean . . . ?' Sergi said, his interest suddenly aroused.

'That most likely the girl didn't get here by herself, somebody else brought her here,' Ferrara said, already thinking ahead. 'And that in any case she wasn't an addict who came to a deserted spot to shoot up, given the kind of area this is and the absence of syringes or any prints suggesting that people were walking near where she was found. That seems to be the first thing we've definitely established.'

If she had been brought here, there were two possibilities: either she had been transported in a car, or she had been carried in someone's arms across the countryside from one of the villas or houses in the area. The nearest were at least six or seven hundred yards away. If she had been carried, it would have had to have been by more than one person, because if there was only one person carrying her, she would have had to have been dragged for long stretches. If on the other hand she had been dumped from a car, then she could have come from anywhere and only one person might have been involved.

Both possibilities had holes in them, but they couldn't be ruled out. That meant they would have to search the whole of the surrounding area.

'I'm sorry, boys, but we haven't finished here yet. We have to comb the area over a radius of at least a mile, and check out all the nearby buildings, discreetly if possible. Send for reinforcements if you need them. I have to get back to the hospital.'

It had occurred to him that he had left without even saying goodbye to Leone, and that a chat with Signora Finzi and some of the other nurses might not go amiss.

It also occurred to him that it was already afternoon and he hadn't had lunch, but he wasn't hungry. Usually when he was on an important case, he skipped meals without even noticing. Perhaps all the cigars he smoked took away his appetite. This time, he was sure it had nothing to do with his cigars, and everything to do with the

45

macabre spectacle he had chosen to observe that morning.

The prospect of going back to the hospital didn't appeal to him, but when had he ever been able to afford the luxury of choice?

*   *   *

Leone had already left: he would have to call him later to apologise. He had better luck with Signora Finzi, who as it turned out was on duty that afternoon.

She was about fifty, tall and thin, with copper-coloured hair and a thin, hooked nose. She wore glasses with thick blue-tinted lenses. She looked like the kind of woman who never smiled, but in the event she was neither hostile nor crabby.

She led him to an empty office, away from the chaos of the waiting rooms. The room was full of metal tables piled high with files and boxes of medication, and several electronic devices were stacked on shelves.

'I'm here about the young girl who overdosed,' Ferrara began.

The woman nodded. If she was surprised, she didn't show it.

'Were you on duty when they brought her in?'
'Yes.'
'When was she transferred to intensive care?'
'Almost immediately. Doctor Carli in emergency immediately realised it must be an overdose and that the girl was in a serious condition. He informed Professor d'Incisa, who had her transferred to intensive care immediately.'

'So it was the professor who admitted her?'

46

'The professor and his team, yes.'

'It was Sunday, is that right?'

'Yes, but there's nothing unusual about that. He's always working. He works too much. I remember he looked especially tired and drawn that morning, and he got quite angry when he saw the girl. He probably hadn't slept a wink all night, and it can sometimes be discouraging when you have urgent cases needing attention and they bring in these people who've been shooting up on a Saturday night.'

'Do you think he should have been working if he was as tired as that?'

The woman pulled a face: the closest thing to a smile Ferrara saw from her. 'Professor d'Incisa has energy to spare, and he's famous for keeping a clear head. And anyway, this wasn't surgery.'

'When they brought the girl in, was she still dressed?'

'I don't understand.'

'I'm sorry, I don't really know how these things work. Perhaps they'd already undressed her in emergency. I assume patients are given gowns to make things easier for the doctors.'

'No. There was no time to change her. We had to intervene urgently. They must have done it later, when she was admitted to the ward.'

'Who would have done that?'

'The nurses on the ward.'

'Do you remember how she was dressed?'

'Of course. Like all young girls—jeans and T-shirt. Cheap stuff, though, the kind you find in a street market. Cheap jewellery, too. She must have been quite poor. A runaway, probably. No one ever came looking for her.'

47

'Do you get a lot like her?'

'More than we'd like to, and more than you'd imagine.'

'A nuisance, would you say?' he asked, thinking of Professor d'Incisa's anger.

'No, Superintendent. I'd never say that. When they come into hospital they're patients, and we're here to take care of them. That's our job.'

'Of course. I only meant that if they take you away from other urgent cases—'

'Even junkies are human beings, and not all of them are the same. It can be discouraging, but they're never a nuisance. That's not just a question of professional ethics, it's a question of conscience.'

'Among these junkies, are there many minors?'

'Yes, quite a few.'

'Even children?'

'I beg your pardon?'

'She wasn't an adult, am I right?'

'Well, not really, but . . .'

'According to the pathologist she might have been fourteen, perhaps even thirteen.'

The woman seemed quite struck by this, and thought about it for a few moments. 'Oh my God, I suppose that's possible. But I thought she was older than that. Being a junkie . . .'

'And that doesn't seem strange to you?'

'To be honest, yes, now that you've told me.'

'So you can understand why I have to ask you all these questions?'

'Oh, don't worry about that. If I can help you in any way . . .'

'Thank you. I have one more question. I didn't find any shoes among the girl's personal effects.'

48

She thought for a moment. 'That's right, she was barefoot.'

'And did that seem normal to you?'

'To be honest, I don't think anyone was bothered about it. The paramedics might have taken them off.'

'As far as you recall, were her feet bruised or particularly dirty?'

Again, the woman thought for a moment. 'No, I'm pretty sure they weren't . . .'

'Thank you. I'm going to try and find out if it was the paramedics who took her shoes off. But if it was, they would have given them to someone, wouldn't they?'

'Of course, to one of the nurses.'

'The strange thing is, she didn't have any bra or knickers on either.'

'I don't understand.'

'Was she wearing any underwear when she was brought in?'

'I really don't know. We didn't undress her. There was no need to when we administered the Narcan, or when we took the blood test and put her on a drip.'

'Were you there all the time they were working on her?'

'Yes, all the time.'

'And in your opinion, was every possible care taken?'

'Absolutely. Professor d'Incisa may have been tired, but he directed his team with total dedication and did absolutely everything that had to be done. I'd swear to that in court.'

Ferrara smiled. 'That won't be necessary. This isn't an interrogation. We're not even investigating a crime. I'm just trying to understand how a child ended up full of drugs in an isolated spot which isn't even a hangout for junkies, and how she ended up here without shoes . . . or underwear.'

'When you put it like that, it does seem strange. Perhaps you should ask the nurses who looked after her when she was taken to the ward. They should know more about the clothes. You'll probably find they've been put somewhere by mistake.'

'I'm sure you're right. Do you remember which nurses?'

'One of them was definitely Elena Scandellari. She's here now, do you want me to call her?'

She was there, too! Could the day, which had begun so badly and continued to get worse, be ending well after all?

'You'd be doing me a great favour. Tell her I'm waiting for her here. You can go back to work. I've kept you too long. Thank you, you've been a great help.'

'If you need anything else, let me know. I didn't think she was so . . .'

'Young?'

'Yes.'

Ferrara wouldn't have been able to swear to it, but he had the impression her glasses had steamed up.

'Maybe she wasn't,' he said, trying to make her feel better. 'We're only guessing. She may have been fifteen or sixteen.'

'Even so . . .' the woman sighed as she went out.

The sigh made Ferrara think she might be feeling guilty that after that first day she hadn't seen the girl again, as if she had failed in her duty to her patient. But perhaps that was unfair, perhaps she had simply had some days off.

*   *   *

Elena Scandellari, who knocked at the door a few minutes later, couldn't have bccn more than thirty. She was buxom and quite pretty, and Ferrara guessed that she was usually lively and cheerful, but at the moment she seemed intimidated to be in the presence of a high-ranking police officer.

'Did Signora Finzi tell you why I wanted to see you?'

'About the clothes?'

'That's right. Apparently the girl wasn't wearing any shoes when she was admitted. Did the paramedics give them to one of you?'

'No, she didn't have any.'

'And she wasn't wearing underwear either, is that right?'

'That's right, signore.'

'And didn't that strike you as odd?'

'Yes, especially as she must have had her period recently. I thought, "Look how these little whores go around these days" . . . I'm sorry,' she added, remembering that she was talking about someone who had died.

'Do you mean she had blood on her?'

'Yes, I saw the bloodstains when they stripped her to change her.'

'Where?'

'On the insides of the thighs. The genital area seemed clean, but as if it had been washed in a hurry, at least that was the impression I had. I remember it well.'

'Were there any bloodstains on her jeans as well?' Ferrara asked.

'I didn't notice.'

It didn't matter. He'd be able to check that out himself, or better still, Forensics would do it for him.

'I see. In the days that followed her admission, did she lose any more blood?'

'No, that's why I thought she must just have had her period. It was probably just finishing.'

'Right . . . Did she have anything in her pockets?'

'A few sticks of chewing gum . . . I also remember a used tissue rolled into a ball. That was it.'

'Did you throw the tissue away?'

'It was rubbish, Superintendent . . .' she said, apologetically.

'Of course. So you cleaned her and put her in a hospital gown.'

'Yes, obviously.'

'And you didn't tell anyone about the bloodstains? You didn't report them?'

'No, I didn't. I thought that was her business anyway, the poor girl. If someone comes in who's been knocked down by a car and their underwear is soiled, I don't tell the whole department!'

Ferrara smiled. It was a slightly bitter smile: that rolled-up tissue might have been able to tell him something. But he certainly couldn't fault the nurse's humanity.

'One more thing. Has Signora Finzi been away?'

'Just for a few days. She came back today.'

For some reason, that cheered him up.

*   *   *

It was a bit late now to go back to Headquarters, so he told the driver to drop him on the banks of the Arno, near where he lived.

On the way, he called Leone's office.

The pathologist greeted him with the words, 'You left without saying goodbye!'

'That's why I'm calling you now.'

'Oh, I see, it's not because you wanted to ask me some questions . . .'

Ferrara smiled. 'Why didn't you become a detective, Leone?'

'For the same reason you didn't become a pathologist, judging by the way you ran off today just when things were getting nasty. The State needs both of us, and God in His infinite wisdom invented the division of labour. So what do you want to know?'

'Everything.'

'Obviously. Okay, let's say . . . today is Friday, tomorrow we start the lab tests, so . . . You can call me again next Friday, all right?'

'Can't you at least tell me part of it?'

'You mean, let's stop joking?'

'If possible . . .'

'At your service, Chief Superintendent. Given what I've seen so far, I think the hospital's diagnosis was correct.'

'So do I, but that's not the most important thing. It's the circumstances in which the drugs were taken that interest me. And there's something else: I've just found out that when the child—'

'I wouldn't necessarily call her a child. You saw her yourself.'

'The girl, then, if you like. When she came into the hospital, she had blood on the insides of her thighs, near the groin. Is it possible to establish if she was having her period or if she'd just finished it?'

'Of course, from the histological test. I'm going to do a biopsy on the sample I took from her uterus. We just have to wait.'

'In the meantime, if—hypothetically—she wasn't having her period, would that mean she had sexual relations very close to the time of her death?'

'Yes, of course, and if there was blood, that would mean those relations were probably violent and repeated, since we know she wasn't a virgin. But we'd have to ascertain that the blood was hers.'

'What if you had a sample?' Ferrara asked, thinking of the jeans.

'We'd be home and dry!'

'Good. What impression did Professor d'Incisa make on you?'

'A competent professional, I'd say, someone who knows his stuff, but a bit of a cold fish. Why?'

'One of my inspectors has been following the case since before the girl died, and he has the feeling the girl might not have been treated as well as she could have been. He said he thought she'd been a bit neglected.'

'So what are you thinking? Malpractice? Well, we won't be able to ascertain that from the autopsy, but it would be useful to have a look at the hospital's medical records. Do you have them?'

'I've put in a request to the deputy prosecutor.'

'If you do get them, make sure I'm sent a copy.

It's possible the doctors there aren't as careful as they should be. I did notice an alteration in the mucous membranes of the nose, and d'Incisa said it was due to the tube they put in. But I've seen similar cases where microscopic analysis has revealed the presence of foreign bodies.'

'And would that be important?'

'If it's what I'm thinking, it'd be curious to say the least.'

'Why, what are you thinking?'

'Well, all the other cases I was talking about were cocaine users.'

For a moment, Ferrara was speechless. 'So apart from the heroin, she may have taken coke, too? At that age?'

'Not only at that age, but not even as a habitual user. But all this still has to be demonstrated. Let's wait for the test results.'

'When will they be ready?'

'I'll see if I can get some preliminary results to you in forty-eight hours.'

*   *   *

They had arrived. He got out of the car and walked along the banks of the Arno. The narrow pavement was crowded with tourists, many of them stopping to photograph the Ponte Vecchio in the nostalgic orange light of early sunset.

He needed that short walk, despite the heat, to try to put the whole tangle of things inside his head into some kind of order. Drugs: too many. Malpractice: possible. Clothes: missing. Sex: too much of that too, probably.

A pair of jeans, a T-shirt with an unknown label,

55

a small imitation gold ring—why did the ring affect him as much as it did? The professor, the pathologist, Ascalchi, Violante, Fanti, the Commissioner who was looking for him . . .

The Commissioner! He hadn't even called him back!

5

'You didn't call him back?'

'No.'

'You mean you didn't even *speak* to him?' Deputy Prosecutor Anna Giulietti insisted. 'You've been out of touch all day?'

'I was busy.'

'I hope for your sake it was an important case. He was beside himself. You know what he said to me when I ran into him in the corridor about five?'

'I can imagine.'

'I don't think you can. He said, "Who does this Ferrara think he is? Always breaking rank, no respect for authority, no *esprit de corps*, no discipline! But I'll get him, one of these days. I'll nail him, like Christ on the cross." Word for word, give or take a comma, apart from a few expletives which I won't repeat because they offend my feminine modesty.' Anna Giulietti sounded half amused and half worried. Outside office hours, her tone towards him these days was increasingly friendly and conspiratorial.

It was just after nine o'clock in the evening and the terrace of Ferrara's apartment was still bathed in the golden light of sunset. The leaves of the bougainvillaea in the arbour glinted. Ferrara and his wife were having dinner there, as they did every evening.

On getting home, Ferrara had immediately noticed the two brown leather bags, packed and ready for tomorrow, and had perked up a little. The prospect of a relaxing weekend with Petra and his friend Massimo made up for all the effort he had put in on what had been an extraordinary day.

His exhaustion must have been obvious because, even before giving him a hug, Petra had asked, 'What did my chief superintendent do today?'—a question she always asked when she saw him in that state.

Anna Giulietti's phone call had come as he was about to take a mouthful of fish and Petra was telling him how she had gone all over town in search of her favourite deodorant and hadn't been able to resist buying him some swimming trunks.

Anna Giulietti had called to find how things had gone with Riccardo Lepri.

'So you saw him today?' Ferrara asked, vaguely surprised because the Commissioner didn't often visit the Prosecutor's Department.

'Gallo sent for him. All very hush-hush. Some kind of summit meeting, I guess. What are you planning to do?'

'I'll go and see him on Monday. I can't go tomorrow, I have a previous engagement, and there's no way I can give it up.'

Petra nodded her approval.

'Maybe you should say you're ill, or just go away on holiday, and he'll forget all about it. But what was he so upset about anyway?'

'Apart from the fact that I was rude to him by

57

not phoning him back, I really have no idea, believe me.'

'Let me know when you find out.'

'Feminine curiosity, eh?'

'Call it professional anxiety about a friend, Michele.'

'Don't worry, I've seen worse.'

'Just satisfy my curiosity, okay?'

'All right. Bye.'

'Bye.'

*   *   *

'That was Anna, wasn't it?' Petra asked.

'Yes.'

'Who were you rude to?'

'The Commissioner.'

'I thought so. Is that what's worrying you?'

'Is it so obvious?'

'*Ich sehe das*, Michele . . . I can see it. When have I ever not seen it?'

'You're right. But it isn't that. I'm always having run-ins with Lepri, but then everything gets sorted out. Basically, he's quite an accommodating person, as long as it suits him. He prefers not to get on the wrong side of anyone.'

'What is it, then?'

Ferrara was almost tempted to tell her about the girl. A woman's sensibility, Petra's sensibility— when Petra was a child, as he knew from her photos, she'd had the same green eyes he imagined that poor girl having, and the same ash-blonde hair—might have been able to help him to see things that he, a man and a Southerner to boot, would otherwise never have thought of. But they

58

had made a tacit rule never to talk about his work and he preferred to keep to it. His wife's question had been a spontaneous expression of her unswerving love for him. He understood that and it was enough.

'Forget about that,' he said, smiling. 'How about showing me those famous trunks?'

'No, no, no,' she replied, flirtatiously. 'Your bag's already packed, and I don't want you messing it up.'

'At least tell me what colour they are,' he insisted, pouring out two half glasses of Friulian Tokai, which he liked for its fruity flavour and its slight aftertaste of bitter almonds.

'Green with blue stripes,' she replied, radiantly.

It reminded him of something, and at first he wasn't sure what it was. Then he remembered. 'Like the ones—'

'Absolutely identical!'

More than thirty years had passed.

Thirty years since they and their inseparable friend Massimo Verga had spent a summer camping on Lampedusa, that dream island with its view over the Isola dei Conigli and the transparent blue sea which would have inspired envy in a coral reef; that island where they had set the seal on their love.

The memories returned, and he could feel tears pricking at his eyes. Petra had been so beautiful, tall as a goddess, merry, full of life. It hadn't been her eyes, or her mouth, or her long slender legs, or her lovely breasts, which had driven him wild. It was her voice. He was crazy about her husky, sensual voice, which sent him into an ecstasy of laughter and adoration every time she mangled the

Sicilian dialect.

It had been a summer that had seen the birth of their love, but a cruel summer too, because in their own self-absorption they did not see in time the fire that was smouldering so close to them.

Ferrara realised it when he left the tent, incredulous at what had happened, and ran down to the beach, breathless with happiness, to tell Massimo, and his friend's glowering look forced him to hold back the river of words bursting inside him. And later, when they were sitting around the fire, roasting potatoes and cuttlefish as big as steaks, and no one said a word, Petra realised, too, and she was stunned, knowing she should feel guilty but unable to do so.

But it was already too late.

Massimo had introduced them, Massimo loved them both. But when he realised that they were a couple and he was the unwanted third part of the equation, he vanished. As soon as they got back to Catania. He vanished for good, and many years passed before the Ferraras met him again, in Florence.

'I'm pleased we're going to see Massimo,' Ferrara said, casting these memories aside.

'Tell me about it. We've hardly seen him since he rented that place in Marina di Pietrasanta. He's never at home.'

'*Cherchez la femme!*'

'That's what I'm afraid of!'

Massimo Verga was an inveterate womaniser. Petra had two nicknames for him: Peter Pan and 'the *tombeur*'—the ladies' man. Perhaps because he had never found a woman who could replace Petra, or more simply because of his innate character, he often fell head over heels in love, but it never lasted long. His love affairs amused Michele but worried Petra, who could see him getting old without a companion. She had another worry, too. He had already squandered a great deal of his inheritance, but she was afraid that sooner or later he would get into even worse trouble.

'Do you want to bet we'll solve the mystery tomorrow?' Ferrara said with a smile.

As he spoke, the telephone rang again.

*   *   *

'It's me again.'

'Anna?'

'Sorry to disturb you, Michele, but it's urgent. It's about this business of the Commissioner and the girl who died in the Ospedale Nuovo.'

'The child?'

'Child? They told me she was a prostitute.'

Rumours travelled fast. Especially the worst ones.

'Who told you that?'

'I can't tell you. We have to meet.'

'How about Monday?'

'I can't. I'll be busy all day, I'm in court and then I have a meeting with some of my colleagues. Tuesday's pretty full, too.'

'So what shall we do?'

'Well, there's tomorrow. I know you have something to do but . . .'

'Tomorrow?' he repeated, looking anxiously at Petra, who responded with an expression of resigned disappointment—the expression of

61

someone who had been in this situation many times before.

'I don't have any hearings, as it's Saturday, but I have to go to Perugia in the morning. I'll be back in the afternoon, though. How about three o'clock?'

Worse still: the whole weekend would be ruined. But Ferrara realised that Anna was making an exception for him, and he couldn't refuse. Especially as it had something to do with the investigation into the dead girl, which he was taking increasingly to heart.

'Okay, tomorrow at three,' he confirmed, with a guilty glance at his wife.

Petra responded with a nod. A bitter nod.

*   *   *

Midnight.

Petra had silently unpacked, put the linen back in the drawers, the beach sandals in the shoe rack, the toiletries in the bathroom, and put away the swimming trunks, still in their cellophane package.

She had said goodnight with a long, affectionate kiss and gone to bed. Ferrara could still feel the kiss on his lips as he paced from the terrace to the living room and back again, trying to work off the tension inside him.

It was a starry night. The noises of passers-by drifted up from the street. From the Ponte Vecchio he heard a burst of laughter: innocent laughter, probably, but to him it seemed mocking.

He took refuge in the living room.

It was a spacious room, divided in two. On one side, the sofas, the armchairs, and a large desk where he often worked at night. On the other, a long, narrow eighteenth-century table, which could be used either as an additional work surface or a dining table when it was too cold to eat outside.

On the walls, paintings of various kinds and provenance: German ones from Petra's family, others from his parents' house, and others they had collected during their long years together.

There were also a number of small tables spread through the two areas, cluttered with framed photographs: one of Petra's passions. They were photos of the two of them, of relatives and friends, and of all sorts of occasions that had taken place over the years. For every photograph, Petra tried with a stubbornness and determination that was quite 'Teutonic'—as he chided her affectionately —to find the most suitable frame, one which reflected the spirit and period of the image. There were old black and white photos, and more recent ones in colour. Ferrara also now had an impressive file of electronic images, but from time to time he liked looking over these fragments of their shared history.

As he did tonight.

And his gaze finally came to rest on one of the photos of Petra as a child. She was about eight or nine, if he remembered correctly. A slight girl, wearing a calico dress that was too big for her, her thin legs peering out incongruously from beneath the skirt, and a pair of plaits that was in none of the other photos. It was a colour photo, the colours rather faded now, and Ferrara noticed, perhaps for the first time consciously, the little ring on one of the fingers of her right hand: an imitation gold ring, with a fake amethyst.

63

6

'Don't you ever go on holiday, Gatto?'

It always amused Gianni Fuschi, the head of Forensics, to use that nickname for Ferrara. It had been given him years before by a woman journalist on *Il Tirreno*, who had become slightly infatuated with his catlike green-hazel eyes and his soft, cautious movements, like a cat ready to pounce. It had immediately been taken up by other newspapers, who never hesitated to use it to mock him, criticise him or just plain provoke him every time the opportunity presented itself. It even circulated among his men: not that they would ever have dared utter it in his presence, but they often used it among themselves, sometimes in a tone of unconditional admiration, sometimes in a teasing way, depending on how well an investigation had worked out, or on the chief's mood at the time.

The only one of his men who never used it, as far as he knew, was Fanti.

But that Saturday morning, Gianni Fuschi didn't seem at all amused when Ferrara visited his office, and greeted him warily.

'What about you?' Ferrara retorted. 'You never take a holiday either.'

'What can I do? You collect a whole lot of rubbish and dump it in my laboratory. Cans, cigarette ends, bottles of all kinds. Do you have any idea how long it takes to examine these things one by one for prints and traces of saliva? And for what? Rumour has it—and of course I always listen to rumour, it's generally reliable—rumour has it you don't even know for sure there's been a crime. Is that right?'

'In a way, yes,' Ferrara admitted.

'Tell me you're kidding or I'll never talk to you again.'

'There's something strange about this case, Gianni. Something ugly, maybe even *very* ugly. You have to help me out.'

'*Something* strange? And do you think that's enough? It's August the fourth, damn it. Don't I have a right to time off like everyone else? Are you trying to appeal to my better nature?'

'You're right. So leave the rubbish, as you call it, and have a look at this for me.' He handed him the little bag.

'What the hell's this?'

'The girl's personal effects. Concentrate particularly on the jeans and see if you find any traces of blood on the inside, especially near the crotch.'

Fuschi made a face. 'Inside? Why, wasn't she wearing knickers?'

'I haven't found any yet, and a nurse at the hospital told me that when she was brought in the insides of her thighs were bloodstained, so it's quite likely that the jeans absorbed some of it.'

'All right, but what good will it do you?'

'It's important, believe me. It'll help us to confirm or deny a theory that arose from the autopsy.'

'Which is . . . ?'

'That she may have been raped. Especially if the histological tests show that she wasn't having her period at the time. And if we find blood on her jeans.'

'May have been . . . if . . . if . . .' Fuschi observed sceptically.

'What else can we do? You know that's the way we work: we theorise, we check things out, we change our minds on the basis of results. All that's necessary, along with a certain amount of intuition and a lot of patience, as well as the extremely valuable technical support we get from people like you. If all the *maybe*s and the *if*s are confirmed, my dear Gianni, we still might not be able to draw the conclusion that she was murdered as well as raped, but we'd be very close.'

'In which case I'd still have to sort through the rubbish, except this time there'd be a reason for it. You see, I win!'

'No, I win, because you'll carry on talking to me after all!'

'Go on, go.'

'Bye. Let me know what you find. Call me at home, call me on my mobile, it doesn't matter. This is urgent.'

'Bye!' Fuschi waved him off.

'For now,' Ferrara said.

*   *   *

It was four minutes to three by the time he got to the Prosecutor's Department, and one minute to three when he knocked at the door of Anna Giulietti's office.

'Come in, Chief Superintendent, please sit down,' she said, in the solemn tone she reserved for their work meetings.

Although they had grown a lot less formal with

66

each other since becoming friends, Anna had insisted that their personal relationship remain strictly confined to their meetings outside the office, on the grounds that they wouldn't be able to deal with each other in a professionally correct way if the friendship factor came into play. And it wasn't only a question of putting it on in front of third parties, it was a rule that had to be observed even when they were alone. Outside, they were friends. Inside, they were colleagues—or even enemies, if their respective roles required it.

To Ferrara, this compromise solution had seemed a bit schizophrenic at first, and he had been sure it wouldn't last. But it had, and he was starting to get used to it—not that he always carried it off as well as she did—and to see that it really worked!

'Good afternoon, Signora Giulietti,' he said, sitting down in front of the imposing narrow walnut desk with its gently rounded edges and its elegant Z-shaped decorations. It was a fine Art Nouveau piece—designed by Van de Velde, she had told him proudly the first time he had complimented her on it—inherited from her grandfather, who had been a notary. She had brought it here from her home in an attempt to make her office a little less anonymous: an attempt echoed today by a colourful bunch of gladioli and lupins in a crystal vase on the windowsill.

'Are they from an admirer,' he asked, 'or was someone trying to bribe you?'

'Don't joke about it. You know perfectly well I don't have a private life. They're from the florists below my apartment, and I paid good money for them.'

There wasn't a trace of sadness in these words, but they were indicative of a solitude which would have been incomprehensible in a woman who was still youthful, beautiful and rich, and belonged to an old and illustrious Florentine family, if she herself had not told him how her profession was everything to her and gave her all the satisfaction she needed in life.

'So, to business,' she continued.

'All right, Anna.'

She glared at him because of his informality. 'I made a few discreet phone calls last night, and now I know everything.'

'Lucky you. I find that the further I go the more I seem to be in the dark. How much can you tell me of what you know?'

'Enough. But first I need to ask you some questions.'

'Go ahead.'

'As you know, I've been asked to oversee the case of the young prostitute who died on August second at the Ospedale Nuovo. I've been told that you're very keen to see it through.'

Ferrara merely nodded. Again the girl was being referred to as a prostitute.

'Could you tell me how far you've got?'

'To be blunt, Signora Giulietti, I still have a long way to go. She was a young girl, almost a child, and we have to take that into account.'

'A child? No one told me that. How old, exactly?'

'No one knows, exactly. But between thirteen and fifteen, sixteen at the most.'

Anna looked angry for a moment, although it wasn't clear who with.

'We haven't yet managed to establish her identity,' Ferrara went on. 'That's why we're leaning towards the theory that she was an illegal immigrant. We still don't know if she was in fact a prostitute. The cause of death was almost certainly a heroin overdose, but we still don't know how she came to take it.'

'And is that why your report suggests homicide as a consequence of the administration of drugs, according to article 586 of the penal code?'

'That's our preliminary suggestion, yes. I'll follow every possible lead, of course, but at the moment homicide seems the likeliest hypothesis. Both the pathologist and the head of Forensics are currently evaluating a number of elements which may indicate that the girl was raped before being killed . . .'

'Raped? A prostitute? Well, it's possible of course, but I hope you're not letting your imagination run away with you, Chief Superintendent. However, I understand your— what shall we say?—your determination, if the poor girl really was as young as that, even if she does turn out to have been a non-Italian citizen. I understand it and I share it. Just as I appreciate the various initiatives you've already undertaken or intend to undertake, and I want you to know you can count on the total support of the Prosecutor's Department. What is not clear to us, however, is what the hospital has to do with it.'

That 'us' did not pass unnoticed.

'What do you mean?' he asked.

Anna Giulietti opened the green cardboard folder she had in front of her and took out Violante's request to see the girl's medical records.

'This seems to be what's causing all the fuss. At least partly. As far as I understand it, we need to answer certain basic questions. Who was this girl, where does she come from, how did she end up where she ended up, and are any third parties directly or indirectly responsible for her death? Am I right?'

'Yes, of course, but the medical records may contain useful information.'

'On her progress while in hospital. But the crime happened *before* she got to hospital. By the time she was brought in, she'd already overdosed and was close to death, wasn't she? And she died of that overdose, you've confirmed that.'

'True, but the results of the blood test that was done soon after she was admitted may tell us a lot of things—'

'Isn't what Professor d'Incisa told you enough? Or can't you just ask him for those particular results?'

'How do you know I saw him?' Ferrara asked, angrily. Now he knew where the description of the girl had come from (Professor d'Incisa had called her a 'whore' during the autopsy). D'Incisa had complained and the complaint had reached Prosecutor Gallo, Anna's boss. And Lepri had been talking to Gallo before his outburst to Giulietti . . .

There was an amused look in Anna's bright blue eyes. 'I told you, Chief Superintendent, I've made my own inquiries. You, though, aren't telling me everything, are you?'

'The inspector who was originally following the case had the impression the hospital neglected the patient,' he admitted, 'and my conversation with the consultant confirmed that impression.'

'I thought as much. You're talking about malpractice, is that it? Do you think there are grounds for opening an inquiry?'

'No,' he had to confess. 'As I said, these are just impressions. But perhaps if we can obtain the medical records and find out more about what led to the overdose, we may also discover—'

Anna Giulietti sighed. 'We're talking about two different investigations, Chief Superintendent. Do you agree?'

'Yes.'

'Of the two, the first is of no great interest to anyone, except for you and now me; the mere possibility of the second has already created a fuss.'

'I don't understand.'

'So you still have no idea why the Commissioner is getting so upset?'

'Because I went to the Nuovo?'

'Doesn't matter. But who's in the hospital?'

'Professor d'Incisa?'

'Yes, but not just him. Other consultants, professors, surgeons . . . *Doctors*, Ferrara.'

'So?'

'Come on, don't play the innocent. Do I have to spell it out for you?'

The puzzlement on Ferrara's face was eloquent enough.

'Come on now! What world do you live in, Chief Superintendent? *Freemasons!* Don't tell me you don't know that in the medical profession, especially here in Florence, it's almost impossible to get anywhere in your career unless you're a member of some lodge or other, official or not!'

It might have been an exaggeration, but there was a lot of truth in it. Everyone knew that many hospital doctors were Freemasons. And that the bonds of brotherhood between them were so strong that they would help each other in secret to protect the reputation of a Mason in trouble with the authorities.

Anna Giulietti's observation moved the investigation into thorny territory. For good or ill, Freemasonry was a powerful institution, which had survived periodic persecutions and demonstrated a resilience and a tenacity capable of defying any government, since governments, by definition, were transitory. An ambiguous institution, but, as far as anyone knew, dangerous only when it deviated from the norm. Officially, it was a perfectly respectable organisation, which, over the course of its long history, had counted a large number of important figures from the political, military, artistic and cultural worlds among its members: Garibaldi, Washington, Lafayette, Beethoven, to name but a few.

His mind was working fast. 'Do you mean Lepri ...?'

'Ferrara, are you still playing the innocent? I don't know if the Commissioner is a Mason or not, it doesn't really matter. All it takes is for those who count in medical circles to exert pressure, and for the pressure to get to Lepri, Gallo, whoever, whether they're part of the Brotherhood or not.'

'And to you, too?'

She smiled enigmatically. 'Does that matter?' she asked. 'As I see it, I'm doing you a favour. The message is clear: an investigation into what went on in the hospital isn't welcome. As we've

72

established, you have two different investigations in progress. Digging in your heels over the second may compromise the first. I have good reason to believe that, if I hold off on granting this request,' she said, pointing to Violante's document, 'you'll be able to continue your investigation into the girl's death without any problems.'

Is there a female lodge? Ferrara wondered. He couldn't tell whether Anna Giulietti—the 'iron prosecutor' as she was known to her colleagues despite her blonde hair and blue eyes—was blackmailing him or helping him. If there was such a lodge, it was very likely, given her illustrious ancestry, that she belonged to it.

'I see,' he murmured.

'I hope so. But I haven't finished.'

'Go on.'

'If the first investigation reveals solid evidence—and I mean solid, I hope we're clear about that—that one or other of the doctors or nurses at the Ospedale Nuovo may have contributed to this patient's death, I expect you to do your duty. Then, and only then, I'll be quite happy to grant the request.'

*　　　*　　　*

It was still early when Ferrara left the Prosecutor's Department and hurried back to his office.

He was not at all disheartened by the line Anna Giulietti had chosen to follow. Freemasonry, inaccessible as it was, might well be a line of inquiry that was worth pursuing. He'd have to be extremely discreet, though, or he risked jeopardising his tacit pact with the deputy

73

prosecutor. It was the kind of operation that required the offices of the incomparable Fanti, and he called him as soon as he got in.

'What is it, chief?' Fanti said, even before he had entered Ferrara's office.

'I need the membership lists of all the official Masonic lodges in Florence . . . and even the unofficial ones, if possible.'

Fanti looked at him, bewildered.

'Don't stand there gawking. Haven't I made myself clear?'

'You've made yourself very clear, chief . . . but . . .'

'But what?'

'Where am I supposed to find these lists?'

'Try Special Operations first. They're interested in these things.'

'And if they don't have them?'

'Have you gone gaga today? Try the internet. Go to a bookshop and buy me all the books you can find on Masonry in Florence. Do what you always do! But be discreet, please. This has to be done in absolute secrecy.'

Fanti was already on his way out when he called him back.

'On second thoughts, don't go to a bookshop. If I need books, I'll buy them myself.' He was afraid that his secretary, to avoid making any mistakes, would buy every book he could find in every bookshop in Florence.

*   *   *

He was about to call Petra to suggest they have dinner at I Palmenti, a restaurant in Montelupo

74

Fiorentino which they both liked, when Fanti came back looking dejected.

'What's happened?' Ferrara asked.

'Chief . . . Special Operations have the lists, but . . .'

'But what?'

'They need a request in writing, otherwise they won't let anything out of their office.'

'That seems okay, Fanti. What's the problem?'

'The request has to be signed by you personally and no one else . . . not even by a civil servant. That's what they told me.'

No chance of being discreet now, obviously.

'I see. All right, forget about it.'

'I'll try the internet, then.'

'No, don't worry.' He had had another idea.

'Are you sure, chief?'

'Yes, I'm sure. You can go.'

Fanti went out, looking mortified, and Ferrara felt sorry for him. But he was already searching for the personal telephone number of the deputy prosecutor in Bologna, Raffaello Petrini, who a few years earlier had investigated some very 'unofficial' Masonic activities, directly implicating the heads of various lodges, and in the process accumulating an impressive mountain of papers.

Ferrara had met him when they were both working in Reggio Calabria and they had developed a great deal of mutual respect.

Raffaello Petrini was only too happy to help, and promised to fax him all the documents he had relating to the Florentine lodges, which he had kept constantly updated.

After that call, he finally phoned Petra.

They agreed to go to I Palmenti (*Are you trying*

75

to be forgiven? she asked. *No*, he lied, *I'm trying to save you having to cook tonight*) and then Petra asked, 'Have you called Massimo to apologise?'

'No, not yet . . .'

'A good thing I thought of it, then. He was most upset, especially as he'd gone to a lot of trouble to book a table at Romano's in Viareggio. Still, he said the reservation wouldn't go to waste, because he'd find someone else to console himself with.'

'Knowing him, we can guess which gender that someone is likely to be, even if we don't know her name.'

'Right,' Petra said, not at all enthusiastically. 'Anyway, call him yourself, please.'

'Don't worry, I will.'

'Good. I'll book a table at I Palmenti. Is nine o'clock all right?'

'Perfect.'

*   *   *

Ferrara didn't get the chance to talk to his friend. First the line was engaged, then he heard the hum of the fax machine in Fanti's office and sat waiting, listening intently, as if his ears could read.

After a length of time that seemed endless, his sergeant finally appeared with about a hundred pages. And they only covered Florence!

'Here are the lists, chief!' Fanti said. He was rather more cheerful than he had been before, even though he knew he had done nothing he could take credit for.

'Thanks, you're a star.'

The document, entitled *The Lodges of Florence*, traced the history of the Freemasons in the Tuscan capital followed by a list of the various lodges and the names of all their members. Several of the names were preceded by the word 'Doctor', but it was clear that this did not always indicate a doctor of medicine, merely the person's academic qualification. Only in a few cases was the profession specified, and there were lawyers, architects, engineers . . . He was not surprised to find the name of Ludovico d'Incisa. At the same time he felt relieved not to see, at least on a first quick glance through the many pages, the name of Anna Giulietti. Nor those of Commissioner Lepri or Prosecutor Gallo.

He closed the file and put it in his briefcase. He would study it at greater leisure when he got home.

*   *   *

Montelupo Fiorentino, a town noted for its ceramics, is located a few miles from Florence. The Ferraras drove there in their old, indestructible Mercedes, which the Chief Superintendent had had for years and couldn't give up.

A restaurant based in a converted mill with a charming period cellar well stocked by the current owners, I Palmenti had become almost a regular destination. Apart from the traditional, earthy Tuscan dishes much loved by Petra, the restaurant was noted for its excellent fresh fish which to Ferrara's palate tasted unmistakably of the Tyrrhenian Sea, especially where it lapped the shores of his native Sicily.

That evening, the owner proudly recommended

77

the *pezzogna*, a rare deep-water fish only found, in season, off the islands of Elba and Capri. Its soft but solid flesh was incomparable and the wine that came with it, an extraordinarily smooth, rich Fior d'Uva from the Amalfi coast, brought out all its flavour.

'I've never eaten anything to touch this,' Ferrara exclaimed, after the last mouthful.

'I bet Massimo doesn't get treated like this at Romano's,' Petra said, pleased to see her husband looking so relaxed. 'By the way, what did he say to you?'

'I couldn't get hold of him,' he replied, clearly embarrassed. He had had all afternoon to try again.

'*Ach du lieber Gott!*' Petra exclaimed, as she often did to express surprise. 'Michele! That's not good enough!'

'I'll call him tomorrow,' he said, winking at her. 'Now isn't exactly the time, is it?'

But she didn't appreciate that wink, which she found a little too dismissive. She felt guilty about her friend and mortified by her husband's thoughtlessness. She loved Italy, her adopted country, but she didn't always like the Italians' devil-may-care attitude, which was so different from German rigour. In important things, she found that rigour—and admired it—in her Michele, so she was all the more disconcerted now by how negligent he had been towards his closest friend. Of course, she realised that he was going through a hard time at the moment. He seemed to her more stressed than usual and she felt sorry about that. But for her, friendship was sacred.

It was sacred for him, too, and now he sat there

78

consumed by regret, in a silence heavy with his wife's disapproval.

The silence was broken by the ringing of his mobile phone.

'It's him!' Petra exclaimed, brightening up.

But it wasn't his private phone, it was his work phone.

*　　*　　*

'Gianni here.'

'At this hour?'

'Why, am I disturbing you? I'm sorry, but I'm working. There's this annoying fucking superintendent I know who makes me do all these absurd things . . .'

'I'm working, too,' Ferrara lied, looking furtively at Petra, who, apart from anything else, couldn't stand lies.

'Then listen to me. The news isn't good.'

'I take it you didn't find anything,' Ferrara said, his heart sinking at the thought that this had been another wasted day.

'No, you don't get it at all. There are bloodstains, and lots of them, and not just bloodstains. There are other stains, too. Transparent ones, which have hardened to a crust . . . almost certainly sperm.'

'Excellent, Gianni!' Ferrara cried, unable to contain himself.

'For you, yes . . . but I'll have to start with the cans again. I can't go any further with the jeans.'

'Why not?'

'Because to continue analysing them, I'd have to get authorisation from the deputy prosecutor.

79

Further tests would destroy the fabric and may be unrepeatable. I have to follow the law. May I ask if there's anyone actually under investigation in this case?'

It was true. In cases where an unrepeatable test needs to be carried out on a person, thing or place which is subject to modification, the Prosecutor must, at the earliest opportunity, inform the person under investigation, that person's counsel and the victim of the crime, specifying the day, the hour and the place at which the test is to be carried out and giving them the chance to appoint their own technical experts, who then have the right to be present when the task is carried out and to make their own observations and reservations.

'Not yet, Gianni,' Ferrara admitted, resigned to the idea that he would once again have to call Anna Giulietti, who had disconcerted him somewhat with her defence of the Freemasons. 'But you're right, we'll have to follow the accepted procedure.'

'So talk to the deputy prosecutor and let me know. In the meantime the material will remain here at your disposal.'

'Thanks, Gianni. I owe you dinner. Ever eaten *pezzogna*?'

'What's that? Vegetable soup?'

'Make a note of it. If I don't buy you *pezzogna* for dinner before the end of the summer, then you really are entitled never to talk to me again.'

'No, the reason I won't talk to you is because you're making me sift through rubbish for no reason, remember that.'

*   *   *

Later, on the way home, Petra felt her spirits lightening, hearing her husband whistle a tune from *The Barber of Seville* as he drove through the night. And so she repressed for the moment what he called—making fun of her—'the unsuppressable Teutonic gene'. It was not until they reached home that, unable to hold back any longer, she again reminded him of his unforgivably thoughtless attitude towards his friend.

7

The first thing Michele Ferrara did on the morning of Sunday August the fifth was to call Massimo. He and Petra were on the terrace, where they were having breakfast: the usual German-style breakfast made entirely with Italian ingredients. Petra often joked that it expressed the alliance between their two countries better than any bilateral treaty. To which Ferrara always replied that it was expressed even better in their marriage.

'"The number you have called is unobtainable at the moment",' Ferrara recited, mimicking the recorded voice he heard.

'He's probably sleeping and took the phone off the hook. Nothing unusual about that. It's Sunday, he's on holiday. He must have gone to bed late.'

'Of course . . . Lucky him. But that means I have to carry my remorse around with me.'

'Good, you deserve it!' Petra said, wickedly. 'I hope he sleeps till midday!'

81

'Too bad if he does,' Ferrara replied, the solemnity of his voice belied by the amused look in his eyes. 'He's going to miss the heartfelt apologies of the head of the *Squadra Mobile*.'

'At least he's having a rest. You should try it some time.'

'Well, right now, I'm going to have a shower,' he announced, finishing the last slice of ham and standing up.

Later, washed and dressed in his Sunday best, he called Anna Giulietti.

After a few fruitless attempts to reach her, he got her on her mobile.

'Michele, why on earth are you phoning me at this hour? And on a Sunday? Is there news?'

'Yes, there is. I know you're not on duty, but I need your help.'

He updated her on what Gianni Fuschi had discovered.

'That's good,' she commented. 'But if it's an unrepeatable act, we'll have to follow procedure.'

'Isn't there any way we can get round it? After all, we don't have anyone under investigation yet, we don't even know who the victim's family are, and we really need a result as soon as possible. You do see that, don't you?'

'Yes, Michele, I do, but you're talking to a representative of the Prosecutor's Department and procedure has to be respected . . . But let me think about it. I'll call you back later.'

'I'll wait until I hear from you, then.'

'I promise I'll call.'

They hung up.

'How about trying Massimo again?' Petra suggested.

Ferrara did so.

The same unfailingly polite recorded message.

'Too bad for him.' He kissed his wife in the doorway. 'See you later.'

'You'll be back for lunch, won't you?'

'Of course, if the Commissioner doesn't kill me.'

*　　　*　　　*

Commissioner Lepri and Chief Superintendent Ferrara often met on Sundays. Sometimes it was a planned meeting—they would take advantage of the fact that it was a quiet day to sum up the week that had just passed and to map out the one ahead—but more often it was by chance: there were so few people in the building, they couldn't help bumping into one another.

That Sunday, they could hardly avoid meeting, and it was up to him to see Lepri first before the Commissioner sent for him or, worse still, pounced on him in his office. Lepri wouldn't be in a good mood if that happened: it would have meant that he had had to come all the way downstairs, and his already ruddy complexion would be quite purple with the exertion.

So Ferrara went upstairs, after a last vain attempt to speak to Massimo. He was calm, and ready for the confrontation. He had decided to try and stay as correct and civil as possible.

Riccardo Lepri was not an irascible person and was more inclined towards mediation than conflict. In face to face discussions, he preferred to win over the other side by appearing flexible and understanding. On rare occasions when he lost his temper, however, he exploded with a vehemence

83

which went beyond all bounds of reasonable behaviour, with consequences that were impossible to predict. Michele Ferrara entered his office ready to be the target of one of these rages.

The Commissioner's welcome caught him completely off guard.

He was sitting at his shiny desk, reading the newspapers. He looked up from them and smiled. 'Ah, good morning, Chief Superintendent. Come in, take a seat. Would you like a coffee? Or would you prefer a nice glass of cold water on a hot day like today?'

'Water would be fine, thanks,' he replied warily. This opening could well be deceptive, he thought, and the explosion was still to come. But he had not noticed any malice or irony in the Commissioner's words.

Lepri poured the water and handed him the glass. Ferrara sat down in the small armchair on the left reserved for visitors.

'Take your jacket off, if you like,' Lepri went on. He himself was in his shirtsleeves, although he had not loosened his collar and his tie was impeccably knotted. 'Florence in August is worse than an oven. No surprise our Dante's best work was the *Inferno*, don't you think?'

Ferrara said nothing, not sure what to reply.

'What are we doing here in August—and on a Sunday, too? Our duty, of course! As ever . . . Always too much to do, eh, Chief Superintendent?'

Here comes the first thrust, Ferrara thought. 'That's why I came to apologise—' he began.

'For what?' Lepri seemed genuinely surprised.

'For not calling you back.'

'Oh, please, that's water under the bridge. I

84

knew you were busy. How could I not? I'm always so busy myself. No, don't worry. All I wanted to know was whether you're making any progress. I hope this thing can be resolved quickly and without fuss. We wouldn't want the world to think Florence is a city full of prostitutes and junkies. Heaven forbid!'

'Thank you for being so understanding. I'm doing my best, but it's rather a complicated case.'

'Go on.'

'We're dealing with a minor, probably an immigrant, most likely not an addict, but in all probability, given what we know so far—and we're still in the very early stages—drugged and raped by one or more people. These same people then took her and dumped her in the place where she was found—either because they thought she was dead, or because she was in a very serious condition. As subsequent events unfortunately demonstrated.'

As he spoke, Ferrara realised that he had lost his reserve and was addressing the Commissioner as if thinking aloud to a colleague.

'A real murder, then,' Riccardo Lepri commented, sympathetically. 'Homicide. A nasty story. Any suspects?'

'Not at the moment. But what we've found out so far would tend to point in the direction of either drug pushers or paedophiles, because although we're not sure of the girl's age we think she could be quite young. We can't rule out the possibility that she was gang-raped or that she was forced to have sex at one of those infamous parties involving adults and children . . .'

Lepri made an irritated gesture. But it wasn't aimed at Ferrara. The existence of these paedophile parties was one of the most persistent urban legends of Florence. It resurfaced from time to time, and in some cases the police had come quite close to getting somewhere, but somehow or other, the whole thing always fizzled out. The reason, Ferrara tended to think, was that the people who organised the parties belonged to the upper echelons of society and could count on protection at high levels.

Lepri was probably thinking the same thing, and shuddering at the thought of the scandal that would be caused by a wide-ranging investigation that led in that direction.

'Let's hope not, Ferrara, let's hope not! Once again, I must impress upon you how important it is to be discreet. You know I trust you. Don't complicate my August, eh?' He wagged his index finger in a jokily threatening manner, then added, 'You said she might be an immigrant?'

'Almost certainly.'

'Poor girl,' he said, and the implication was, 'Weigh it up: an insignificant illegal immigrant on one side, the reputations of the finest names in the city on the other.' But he didn't say this. It was up to Ferrara to draw his own conclusions.

*   *   *

Ferrara walked back downstairs feeling slightly confused. He was actively pursuing the train of thought set in motion by the hypothesis of the paedophile parties, which had been on his mind ever since Leone had aired the possibility that in addition to heroin the girl might also have taken cocaine. The use of cocaine was more widespread among the well-to-do, which would tend to push the idea of a gang rape into the background. But this train of thought risked derailing the whole investigation. It hadn't even been demonstrated yet that the girl was raped by several people, and there were other lines of inquiry that still needed to be followed up before he could concentrate exclusively on this one.

What confused him was the almost religious care with which both he and Lepri had avoided the subject of the Ospedale Nuovo. For his part, he had not wanted to set a bad example after Lepri had downplayed the question in such a lordly manner. Clearly, the reason he had been looking for him on Friday was to advise him, in response to pressures it wasn't hard to guess at, that he should be tactful in dealing with the doctors. And yet today he had called the episode 'water under the bridge'. Ruling out a direct connection between Leone and Lepri or Gallo—and he had to rule it out—that could mean one of two things. Either d'Incisa had assumed that Ferrara had tacitly agreed to his implicit request to go easy on the hospital staff, and had reassured the Commissioner, through the prefect. Or else Anna Giulietti had reassured Gallo that Ferrara wasn't going to interfere, and then Gallo in his turn had . . .

Or both of these, why not?

Either way, it all pointed to the influence of the Freemasons . . .

*   *   *

When Ferrara reached his floor, he did not stop

but continued downstairs, went out into the street, and set off for the Verga bookshop in the Via Tornabuoni. In August, because of all the tourists, the shop stayed open on Sundays.

And given that he was going there, even if Massimo wasn't there, he decided to try calling him again.

'*The number you have called is unobtain—*'

'For fuck's sake!' he swore, angrily cutting off the call.

Rita Senesi, Massimo's assistant and factotum—it had never been clear whether she was more devoted to the shop or to its owner—greeted him in her usual cheerful and slightly flirtatious manner. 'Hello, Chief Superintendent! At least you aren't on holiday.'

'No, Rita, if only,' he replied. 'But your boss seems to be, and what's more he keeps his phone turned off so that no one can reach him.'

'Ah, so you've noticed that, too?' she said, indignantly.

'I've been trying to reach him all day.'

'He's a bit absent-minded—what can we do? He must have forgotten to switch his mobile on. But he has to be here tomorrow, whatever happens. We have to do the accounts! Is there anything you want me to tell him?'

'Just for him to get in touch, at least with the few friends he still has left.'

'Don't worry, Chief Superintendent, I will.'

'Good. Mind if I have a look around?'

'Be my guest. Can I help at all?'

'I'm looking for something about Freemasonry.'

'About time.'

'What do you mean?'

'That it's never too late . . .'

'For what, Rita? What are you talking about?'

'To join, of course.'

'Come on, don't talk nonsense. Do you really think—?'

'They all come in here pretending to be "scholars", researching the "phenomenon", as they call it. In my opinion, for what it's worth, they're swotting up for their exams! I don't know much about it, thank Heaven, but it seems to me that these days belonging to a lodge is worth more than having a degree.'

'You're not going to tell me that Massimo . . .'

'Don't ask me, ask him!'

'Go on, show me the books.'

* * *

He arrived home with a bag full of books, feeling distracted and listless.

Petra had put on a CD of Italian arias sung by Cecilia Bartoli to accompany dinner, and that was fine with him. There was a kind of nostalgia in the air that put him in the mood for confessions.

'You know what I think?' he said, sipping his Terra dei Forti Pinot Grigio. The sounds of the city rose from the street, muffled by the rustling of the leaves in the arbour.

'What, Michele?' she asked, as considerately as ever.

'That I'm isolated. I don't *belong*.'

'What do you mean?'

'I don't know, exactly. But it's as if everyone in this country is part of something: the church, a political party, the Mafia, the Freemasons . . . I'm

89

not. The police, yes. I believe in that. But is it enough? Then you discover that perhaps the Commissioner is under pressure from God knows who, your best friend may be a Mason, the deputy prosecutor takes her instructions from some superior body we can't even begin to imagine, and I—I'm there, in the middle, like a skittle in a game of bowls I have no control over.'

'That's enough now, Michele,' Petra said sternly. 'I don't know what you're talking about and I don't care. I don't care because I know one thing: you do belong. You belong to me just as I belong to you. And we both belong to our families, and to our friends who are dear to us and count on us. It's all the rest that doesn't count. Why should it count when the rest of the world is at each other's throats for a piece of bread or an oil well? You want to talk about what's wrong with your country? It's my country, too, you know. And I love it. But I also love my Michele and I know, because I know him, that he'll do what his heart tells him to do. And that's enough for me, Michele. If only it were enough for you—'

He did not have time to reply because the phone cut into Petra's words, making them both jump. This daily interruption of lunch was becoming a habit. Not that she was doing it deliberately, but it was Anna Giulietti again.

'I think I've found the solution.'

'What is it?'

'Ask Fuschi if it's possible to analyse just a small part of the stained fabric . . . It's important that he doesn't ruin the whole of it. Do you understand?'

'Yes, of course.'

'If that's okay, tell him to come and see me

tomorrow, at eight on the dot, and I'll give him the order to proceed according to Article 359 of the code of criminal procedure, not Article 360. In other words, I'll ask him to ascertain the exact nature of the biological or organic stains on the jeans and anything else he can find, like the blood group, the DNA . . . That way we'll at least have something we can use in the investigation. Then, if need be, for the rest of the material, we'll follow Article 360 to the letter.'

She seemed even more excited than he was.

'I understand, Anna—it's an excellent solution!'

'But please make sure he comes tomorrow at eight sharp.'

'Without fail. Have a nice Sunday.'

'You, too.'

Then he phoned Gianni Fuschi, who was not at all pleased.

8

At the Monday briefing, all the men Ferrara had at his disposal for this case were present: Ascalchi, Violante, Sergi, Inspector Venturi and the head of Narcotics, Luigi Ciuffi, whom he had decided to involve directly after Ascalchi had filled him in that very morning. Plus, of course, Fanti in his usual capacity as secretary.

At the end of a brief run-down of the facts and his own deductions and theories, Ferrara asked, 'Anything new on your side?'

'We haven't yet received authorisation from the Prosecutor's Department to get hold of the medical records,' Violante said.

'I know Deputy Prosecutor Giulietti is very busy. We can't rush her, we just have to be patient. For the moment we have to concentrate on what happened before the girl was found. To start with, Violante, see if you can find out who made the call to the emergency services. Then talk to the paramedics, ask them how the girl was dressed, and if they noticed anything suspicious in the vicinity. Anything else?'

There was a brief silence, then Fanti cleared his throat.

'Yes, Fanti?'

'I don't know if this is the right moment . . . but you asked me to look for that name "Steaua Rosie", you remember?'

'Yes, of course. Well?'

'It's Romanian, chief. It means "red star". I found out it's the only company in Moldova making T-shirts, blouses and underwear, and its head office is in the capital Chisinau.'

'Good work, Fanti—how did you manage that?'

'The internet, chief, and a few calls to colleagues in Interpol.'

'Excellent. Well, this may not be absolute proof, but it does tend to confirm the hypothesis that we're dealing with an illegal immigrant—if not actually Moldovan, certainly from some country in Eastern Europe, perhaps a slave of one of those damned people traffickers. I can't really see an Italian tourist going to buy clothes in Moldova, can you?'

They all shook their heads.

'I have a suggestion,' Ascalchi said. 'Instead of constantly calling her "the girl" or "the immigrant" or whatever, why don't we call her "Stella"?'

Ferrara liked that touch of humanity on the part of the sceptical, easygoing Roman.

'We could call the case "Operation Stella",' Luigi Ciuffi said.

'Done,' Ferrara approved, smiling. Then, addressing all of them, 'Any other theories, ideas, leads to follow?'

'I've given this case top priority,' Ciuffi resumed. 'I'll see if my boys can get anything more specific from the dealers. Most of them are Tunisians, Algerians, Moroccans, and Albanians. We'll start with the areas best known for dealing— Santa Maria Novella, Santa Croce, Santo Spirito— and then radiate outwards to cover the whole city and surroundings. It won't be easy work.'

'When is our work ever easy?' Ferrara observed, more to himself than to his men.

'At the moment I have a team keeping an eye on two Albanian brothers,' Ciuffi went on. 'According to one of my informers, who I trust, the two of them are supposed to be going outside Florence to get new supplies. It seems they're rising stars, for what it's worth.'

'Let's hope so. Is that all?'

'Yes, as far as I'm concerned.'

'Good. Venturi, I want you to link up with the Juvenile Division and find out all you can about what's happening on the paedophile scene. Check up on the youth gangs, too, see if there have been any sexual crimes reported recently, even just suspicion of attempted gang rapes.'

'Yes, chief,' the inspector replied.

'Ascalchi, I want you to link up with Vice and check out the prostitution angle, especially where immigrants are involved.'

Considering that he had covered all the main areas of inquiry and happy to see the newly christened 'Operation Stella' properly launched, he closed the meeting with his customary 'Any other questions?' to which, as usual, no one replied.

*   *   *

Just after eleven o'clock, Fanti handed him a file.

He kept his word, Ferrara thought, seeing the heading:

DOCTOR FRANCESCO LEONE
UNIVERSITY OF FLORENCE
DEPARTMENT OF ANATOMY, HISTOLOGY
AND FORENSIC MEDICINE
SECTION FORENSIC MEDICINE

He started reading.

1. *Having read the documents and examined the cadaver, we have established that the death of this unknown young person, which occurred in the resuscitation unit of the Ospedale Nuovo, took place at about 16:00 hours on 2 August 2001.*
2. *The anthropometric examination and the X-rays have led us to the conclusion that the young woman had reached 14 but not yet 16. This was confirmed above all by the rate of bone calcification and the dentition (presence of the seventh but not the eighth).*
3. *The examination of the body before dissection*

94

revealed among other things that the young woman had had sexual relations, including anal relations, confirmed by the discovery of semen, on which laboratory tests will be carried out.

4. *The autopsy did not reveal any significant evidence that death was due to trauma. Elements emerged in the course of the autopsy which, taken in conjunction with the medical report and the observations of the consultant, Professor d'Incisa, would seem to confirm that death was consistent with an overdose of heroin (there should however be further clarification on this point once the histological tests have been completed). This overdose did not cause death immediately on consumption but led to encephalic disorders, principally anoxic, irreversibly compromising the cerebral functions, causing death after five days in a state of irreversible coma.*

5. *In the course of the autopsy, samples were taken of hair, nails, body fluids, sections of encephalus and liver, as well as fragments of all the organic remains, for the appropriate chemical and toxicological tests.*

6. *It has emerged from the first results that the young woman had not menstruated. The biopsy of the uterus revealed that the endometrium was thickened, which was why the menstrual cycle had not yet appeared. Histological examination of the mucous membranes of the nose revealed the presence of traces of cocaine, mixed with another substance, on which tests are currently in progress.*

95

7. As soon as possible, a complete report on all
    the results of the histological and toxicological
    tests will be issued.

Also included in the file, scribbled in pen, was a
Note for Chief Superintendent Ferrara:

*As regards sexual relations, the
signs are quite evident and
demonstrate that the young
woman had probably had them
shortly before being taken ill. In
that case, the cocaine may have
acted as a stimulant.*

Ferrara lit a cigar and puffed at it, feeling a
certain satisfaction. It was a rueful, purely
professional satisfaction, which did not in any way
lessen the sorrow he felt over the fate of the child
they had decided to call Stella.

*   *   *

Violante came back early in the afternoon from his
visit to the emergency services. He confirmed that
Stella had been found wearing jeans and T-shirt,
but no shoes. The paramedics didn't know
anything about her knickers or bra, nor had they
been struck by anything unusual in the vicinity.

The switchboard operator had not been able to
say anything about the man who had made the call.
The fact that he was a man was the only thing they
were fairly certain about. The call had come in at
about 6.45 on the morning of 29 July. It had been a
short call, and there was no recording of it, either

96

because the tape recorder had not been working or because of an oversight.

'We have to go further, Violante. What we need urgently from the Prosecutor's Department is authorisation to ask the phone company for a record of the emergency call and where it came from. And if it's a mobile phone, we need the name of the registered user and the identifying signal of the cell in the area affected by the outgoing call.'

'Okay, chief.'

All police forces were now aware that mobile phone records could very often be important, and sometimes even decisive, in an investigation, especially in identifying the contacts of a crime victim or a suspect. Even though the logs did not reveal anything of the contents of calls, they did indicate the date, the hour, the duration in units/seconds, and the area affected by the call, which allowed the police to identify individuals who might otherwise have remained unknown.

*   *   *

It was already five thirty. Massimo Verga was probably in his bookshop. Ferrara decided to go over there. It would be much better than phoning: he hadn't seen him in a while and it would be nice to greet him in the flesh.

The Via Tornabuoni was not too far from the Via Zara, and he preferred to walk even though the heat and humidity were still unbearable.

He found Rita doing the accounts together with the two other assistants. Massimo had not yet shown up, and she could not conceal her anxiety.

97

'Have you tried calling him?'

'Of course I have, Chief Superintendent! His phone's always switched off, there's no way to talk to him.'

'Isn't there a phone where he's staying?'

'Who knows? I don't have the number. Do you even know where he's been staying?'

It was true: they knew he had rented a place in Marina di Pietrasanta, but they had no idea of the address. It was supposed to be a surprise, he had said.

'He may have got caught up in traffic, you know how it is in summer . . .' he said, in an attempt to reassure her. But it was Monday afternoon, and if anything the traffic would have been going to the sea, not coming back to the city.

'Let's hope so . . .' she said, although she knew as well as he did that it was unlikely.

'Well, if he comes in or phones tell him to call me.'

'I will, Chief Superintendent.'

*   *   *

With one thing and another, it was nearly seven by the time he got back and he was surprised to find Fanti still there.

The sergeant lived in Prato. If he didn't hurry, he would miss his usual train. Normally he never left later than six-thirty.

'Fanti, what are you still doing here?' he said teasingly, but then realised that the sergeant was looking unusually solemn, and paler than usual. 'What's the matter? Has something happened?'

Without saying a word Fanti handed him a piece

98

of paper with the words *Urgent memo* in the top right-hand corner.

Request help in search for Simonetta Palladiani née Tonelli, born Carrara 17.11.1967, and Massimo Verga, born Catania 10.10.1949, owner of bookshop of same name in historical centre Florence. Said persons believed missing after suspicious death of Ugo Palladiani, born Florence 30.01.1940, husband of aforementioned Simonetta Palladiani. Death probably occurred night of Saturday 4 and Sunday 5 August and discovered this morning.

Police Headquarters Florence, to whom copy of present memo is sent, are asked to supply information regarding aforementioned Massimo Verga who, according to the Interior Ministry data bank, was interviewed at aforementioned Police Headquarters in 1970. Memo sent urgently by order of Public Prosecutor's Department Lucca.

Signed Marshal Angelo Belsito, Commander of Carabinieri station Marina di Pietrasanta.

Ferrara collapsed onto one of the visitors' chairs, closed his eyes and grasped the edge of the desk.

His head was spinning.

9

During the restless and often sleepless nights that followed, Ferrara had time to reflect on certain assumptions which are taken as gospel truth, but clearly are not. One of these is the common belief that among the many misfortunes which could befall the relatives, friends or close acquaintances of a police superintendent, that of being suspected, let alone actually accused, of a serious crime is completely impossible.

Why do we assume this? Probably because every police officer believes that those he knows are honest people and that, given his choice of career, they could only be on the side of the law. But even though life had taken it upon itself to show Ferrara that this eventuality was possible, he continued to consider it unlikely, and this gave his days the hallucinatory feel of a nightmare. He had to make an effort to keep a clear head, which had never been as necessary as it was right now.

Another deeply rooted belief now being shaken—with consequences that for him, a true Sicilian, would be devastating—was the sacred, indestructible value of friendship.

Of course he and Massimo Verga were very different. But only in the external choices they had made in their lives, in much of their behaviour and perhaps—although he wasn't sure of this—in their political beliefs, which they had always avoided talking about for fear of discovering they were either too similar or too different. What united them were much more deeply held values, which

100

had brought them together and cemented their friendship despite misunderstandings and absences. It hurt him now to think back to those difficult days following his engagement to Petra, which had ended with Massimo leaving Sicily for good. And it made him melancholy to think that one of the things that united them and would always unite them was their love for the same woman, which Massimo had sublimated into his inveterate Don Juanism.

The hours which had followed his reading of that incredible memo had been unsettling and interminable.

Good old Fanti had refused to take his train ('I'll sleep here, chief, don't worry, this isn't the first time'), had grabbed the phone and had called the Carabinieri station in Marina di Pietrasanta, only to find himself up against a brick wall in the shape of a guard who was 'not authorised to report the movements, let alone the mobile phone number, of Marshal Belisto, not even to the President of the Republic in person!'

'In my opinion, the bastard was enjoying it,' Fanti reported to Ferrara. 'Always ready to cooperate, those Carabinieri.'

Ferrara was not surprised: the Carabinieri had never been very co-operative towards the police. Even when they did manage to get something out of them, it was like squeezing blood from a stone.

'Did you tell him the call was from me?'

'Of course, chief, but he didn't give a damn, I'm sorry to say! On the contrary—'

'Did you tell him that they should call me back as soon as possible, even on my mobile or my home number?'

'Yes, chief.'

'Good, we just have to wait and hope. The thing I find strange . . . I never heard anything about Massimo being investigated in 1970.'

'That was a long time before you arrived, chief. Who knows where you were in 1970!'

'Right. Well, seeing that we have to wait anyway, can you do me a favour? Go to records and get out his file. Now that we know it exists, let's see what he did that was so terrible . . .'

By the time Ferrara had phoned home and told Petra he would be late, without mentioning the real reason, Fanti was already back with a thin file from 1970. The very sight of it set his mind at rest. He knew what a real criminal's file looked like, and this certainly wasn't one of them.

He opened it.

There were just a few sheets of paper inside, yellow with age.

Massimo Verga had been picked up by officers of the Political Division at a house in Florence used by the Communist Party and frequented by intellectuals involved in the student and worker protests of the time. As he had no criminal record and had never been implicated in any crimes, there had been no further investigation and the file had been closed and never opened again.

Nothing to worry about there.

He walked into Fanti's office. He didn't have the heart to call him again. Fanti was always ready to work overtime, to take on any chores he was asked to, and Ferrara felt he owed him that courtesy at least.

Fanti was busy zapping between the local TV channels searching for news of the case in Marina di Pietrasanta. But there was nothing. It was too late: nearly eleven o'clock.

'Forget about that. Why don't you call our people in Viareggio? They should know something, as it's so close.'

'I've already done it, chief, but they don't know much. Just that Ugo Palliadini's body was found in a villa belonging to his wife, a beautiful woman, quite well known in the area, who's gone missing. The Carabinieri were called in, but as usual they aren't saying anything, even to the local police.'

'This Palladiani,' Ferrara said. 'Have we come across him before?'

'I don't know, chief, I don't think so,' Fanti replied, embarrassed. 'I can take a look in records, if you like . . .'

'Try that. And if he doesn't have a criminal record, check out anything else we have on him. Even applications for passports, licences, weapons permits. Find out all you can.'

'Yes, chief.'

'Check on his wife, too, this Simonetta who went missing with Massimo.'

'I'll get right on it.'

'You won't find much at this hour. Go to sleep now, I'm going home. It's unlikely this Belsito will call back tonight.'

'How shall we answer the memo?' Fanti asked, anxiously.

'I'll deal with that tomorrow. For now, let's keep them guessing.'

*   *   *

Petra was waiting for him on the terrace, with his

dinner ready despite the hour. This time he had to tell her.

For a long time they sat in silence, without touching the food, under a starry sky which had lost all its magic. They were both absorbed in their memories of Massimo, both trying to make sense of the most difficult moments of their friendship, both full of remorse and regret.

A year older than Ferrara, passionate about art, music and philosophy, Massimo Verga had considered himself, from the start, a spiritual guide to his younger contemporary. They had met in their schooldays, and a strange but deep friendship had grown up between the cleverest, most handsome, elegant, self-confident and unconventional heir of a rich, aristocratic family from Catania and the stubborn, somewhat reserved son of peasants from the slopes of Etna, solid people who clung tenaciously to that unforgiving land, to traditional customs and to their own children.

Petra had met Massimo during a holiday in Sicily, her first holiday without her parents, who had stayed behind in Germany. She remembered him as a charming young man with noble features and a thin moustache which had reminded her of the Sicilian writer Elio Vittorini. It was her fascination with Vittorini that had made her choose to study Italian literature at the University of Heidelberg and to visit Sicily as soon as she could. She had been enchanted by the place and its mixture of cultures. It was an island where the wind from the East, tantalising and full of spices, caressed the columns of classical Greek temples.

In those days, foreign women, especially the tall,

slim, blonde, green-eyed Nordic type, literally turned heads in Sicily. Young Sicilian men, driving around in couples on their wobbly Vespas, were so distracted by these women—it would have been a 'mortal sin' not to look, and whistle, too—that they would sometimes lose control of their vehicles and come close to knocking down a pedestrian or crashing into a lamp post. Great times, which Petra remembered with affection and a touch of melancholy. She had liked Massimo immediately, but it had not been because of him that she had decided it would be better to continue her studies right there. It had been because of the shyer, more introverted but level-headed Michele, to whom Massimo had proudly introduced her.

What had followed—Massimo's 'flight', their long separation until many years later, when any possible resentment had gone, their meeting again in that city in central Italy which had adopted them—now hung over their silence like a shadow. What had become of him all that time? What had he been up to, apart from squandering his inheritance on love affairs?

They realised—and it was perhaps the first time they had become so acutely aware of it—that Massimo had always been vague about his various flings. He had generally limited himself to making backhanded compliments about the inexplicable beauty of women. Women were a mystery; a mystery he usually summed up by solemnly quoting the humorist Campanile: 'Do we like women because they are wonderful, or do they seem wonderful because we like them?' They were divine creatures he simply couldn't resist, nor would he ever want to. Comments like these had always amused Michele and worried Petra.

They also felt remorseful over last weekend's missed rendezvous. None of this would have happened if they had been with him on Saturday night for their long-planned get-together. So their silence was tinged with embarrassment. They even avoided looking each other in the eyes, each afraid of seeing in the other his or her own self-accusation.

In the end, it was Petra who broke the silence. 'You must do something, Michele.'

'I'm trying to think what,' he murmured.

Her eyes were on him, and there was no hint of that smile he loved so much. 'I know,' she said, 'but it's not enough. This time I'm the one asking you not to spare yourself, to do whatever it takes. And you have to see it through to the end. Whatever happened, he had nothing to do with it.'

'I know that!' he burst out, almost angrily, and immediately regretted it, fearing that his anger might betray a doubt, an uncertainty he was sure he didn't feel. Of the two of them, she was the one who might have doubts: she had always been afraid that Peter Pan's love affairs would end up getting him in serious trouble one day.

'Of course he had nothing to do with it,' he said, trying to downplay his outburst.

Petra said nothing, but looked at him sadly, her eyes glistening with tears—and it was not like her to cry.

*　　　*　　　*

The following morning there was nothing in the newspapers, apart from an extraordinarily vague article in the Livorno daily *Il Tirreno*.

MYSTERIOUS DEATH OF A FLORENTINE
THE CARABINIERI ARE INVESTIGATING

The Carabinieri in Marina di Pietrasanta, in collaboration with the provincial command in Lucca, are investigating the death of Ugo Palladiani, the Florentine director of a public relations company, who died in mysterious circumstances in a villa owned by his wife, the well-known cultural organiser Simonetta Palladiani. His body was found by the housekeeper yesterday morning in the ground floor drawing room at the foot of the stairs leading to the first floor. According to the housekeeper, one of the guest rooms, occupied by Ugo Palladiani, was in a state of disorder, as if a fight had taken place there, although no objects of value were found to be missing. Adding to the mystery is the absence of the villa's owner, whose bedroom was found to be perfectly tidy, just as the housekeeper had left it on Saturday morning. We have tried to find out more for our readers from the Carabinieri, but for some reason they have not been forthcoming with information—wrongly, in our humble opinion. Rumour—how trustworthy we do not know—suggests that the results of the autopsy, which took place yesterday afternoon, support the theory of a possible homicide.

The mere mention of the word made Ferrara's cigar taste sour.

That would put Simonetta Palladiani, who is missing, in a particularly sensitive position. Simonetta Palladiani is well known on the Versilia coast for her tireless activities in the social and cultural field: for the past two years she has owned the Archivolto art galley in Forte dei Marmi, where talented young painters and sculptors exhibit their works; she has been a member of several literary prize juries, and she has helped to organise festivals and other social and cultural events. In this she has had the support of her husband. The couple are separated but still married and appear to have been on excellent terms. While the Carabinieri carry out their duties, we can only express the hope that Simonetta returns soon to brighten our days and nights on the Versilia coast with her usual enterprising spirit and her luminous smile. C.P.

A strange article, he thought.

He would have liked to talk to that journalist. To judge by his criticism of the Carabinieri and the familiarity with which he referred to Simonetta Palladiani, about whom he talked in such flattering tones—without once mentioning Massimo Verga, Ferrara had noted—he probably knew a lot more than he said.

But was the 'he' a 'she'? he thought suddenly. Didn't the initials C.P. at the end of the article belong to Claudia Pizzi, the very same woman who had given him the nickname Il Gatto?

For now, there were other things that needed to be done. He picked up the receiver and asked the switchboard operator to get him the commanding officer of the Carabinieri station in Pietrasanta. 'Tell him it's me and put me through only when the marshal himself is on the line.'

'Of course, chief. I understand.'

A few minutes later, the phone rang and he lifted the receiver before Fanti could do so.

'Chief, Marshal Belsito to speak to you.'

'Hello?'

'Marshal Angelo Belsito here.'

'Ah, Marshal, hello. This is Chief Superintendent Ferrara, head of the *Squadra Mobile* in Florence.'

'Nice to hear from you. I know you tried to reach me yesterday and I'm sorry I didn't call you back, but we were very busy until late last night. What can I do for you?'

'I was hoping to talk to you, Marshal, because I received your memo. Now I've just been reading in *Il Tirreno* that this could well be a murder case and I wanted to find out more.'

'We're still in the early stages,' the marshal replied, vaguely. 'As I'm sure you realise, it's still too early to speculate.'

The allusion to a possible murder, especially coming from the head of the Florence *Squadra Mobile*, must have made a spark of the age-old rivalry between the police and the Carabinieri flare up in the marshal. Since the case had been reported to the Carabinieri, it belonged to them, and the marshal was clearly determined to defend

109

his jurisdiction.

'Of course,' he continued, 'we know a man is dead and his wife is missing. As is her lover, Massimo Verga. All we need from you, Chief Superintendent, is routine information on the two of them, as is normal. Nothing else, at least for now.'

'Yes, of course, Marshal, that's what I understood from the memo,' Ferrara replied, coldly. This was the first he had heard about Massimo being Simonetta Palladiani's lover, and the news naturally increased his anxiety. 'But what exactly do the results of the autopsy say?'

'I'm sorry, Chief Superintendent, but I'm not authorised to tell you that. You know how these things are. I'm sure you understand. Do you mind my asking why you're so interested?'

'Because Palladiani is from Florence, and so is Massimo Verga. In fact, I don't think Signor Verga is someone who could ever have been involved in something like this except by chance. In my opinion, he's completely innocent.'

'Why, Chief Superintendent, do you know him?' the marshal asked after a very slight pause. Ferrara realised that he suddenly seemed to be paying close attention.

'Yes I do, Marshal. I know him very well. In fact, I've known him a long time . . . and I'd vouch for him with my life!'

A long pause followed. Then Marshal Belsito, now in a more official tone, said, 'Perhaps, Chief Superintendent, since we're dealing with a friend of yours, you'd be able to come here so we could talk to you.'

You bet I could! Ferrara thought. 'No problem,

110

Marshal . . . I could come right now. Will you be there?'

'I'll be waiting.'

'I'll see you later, then. As soon as I get there.'

'I'll be waiting,' the Marshal repeated, in a curt, formal tone. To Ferrara it sounded more like a threat than a promise.

10

The Carabinieri in Marina di Pietrasanta occupied a small, red, two-storeyed villa one block from the sea, where two side streets met. On the small balcony at the back, washing was hanging out to dry. The front was separated from the street by a small, well-tended garden protected by a low white perimeter wall.

The driver double-parked in front of the side gate. The word *Carabinieri* was on the name plate next to the entryphone, while the blue and white sign was inside, above the main door. A woman in a sarong passed Ferrara, pushing a pram, with a little boy and a smaller girl in bathing costumes attached to the sides by leads. Around her waist, the girl was wearing a plastic life preserver shaped like a duck, and the pram was full of beach toys.

Ferrara rang the entryphone.

A sentry appeared almost immediately.

'I'm the head of the *Squadra Mobile* in Florence,' Ferrara said, showing the badge that said *State Police—Chief Superintendent* at the top, and just under it a photo of himself in plain clothes.

'Please come in, Chief Superintendent. The Marshal is waiting for you.'

In the small waiting room, the air conditioning was full on. The room was sparsely furnished, and the only decorations on the walls were prints commemorating the deeds of the Carabinieri. A few in-house magazines lay on a low table in front of an imitation leather sofa.

The sentry left the room for a few minutes, then came back and asked Ferrara to follow him.

The commanding officer came towards him and held out his hand as soon as Ferrara entered his office. 'Marshal Belsito.'

Of medium height and solid build, he was probably closer to sixty than fifty. The most salient feature of his deeply lined face was his thick grey moustache, drooping at the ends: the classic image of the provincial marshal.

'Pleased to meet you,' Ferrara replied. There was no need to introduce himself as the sentry had already announced him.

'And this is the captain,' Belsito said, introducing a young man who had risen from an armchair and approached them. He was about thirty, and so tall that he towered over both of them. He had a severe blond crew cut and, with his athletic physique, looked naturally elegant in his impeccable uniform.

'I'm Captain Renato Fulvi, and for some months now I've been commander of the detectives' unit in the Lucca provincial command.'

He had a northern accent, perhaps Piedmontese.

'Pleased to meet you. Chief Superintendent Ferrara, head of the Florence *Squadra Mobile*.'

'Please take a seat, Chief Superintendent,' Marshal Belsito said, indicating one of the two visitors' armchairs in front of the desk.

Ferrara sat down, and so did the two carabinieri: the marshal in the other armchair and the captain behind the desk, where the marshal should have been sitting. It was a strategic arrangement, surely deliberate, which he didn't like. It seemed to be intended to make him feel like an ordinary citizen who had been summoned by them to be interrogated.

As if to confirm this, the captain, without any preamble, not even the polite formulas expected in a meeting between colleagues, went straight to the point and asked his first question. It was as if he wanted to make it clear that in these circumstances matters of rank were unimportant. And Ferrara did not know if he should be irritated or even more worried about Massimo's position.

'The marshal tells me Signor Massimo Verga is an acquaintance of yours, Chief Superintendent. Or should we say . . . a friend?'

'He's a very good friend of mine,' Ferrara replied, dryly. 'That's why I'm here, isn't it?'

'I thought you were here to find out what happened in the villa where your friend was staying?' the captain said, giving the marshal what seemed to Ferrara a vaguely smug look. Ferrara was feeling increasingly irritated.

'That, too, now that you've told me he was staying there,' Ferrara said. 'I didn't know before.'

'But you're a police officer,' Captain Fulvi replied in an unbearably pedantic tone. If it bothered him that he had given away a piece of information, however trivial, which Ferrara had not known, he did not show it. 'And you should know that we're dealing with the case, not the police.'

This was debatable: for certain types of crime, Marina di Pietrasanta was within Ferrara's jurisdiction. But he preferred to let that go. He decided instead to try a friendlier approach.

'Of course I know that, Captain. I have plenty to do in Florence, believe me, I have no intention of meddling in this case . . . But, as I said, Massimo Verga—'

'—is a friend of yours, we understand that. But for us he's a citizen like any other and will stay that way until our investigation is complete.' It was clear from the captain's tone that, as far as he was concerned, Ferrara had adopted completely the wrong tactic. 'You know perfectly well that while it's in progress, there are no friends, or friends of friends.'

The assertion was so blunt and, since it was uttered in the presence of another member of the Carabinieri, so serious that Ferrara was surprised he managed to control himself. If he hadn't, he could happily have hit this arrogant young man whose only training had probably been in some safe barracks in the north where he'd been stuffed full of theory. Perhaps it was only the sense that this was part of his strange nightmare which held him back. He simply stared in astonishment at the two men.

Why had his relations with the Carabinieri always been stormy? He thought he had left behind him for good those long-gone times when he had taken his first steps as a detective.

The episode was fresh in his mind.

114

It was in Catanzaro. His chief had given him the job of delivering an arrest warrant. 'Go after eight in the evening,' he had said. 'The man's on probation and is supposed to be at home by then.' The man was a well-known Mafia boss, and Ferrara had gone to his home, trembling somewhat but determined to carry out this important mission—one of his first—to the best of his ability. He had knocked at the door and the small, unassuming woman who opened it had said that her husband wasn't there.

'That's not possible, signora. You husband is on probation and has to be at home at this hour!'

'He's gone to the Carabinieri with his lawyer, signore,' the woman had replied.

So Ferrara had gone straight to the Carabinieri.

The sentry had tried to stop him going in, saying that the marshal was busy and could not be disturbed, but he had simply ignored him. The marshal had not been well pleased by the intrusion. He had two men in his office, both smartly dressed in dark pinstriped suits, so that Ferrara had not been able to tell at first which one of them was the man he had come to arrest.

He had ignored the marshal, walked up to the two men and, recognising one of them as the Mafia boss, addressed him directly.

'You have to come with me. I have a warrant here for your arrest.'

'I knew this was coming,' the man had replied confidently, 'but I can't go with you. The reason I came here with my lawyer was to present a medical certificate.'

'I find you here, instead of at home in your bed,' Ferrara had retorted, in a similarly confident and determined tone. 'If you're fit enough to come here, you're fit enough to come with me.'

'I've just had an operation. I'm full of stitches. There's no way I'm getting in a car. If anything happens to me the responsibility will be yours.' The Mafioso's gaze had turned threatening.

'I'm perfectly happy to take that responsibility. Now come with me.'

At that point the marshal, who was still on his feet behind the desk and had remained silent until now, had objected. 'Really, I—'

But Ferrara had not let him finish his sentence. 'We're wasting time here.' He had turned to the officer who had come with him. 'Sergeant, the handcuffs.' The sergeant had gone up to the Mafioso, taken him by the arm and led him away.

The Carabinieri had kicked up a major fuss over this incident. A Mafia boss had been arrested right inside their building—not by them, but by the police. The head of the Reggio Calabria *Squadra Mobile* had had the unenviable task of smoothing things over. He had persuaded Ferrara to agree to the marshal countersigning the report.

'Only because you ask me and you're my boss,' Ferrara had said. 'If it was up to me, I wouldn't let him sign. But I just follow orders.'

*   *   *

'Could you tell us what kind of man your friend is?'

The captain's voice seemed to reach him from a long way away, jolting him out of the memories which had suddenly crowded into his mind.

'Tell me something, Captain,' he replied,

116

incredulous. 'Is this an interrogation?'

He had conducted many interrogations, but had never been interrogated himself. Was this, too, part of the nightmare?

'This is strictly off the record, Chief Superintendent. For the moment all we need is a little background information. And you did come here of your own free will. Unless . . .'

'Unless what?' Ferrara asked, seeing that the captain was taking his time finishing the sentence.

'Unless the deputy prosecutor who's coordinating the investigation subsequently decides it's necessary to take a formal statement from you. But if that's the case, we'll inform you in due course.'

We'll inform you in due course! Not 'We'll let you know' or something similar. The words could not have been more official, and Ferrara felt as though he had been punched in the stomach.

He knew the law. He knew that if the deputy prosecutor decided to request a formal statement, he would receive a written summons to appear, and he would have at least three days to comply, as laid down in the rules of criminal procedure.

'I have no problem making a statement, Captain. I came here voluntarily to talk to you about Massimo Verga in the hope that it would help the investigation, perhaps speed things up. I didn't want you to waste valuable time on false leads. And I remind you that, as a detective and as head of the Florence *Squadra Mobile*, which, as I'm sure you know, has jurisdiction here for some crimes—'

'Of course we know, Chief Superintendent,' Captain Fulvi cut in, clearly galled by Ferrara's implicit criticism of the slowness of the investigation. 'But in this case the investigation is totally within the jurisdiction of the Carabinieri, as authorised by Deputy Prosecutor Lupo of the Prosecutor's Department in Lucca. We're grateful to you, thank you, but we don't need help from Florence. We can call on our special operations divisions for reinforcements, if necessary.'

Ferrara recognised the name of the deputy prosecutor as someone he knew, and that reassured him a little, but he preferred not to show it. He adopted a more docile tone, realising that the important thing was to try and get out of here as soon as possible, away from a situation which was becoming increasingly absurd.

'Captain, tell me what you want to know,' he said with feigned resignation. 'I'm at your disposal.'

'All right, Chief Superintendent. I'll repeat the question: what kind of man is your friend Massimo Verga?'

Meanwhile, the marshal had taken a few sheets of white paper and a pen from a drawer, ready to take down Ferrara's answers. Even if this wasn't a real interrogation, the statement would end up as an entry in police records, signed by the two Carabinieri, and would be passed on to the deputy prosecutor in charge of the investigation.

'To me, and to the many people who know him, he's a highly regarded person, and a very hard worker. For some years he's been the owner of a thriving bookshop in the historical centre of Florence, which numbers some of the most distinguished people in the city among its customers. Massimo Verga himself is a highly

118

cultured man. He's never been in trouble with the law, apart from one juvenile episode of no importance, as I'm sure the marshal will already have ascertained. If he hasn't done so, I can provide all the paperwork.'

'Do you think he may have had any questionable associates?' thc captain asked, ignoring this barb.

Did Fulvi include him in that description? Ferrara wondered, with bitter amusement.

'I don't know of any questionable associates. If I'd suspected he had any, I wouldn't have kept him as a friend, as I'm sure you can imagine.'

The captain nodded, and Ferrara had the feeling he had realised what an inappropriate question that was to ask a policeman, let alone the head of the *Squadra Mobile*.

Renato Fulvi was silent, as if pondering his next question. Then he exchanged a quick glance with Marshal Belsito, and it was the marshal who asked the next question.

'Chief Superintendent, do you think your friend and Signora Simonetta Palladiani were romantically involved?'

Now we're getting to it, Ferrara thought.

'No,' he said, 'but it wouldn't surprise me if they were lovers, as you told me on the phone.'

The glance of disapproval the captain gave the marshal did not escape him. They were equal now, as far as giving away information went.

'You see,' he continued, 'Massimo Verga has never married, and has had lots of affairs. He has a weakness for women, as do many Italian men, but I don't think that counts as a crime and none of his girlfriends have been . . . questionable.'

'But adultery can get people into trouble,' the captain said. 'Signora Palladiani was a married woman.'

'Not really, according to today's edition of *Il Tirreno*. She and her husband were separated, I think it said.'

The captain looked at him with what at last seemed to be sympathy.

'Don't you think you're clutching at straws, Chief Superintendent?' the marshal said. 'They had never divorced. We're not exactly sure what kind of relationship they had. We'll find out, but for the moment what we know is that the three of them were there that night in Signora Palladiani's villa in the Via Roma—' (two-one to the marshal, Ferrara thought: another piece of information he hadn't known before) '—the husband, the wife and the wife's lover. Now one of them is dead, and the other two are missing.'

In his place, Ferrara thought, he might have come to the same inescapable conclusion.

'It isn't possible, Marshal. Massimo Verga isn't a criminal and would never ever . . .'

'What?'

'Massimo Verga wouldn't hurt the proverbial fly . . . believe me.'

'Do you have any idea where he might have gone?' the captain asked, seemingly determined to continue with what was turning out to be a genuine interrogation. 'Do you know of any contacts he has, either in Tuscany or elsewhere, who might be sheltering him?'

'I have no idea . . . Massimo is not the kind of person to have secrets. The fact that he's missing worries me a lot. If you can't find him, it must

120

mean something serious has happened to him. Do you understand, Captain? Something that's stopping him from getting in touch with anyone . . .'

There was such distress in his voice that the captain paused for a long time before continuing.

'Last night, a patrol went to his apartment in Florence, but there was no one there.'

'He lives alone, Captain . . .'

'Does he have any relatives in Florence?'

'No. His only relatives are in Catania, which is where he was born.'

'We've already contacted our Sicilian colleagues,' the captain said.

'Let me ask you something. Do you really think Ugo Palladiani was murdered?'

There was another, longer pause.

'We're certain of it.'

Ferrara felt his strength fail him. 'Why?'

Fulvi thought about it, then replied, articulating his words clearly, 'Chief Superintendent, I don't think you've quite understood. We're the ones asking the questions!'

This was the last straw. All the frustration Ferrara had been feeling during this ridiculous conversation boiled over. 'No, Captain, you're the one who hasn't quite understood,' he began, his voice gradually becoming louder as he went on, although he had no idea where this outburst would lead. 'First of all, you seem to have forgotten that I'm not some street vendor you can push around, not some pickpocket on the beach, not some rowdy drunk. I'm the head of the Florence *Squadra Mobile* and I won't tolerate an officer of the law getting a kick out of throwing his weight around. There's a man out there who may be in grave danger. If he isn't already dead, seeing how much time you've wasted so far!'

The captain had turned purple. 'I won't stand for this, Chief Superintendent!' he retorted.

'This conversation is over. Don't think I'll hesitate to complain to the Director of Public Prosecutions, if necessary.'

'That'll make two of us, then.'

'Let the best man win!'

*   *   *

'Go all the way along the Via Roma and stop when you see the Carabinieri,' Ferrara said to the driver. He was still furious.

The villa was not hard to spot. The Carabinieri were guarding it, as he had expected. But there was no point stopping.

Above the high perimeter wall rose a canvas barrier stretched over steel scaffolding, which completely blocked the view. He decided he would have to come back.

11

Despite flashing his light and sounding the siren, it took Ferrara more than an hour and a half to get back to Headquarters. On the way, he received two phone calls. One was from Petra, whom he told everything. The other was from Rita Senesi, and he told her he hadn't heard from Massimo either, but he was looking into it and she shouldn't worry. As a piece of advice it was as stupid as it was pointless, but he did not yet feel like filling her in on what had happened, communicating his own anxiety to her, when she was already anxious enough.

He himself had called Fanti, but he wasn't in. He had then asked the switchboard operator to get him the phone number of *Il Tirreno*. He spoke first to the local news editor, without much success, then to the chief editor, who confirmed that C.P. did indeed stand for Claudia Pizzi. But she was out on a job that day. He finally managed to obtain her mobile and home numbers. She lived in Carrara. The mobile seemed to be switched off, and when he tried her home number all he got was an answering machine. He left a message, asking her to call him back.

He was still beside himself when they finally got to Headquarters. He hurried along the corridors like a cyclone, screaming 'Fanti!' before he had even crossed the threshold of his office.

No reply from the sergeant.

'Fanti!' he repeated, entering the office and walking to his desk. 'Where the hell is he hiding himself?'

It was clear that the sergeant wasn't in his office. What Ferrara found instead was a note telling him that he would be away all morning checking various things—*It's almost three in the afternoon!* he thought—and that Dr Francesco Leone had called twice.

'Of course!' he said to himself in a low voice. 'Operation Stella.' He had forgotten all about the dead girl. But he called Leone, perhaps in the secret hope that he had discovered something which would miraculously solve the case, leaving him free to devote himself to his missing friend.

'Thanks for the report, Doctor. It's been very useful.'

'Don't mention it. And I have something else to tell you about the girl.'

'Stella,' Ferrara said.

'Ah, was that her name?'

At that moment, Fanti returned, waved to him in greeting, and went into his room to switch on the computer.

'No. I don't know. That's what we decided to call her.'

'Good for you! Well, Stella wasn't an addict, that's definite.'

'How do you know?'

'From the analysis of the hair and the toxicology tests, which we've just finished. In habitual drug users the drug leaves a deposit on the hair; hers was as pure as an angel's. Same thing when we tested the bile and liver samples, neither of which showed any trace of addiction. She was clean, Chief Superintendent. But the bile and liver did show the presence, although in minimal traces, of benzoylecgonine, the metabolite of cocaine—which indicates that at about the same time she consumed opiates, the girl . . . what did you call her?'

'Stella.'

'Right . . . Stella had also taken cocaine.'

'Confirming what you found in the mucous membranes of the nose.'

'Precisely.'

Ferarra could distinctly hear Fanti tapping away at great speed on the keyboard of the computer in

124

the next room, through the thin walls.

'So she was drugged and raped.'

'That's for you to establish. I supply the facts, you make the deductions.'

'Anything else?'

'Isn't that enough?'

'More than enough. Thanks, Leone.'

'Just doing my job.'

*   *   *

There was a knock at the door while he was still replacing the receiver.

'Fanti, who is it?' he cried, and immediately added, 'Fanti! Where were you before?'

The sergeant ran to the door, then back to Ferrara's desk.

'It's Chief Inspector Violante, chief,' he said, looking pained and worried.

'Send him in, but first do you want to tell me where the hell you've been?'

'Checking up on Palladiani, chief,' Fanti replied. 'Like you told me,' he added, almost under his breath.

'Oh, I see. Good for you. What did you find out?'

'Several things, chief.'

'Go on.'

'Now? What about Chief Inspector Violante? Anyway, I'm still collating the material. If you like, I could prepare a preliminary report. It'll be ready in half an hour at the most.'

'All right. Send Violante in, and bring me the report as soon as he's gone.'

'Okay, chief.'

*   *   *

'Good afternoon, chief,' the inspector said, sitting down.

'Do you think so?' Ferrara replied.

'I'm sorry?' Violante said, not understanding, or more likely not hearing.

Ferrara raised his voice. 'I said, do you think it's so good? Not to me it isn't! Never mind—do you have any good news for me?'

'Well, chief, we were in touch with the phone company several times this morning and finally got a reply from them.'

To get himself back on the wavelength of the Stella case, Ferrara looked through Violante's correspondence with the Prosecutor's Department and with the phone company. He noted that Anna Giulietti had sent copies of everything to her colleague, Deputy Prosecutor Erminia Cosenza, who was dealing with other overdose cases being investigated by Narcotics. This at least cheered him up: he knew how important it was for prosecutors to coordinate their investigations, since even apparently unrelated cases sometimes turned out to have something in common.

'Good. Go on, I'm listening!' he said to Violante, who had been waiting while he read.

'Whoever made the call made it from a public phone booth a few hundred yards from the place where Stella was found, quite close to a bar, which was still closed when the ambulance arrived. A five-thousand-lire phone card was used for the call. The phone company have supplied us with the serial number.'

'That's good. Have you identified the owner?'

'Unfortunately, not yet. There are no names on phone cards.'

'I know that, Chief Inspector, but they're made to be used.'

Violante gave him a blank look.

'You have to put in another request immediately.'

'Go on, chief.'

'We know for certain that the call was made at 6.45 a.m. on July twenty-ninth. We need the records of the phone booth to see what calls were made just before and just after that one.'

Violante was starting to understand. A few years earlier Ferrara had managed to identify the killer of a prostitute in that way. But in that case the killer had stupidly telephoned his wife and then his victim just before going to see her and killing her, whereas now they were dealing with a single emergency call.

'Just before and just after, chief, meaning . . . ?'

'At least half an hour before and half an hour after,' Ferrara said.

'Okay. I'll get on to it right away, but it may take a few days, maybe even a week, before we get an answer.'

It was true: it could well be that long, because it took several days for the phone company's computer data to be completely updated. Worse still, if the technicians at the phone company thought the police were investigating some trivial case—nuisance calls, something like that—they took even longer.

'I know, Violante. But the sooner you put in the request, the sooner you'll get the answer. You just

127

have to keep on at the phone company, keep reminding them this is a homicide investigation.'

'All right, chief,' Violante said, making as if to stand up.

'Wait, I haven't finished.'

'Go on, chief.'

'We also need the records for the phone card. We need to know if the caller used it before or after, which phones he used it from, and who he called.'

'Okay, chief.'

Violante left the room.

*   *   *

Fanti came in and handed him his report. 'Would you like a coffee, chief?'

It was only then that he realised he hadn't eaten or drunk anything all day. The Carabinieri hadn't even had the courtesy to offer him a coffee!

'Why not?' he replied, forcing himself to smile and take advantage of this break to try and relax. 'And see if you can get me a sandwich, too. But I want a good coffee, okay, Fanti?'

'As always, chief,' Fanti said, withdrawing to his own office.

The taste of Fanti's coffee tended to vary. Whenever Ferrara had remarked on this in the early days, Fanti had tended to reply with an enigmatic smile, like someone who knows a secret he has no intention of revealing, even under torture. Then one day, he had yielded to Ferrara's insistence and had explained that he used different blends, from different manufacturers, which he then blended before putting in the filter. A blend

128

of blends: that was the secret and the reason for the sometimes alarming variability of the coffee he so thoughtfully served to his chief.

His secretary really was unique, Ferrara had thought, with a laugh. He was lucky to have found him, because he couldn't have invented someone like that.

Cheered by that memory, he opened the file. He was still immersed in it when Fanti returned with a ham roll and the coffee. The sergeant did not dare to interrupt him. He almost tiptoed in and carefully placed the tray on Ferrara's desk. Ferrara continued reading as he ate and drank. The coffee was bland and slightly watery.

UGO PALLADIANI/SIMONETTA PALLADIANI NÉE TONELLI—COLLATION OF OFFICIAL DOCUMENTS AND REPORT

Subject 1
UGO PALLADIANI, originally Folco, born Florence 30/01/1940, resident there, at 680 Via della Vigna Nuova.
*   Identity Card AE 6149065 issued Town Hall Florence
*   Passport B 031285 issued Police Headquarters Florence [see appendix A]
*   Driving licence AB Florence 0784612
*   Weapons licence 468905 79 issued Police Headquarters Florence
*   Administrative documents: see appendix B
*   Various: see appendix C

REPORT:

Subject 1 comes from a family of rich Florentine textile merchants. Only son. Cavour Senior High School 1954-58, Bocconi University Milan, 1959-63. Studies interrupted by death of father. Takes over family business in crisis. Business declared bankrupt [see appendix B subsection 4] 1965.

1965-76: details missing at present time [presumably devoted to social life: see appendix C subsection 3].

1976: marries Susanna Spotorno, wealthy Roman retailer, owner of two clothing shops in the capital: one in the Largo Argentina and the other in the Via Cola di Rienzo.

Following his marriage, embarks on clothing business, successfully but briefly [Note: these are the years of the Gucci crisis and Ugo Palladiani appears to realise that new developments will be in casual clothing, as turns out to be the case. But he seems unable to adapt to the changes of the Eighties and the trend in designer casuals. He continues with mass produced clothing, inevitably losing out to more prestigious brands which capture the market during these years].

His financial failure does not prevent subject from continuing to lead an extravagant life [see appendix C subsection 2].

1986: divorces Susanna Spotorno.

1989: marries Simonetta Tonelli [see subject 2].

1991: declared bankrupt by the court of Florence [see appendix B subsection 1] [Note: declaration is evidence of extent of Subject 1's debts].

1994: subject settles debts and founds a public relations company, UP Communications Ltd, based at 680 Via della Vigna Nuova. Substantial profits up to and including year 2000.

Subject 2
SIMONETTA PALLADIANI NÉE TONELLI, born Carrara 17/11/1967, residing 135 Via Roma, Marina di Pietrasanta (Lucca).
* Identity Card details requested from Town Hall Pietrasanta 07/08/01
* Passport B 031285 issued Police Headquarters Lucca
* Driving licence information requested Prefecture of Lucca 07/08/01
* Weapons licence: None
* Various: see appendix D

REPORT:
Subject 2 is a woman with an active social life [see appendix D].

At this stage of the investigation, there is no available information on her family and education.

1989: marries Ugo Palladiani.

1996: moves from Florence to Marina di Pietrasanta. Active presence in cultural and social life of Versilia coast, not Florence [Note: civil marriage still valid. Maintains friendly relations with husband]

131

[see appendices C and D].

Report compiled in accordance with your instructions
Signed: Sergeant Nestore Fanti
Florence, Tuesday 7 August 2001

Appendix A was an old, invalid passport that had been returned to Ugo Palladiani when he had applied for a new one.

He opened it.

He studied the photograph for a long time. Despite his age, Palladiani looked relaxed, well groomed, a man who took care of his appearance. He wore his greying hair rather long, like an artist. Perhaps he had been one of those men who are convinced they will always be young.

But he did not recognise the face. He had certainly never met him: he had a photographic memory and would surely have remembered him. But it was strange, because the name . . .

The other appendices were a report that he owned three hunting rifles; the hunting licence itself; a report of the theft, two years earlier, of his car, a Mercedes CLK; balance sheets; declarations by the Bankruptcy Tribunal and various newspaper cuttings (appendices C and D), either showing him at various social occasions alone or with his wife, or reporting events on the Versilia coast, at which Simonetta Palladiani appeared with various people, but never with her husband.

There was no doubt that Simonetta was a very beautiful woman. She was tall and sensual, and in some of the photos she looked more like Ugo's daughter than his wife.

Even knowing Fanti's diligence and meticulousness, Ferrara could not help wondering how he had managed in less than twenty-four hours—six or seven if he had followed his advice and had gone to sleep the night before—to gather such an impressive body of information. Fanti had done an extraordinary job, and although Ferrara was usually sparing with his praise, this time he couldn't help telling him.

'Fanti,' he called.

Fanti came in looking anxious, as if expecting to be reprimanded. 'Yes, sir?' Fanti replied.

'Excellent work, Fanti. Congratulations!'

Fanti blushed visibly. 'But it isn't finished, chief . . .'

'I know. Don't worry about that. What I'd like to know is how you found out all these things. I don't mean what's in the documents. I'm talking about all these "notes", the story of his clothing business . . . Who did you get that from?'

'From a neighbour, the Contessa Servi,' Fanti said, with legitimate pride. 'Don't you remember, chief? The old lady who came to us in June to report a theft from her apartment.'

Ferrara remembered her well: a sprightly old lady, dressed the way women of good families used to dress. Commissioner Lepri had asked him to take her off his hands.

'The Contessa Servi's apartment,' Fanti continued, 'is in the very same building where Ugo Palladiani lives, on the same floor.'

'Lived,' Ferrara corrected him.

'Yes, chief, lived.'

'And his company also has its offices there, doesn't it?'

'No, the offices of the company are on the ground floor, and the apartment's on the second floor.'

'Did you go to the offices, too?'

'No. Or rather yes, but they're closed for the holidays.'

'A thriving company, according to the balance sheets. I wonder how he managed to recover, after so many disasters . . .'

'Maybe his second wife was rich.'

'There isn't much about her, is there?'

'I'm still investigating, chief . . .'

'Didn't the contessa tell you?'

'What?'

'If she was rich.'

'I didn't ask her,' he admitted, mortified.

'Don't worry, it doesn't matter. You did an excellent job, as I said.'

'Thank you, chief.'

Ferrara fell silent, lost in thought.

'May I go?'

'Of course . . . Oh, just a moment, Fanti.'

'Chief?'

'I'd like you to get hold of Superintendent Rizzo. Tell him I'm sorry, but I need him to interrupt his holidays and get back here as soon as he can.'

'As soon as he can? What does that mean?'

'It means as soon as possible, Fanti. In fact, right away.'

'I'll get on to it now, chief.'

He left the room.

*   *   *

134

Ferrara went back to the file, concentrating this time on the financial affairs of Subject 1, as Fanti had dubbed him. He could not understand how he had managed to recover from a setback which would have floored businessmen a lot more hardened than Palladiani seemed to have been, how he had bounced back and established his PR company. Even with a rich wife, it couldn't have been easy.

What if Ugo Palladiani had been in debt to a loan shark, and was murdered because he couldn't pay? he wondered. It was pure speculation, not too far-fetched—there were an alarming number of similar cases—but speculation nonetheless. It did have the advantage, though, of clearing Massimo.

Finding Massimo—finding him alive—was unfortunately another matter, he thought with a pang in his heart.

He dismissed the implications of this last thought and tried to concentrate on practicalities.

First of all, he had to ascertain if Simonetta Tonelli was a rich woman. It might be worth having a chat with the Contessa Servi, who gave the impression that she knew a lot.

'Fanti!' he called.

'Chief . . . I haven't been able to reach Rizzo.'

'Keep trying. But that's not why I called you.'

'Go on, chief.'

'Phone the contessa and ask her if I can go and see her. Today, if possible.'

'I'll get on it right away.'

Fanti went out and Ferrara looked at his watch, sighing as he did so.

It was 4.01.

Rita Senesi hadn't phoned. It was time to call

135

her and tell her what had happened.

12

There were so many people in the streets,
constantly slowing down the car, that Ferrara
asked the driver to let him out in the Via Cavour
and walk the rest of the way. He cut through the
queue of tourists waiting in line to get into Santa
Maria del Fiore, saying, '*Pardon*, excuse me, *bitte*,
permiso!' and thinking that he would soon have to
learn how to say it in Japanese and perhaps even
Chinese, and walked around to the other side of
the baptistery like a sailor in a storm-tossed sea of
people. Not only were there the crowds to contend
with, and the chaos in marked contrast to the
harmonious lines of Giotto and Brunelleschi's
architecture, there was also the stench from the
horseshit deposited by the animals pulling
the carriages, a stench made all the worse by the
heat.

He crossed the Piazza della Republica to the
Via degli Strozzi and he could not resist a glance in
passing at Giambologna's grim little devil at the
corner of the Via dei Vecchietti. He wondered if
that devil, too, felt lost in the middle of all the
crowds. Perhaps he was the one who had
summoned them, and was now thoroughly
enjoying the spectacle.

The building in the Via della Vigna Nuova was
as imposing, solid and aristocratic as the street
itself—today the heart and drawing room of the
city—one of the two streets, the other being the

136

Via della Vigna Vecchia, which Ludovico de' Medici, lover of good wine and good food, had named after the vines in 1477.

The caretaker, a fat man made haggard by the heat, must have left the jacket of his uniform in his lodge and was idling in shirtsleeves beside the front door, looking vaguely dazed. He didn't even ask for Ferrara's name, just told him which floor to go to.

The lift was a heavy black iron structure which squeaked as it ascended. It smelt of wood, and had an ornate interior, with a small bench upholstered in red velvet. The velvet was frayed, which seemed to Ferrara to complement the slowness with which the lift moved.

A black man in white livery opened the door, and led him into an elegant air-conditioned drawing room. The furniture was antique, some of it English and some of it nineteenth-century Florentine. Big mirrors on the walls displayed the reflected images of old master paintings, mostly landscapes and religious subjects.

'Very punctual, Chief Superintendent, please sit down!' the contessa said in greeting, dismissing the servant with a slight gesture of the hand. He was immediately replaced by a woman in a white starched cap and apron, with olive skin and oriental features, carrying cups, teapot and cakes on a silver tray, which she placed on a large glass table next to the sofa.

'You're just in time!' the contessa continued as the maid poured the pleasantly spicy infusion in the cups and withdrew without a word. 'I hate having tea alone . . . Or perhaps you'd prefer coffee?'

'Tea will do very nicely, thank you, Contessa.'

He remembered her well. She was tiny, angular, and very pale: a pallor her discreet make-up could not quite conceal. Her vaguely blue-tinted hair was perfectly groomed, as if she had just come from the hairdresser. She was wearing a light silk dress and a few discreet jewels which betrayed her elevated rank without shouting it to the rooftops.

'I hope these cakes are to your taste, Chief Superintendent. They're from Sicily.'

Her manner was coquettish, and her eyes sparkled.

'Very much so.'

'Please help yourself, Chief Superintendent. It's always a pleasure to be with civilised people, and that happens more and more rarely, don't you find? I go out less and less. I'm sometimes invited to social events, but I find them increasingly boring and pointless. Things aren't the way they used to be. We live in an ugly world, and it'll get worse, take it from someone who went everywhere for as long as I could, when my poor husband was alive. The ugliness is increasing. You're not safe within your own four walls any more, I think you know what I'm referring to . . .'

'Yes, of course.'

'It's a shock, I can tell you that, to discover that strangers have been rummaging among your things, not to mention the damage . . . You don't know how much I miss those folding kidskin fans! They were part of my life, a rare collection, an heirloom, did you know that?'

'Yes, Contessa, you told us when you reported the theft.'

'Of course, it's just that it rankles with me so

138

much . . . By the way, is there any news?'

'Still nothing—but we're working on it. They must be having problems offloading them. We'll get them sooner or later, don't worry.'

'Do you think so?'

'With that kind of robbery, unless it's been carried out on commission, the thief usually has a great deal of difficulty selling the stolen goods.'

'Let's hope it's as you say, Chief Superintendent, and that you manage to get them back. I'd be so grateful! But you haven't come here to listen to me grumbling. So tell me, to what do I owe this pleasant visit? Mind you, I think I can guess.'

'I'm sure you can, Contessa. I'd like to continue where my secretary left off.'

'If possible. I think I told him everything, though . . . What a nice young man!'

'Did you know Ugo and Simonetta Palladiani well?'

'Fairly well. We didn't see each other socially, if that's what you mean, but I've been living in this building since I was born and the Palladianis have always been our neighbours.'

'So you knew Ugo when he was born?'

'Practically, yes.'

'What kind of man was he?'

'A tearaway, I'd say. A handsome child who became a handsome but spoilt teenager. Then a handsome adult, but still spoilt! Expensive cars, girls, all that kind of thing.' She chuckled. 'When he was young and when he wasn't so young.'

'A rich man's life, in other words. Did they have a lot of money?'

'The family, yes, but when Folco, the father,

died, he left them rather badly off. Ugo took over the business, not very successfully. He never lacked for anything, though, I can assure you of that.'

'He seems to have had rather a lot of ups and downs before he started his PR company.'

'Not in his social life, though. Endless parties and expensive dinners. And what's PR, anyway? Is that a serious profession? You tell me . . .'

Ferrara ignored the remark. 'As far as you know, is his second wife rich?'

'Who, Miss Forte dei Marmi?' the contessa exclaimed immediately, and laughed. 'Come on, Chief Superintendent! A nobody who likes to think she's a somebody. Pretty, yes, he always liked them pretty! But rich, no! The classic cover girl who marries an aging man. Someone without a name . . . Tonelli or something like that, just imagine! A drunken father, a miner or something, over in those parts, where the marble quarries are, you know? No, no, Ugo Palladiani never had a cent from her. Quite the contrary, trust me!'

'And yet he miraculously recovered from a serious financial crisis when his clothes business failed.'

'I'm sorry, Chief Superintendent, but I couldn't tell you anything about that, apart from the fact that I was as surprised as you are. Someone, I can't remember who, said he must have had help from somebody, but no one ever knew who or why. At least I never did . . .'

She did, however, seem an unusually well-informed woman. He wouldn't have used the word 'gossip', only out of respect for her title and age, but he certainly thought it.

'Who might know?'

'I'd tell you if I could, but believe me . . .'

If I don't know, then I don't hold out much hope for you was the clear message. But that didn't rule out—in fact, it reinforced—the idea that he had been helped by loan sharks.

'Contessa,' he said, standing up, 'I shan't bother you any longer. Thank you for your hospitality.'

'Oh, nonsense. It's been a pleasure. Come back whenever you like. I always like having visitors.'

She rang a little silver bell to summon the maid.

'Jacqueline, show the Chief Superintendent out. Goodbye, give my regards to the Commissioner . . . and don't forget those fans!'

'Don't worry,' he said as he walked away.

The same thing he'd said to Rita Senesi.

*   *   *

Back out in the street, Ferrara was hit by the hot wind that was beating down on the city without bringing any relief.

He switched on his mobile. There was a text message from Rizzo, telling him he'd be back in the office the next day.

The only good news he'd had all day. He would delegate the Stella case to Rizzo, and devote himself body and soul to the search for Massimo, which meant to the murder in Marina di Pietrasanta, and he didn't care if it was within the Carabinieri's jurisdiction or not.

He decided to return home.

As he walked in, he heard the sound of a saxophone in the background, and recognised Billie Holiday's recording of 'The Man I Love'.

141

Petra often played Billie Holiday to relax when she had a lot on her mind.

They didn't say much to each other that evening. She only had to look at his face to know that there was no news.

After a cold dinner of ham and cheese, eaten quickly, Ferrara sat down at his desk to have a last look at the Stella file before he passed it on to Rizzo the next day. Keeping himself busy was the only way to exorcise, for however short a time, the spectre of his friend's absence, which hung in the air, making the apartment feel cramped and inhospitable.

He had written a memo headed *For Francesco Rizzo*, summarising the case to date and listing suggestions as to the direction he thought the investigation should take, and was now studying the report on Freemasonry, when his work mobile rang.

'Is that you, Chief Superintendent? I'm sorry to call you so late.'

It was a woman's voice, young and self-confident.

'Thanks for calling me back, Signorina Pizzi.'

'It's more than a duty, it's a pleasure. We haven't spoken in quite a while. Are you still angry at me over the Gatto thing?'

'I've never been angry with you. And anyway . . .'

'Yes?'

'Whether I like it or not, it's become a kind of trademark, you must have seen the other newspapers . . . And it's not just the newspapers. The only person who absolutely refuses to use it is my wife. But I'll tell you this—there are situations in which I'd prefer to be a cat rather than a police officer.'

'Is this one of those times?'

'I'm going through a bad patch, yes.'

'That makes two of us, then. But you didn't call me to cry on my shoulder, I suppose.'

'You're right. I read your article about the death of that Florentine businessman in Marina di Pietrasanta and wanted to know a little more.'

'But aren't the Carabinieri handling the case?'

'Yes, they are. Let's just call it professional curiosity, shall we?'

She was a journalist after all and he couldn't tell her too much, couldn't tell her what he was really worried about. If he did, he'd find his name mentioned in connection with the case the very next day on the front page of *Il Tirreno*. He could already see the headline, across four columns: MYSTERY MAN FROM MURDER VILLA IS FRIEND OF FLORENCE *SQUADRA MOBILE* CHIEF.

'All right, let's call it that,' she said. 'I smell a conflict of jurisdiction. In that case, don't leave me out . . . when the time comes, of course. But if Il Gatto himself has called me, that must mean the homicide theory is no longer just a theory. Am I right?'

He decided it was safe to give that much away. 'If you don't mention your source, affirmative.'

'Don't worry, I won't. I don't think the Carabinieri would like it, do you?'

'Good girl.'

'Anyway, I was expecting it. This is a nasty story, Chief Superintendent. Much nastier than it seems.'

'In what way?'

'I won't say too much now. Read my newspaper.

143

I'm just finishing the article . . . as long as they don't censor it! I'm adding powder to the fire—and when it explodes it'll be louder than carnival!' There was pride in her words, but her tone was weary rather than amused.

'I'll do that. But can you tell me anything about Simonetta Palladiani?'

'What do you want to know?' she replied, a touch cautiously, her voice cracking slightly, as if embarrassed as well as weary.

'You wrote about her as if . . . you knew her well. Did you know her?'

'We were classmates. We grew up together.'

'I see,' Ferrara said, thinking of himself and Massimo: schoolfriends who had grown up together. 'And do you have any idea where she is?'

'If only I knew!' she said with a sigh. An anxious sigh? Ferrara wondered.

'Could she have gone on holiday?' he suggested. 'Before her husband died, perhaps?'

'No, Chief Superintendent. Unfortunately she was there that night.'

'How do you know?'

'The housekeeper told me. She was the one who told me everything, in fact. I got fed up waiting for the Carabinieri!'

'What's the housekeeper's name?'

'Grazia Barberi.'

'And do you know where she lives?' Ferrara insisted, making a note on a piece of paper.

'In Pietrasanta, right at the top. The Via Martiri di Sant'Anna, a pink building, five storeys high, you can't miss it.'

'What kind of person was Simonetta Palladiani?'

144

'Why do you say "was"?' Claudia protested, her voice breaking with emotion.

'I'm sorry, it just came out. It was only because she hasn't been found yet . . . Are you very close?'

'We used to be, but I didn't see anything of her after she married that guy and went to Florence. We spoke a few times on the phone when she moved to Marina, but we've never seen each other again. If there really was a murder, she has nothing to do with it, believe me . . .'

The same certainty he felt about Massimo!

'Was there anyone else in the villa?'

'So you know that, do you? Yes, a man from Florence, her latest boyfriend apparently.'

There were still so many things he would have liked to ask her, he might have been on the phone for hours. Talking face to face was always preferable. A particular intonation of the voice, lowered eyes, a hesitation, could say more than a thousand words spoken at a distance.

'Listen, signorina, could we meet?'

She seemed to think it over. 'Yes, I'd like that— it might be useful to both of us,' she answered finally. 'When?'

'How about tomorrow?'

'I can't do it in the morning . . . I could manage late afternoon. How about an aperitif at the Twiga in Marina di Pietrasanta?'

'What's that?'

'Chief Superintendent! Don't tell me you still go to the Capannina? The Twiga's the hottest place in town! Footballers, models . . . the crème de la crème!'

'Wouldn't we be a bit too visible?'

'If we need privacy we could always walk along

145

the beach, far from prying ears.' She wasn't being flirtatious, but establishing a worried complicity.

Ferrara sensed a kind of urgency no different from his own, and he felt less alone.

'Is five okay?'

'Let's say six.'

He started looking through the file on Freemasonry again, but couldn't concentrate. What was it that Claudia Pizzi had found out? What had she meant about an explosion? The first thing next morning, he absolutely had to read *Il Tirreno*.

He lit a cigar and skimmed through the lists of members as if reading the phone book. One of the best books to send you to sleep, his friend Massimo had once suggested to him: a lot of characters and no plot. Except that he had already lost sleep on Monday night and tonight would be the same, even with all the phone books in Italy.

Especially after the name that suddenly leapt off the page, going through him like an electric shock: Ugo Palladiani, born in Florence on 30 January 1940, was a member of the Concorde lodge!

13

Michele Ferrara could not wait until he got to the office, where the newspapers would be waiting for him, but bought a copy of *Il Tirreno* at the newsstand near where he lived before getting into his service car.

He leafed through it while the driver dodged the pedestrians as he did every morning, and when he reached the last page he started again from the first, with no better luck. The only item about the death of Ugo Palladiani was a brief recap of the case, unsigned, which added nothing new, illustrated by a photo of the impenetrable exterior of Simonetta's villa, guarded by the Carabinieri. No sign of Claudia Pizzi's explosive article. Had they censored it as she had feared? He thought of calling her but dismissed the idea. She had told him she would be busy and anyway she would tell him everything, at greater length, that evening at the Twiga.

Besides, they'd already arrived at Headquarters and he had to get out of the car.

He started going through all the newspapers as soon as he was in his office. Fanti asked him if he wanted a coffee, and he said yes. The other papers had picked up on the news by now, and went into it in greater depth than today's *Il Tirreno*. There were photos of Simonetta and her various activities, and *La Reppublica* and *Il Corriere della Sera* already mentioned the homicide theory. *Il Corriere della Sera* even carried a short interview with Captain Fulvi, who was non-committal but praised Belsito's efforts and implied that the Carabinieri would soon solve the case.

None of the papers mentioned Massimo Verga, and Ferrara wondered if that was a good or a bad sign. He leaned towards the latter, though: it suggested a strategy on Captain Fulvi's part to make the suspect drop his guard while his men, with Belsito at their head, tightened the circle around him. An old trick which sometimes worked when you weren't dealing with hardened criminals.

He tried to dismiss the thought, concentrating

147

on the daily routine, which he wanted to get out of the way as quickly as possible so that he could devote all his time to the only case that interested him. But his mind kept going back to that Masonic list which included the name of Ugo Palladiani. What were the implications of that?

The first and most obvious, which had occurred to him during another sleepless night, was that 'the Brotherhood' had rescued Palladiani from financial collapse. He didn't like it very much, because it would put paid to the already flimsy idea of the loan shark, but you couldn't base a case on an aesthetic preference, and whether he liked it or not, it would have to be gone into.

He put aside the files and took the membership lists out of his briefcase.

The Concorde lodge had fourteen members, twice the minimum necessary to constitute a lodge. He looked at the professions noted down next to the names. Apart from Palladiani, there were three lawyers, an engineer, a headmaster, a professor, two doctors of medicine, a commercial accountant, two shopkeepers and two industrialists. A depressing list: in theory all of them could have had the means. He wished he could have had Anna Giulietti's help to interview them, but the Palladiani case didn't come within her jurisdiction—it was under that of the Prosecutor's Department of Lucca.

This reminded him that the Carabinieri had mentioned that the deputy prosecutor was Armando Lupo, an old acquaintance from his days in Sicily. Ferrara had not even known that he had been appointed to Lucca. They had worked well together in the past, but that was of no advantage

148

to him now, because he wasn't dealing with the murder in Pietrasanta and the Carabinieri were.

He fell back again on the last resort. 'Fanti!'

'Yes, chief?'

'Can you photocopy this page and try to find out all you can on each one of them, apart from Palladiani of course. See if they have criminal records, if there are any lawsuits against them, and most importantly how they're doing financially. But please keep this to yourself! No official requests, no checking of bank accounts or anything like that, for goodness' sake. Only what you can find out without attracting attention. Get Venturi to help you.' Venturi was the man in the *Squadra Mobile* who knew everything that had ever happened: he was a walking archive of dates and names. 'But I don't want him to breathe a word of this either, got that?'

'Don't worry, chief.'

'Good. Has Rizzo arrived?'

'Not yet.'

'Send him to me as soon as he gets here.'

Once Fanti had left the room, Ferrara went back to his files.

*   *   *

He had just finished dealing with the most urgent matters when Francesco Rizzo appeared. Ferrara felt relieved. A big, reserved man, with eyes that tended to be evasive, Rizzo was unfailingly loyal and generous. He gave Ferrara a sense of security. Right now, he needed him desperately.

'I'm sorry if I've ruined your holiday, Francesco,' he said, noticing immediately that

149

Rizzo hadn't even had time to get a tan.

'What's going on?' Rizzo asked, sure that whatever it was must be serious.

Ferrara filled him in, and gave him all the documents and the memo he had prepared. Rizzo looked over the memo.

OPERATION STELLA
—Complete the map detailing all the buildings in the area where the girl was found.
—Wait for the authorisation to see Stella's medical records and have them examined by Dr Francesco Leone.
—Follow up the tests on Stella's clothes currently in progress by Forensics.
—Follow up the development of all lines of inquiry already begun (drug dealers, paedophiles, illegal immigrants).
—Assess whether it is necessary to involve the Juvenile Division further in the investigation.
—Follow up checks on the phone card used for the call to the emergency services.
—Follow any other leads as you see fit.

'If I'd read about this, chief, I'd have come back straightaway without waiting for Fanti to call me.'

'It hasn't been in the papers. When they found her, she was just one more junkie, that's not news, and when she died she was one more dead person in a hospital with more than a thousand patients.'

'Maybe it's better that way . . . All the same . . .'

'Go on, Francesco.'

'I was thinking we could put out a press statement, with Stella's description and photo . . . unless you've already done it.'

'No, it didn't seem appropriate. Besides, as she's a minor, we have to proceed with the utmost caution . . .'

'I know, but at this point publishing the photo may be of use to the investigation. It may be that someone will come forward, even if only through an anonymous phone call.'

'You may be right, but you'll have to ask Deputy Prosecutor Giulietti for authorisation.'

'You want me to do it?'

'Yes, Francesco. From now on, Operation Stella is all yours. I have something else to see to.'

And he told him about Massimo Verga's disappearance and the murder in Marina di Pietrasanta.

'Incredible,' Rizzo commented, genuinely concerned. He was a man of few words, but as down-to-earth and solid as his physique.

'Incredible but true, unfortunately. So you understand why I can't handle the Stella case as well? Apart from the time factor, my heart isn't in it.'

'Of course!'

'I'm going to the Versilia coast today to talk to the journalist who's been covering the case. And I may stay there for a few days.'

'If you need us, chief, we're here.'

'Thanks, Francesco, I know.'

'What about Commissioner Lepri? What shall I tell him?'

'Don't worry, I'll deal with him. I'll go and see him now and explain the situation. Apart from anything else, we have jurisdiction over Pietrasanta for certain kinds of crime, and anyway the victim lived in Florence and had his business here.'

'Let's hope he understands that and doesn't just say that the Carabinieri are dealing with it,' Rizzo said.

Prophetic words.

*   *   *

As soon as the green light came on, giving him the go-ahead to enter Lepri's luxurious office, Ferrara was hit by an unstoppable torrent of words.

'How much longer will I have to keep calling you to order, Chief Superintendent? Don't you realise your work is here, in the most important city in Tuscany, a showcase of interest to the whole world? You have duties, you can't do everything off your own bat, trampling on the rules and cheerfully ignoring the hierarchy!'

He was purple. Ferrara had never seen him like this.

'I don't—' he began.

'"I don't" what? First you get the doctors at the Ospedale Nuovo all worked up, but I close my eyes to that. Then you interfere in a Carabinieri investigation, in another town to boot, and I have to hear about it from Rome, where they may well be starting disciplinary proceedings! Well, let me tell you this: if they do, I'm not going to save your skin. On the contrary . . .'

Captain Fulvi is good, Ferrara thought.

'I haven't interfered in anyone's investigation,' he said, adding mentally: *so far*. 'I went there at their request to talk to them about an acquaintance of mine.'

'Oh, yes, Massimo Verga, the heartbreaker, the *intellectual*,' Lepri said, contemptuously. 'Watch

152

out for that one! I've been making inquiries, you know. A subversive! You make a good couple! So, you "haven't interfered" . . . Oh no! It wasn't you who questioned the Contessa Servi, it was your double. And it wasn't your secretary, Fanti, who gathered information on Ugo Palladiani, the victim of the murder thc Carabinieri are investigating. He also has a double. Florence is full of doubles!'

The Contessa Servi was good, too. Well, he should have expected it. Contessa or not, she was a gossip.

'It's true, I went to see the Contessa—'

'And I'm sure it wasn't to talk about the robbery, which strangely enough you haven't solved. I had to listen to all her complaints. The thieves are living it up in Florence, Ferrara, and you go to Pietrasanta to bother the—'

'A friend of mine is involved in that case.'

The Commissioner leaned back in his armchair, exhausted. 'We've talked about that, Chief Superintendent, I don't want to hear any more. Drop the Palladiani case. That's an order. The Carabinieri are dealing with it and they're the only ones who should be dealing with it. If I find out you're anywhere near there again, for any reason, I'll take measures that'll make you regret it, I assure you! And make sure you don't bother the Contessa again . . . unless it's to restore her bloody fan collection to her!'

'Don't worry, I won't bother her. In fact . . .'— the idea came to him as he spoke—' . . . the reason I came to see you was to tell you that I'm taking a few days' holiday.'

'Good idea. Yes, go. I think you need it. You

153

never take a break. It'll do you good. Go, go. Get as far away from here as you can!'

*   *   *

When he got back to his office, he summoned all his men and told them that he was putting Rizzo in charge. They all guessed the true reason for this sudden 'holiday'. The team's bad mood was tangible.

It was then that Ciuffi of Narcotics, as if to relieve the tension, said, 'Chief, we may be about to nab those two Albanians I told you about on Monday. They're on their way back to Florence, together with a Florentine we think they're in cahoots with. They left this morning, stopped rather suspiciously in the Versilia service area on the A12 autostrada, carried on as far as the tollbooth, then turned round and started back. I've given orders to the traffic police to stop them for a routine check as soon as they've passed the Lucca tollbooth. Some of our people will be with the patrol. If they're carrying what I think, those three are well and truly fucked!'

'Well done, Ciuffi. It certainly doesn't seem normal for someone to go for a little drive along the autostrada and then just turn round and come back! Did you see what they were doing during their stop?'

'Almost nothing. They parked in the heavy goods vehicle area, and were practically hidden in the middle of all the lorries. Our people couldn't go any nearer for fear of being spotted. But they did see them load a spare tyre in the car, so in my opinion we're on the right track. The whole scene

154

was captured on video and in still photos. We'll be having a good look at them.'

'Good. Who knows? Once you've got the three of them, you may even be able to get them to give us a lead on the dealer who supplied the drugs that killed Stella . . .'

'Possible . . . But these are tough cookies.'

'I'm sure they are, but you know what they say? Where there's life there's hope.'

Ciuffi smiled. 'They also say "That'll be the day".'

'Whatever happens, report back to Superintendent Rizzo, he'll know what to do.'

'Right, chief.'

'And if you need any of the team, they're here.'

Everyone nodded.

*   *   *

While Petra packed, Ferrara started phoning around in search of a hotel that still had a room available even though it was high season. At the fourteenth attempt, he had a stroke of luck: a room had become available that very day at the Principe, one of the best seafront hotels in Marina di Pietrasanta.

They arrived early in the afternoon. They had spent the whole journey in silence, not even playing music, as neither of them felt in the mood for it.

Once they had unpacked, they went out for a stroll along the seafront.

It was very hot, but for Petra it was an attempt to take her mind off things and for Ferrara a chance to have a look around. They went as far as the Twiga, which was on the border between Marina di Pietrasanta and Forte dei Marmi, and could be recognised by its logo, a giraffe's head, on a banner. Just before they got there, Ferrara saw Simonetta Palladiani's villa again. It was no longer being guarded, but it had been sealed.

The sun was high. Cars, mopeds and lots of bicycles sped along the street. The entrances to the bathing establishments, some of them quite elaborate and imaginative, blocked the view of the sea, which was glimpsed only through the odd gap. The beach was packed.

On the way back they stopped in front of the villa and peered, like any two curious passers-by, through the cracks in one of the two solid wooden gates, one giving access to the drive leading to the garage behind the house, the other to the small, well-tended front garden. The house itself was a handsome pale ochre building. There were two side wings, each two storeys high, set slightly back, flanking a central one-storey section topped by a broad terrace beyond which a corridor joining the side wings was visible. The dark green shutters were closed.

'A pity about that thing,' Petra said, pointing to the canvas-covered scaffolding which towered over the perimeter wall. 'It blocks out the view. What's the point of having a house facing the sea and then not being able to see it?'

'Yes,' Ferrara agreed, at a loss for an explanation. It seemed unlikely that it was an attempt to shield the villa and its occupants from prying eyes, and he noticed that this wasn't the only villa protected like this.

The mystery was solved by the porter at the

Principe when they got back to the hotel. The canvas was a special material which let those inside see out but prevented sand and salt, blown in on the wind from the sea, from corroding the door and window frames, or at least slowed down the effects.

It was nearly time for his appointment. Ferrara suggested to Petra that she take advantage of the hotel's swimming pool, said goodbye to her, and set off for the Twiga.

*   *   *

The cars parked in the palm-shaded car park of the Twiga Beach Club made it very clear that this was an exclusive venue.

Young waiters and waitresses, all in yellow T-shirts bearing the club's logo, were serving aperitifs to members sitting around low tables in surroundings decorated in African style. A beautiful girl came up to him and asked him if she could help him, in such a way as to make it clear to him that if he wasn't a member, and didn't intend becoming one, he wasn't welcome. He told her he had an appointment with someone and she asked who. The name Claudia Pizzi meant nothing to her, but a man who was just passing, and who also seemed to be part of the staff, heard him and butted in.

'She's a journalist on *Il Tirreno*. She told me last night she'd be coming in for an aperitif with a friend. Show him to the Chiringuito.'

'Follow me,' the beautiful girl said, and led him past the swimming pool. The pastel shades of the huts, each one a different colour, were reflected

157

on the surface of the water. They reached a bar covered over by a straw roof, at the very edge of the beach. Two barmen in identical T-shirts were serving.

He ordered a soft drink and watched the members sunbathing or relaxing in the shade of wide, elegant white tents, each supported at the sides by four wooden poles. Each tent contained two deckchairs, two sunbeds, a director's chair and a small table. He didn't even want to think how much it cost to spend a day here, let alone the whole season.

What he thought instead was that for the first time he was truly alone: alone to confront what was probably the most difficult mission of his life. The journalist he was waiting for might be the only ally he could count on. She certainly seemed to have the same respect as he did for the value of friendship.

But she was late. He looked at his watch. It was 6.14.

At 6.30 he started to get worried, and at 6.40 he tried to call her on her mobile but either there was no network or the phone had been turned off. At 6.55 he phoned the newspaper but they told him they hadn't seen her all day. He tried her home number and got the answering machine as usual. Once again, he left a message asking her to call him, adding this time that he was staying at the Principe and giving the number of the hotel.

At 7.15 his mobile rang.

'Ferrara!' he said, hoping that his tone made it clear that even if she was a woman she didn't have the right to make him wait so long.

'Am I disturbing you, chief?'

It was Rizzo.

Were they already starting to bother him from the office?

'No, not at all. What is it?'

'It's sensational, chief! Ciuffi caught those Albanians red-handed. And what a haul!'

'How much?'

'Ten kilos of heroin, chief! Ten kilos!'

Ferarra let out a prolonged whistle. It really was sensational, the kind of coup that rarely happens in the life of a policeman, and only if he's very lucky. 'Have you told Lepri?'

'I thought you'd want to do it.'

'I'm on holiday, Francesco.'

'But . . .' his deputy tried to insist, knowing full well that if he did so, he would end up getting the credit for the operation.

'No "but"s. You tell Lepri, but first put me through to Ciuffi, if you can.'

'Sure, he's right here. Hold on a second.'

'Good evening, chief.' Ciuffi sounded rather emotional.

'Congratulations, Ciuffi. Excellent work. I hope you still have wall space left to cover with newspaper articles!'

'We haven't informed the media yet.'

'I'm sure Lepri will see to that, don't worry. It's only right that your work is publicly acknowledged.'

'Thank you, chief.'

He was about to say goodbye, when he remembered Stella. 'One more thing, Ciuffi.'

'Yes, chief?'

'As soon as possible, put in a request to the deputy prosecutor—it's Cosenza, isn't it?—for

159

authorisation to bug the Albanians' cell, unless you've already thought of it.'

Listening to the prisoners' conversations might give them useful information, especially on the source of the drugs and the names of any accomplices. But Ferrara also hoped they might be able to kill two birds with one stone and learn something that would help them in the Stella case: although he was no longer dealing with it directly, it was still on his mind. *That'll be the day*, Ciuffi had said, but maybe the day was coming.

'Not just the Albanians, chief. There's also the guy from Florence, Emilio Zancarotti. The three of them are in the same cell.'

'Better still. Maybe they'll talk in Italian, not just in Albanian!'

It was already after seven thirty. He paid and left.

14

The newspapers on 9 August did not mention any significant new developments in the Ugo Palladiani case, although all of them, including *Il Tirreno*, took it as an established fact that it had been murder. *Il Tirreno* tried to recapture the ground lost the day before, with a long article by someone other than Claudia Pizzi. He called the editorial offices, but it was early and they told him she wasn't there yet, so he tried her home number, without success.

He tried again a little later, while he was having breakfast with Petra in the still half-empty dining room, but just got the answering machine as he had the previous evening. He did not bother leaving a message. He immediately dialled Claudia's mobile number, which rang for a long time without being answered. He assumed she was in her car, on her way to the newspaper. She must have had the phone in her handbag along with a thousand other things, like all women, and in all probability did not even hear it. But she would see that he had called and would phone him back, so it was best not to insist and to concentrate on his next move.

What should it be? He decided he did not have much choice. Too bad if the Carabinieri found out.

*   *   *

He left his car in a car park near the Piazza Carducci, one of the gateways to the 'Athens of Italy' beloved by the poet Carducci. A marble plaque on the wall quoted a sentence from one of his letters: 'What I like about Pietrasanta: a beautiful town, with a unique square, a big city cathedral and the Apuan Alps in the background.'

The square and the cathedral were right there, but to find the Via Martiri di Sant'Anna he had to ask his way several times, walk the whole length of the Via Mazzini to the other side of town and then through part of what until a short time before must have been the outskirts, with fields all around.

Once he was there he had no difficulty in spotting the apartment building Claudia had described. The other buildings were all villas.

There   were   two   entrances   with   two

161

entryphones, and next to one he saw a handwritten card that said *Barberi*. He rang the bell.

Once, twice, three times. At the third long ring a man's voice answered.

'If you're the press, you can shove off,' the man almost yelled, clearly exasperated by the harassment he must have received from journalists. Ferrara knew how persistent and annoying they could be, especially in a small town like this where nothing usually happened.

'I'm not the press,' he replied, gently but determinedly.

'Who are you then?'

He did not reply immediately. Was it better to identify himself, or pretend to be someone else? He could say he was an estate agent interested in Simonetta Palladiani's villa, or a holidaymaker looking for a housekeeper, or else . . .

The man did not leave him time to decide. 'Who are you? Are you still there?'

'Yes, I'm still here.'

'What do you want? Leave us alone.'

'I'm a police officer,' he said quickly before the man could continue.

'What do you want?'

'I need to talk to Signora Grazia Barberi.'

'My wife spent two whole days with the Carabinieri . . . What do you want now?'

'Perhaps you could open the door, and then I'll explain.'

'Wait . . . I'll come down.'

Ferrara was afraid the man would take the time to phone the Carabinieri and find out who this visitor was, but he soon heard the click of the lock and the door opened.

'Signor Barberi?'

'Yes,' he said. He was an elderly man, short and slight, with white hair and a thin moustache, also completely white.

'I'm Chief Superintendent Ferrara.'

The man looked him up and down. 'I've read about you in the papers,' he said at last, almost disappointed. 'I imagined you differently.'

'In what way?'

'Bigger . . . taller . . .'

It wasn't the first time he had heard this. It was as if his media fame had made people think he was larger than he really was.

'Please come in,' the man said.

They climbed to the first floor.

Grazia Barberi was waiting at the door of the apartment. She was shorter, stockier and younger than her husband.

Ferrara introduced himself.

'I was just making some coffee. Would you like a cup?'

'Yes, please.'

They sat down around the Formica table in the kitchen, which was modest but pleasant and very tidy. The wide-open French window looked out onto a small balcony full of flowers and aromatic herbs and let in just enough air to cool the room.

Grazia lit the stove beneath the Neapolitan coffee maker.

'It's an honour for us to have you in our home, Chief Superintendent,' the husband said. 'To what do we owe this visit?'

'As I'm sure you've guessed, it's because of what happened in Simonetta Palladiani's villa.'

'A terrible thing . . . We've been living here for

more than twenty years and nothing like this has ever happened before. This is a quiet place, a holiday destination . . . People come here to enjoy themselves.'

'That's why we'd like to clear this up.'

'And you've come all the way from Florence,' the man commented, not knowing whether to feel flattered or surprised. 'But my wife already told the Carabinieri everything. Aren't they good at their jobs?'

'Oh, no, they're very good. It's just that—'

'Have your coffee,' Grazia Barberi interrupted, saving him from embarrassment. She handed him the sugar bowl and a steaming cup. She gave one to her husband, too, and sat down at the table with her own.

'Well, if you're taking an interest,' the man said, 'the case is sure to be solved soon. I know you're better than—'

His wife silenced him with a nasty look.

'Signora Barberi, I realise you've already been interviewed by the Carabinieri . . .'

'Two days running, endlessly going over the same things. I told them everything I could, didn't they say? Maybe not, or you wouldn't be here.'

'I prefer to hear it from you, signora. Perhaps now, talking to me, you . . .'

'Yes,' the woman said, looking closely at him.

'Are you willing to help? You'd be doing me a great favour.'

For a few seconds more, Grazia Barberi kept her eyes fixed on his. Then, as if satisfied with what she saw, she said, 'If I can.'

'Thank you. Would you mind if I took a few notes?'

'Not at all. It's your job.'

'Good . . .'

Grazia Barberi began her story with Ugo Palladiani's arrival at the villa halfway through Saturday morning. She had only seen him a few times before in the five years she'd been working for Simonetta.

'He arrived unexpectedly. She wasn't pleased.'

'Why? What did they say to each other?'

'They immediately started quarrelling. I didn't catch more than a few words, because at that moment I went into another room . . . I heard them shouting. Simonetta was having a go at him for arriving like that without telling her first.'

'And what did he say?'

'He started shouting, too . . .'

'Did you hear what he was saying?'

'Not much . . . just a few words.'

'What were they?'

' "I'm staying here tonight, I'm at the end of my tether . . . Go ahead and have a good time with your latest boyfriend, do whatever the hell you like, but I'm sleeping here, then tomorrow I'll piss off . . ." Something like that, I'm sorry but that's the way they speak. That was the gist of it.'

'Does the signora have many lovers?'

'No . . . well . . . not all at the same time. I mean, what can I say? She's had a few men in the past few years, yes . . . but it's normal, I think. A beautiful woman like that. She was practically separated from her husband, you know. They hadn't lived together for years.'

'I understand. What happened then?'

'Nothing. She slammed the door and went out, and he put his bags in one of the guest bedrooms

165

upstairs.'

'You say she went out? Did she leave the house?'

'In a way . . .' she said, somewhat reticently.

'Would you mind being a little clearer?'

'Well . . . I told the Carabinieri this, but not the journalists. You know . . . I didn't want them to think . . .'

'I don't understand, signora.'

'She went to the guest flat, behind the house, next to the garage, which was rented all summer to a man.'

'Her lover?'

'Do I have to say . . . ?'

'Yes, signora, if you want to help them. You were right not to tell the journalists, but you have to tell me. The man's name is Massimo Verga, isn't it?'

'How do you know that?'

'Because he's a friend of mine,' he said, looking her straight in the eyes as she had looked into his. 'A very dear friend of mine.'

The revelation had a strange effect on Grazia Barberi. She seemed almost relieved, as if something she had previously only sensed had suddenly become clear. 'So that's why you're interested. The Carabinieri don't even know . . .'

'That's right. And I have to ask you a great favour.'

The husband looked puzzled. He didn't quite understand what was happening.

'Go on.'

'If possible, I'd prefer it if they didn't find out I was here.'

Husband and wife looked at each other in

silence.

'All right,' she said finally. 'If they don't ask us, we won't tell them.'

Ferrara heaved a sigh of relief. He liked this woman, who seemed to go straight to the heart of things.

'Thank you. Can we go on?'

'That's all I know about that day. On Saturdays, I finish at one, so I left.'

She had returned to the villa on Monday at about nine in the morning. She had found the door locked as normal. She had opened it and gone in. Everything was dark inside, and she had assumed that the signora was still asleep.

She had opened the windows in the hall and had gone into the kitchen, which she had found more or less as tidy as she had left it. As she usually did, she had made coffee and taken it up to the signora in her room, intending to wake her up. But the signora wasn't there; the bed was made and the room was tidy.

Not knowing what to do at first, she had finally made up her mind to go and see if Ugo Palladiani was still there—she had noticed his car when she arrived, and when someone was in the state he had been in, you never knew. If he was awake, she would give him the coffee she had made for Simonetta.

The bedroom was in the other wing of the house. The door was open and the light was on. She had gone in. The room was in a mess, more even than you'd see in a bachelor flat, but Simonetta's husband wasn't there.

That was when she had started to be afraid. The house was too big, too empty and silent: something

167

strange was going on. She had thought of calling her husband, but had decided against it. He would only make fun of her.

Summoning up all her courage, she had gone as far as the main staircase which led to the living room on the ground floor, switching on the lights as she advanced. From the top of the stairs, she had turned on the big chandelier. That was when she had seen Ugo Palladiani, lying on the floor in an unnatural position, his face purple, his eyes wide open and glassy. She had fainted.

'When I came to, he was still there,' Grazia went on, 'and I realised it wasn't just a bad dream.'

'What did he look like? Were there any bloodstains? Anything that suggested that something violent had happened, that he'd been attacked?'

She closed her eyes as if she wanted to blot out the memory. 'I don't know . . . All I remember is the eyes . . .'

'All right. What did you do when you got over that first shock?'

'I cried for help . . . but no one came. I was scared.'

'No one heard you? A neighbour, a passer-by?'

'You don't know the place! The villa's so large . . .'

'I understand,' Ferrara said. At that hour and with all the traffic, he thought, it would have been difficult for cries from inside the villa to filter beyond the garden and the perimeter wall. But if Simonetta and Massimo had been in the guest flat, they should have heard her. He did not say that. 'And then?'

That was when she had phoned her husband,

168

who was retired and was at home at the time, and told him to call the Carabinieri and then come over to the villa immediately. By the time he arrived, the Carabinieri were already there.

'Did they check the guest apartment?' he asked.

'Yes, of course,' the husband replied.

'And Signora Simonetta and Massimo Verga weren't there?'

'No, they weren't anywhere,' she said, disconsolately.

'You told me you've been working for the signora for five years, is that right?'

'Yes, ever since she moved to Marina di Pietrasanta . . . That was in 1996. I remember that because it was the year our daughter graduated.'

'So you know her well.'

'I don't want to boast, but she really trusts me. She treats me like one of the family. But I suppose what you're trying to ask is if I think she's capable of killing someone?'

Ferrara had to admire her again. The woman was intelligent.

'Grazia,' her husband said, 'the superintendent has to do his job.'

'Of course . . . everyone's doing their job. But I can assure you, Superintendent, Signora Simonetta wouldn't hurt a fly. She's too good!'

'How do you account for the fact she's missing?'

'I don't know what to say. I'm sure she didn't kill Signor Ugo and then run away. That's what the Carabinieri think. They questioned me about that for hours and hours.'

'Does Signora Simonetta have any business interests in the area?' He looked at both of them as he asked the question, as if to make it clear that

169

he was expecting an answer from both.

It was the husband who replied.

Ferrara already knew part of the answer. Simonetta Palladiani was interested in art and owned a gallery in Forte dei Marmi, where she often, especially in summer, organised exhibitions of paintings and sculptures by a mixture of local artists and those from further afield. Grazia's husband also told him that Simonetta's parents, who had died some years earlier, had held the lease on a number of marble quarries and that the lease had passed to her, but she had never been directly involved with the business.

'What do you mean?'

'Well, they were practically abandoned. I don't think they produced anything.'

*   *   *

It was almost two by the time he got back to the hotel.

He found Petra in a little room next to the foyer, in front of the TV, and he felt a pang in his heart. Petra hated television, and now here she was, spending hours watching shows that did not interest her in the least, as if she was trying to send herself into a state of oblivion, or as if she was expecting some news which would free her from the nightmare into which they had both been plunged.

'I'm sorry, darling,' he said, and from his tone of voice she knew that there was nothing new to report.

The local TV news was just coming on, and Ferrara sat down next to Petra to watch it.

170

The summary began with the local political news. But then the next item was a report on a brilliant operation by the Florence *Squadra Mobile*, which described in great detail the various phases of the capture of two Albanians and an Italian, who had been found in possession of ten kilos of heroin, hidden inside the spare tyre of the car belonging to the Italian, one Emilio Zancarotti.

'The operation,' the newsreader said, over images of Ciuffi holding up the ten bags they had seized, 'was carried out by the Narcotics Division under the command of the head of the *Squadra Mobile*, Michele Ferrara, and is believed to be among the largest seizures of heroin recorded in Tuscany in the past few years. Florence Police Commissioner Riccardo Lepri has been congratulated by the Minister of the Interior and the Head of the State Police and has himself congratulated Superintendent Francesco Rizzo, deputising for Michele Ferrara who is currently on holiday.'

Ferrara smiled bitterly. Obviously Lepri wasn't going to congratulate him personally. But he hoped that at least the Commissioner would ask the minister to award a commendation to Luigi Ciuffi, and perhaps to Rizzo, too. He probably would—that way he could clear the way for Rizzo becoming Ferrara's successor!

Deep down, he wouldn't mind. Rizzo deserved it, and besides, perhaps the time had come for Ferrara to take early retirement and enjoy life with Petra. There were so many places around the world he'd always dreamed of visiting . . .

Not before finding Massimo, though.

*   *   *

They were about to get up and go to the hotel restaurant for lunch, even though neither of them was hungry, when the head receptionist came up to them.

'Telephone, Chief Superintendent. They're asking for you.'

'Do you know who?'

'Brizzi, Pizzi . . . I didn't quite catch it.'

At last! he thought.

'Hello?'

'Is that Chief Superintendent Ferrara?'

But it wasn't the young, self-confident voice he knew.

It was a man's voice.

15

Claudia's father, Amilcare Pizzi, had tried to reach her several times by phone. Worried, he had finally made up his mind to go and see her in the small apartment in Carrara where she lived alone. He had a set of keys in case of emergency. He had rung the bell several times, but receiving no reply, had gone in. Everything in the place was neat and tidy, but Claudia wasn't there. He had walked around for a while without knowing what to do until he had noticed a red light flashing on the ancient answering machine. There must be some recorded messages.

He wasn't sure at first if he should listen to

them. He had no wish to spy on his daughter's private life. But then he had convinced himself that this was an emergency. There were several messages: from her boyfriend, from a girl friend, from colleagues at the paper, from her editor who was waiting for her, and one which had particularly struck him and increased his anxiety—from Chief Superintendent Ferrara.

That was why he was calling him now.

'Do you know where she is, Chief Superintendent?'

'No, I'm looking for her, too.'

'Is she in any trouble?'

'Not as far as I know. We were supposed to meet last night in Marina di Pietrasanta to discuss an article she told me she'd written.'

'And she didn't show up?'

'No . . .'

'And she didn't even let you know?'

'No, that's why I called her.'

There was a pause.

'It's not like her. Just as it's not like her to vanish without telling me . . . I'm afraid . . .'

Ferrara was starting to be afraid, too. 'Try not to worry . . . Listen, are you still at your daughter's apartment?'

'Yes, I'm calling on her phone.'

'Can you wait for me?'

'If you like.'

'Just stay calm, and I'll be there as soon as possible. Give me the address.'

He hung up, threw his wife a kiss, and left the hotel. Petra went back to the television room.

*   *   *

He pushed the Mercedes to the limit on the autostrada between the coast and Carrara. The car responded as efficiently as ever, but to him each mile seemed endless and he hooted his horn loudly trying to get into the fast lane. Big cranes sped past on his right, moving the huge square blocks of marble to the depots. In the distance he could see the mountains, the quarries excavated over the centuries looking like layers of fake snow laid over the wounds in the exposed stone.

From time to time, he tried Claudia's mobile again, but there was still no reply. He imagined her father was doing the same thing.

At the Carrara exit, he hesitated for a moment, then decided to turn left and climb towards the town. He found the address the man had told him, in the Via Verdi, left the Mercedes double parked, unlocked and with the keys inside, hurried to the apartment building and ran up the stairs.

Amilcare Pizzi was waiting for him in the doorway of the apartment. He was a tall, bald man, who looked as if he was at the end of his tether. 'You were quick,' he managed to say.

'I've been trying to call her on her mobile.'

'So have I.'

'Mind if I have a look around?'

'Please, go ahead.'

The apartment was small, airy and very tidy. There was little furniture, but what there was was of good quality. There were many books, magazines and newspapers, and a modern computer. Ferrara looked closely at the large white desk, which had one long drawer.

'Is it all right if I open this?' he asked.

174

'Of course.'

'Or perhaps it would be better if you did it? This isn't my apartment and I feel as if I'm putting my nose in someone else's business.' He was lying in order not to make the man suspicious. Pizzi would have been even more alarmed if he had realised this was a precaution in case the Carabinieri later checked.

'I understand, but it's necessary, isn't it?' the man said, opening the drawer. It contained a small diary, a few reams of extra-thick paper, some neatly arranged pens and pencils, and some cosmetics. The drawer was very deep, and Claudia's father pulled it out some more. There was a digital camera, various kinds of batteries and some manuals for computers and electronic equipment.

'You can close it now.'

As he did so, Pizzi encountered a strange resistance.

'Wait!' Ferrara said.

He bent down. A brown envelope fixed with tape to the bottom of the drawer had come away on one side and was hanging down. He pulled it out. It wasn't sealed. He opened it and took out two photos.

They were both photos of the same mountain. One of the two was a closer shot, showing an area that had been excavated, with two lorries in operation, one of them a tanker lorry. No signs or licence plates were visible on either of the lorries.

'I don't know what these photos are,' Claudia's father commented without waiting for Ferrara to ask him.

So why was she keeping them hidden?

175

'Do you mind if I take them?' Ferrara said. 'I'll give them back.'

'Take them, please. I'm sure you'll get them to her.'

'You have my word.'

There were many other things he would have liked to do—switch on the computer, study the diary, listen to all the messages on the answering machine, and so on—but he had already wasted too much time.

'Signor Pizzi, I'm sure nothing's happened to your daughter, but just to be on the safe side . . .'

'It's better to call the Carabinieri, right?'

The barracks was just round the corner, in the Via Eugenio Chiesa.

'I'd rather go to the police. I saw the station in a square not far from here. Someone there is bound to know me.'

'That's the town hall square.'

'It's really not far. Shall we go?'

'You'd come with me?' Pizzi asked, surprised.

'Of course.'

'Thank you.'

*   *   *

For some offences, such as drug trafficking and kidnapping, the police in the province of Massa-Carrara did not come under the jurisdiction of Florence but, even though it was still in Tuscany, under that of Genoa. It was an anomaly which in these circumstances might be to Ferrara's advantage.

The Carrara police were commanded by Superintendent Giuseppe Lojelo, a youngish, calm-looking man, who greeted him with a big smile.

'I'm honoured, Chief Superintendent. I've heard so much about you, it's a real pleasure to meet you in person. And congratulations on today's operation.' Obviously he had seen the TV news. 'You're on holiday, aren't you?'

'Yes. But I'm worried about a friend of mine, a journalist on *Il Tirreno* who lives here in Carrara, Claudia Pizzi. This gentleman is her father.'

'Pleased to meet you. What's happened?'

'She's been missing from home since yesterday,' Signor Pizzi said.

'Does she live with you?'

'No, she lives alone. But we phone each other practically every day.'

'And yesterday evening she didn't show up for an appointment she had with me,' Ferrara said.

'Well, it is summer. Maybe she went out with some friends. How old is she?'

'Thirty-four,' her father replied promptly.

'Is she married?'

'No.'

'Any boyfriends?'

'There is a young man . . .'

'Have you tried calling him?'

'Listen, Superintendent,' Ferrara cut in. 'We've already tried everything we can. The reason I'm here with Signor Pizzi is that I think it'd be a good idea to start searching for her without wasting any more time.'

'If you say so. But what do you want me to do? Perhaps the best thing is for the gentleman to report his daughter missing, as per normal, and give us a description and anything else that could

177

be useful . . .'

'He'll do that, of course. But in the meantime, his daughter's mobile is ringing and there's no reply. I think it would be a good idea to get authorisation from the Prosecutor's Department to put an urgent trace on the phone.'

The staff at the phone company would be able to locate Claudia's mobile through its IMEI number—the fifteen-digit code unique to each phone—provided it was still switched on and the battery had not run out. They would call the mobile, and the signal would be picked up by an ultra-sophisticated device which would indicate on a monitor within which cell the phone was located. If this was not enough because that particular cell covered a wide area—several miles, for example— which could happen if the phone wasn't in a city but in an isolated area, another sophisticated device would be used to locate it within a margin of error of only a few yards.

Superintendent Lojelo looked at Ferrara incredulously. 'You're saying I should . . . ?' It was a big step to take and it might cost him dearly if this turned out to be a false alarm—for example, if the woman turned out to have simply gone away somewhere with a lover. The deputy prosecutor would never forgive him for the costs in manpower and money incurred by such a technical procedure.

'Yes, Superintendent, trust me on this.'

'But—'

'Excuse us, Signor Pizzi,' Ferrara said, drawing his colleague aside, out of earshot.

'Use my name if it helps, Superintendent. Tell them the request came from me. The thing is, this disappearance may be related to a very serious case that could also have implications for an investigation we have under way in Florence.'

'Well, if you put it like that . . .'

'In the meantime Signor Pizzi can go through all the necessary formalities with you. I have to get back to Marina di Pietrasanta'—he was thinking of Petra—'but I'll keep in contact. Let's exchange phone numbers.'

They did so, and he added the phone number of the hotel to his business card. 'I'll call you soon to see if there's any news, if you don't mind.'

'Of course, Chief Superintendent.'

'And you can call me at any time, understood?'

'Absolutely, don't worry.'

Superintendent Lojelo handed them over to a sergeant who immediately sat down at the computer to write up the missing persons report.

'I have to go, Signor Pizzi, but try to keep your spirits up. As you can see, Superintendent Lojelo is already on the case. You'll see, they'll find her soon.'

What he did not tell him was that the mobile might have been mislaid somewhere, so that even if they found it, Claudia might be miles away. But no one had picked it up, which was strange in itself, and even if she wasn't in the same place as her mobile, he was becoming increasingly worried about her, so was pleased to get a search for her under way.

'Let's hope so,' her father replied, with forced optimism.

'Call me if you need to. You have the number of the hotel.'

*   *   *

179

He did not find Petra in the television room or even in the swimming pool. She was in their room, reading one of the German novels she always brought back from her trips to Germany: they often went there together, especially at Christmas time, which was a period that always made her feel homesick for the smell of vanilla and cinnamon from the desserts her mother made.

But she might not even have been reading. He noticed that her eyes had misted over.

Petra was a practical, down-to-earth woman, and many were the times she had give him moral support when he had felt discouraged. But now she seemed lost, almost numb. It was a sight Ferrara found hard to bear.

'Come on, get dressed. We're going out to dinner.'

'Can't we eat in the hotel restaurant?' she protested, listlessly.

'Don't even think about it. Have you seen the menu? No way. We're going to have dinner in a good restaurant and that's an order!'

'If you like, Michele.'

She had to make an effort, and was not good company on the car ride, but she seemed to come back to life a little when they were in the little square of the 'Athens of Italy', struck by the strange, disharmonious beauty of the place and distracted by the cheerfulness of the people crowding into the bars and restaurants.

Petra was interested in the plaque for the poet Carducci, but was rather less enamoured of the brick bell tower which threw a shadow over the cathedral with its clear white marble façade. They visited a few art galleries then had dinner at the Trattoria San Martino, where the food and wine were authentically local and very good.

Ferrara phoned Lojelo, as agreed, and learned that the Prosecutor's Department had authorised the trace and the phone company was already at work. There was nothing else he could do.

He just had to wait for them to locate the phone.

*　　*　　*

He received the kick in his back soon after he had lain down, and he did not have time to react before he felt the weight of the Italian on him.

'You, leave him alone—leave him alone!' Alex yelled, going to the aid of his brother and trying to separate the two bodies.

It didn't take him long. Even though Emilio Zancarotti weighed almost two hundred and twenty pounds, all of it muscle, there were two of them. It was rather more difficult to stop Nard retaliating and keep the two men apart.

'No be stupid!' Alex said. 'Want to finish up separate cells?'

'That's fine by me,' Zancarotti said, 'if it means I don't have to see him any more.'

'Nothing to do with me!' Nard protested, returning to his bunk.

'Do you hear him? Do you hear him? Did I tell him or didn't I to put on his seat belt? Did I tell him or not? A thousand times, I must have told him . . .'

Alex said nothing.

'He got us caught and now we're fucked, am I

181

right?'

'*Qetesi!*' Nard cried.

'What the fuck did he just say?'

'He say shut up, no pay attention . . . He scared.'

Inspector Oliva of Narcotics held his breath, hoping they wouldn't stop there.

He was in a small room on the same floor of Sollicciano prison as the warden's office, a long way from the cell where the three men were, but as soon as he'd heard the first words, he had stood up from his chair, gone to the listening post and put on the headphones. He didn't want to lose a single word of what these men were saying.

The Albanian brothers Alex and Nard Dakaj had been living in Italy illegally for several months. They had been arrested several times for dealing, found guilty and deported, but each time they stubbornly returned to Italy with different papers. They had so many aliases, they probably didn't know their real names themselves by now.

The third occupant of the cell was a Florentine, Emilio Zancarotti, the owner of the car, and its driver when they had been stopped by the traffic police.

Narcotics had had their eyes on them for several weeks after a tip-off from an informer, a young Romanian prostitute who'd had enough of Alex's violence and had turned herself over to the police in Montecatini, who had then contacted Narcotics in Florence.

The brothers had turned out to be regulars of a bar in the Santa Croce area, run by Emilio Zancarotti, who was already suspected of collecting money from criminal activities and sending it to Albania, where it was used to buy drugs for the European market and women to work as prostitutes in Italy. But it was not clear who he was working for. Under authorisation from the deputy prosecutor, Ciuffi had done bank and postal checks on him, but so far they had not produced any results. Since Ferrara had asked him to hclp on Operation Stella, he had increased the surveillance on the three men.

That night, in the confines of their narrow cell, they continued to trade accusations and threats, but did not come to blows. At about midnight, once all their frustration and anger had finally been vented and they fell silent, except for their snoring, Inspector Oliva started transcribing, word for word, what he had heard and recorded.

16

They were both awake, after yet another sleepless night spent trying to suppress their anxiety and brooding over memories and regrets, when the receptionist put through Lojelo's call.

'They've located the phone. It's near the quarries, over towards Bedizzano. We're on our way there now.'

'I'll join you,' Ferrara said. 'How do I get there?'

'After Carrara, follow the signs to Colonnata. Make sure you take the road that goes to Bedizzano.'

'I'll be there,' he said and hung up.

'Can I come, too?'

Ferrara looked at his wife. It was the first time she had ever asked to be present at a police operation. He could understand it if they had been going to find Massimo, wherever he might be and if he was still alive, but this . . .

Petra's face was drawn, with deep rings under the eyes. She had taken to wearing her blonde hair drawn back, and her complexion was even more pale and transparent than ever. She looked as if she had aged a few years in a couple of days. But Ferrara loved her just as much, if not more: with sudden emotion, he realised that the passing of time and the difficult period they had been going through had not in any way diminished the beauty of that face, but rather gave it an authority consistent with the resolve and steadfastness of her character, which had been such a boon to him over the years.

There was no imploring in her bright green eyes: it had not been a request, more a statement.

'But Petra . . . it's only the journalist we're looking for. Most likely all we'll find will be the mobile phone, abandoned somewhere. It'll be just one more line of inquiry that leads nowhere, but unfortunately we have to follow it up. It doesn't have anything to do with—'

'I can't just stay here all day, sitting in front of that stupid TV set, *mein Gott*! And don't think I want to go to the swimming pool or the sea . . .'

Ferrara resigned himself. There was almost certainly no danger: if the mobile was still ringing, it was unlikely that Claudia had been kidnapped or anything like that.

They got dressed quickly.

By 6.15 they were already on the autostrada, and half an hour later they were climbing the curving road from Carrara towards Colonnata.

184

The landscape was dramatic, perfectly in tune with their state of mind. As they got closer to their target, the deep scars the hand of man had inflicted on the mountain over the centuries became more evident, gaping chasms that were almost blindingly white appearing in the first light of the August sun.

It was still early, but there were already a few tourist coaches on the road, slowing them down.

Three police cars were parked at the Bedizzano exit, where the road meets the lorry lane also coming from Carrara. There was only one police officer beside them.

Ferrara parked the Mercedes on the right, leaving space for any vehicles coming from the branch road to manoeuvre, and got out. Petra followed him.

'I'm Chief Superintendent Ferrara,' he said, showing his badge.

'Superintendent Lojelo is waiting for you up there,' the officer replied.

'How far?'

'About half a mile. But the road is narrow, I don't know if you'll have room for your car. Do you want me to drive you up there?'

He looked at Petra, who shook her head.

'I prefer to go on foot, thanks.'

They set off.

To the right, the hill sloped upwards, thick with oaks and ilexes; to the left it descended in a series of stone embankments above sudden precipices. They had more than half a mile to climb, perhaps as much as a mile, and it was hard going because of all the bends. But by the time they realised that, it was too late to turn back.

As they got closer, they caught occasional glimpses of police uniform through the vegetation on either side: that was where the officers were busy searching.

After a last bend, more or less halfway between Bedizzano and Carrara, they came within sight of a low corrugated iron building painted yellow, a souvenir stand, in front of which was an open space where two cars were parked. One was a police car, and Lojelo stood beside it with his mobile stuck to his ear. The other car was a dark green Renault Clio.

As soon as Ferrara had joined him, Lojelo pointed to the Renault. 'That's Claudia Pizzi's car,' he said. 'It fits the description her father gave us and the licence plate is registered in her name.'

A bad sign, Ferrara thought, as Lojelo tried his mobile again.

'I keep calling at regular intervals,' he explained. 'Fortunately the battery is still working, but the signal is weak. I hope she hasn't put it on vibrate and one of my men hears it. It's been located to somewhere around here, but not to an exact spot, and as you can see this is a very wooded area. It won't be easy. The only hope is if we hear it ringing.'

Just as Lojelo was about to switch his phone off, Petra, who had lingered to look at a small altar fixed in the rock and adorned with buttercups, probably in memory of someone who had died in a road accident, heard a faint ringing.

'Try again, Superintendent!' she cried, coming forward a little.

Lojelo did so, as Ferrara joined Petra.

The ringing was clearer now, although still

distant.

The ground to the right of the rock fell away steeply in an almost vertical trench between the trees and the undergrowth, which was fortunately not too thick at this point. Two electricity cables, or perhaps phone cables, were stretched across the opening of this trench, just above the ground.

Lojelo called to one of his men.

'Go down, but take care. I'll keep the line open.'

The officer came back up a little while later holding a leather shoulder bag, which he had found about twenty yards lower down, snagged on the branch of a bramble bush. Inside, among other things, were the mobile and a wallet containing Claudia Pizzi's ID.

'We have to look further down,' Ferrara said. 'Is there anyone you can call for help?'

'There's a Carabinieri station here in Bedizzano . . .'

'Better to call the Forest Rangers, they know the area,' he said quickly. 'And an ambulance.'

*　　　*　　　*

Claudia Pizzi's body was found almost at the foot of the precipice with five bullet wounds in her back. Retrieving it was a long and laborious operation. The body could not be moved until the forensics team arrived from La Spezia. Claudia was still holding the strap of a Nikon with a powerful telephoto lens. Both the camera and the lens had been broken in the fall.

While waiting, Lojelo and Ferrara questioned the woman who ran the souvenir stand, but didn't get much out of her. It turned out that the Renault

187

had been parked there all the previous day. The woman had seen it when she had arrived and it was still there when she had left in the evening.

'Why didn't you call the police? Didn't you think it was strange?'

'A bit,' she admitted. 'No one usually stops here that long. How was I to know? Maybe it was someone who'd gone on an excursion in the woods . . . Then I thought, what was it doing there, taking up all that room? Seeing it again this morning, I'd probably have started getting worried.'

They obviously weren't going to get anything else out of her.

Later, after the ambulance had driven off with the body, it was Lojelo who said, grimly, 'We'll have to tell her father.'

'We'll see to that,' Ferrara said, encouraged by Petra. In such circumstances, a female presence can be a great help: compassion is a feminine trait, and a man accepts it without feeling that he is being pitied.

*   *   *

Before they got to Amilcare Pizzi's place, Ferrara phoned *Il Tirreno* and asked to be put through to the editor. He told him the news and then asked him about the piece which Claudia had been putting the finishing touches to on the night of the 8th, but which had not appeared the following day.

The editor, shaken by the news, told him he knew nothing about it, but he would find out and call him back. But he could assure Ferrara of one thing: the article definitely hadn't been censored, his paper never did that.

He phoned back ten minutes later, as Ferrara was parking. The reason the article hadn't appeared was that the local news editor had decided it had wandered off the point and was full of hasty judgements unsupported by evidence.

'Can I talk to him?'

'Of course. Hold on, and I'll put him through.'

After a little while, a younger voice came on the line. 'Francesco Gustavino speaking.'

Ferrara put him in the picture.

'I'm speechless,' was all the man could say.

'I know how you feel. I knew her, too. It's terrible to think that someone so young has gone. But you can help me.'

'Tell me how.'

'Why didn't you publish her last article?'

'From a professional like her, it was far too personal. Reading between the lines, she seemed to be attacking the Carabinieri and hinting at all sorts of things without really explaining them. I thought it was all a bit cryptic. I was planning to talk to her, to get her to clarify some parts of it. I really wanted to feel that we could support her in what she was saying, but I didn't get a chance to talk to her. I tried to reach her the other day when I got the piece, but there was no reply. I tried again yesterday, but still couldn't reach her.'

'What exactly did the article say?'

'Basically that the case was somehow related to the marble quarries. Claudia had been interested in that area for a while. She kept saying she wanted to do a big story on it. But the connection she was making in that article between the murder in Marina di Pietrasanta and whatever she had

189

discovered, or hoped to discover, in the quarries seemed a bit forced to me . . . It's as if she was trying to fit the murder into a preconceived theory.'

Ferrara knew exactly what he meant. For a detective, too, there is always the risk of bending the facts to fit a theory he finds hard to give up. It was a risk he himself always tried to avoid by not neglecting any line of inquiry and constantly reviewing, as objectively as possible, the whole process that had led him to that theory—calling it all into question if need be.

'But she did die near the quarries,' he said.

'Yes,' the news editor murmured bitterly.

'Could you send me the article?'

'I don't know . . . Now that she's dead . . . It's Claudia's material . . .'

'Signor Gustavino—It is Gustavino, isn't it?—do I need to say it again? Claudia Pizzi died, in fact was murdered, near a quarry, and her article mentions the quarries. And do I need to remind you that I'm a police officer?'

'I'm sorry, it's just that it's so—'

Ferrara cut him short, giving him the email address he could send the article to.

*　　*　　*

Claudia's father burst into tears, which may have stopped him from fainting. He had gone as pale as the purest marble and Petra quickly went and looked in the dining room sideboard for a liqueur and a glass.

His wife had died the year before; his son— Claudia's older brother—had emigrated to

190

Australia, and now he was alone, without any real reason to carry on living. His daughter had been everything to him, he admitted in despair.

Only much later, thanks to Petra's comforting words, did he feel up to going with Ferrara to Claudia's apartment. Ferrara wanted to have a better look at it with the help of Lojelo and his men.

'Are you sure you'll be okay? If you like, you can give me the keys.' He had to say it, although the presence of Claudia's father would be very useful.

'No, I want to be there.'

They got to the apartment at the same time as Lojelo and the forensics team. Amilcare Pizzi opened the door, and they went in.

'I hope you don't mind,' Ferrara said, 'but as I'm sure you'll understand, this time we really have to check everything.'

'If it helps the investigation, do whatever you have to do. I want you to get them . . . whoever they are.'

The forensics team got down to work. It didn't take long, especially as far as taking video and photographic evidence was concerned, since it was a small apartment. The furniture and objects were so clean and tidy, with hardly a trace of dust, that any prints were invisible to the naked eye. They first had to be enhanced by spreading a special silver-grey aluminium powder with a paintbrush over the surfaces, then lifted with black adhesive tape, and finally photographed.

They then proceeded with the search, the results of which would be reported to the Prosecutor's Department, along with the first documents relating to the finding of the body.

There were a large number of books, magazines, newspapers, notepads and exercise books, as well as diaries used more for notes and memos than to record appointments. Writing down news items and notes for articles on the pages of a diary was an old habit of crime reporters.

Among the diaries was one from this year.

It was from the Florence Savings Bank.

Ferrara started leafing through it, from the beginning. He noticed that some pages had been left blank, as if Claudia Pizzi hadn't worked on those days or else had used a real notebook.

He got to August.

Here the notes came thick and fast, day after day, as if Claudia Pizzi had lived very intensely during this last period. There were phrases which Ferrara surmised had been spoken to the journalist by informers or witnesses, some indicated with a letter. Grazia Barberi's statement, for example, which Ferrara recognised, was indicated with a capital G.

He also noticed that Simonetta Palladiani's name appeared several times, and next to it one or two question marks. Massimo Verga was not mentioned by name, but there was a reference to a 'bookshop owner from Florence' who had rented the guest apartment.

There were also some numbers which seemed to refer to particular quarries.

Suddenly he was struck by a phrase written on a sheet of squared paper tucked inside the cover: *Check presence Sicilian companies in Tuscany.* Why specifically Sicilian companies?

'Let's take all the diaries and notebooks away,'

192

he suggested to Lojelo. 'We need to have a proper look at them.'

'What about the computer?' Lojelo asked, pointing to the Toshiba laptop on the desk.

'That too . . . and the disks,' Ferrara replied. Then, turning to Amilcare Pizzi, 'Signor Pizzi, for the moment we have to take all this material away. You'll get back whatever we don't need.'

Pizzi nodded.

Ferrara turned back to Lojelo. 'You should have this, too.' He handed him the envelope with the two photos which he had found on his previous visit.

Lojelo gave him a puzzled look.

He explained how he came to have the envelope, and said, 'I'll put it in writing.'

When at last he said goodbye to Lojelo, he asked him not to give his name to the press.

*   *   *

They got back to the hotel in the afternoon. There were no phone messages, a sign that nothing of any particular importance had happened in Florence. As soon as they were in their room, Ferrara switched on his laptop and checked his email. There were no messages from the office—he didn't know if he felt relieved or sorry—but there was Francesco Gustavino's email with Claudia Pizzi's article as an attachment.

He read it.

We learn from a reliable source that Ugo Palladiani was murdered. Ferrara shuddered. Obviously she had finished writing this after talking to him. *It has also been ascertained that a third party was present in Simonetta Palladiani's villa, a bookshop owner from Florence who had been renting the guest apartment and who also seems to be missing. Given that there is already a rumour that the owner of the villa and the tenant were more than 'just friends', we seem to be getting into the oldest, most obvious story in the world, still all too common in our little country: the eternal triangle!*

So, while the Carabinieri, who are only doing their duty, ponder what they probably consider the flight of two homicidal lovers, the hope that they will ask themselves some searching questions seems to be vanishing into thin air. Questions such as why the husband of a woman who still holds the lease on a number of marble quarries saved by a Sicilian businessman was killed. Questions such as how this businessman somehow managed to make a success of these quarries—Nos. 206, 219 and 225—which everyone in the area assumed were exhausted, and which had ruined the woman's parents. And our astute Carabinieri have not even noticed the strange coincidence that the disappearing tenant also just happens to be Sicilian . . . These may perhaps be the idealistic ravings of the present writer, who will never believe in the guilt of Simonetta Palladiani—a woman who has been nothing but an asset to this area—but is instead convinced that the activities of the Saviour of the quarries ought to arouse suspicion.

'Should "saviour" be spelt with a capital letter like that?' Petra asked, reading over his shoulder.

'No . . . Perhaps she was trying to be ironic, comparing this Sicilian businessman with Jesus Christ . . . or perhaps it's just a typing error, you know how it is when you write quickly on the computer. I do it all the time.'

'If it is an error, it's the only one,' Petra commented.

But Ferrara was already on the phone.

'Superintendent Lojelo? Ferrara here. Would it be possible for you to find out who manages quarries 206, 219 and 225?'

'Of course. Has it got something to do with the murder?'

'Quite possibly. I'm emailing you the last article Claudia Pizzi wrote. It never appeared, and when you read it you'll understand why.'

'Thank you, Chief Superintendent. You're doing us a great favour.'

Immediately afterwards, Ferrara called Fanti.

'Try to find out all you can about Sicilian companies operating in Tuscany over the last ten years . . . no, make that fifteen years.'

'All of them?' Fanti asked in surprise.

'How many there are, what line of business they're in, where they're distributed. That's all I need for now.'

'Ah,' Fanti replied—it was hard to tell whether he was relieved or not. 'I'll get right on to it. But . . . when are you coming back, chief?'

'Never . . . No, of course I'll be back, but I don't know when. Why, aren't you getting on with Rizzo?'

'It's not that, chief . . . But is everything all right there? Are you making progress? Do you need anything else?'

'No, that's all for the moment. But please, Fanti, call me when you have the information or send it to me.'

'Okay, chief.'

As soon as he had hung up, Ferrara looked at his watch and decided the time had come to make a call he had been putting off for too long.

17

ALEX: You, leave him alone—leave him alone!

[sounds of a scuffle]

ALEX: No be stupid! Want to finish up separate cells?

ZANCAROTTI: That's fine by me if it means I don't have to see him any more.

NARD: Nothing to do with me!

ZANCAROTTI: Do you hear him? Do you hear him? Did I tell him or didn't I to put on his seat belt? Did I tell him or not? A thousand times, I must have told him . . .

[brief pause]

ZANCAROTTI: He got us caught and now we're fucked, am I right?

NARD: [incomprehensible]

ZANCAROTTI: What the fuck did he just say?

ALEX: He say shut up, no pay attention . . . He scared . . .

ZANCAROTTI: Poor thing, is he trying to get to sleep?

ALEX: He scared, scared! Me scared also.

ZANCAROTTI: I swear I'll kill him when we get out of here . . . I don't give a fuck that he's your brother.

ALEX: *He* kill all of us first, Emilio. Not forgive.

ZANCAROTTI: Nor will Zitturi—we've fucked it up for him, too.

ALEX: He not find us in time, we dead first!

[long silence]

ZANCAROTTI: No, I'll kill him first!

NARD: [incomprehensible words]

ZANCAROTTI: I'll kill him.

ALEX: He say quiet or he strangle you. He can do it.

ZANCAROTTI: Me too.

ALEX: He my brother, Emilio. Maybe we stronger than you.

[Long silence. After forty minutes, sounds of snoring.]

* * *

Francesco Rizzo finished reading the prison transcript and concentrated. With a red felt-tip pen he underlined the 'he' in 'He kill all of us first' and drew a circle around the word 'Zitturi'. Then he called Inspector Venturi, who was particularly good at searching through the records, Ascalchi and Ciuffi. It was 9.30 on Friday 10 August. At that very moment, Chief Superintendent Ferrara was waiting for the firemen to recover Claudia Pizzi's body from the bottom of the gully.

'One of them must be the supplier and the other one the person the drugs were meant for,' Rizzo said to Venturi. 'By getting caught, they've screwed both these people, and now they're scared. It may play into our hands. They might be ready to cooperate rather than get themselves killed.'

'The Italian maybe,' Ciuffi conceded sceptically. 'The Albanians won't talk—they're tough, I know

197

them. Even Zancarotti will be hard to crack. He won't want to lose face, he has too much to lose. With the time it'll take to go through the courts and maybe a good lawyer . . .'

'Couldn't we infiltrate someone into the cell before the lawyer gets them out?' Ascalchi asked.

'Not a bad idea,' Ciuffi said. 'I could get one of my men out of mothballs. They're good at blending in and they may be able to get them to talk. It's worth a try, even though I don't hold out much hope. It was a major operation. We're talking here about big shots, really dangerous people. These guys are just couriers, it won't be easy to get them to open up. You've seen how scared they are already . . .'

'Let's try all the same,' Rizzo said. 'Does the name Zitturi mean anything to you?'

'No, never heard it before.'

'Venturi, that's up to you. Go through the records. If necessary, check out all the Zitturis in Italy. It isn't a common name—maybe with a bit of luck . . .'

'All right, chief,' Venturi replied, immediately adding, 'provided he's Italian. This is an international gang. What if he's Greek or Moroccan? Maybe they pronounced the name wrong.'

'Then we're fucked. But I see your point. You'll have to check with Interpol as well.'

'Yes, chief.'

'What's going to be more difficult is identifying the guy they refer to as "He". He must be the Albanians' boss. Any ideas, Luigi?'

'Nothing at the moment. We're analysing the two brothers' mobiles and have asked Deputy

198

Prosecutor Cosenza for authorisation to put a trace on the last calls they made and received. All my men are on the alert, and we're hoping to get something from our informers. A job as big as this doesn't go unnoticcd, there may have been a leak.'

'Perfect,' Rizzo said. 'I don't think there's anything else for thc moment. You can all go.'

*   *   *

A little while later, as he was going to see Fanti to ask if there was any news of Ferrara, Rizzo was stopped in the corridor by Chief Inspector Violante.

'I was just coming to see you. We've identified the owner of the phone card which was used for the emergency call. The Stella case, you know?'

'Yes, of course. Who is it?'

'His name is Pietro Franceschini and he lives in San Michele a Torri, not far from where the girl was found, but more towards Montelupo, in the Via Canto delle Gracchie. We've called him in. Do you want to talk to him?'

'Sure, let's go.'

He followed the inspector to his office, where Sergi was just offering coffee to a man and a woman. They were both middle-aged and rather nondescript. They both looked disoriented and intimidated by their surroundings.

After the usual introductions, Rizzo asked the man if he had been the person who had called the emergency services on the morning of 29 July.

Pietro Franceschini bowed his head in embarrassment and did not reply.

'The call was made from a public place with a

phone card,' Violante said, in a gentle but firm tone. 'The same card that was used to call your home three times, your mother twice and your sister three times.'

The woman—the man's wife, whose name was Rita, shook him lightly by the arm. 'Answer them, Pietro.'

'Tell us the whole story,' 'Serpico' said, in a conciliatory tone. 'If you haven't done anything wrong, you have nothing to be afraid of. We're not accusing you, we just want to know.'

'I didn't do anything,' the man said in a low voice, his head still bowed. 'I . . . I don't know anything.'

'Violante, Sergi, would you mind leaving the room?' Rizzo said. It had occurred to him that the presence of so many officers was making the couple even more scared and uncomfortable. 'I'd like to talk to these two people alone.'

'Listen, Signor Franceschini,' he resumed as soon as the others had gone, 'we don't have anything against you. On the contrary! As far as we know, you simply did your duty as a citizen. You called the emergency services because someone needed help. If anything, you should be rewarded, not scared. That morning, a girl lay dying on the Scandicci road and someone used his phone card to make an emergency call. You didn't lose that card, because the calls my colleague mentioned were made before and after July twenty-ninth, do you understand? So if you don't want to talk, I can only assume that you were the one who put the girl there . . .'

'No, officer, I swear!' the woman screamed. 'It wasn't him . . . It was nothing to do with us. Pietro,

Pietro, tell the superintendent! Oh, holy Mother of God.' She started to cry. 'Why don't you speak? Why don't you say anything? Seeing as they already know . . .'

'I made the call,' the man admitted in a low voice.

'I know. Why didn't you want to tell me?'

The man looked up at Rizzo, a lost expression in his eyes. 'We're simple people, we don't interfere in other people's business. We've never had any dealings with the police, we're clean . . . I did what I had to do, and that's it . . .'

'I understand, don't think I don't. I was scared, too, the first time I set foot in this place,' Rizzo lied. 'We're the ones who hand out fines, who punish people . . . But do you know why we do it? To protect you, not to persecute you. I know, that's not the impression we give, and sometimes we make mistakes, too, and make things worse. But in general we don't, and what you don't see is all the things we do to make life better for you . . . Listen to me, Signor Franceschini. Trust me, tell me the whole story, and everything will be all right, you'll see.'

'I didn't do anything. What do you want me to say?'

'What happened that morning?'

'I went with my wife to church, the parish church of Santa Maria in the Piazza Cioppi in Scandicci . . . Isn't that right, Rita? You tell him, then he'll believe me.'

'It's true, officer.'

'What time was that?'

'Before seven. My wife likes to go to mass early because we have a lot of things to do: feed the

201

animals, clean the vegetable garden . . .'

'Of course, go on. You went to church and then what?'

'No, it was before we got to church, on the Via di Mosciano, the scenic bend, you know? The one on the road, after Domenico's restaurant . . . I mean, after the bend, after the fork for San Martino alla Palma . . . just past it . . . I had to stop because . . .'

'Because . . . ?'

The man looked shamefaced. 'I had to relieve myself . . .' he admitted at last, turning red.

'It often happens to him in the morning,' his wife explained. 'He's a little incontinent, you know . . . He's being treated for it.'

He gave her a scathing look.

'Nothing wrong with that,' Rizzo said. 'It's not a crime. And then?'

'I went to the side of the clearing and did what I had to do, then as I was zipping up I saw something a little further along, to the left. It looked like a hand sticking out. I couldn't see it clearly, because it was just after the bend, when the wood starts to slope away.'

'And what did you do?'

'Well, I went to see what it was.'

'Did you go too, signora?'

'No, no. I stayed in the car. I was wearing my Sunday best. I didn't want to ruin my shoes . . .'

'Did you find the girl?' Rizzo asked, addressing the man again.

'Yes, she was on the ground. I thought she was dead . . .'

'Did you go up to her?'

'I went a bit closer. She didn't have any shoes

202

on. I saw she was breathing . . . so I ran back to the car and called the emergency services from the first phone booth I could find.'

'Which was the right thing to do, as I said. Did you notice anything while you were still in the clearing?'

The man hesitated, and bowed his head again. 'No . . . nothing . . .'

It looked as if the woman was on the point of urging him to say more, but in the end she kept silent.

'Did you see anyone in the vicinity? Were there any cars parked nearby?'

'No.'

'Did you see her shoes anywhere? Was there anything around that might indicate how she'd got there? A moped, for example?'

The man shook his head.

'So you really can't tell me anything else?'

'No, officer,' Pietro Franceschini replied.

'All right. You can go for now. But first I'll have to take a written statement, Signor Franceschini. Please be patient . . . you've been a great help to us. Please, if you'd like to go into the waiting room.'

Glancing at his wife, the man nodded.

*   *   *

After the couple had gone out, Sergi and Violante came back in. Rizzo was just bringing them up to date when there was a knock at the door.

'Come in!' Violante said.

'It's Signor and Signora Franceschini again,' the officer who opened the door said. 'They want to speak to you.'

'Again?'

'They were halfway down the corridor, talking non-stop, then they asked me if they could see you again straightaway. They said it was urgent.'

'Send them in.'

Hesitantly, with a guilty air, the husband and wife came back in.

'Would you rather we were alone?' Rizzo asked.

The man shook his head. In his hand, he was holding a white handkerchief rolled up in a ball.

'I forgot to tell you . . . to tell you . . . I found this in the clearing . . . near that girl.' He held out the handkerchief.

Rizzo opened the improvised wrapping.

There was a small object inside.

Still holding it with the handkerchief, he lifted it to see it better.

It was a gold cufflink with a broken clip. Engraved on it was an elaborate design with an unusual symbol:

18

Michele Ferrara got to Lucca just before five o'clock on Friday afternoon.

Deputy Prosecutor Armando Lupo had sounded more formal and more reticent than Ferrara had expected when he had telephoned him to say hello and suggest they meet. That was why he had not told him the real reason for his visit—he simply said that, being on holiday in Marina di Pietrasanta and hearing that Lupo was now working in Lucca, he'd just like to drop in and say hello. Lupo's reaction suggested that he had been forewarned by the Carabinieri, and Ferrara felt slightly nervous as he got closer to his destination.

The Prosecutor's Department of Lucca was housed in a handsome one-storey red-brick building in the Via Carducci, next to a pay car park, which was where he left his car. It was temporary accommodation, but looked as if it might end up being permanent, given how long it was taking to convert the former Galli Tassi complex in the centre of the city into prestigious new offices.

Ferrara walked in beneath the plexiglas roof and gave his name. He was led to Lupo's office. Lupo greeted him in the official manner their respective roles dictated, but there was nevertheless a certain warmth in the greeting.

The room was quite small and dark, so much so that even in the middle of the day it was necessary to keep the white neon light on. The furnishings were modest: a desk with a computer and printer,

205

a few chairs, a bookcase, a sofa and two small armchairs all crammed against each other without enough space between them to move around in. Files were piled up in every corner and even strewn over the floor. Ferrara and Lupo took their seats as best they could.

'So you left Sicily too,' Ferrara began.

'A few months ago. Actually, I had to . . . I'll leave you to imagine the reasons, Chief Superintendent.'

That wasn't hard to do. He knew Sicily well, and he knew the difficulties that servants of the State, judges and policemen especially, had to confront every day, often jeopardising their own safety and that of their families. And he knew how hard a young deputy prosecutor had to fight against the Mafia in an area—the province of Palermo—which had always been particularly dangerous.

'I hope you like it here.'

'I'm getting used to it. How about you, how do you find Florence?'

'Florence isn't Palermo. Life's good, though I have to confess I often feel homesick for Sicily.'

'Oh, yes! There are wonderful places in Sicily. A pity about the crime, though . . .'

Lupo broke off and was silent for a few moments. It was pointless to dwell on a subject that was painful to both of them.

'Can I offer you a coffee?' he asked.

'Yes, I'd like that.'

While they were waiting for the coffee to be brought in, Ferrara asked, 'Do you remember the case of the massacre in the Via Rosselli?' He was alluding to an event they had both lived through, in an attempt to re-establish the relationship they once had, which he needed desperately now.

'How could I forget?' Lupo replied. 'It's one of those things that really mark you when you're a prosecutor. And even after all this time, I have to tell you, I admired you a lot. You really did a good job.'

'My colleagues, too.'

'Oh yes, of course, that goes without saying.'

One April morning ten years earlier, a group of ruthless hitmen had opened fire on a car in the Via Rosselli, in Palermo, killing an entire family: a husband, wife and two children, both minors. Ferrara, in collaboration with his Sicilian and Calabrian colleagues, had managed to identify and arrest not only the hitmen—one of them a Calabrian, on loan from the Calabrian Mafia—but also the people who had sent them. At the time, Lupo had only recently entered the magistracy and was serving his apprenticeship in the Prosecutor's Department of Palermo. His superior was in charge of the investigation, and he had assisted him with all the enthusiasm of youth.

After the coffee, and the silence that followed this brief evocation of the past, Ferrara judged that the moment had come. 'I didn't come here just for the pleasure of seeing you again,' he said.

'I thought as much . . .' Lupo replied, his face darkening: it was a handsome, open face, still young but already deeply furrowed. 'And with all due respect, Chief Superintendent, I wouldn't like this meeting to be a source of embarrassment. You're on holiday, but I'm not and I have my job to do. Perhaps we could meet another time. I could come over to Marina and we could go for a swim . . .'

Stung but not surprised, Ferrara looked him straight in the eyes. 'It's not my intention to cause you any embarrassment. And in fact I need you to do your job, not to have a swim. Not that I wouldn't like that, even though I don't think you'd appreciate the sea around here after Sicily.'

'There's no need to beat around the bush, is there, Chief Superintendent? Not you and me. As I'm sure you must realise, I already know that you've involved yourself in an investigation by the Carabinieri, a murder investigation in which a friend of yours is a prime suspect. I also know that your behaviour hasn't exactly been exemplary, and that a request has gone through for disciplinary proceedings against you. Believe me, I felt sick when I heard about all this: sick at the thought that a friend of yours was so deeply involved, and even sicker when I was informed that Captain Fulvi had put in an official complaint about you. I tried to dissuade him, but it was too late. I'd have preferred not to be the person given the task of coordinating this investigation. It's the worst thing that's ever happened to me. But it's happened, so what can I do?'

'I'm glad it's you,' Ferrara said. 'Don't worry about me, you carry on. I trust you. Do your duty, see it through to the end, don't let anyone else influence you—and that includes me—and I'm sure everything will work out fine.'

Lupo looked at Ferrara as if he was putting on an act, or didn't really understand the gravity of the situation.

'Whatever happened in that villa,' Ferrara went on, 'Massimo Verga had nothing to do with it. He can't have been the one who killed Ugo

208

Palladiani.'

Lupo was sympathetic. 'I'd have said the same, if it had been my friend. In fact, I'd go further: as far as I'm concerned your friend is innocent until we have evidence to the contrary. The problem is that while we're sitting here talking, the evidence is piling up . . . Unfortunately, sometimes reality is a lot tougher than our illusions. I understand, but I beg you, don't make my task any more difficult than it already is . . .'

Ferrara weighed his words before answering. Then, slowly and emphatically, he said, 'I'm not harbouring any illusions. I've always had my feet planted firmly on the ground, and I know what I'm saying. Massimo Verga is a profoundly honest man. The fact is, the case is much more complicated than it seems. There was a journalist who realised that, who's now been murdered. Do you know anything about that?'

Armando Lupo frowned. He didn't want to get drawn into this. It might well be a trick to gain time, which was something he had feared from the start, knowing Ferrara's catlike shrewdness. But the news was difficult to ignore.

'What do you mean? No, I didn't know.'

'We recovered the body this morning—you'll read about it in the papers tomorrow.'

'But didn't you say you were on holiday?' Lupo asked, and it was hard to tell if he was surprised, being ironic, or frankly annoyed.

'Forget about that,' Ferrara replied, and he told him everything, from his first phone call to Claudia Pizzi to the sad outcome.

'Have you brought the article with you?' Lupo asked, after what seemed to Ferrara like a very long pause.

Ferrara handed him a disk. 'I'm sorry, but I don't have a printer at the hotel . . .'

Lupo stood up, went to the computer, put the disk in, and opened the file. As he was reading, Ferrara stood up in turn and without being invited went and sat down in one of the small armchairs facing the desk.

'Well?' he asked anxiously, as soon as Lupo took his eyes off the screen.

'Where did you say this poor woman's body was found?' Lupo asked, turning to him with an inscrutable look on his face.

'On the road to the quarries, above Carrara.'

'That means it's within the jurisdiction of another Prosecutor's Department—Massa-Carrara.'

Ferrara felt himself being plunged back into the same old nightmare. Was it possible Lupo intended to wash his hands of this, like Pontius Pilate?

'I know that, but doesn't it seem obvious to you that there might be a connection between the two murders?'

'According to you. It was a theory, and notice I say "theory", dreamed up by a reporter on a provincial newspaper, someone desperate for a scoop. Where's the evidence?'

'It's up to us to find it,' Ferrara said, and immediately corrected himself, 'us and the Carabinieri. I know perfectly well it's just a theory, but it's a theory that got Claudia Pizzi murdered!'

Lupo seemed to hesitate for a moment. 'Yes . . . and as usual it's the Mafia's fault! Is that what this journalist was trying to prove? What do you want me to say?' He shrugged. 'My advice is to contact the Prosecutor's Department of Massa-Carrara. Don't you think this Pizzi woman could have been . . . a bit out of control?'

'What do you mean?'

Lupo leaned back in his armchair, and sighed deeply. 'Surely you of all people should understand that . . . You maintain that Massimo Verga is an honourable man, and I want to believe you even though it has still to be proved, and then you bring me an article in which he's virtually accused of murder. On the basis of a prejudice, a cliché we're both familiar with. Massimo Verga is a Sicilian, *ergo* he's a Mafioso, *ergo* Ugo Palladiani was killed by the Mafia, not by his wife . . . Apart from the fact that according to this theory your friend is still a suspect, in my opinion it's also an insult to a whole region. We both know how much Sicily suffers from the presence of the Mafia, but fortunately the vast majority of the population are not Mafiosi. No, Chief Superintendent, I can't help you . . . all I can do is give you some advice. Trust me when I say it's sincere. I feel I owe it to you because of the esteem and respect I have for you. My advice is to drop the Pietrasanta case; the Carabinieri are dealing with it and they're making progress, I can assure you of that. If your friend is innocent, he has nothing to fear, I promise you. And if he gets in touch with you, advise him to give himself up, please.'

There didn't seem to be any point in continuing to argue his case. It was obvious that Lupo had made his mind up and didn't intend to change it, not even for a policeman he said he respected.

'I'll even bring him in myself,' Ferrara said. 'You

211

can count on it.'

*   *   *

When he got back to the hotel, Petra just had to look at the expression on her husband's face to know that now was not the time to ask questions. And he did not give her any answers. They were for him to figure out during what looked certain to be another sleepless night.

That evening they did not have dinner.

They walked down to the beach and then set off along the foreshore, holding hands and not saying a word.

They walked towards the lights of the port of Viareggio beneath the stars, then turned back and went the other way as far as Forte dei Marmi. By the time they were back in Marina di Pietrasanta, they were both exhausted.

Ferrara opened two deckchairs he found propped against the wall of the hotel's bathing establishment, and threw himself down on one of them, like an empty sack. Petra left him, went inside the hotel, and soon came back with two thin blankets. She laid one over his legs and then sat down and covered herself.

In the darkness she searched for her husband's hand, and held it tightly as if by doing so she could unburden him of his mental anguish.

Ferrara saw again Lupo's furrowed brow, the shrug that seemed to admit that he could do nothing for him, the look of sympathy he had given him as he walked him to the exit, the kind of look you give someone who's defeated.

Above all, he kept hearing those brief phrases

which Lupo had come out with, which had unwittingly been like knives piercing his skin: *a friend of yours is a prime suspect . . . a friend of yours was so deeply involved . . . while we're sitting here talking, the evidence is piling up . . . the Carabinieri are making progress, I can assure you of that . . .*

The words went round and round in his head until, unable to fight any more, he closed his eyes.

In the half-sleep that preceded a sleep beset with nightmares, his last thought, perhaps an unconscious balm to distract him from his obsession with his friend, was that he hadn't heard from the office all day and had no idea how another murder investigation, the Stella case, was going.

19

Heraldry was the last thing in the world Inspector Riccardo Venturi would ever have thought he'd have to deal with when he joined the police force. He was the son of poor peasants from the Agro Pontino who had only ever known three coats of arms, the arms of Savoy, the Fascist emblem, and the shield of the Italian republic. He had only a vague idea that once upon a time, the counties, principalities, marquisates, bishoprics and other subdivisions of Italy had produced them in abundance, and that there were still a lot of people who liked to show them off, and even more people who aspired to have one.

To him, the servant of a country which was now and forever republican, this seemed a ridiculous, outdated aspiration, and those who had them sewn on their shirts or engraved on their cufflinks—another relic of a bygone era, in his humble opinion—were pathetic.

And yet here he was, this Saturday morning. First, he had gone to see Rizzo to hand over the pile of lists, papers and maps he had assembled relating to properties in the area where Stella had been found, as Ferrara had asked him to do before leaving. Now he found himself going around libraries, archives, second-hand bookshops, searching for someone to throw light on that cufflink. Superintendent Rizzo had had the cufflink photographed, and the photograph enlarged and distributed to everyone in Headquarters, so that they could all get to work and identify the coat of arms and the symbol as quickly as possible. If in addition to identifying the symbol they could also discover the name of the man who owned the cufflink, better still. This was the best lead they had had so far in the hunt for Stella's killer.

In the light of this new clue, the results of his researches into the buildings in the area where the girl was found had been hurriedly brushed aside.

They all had the photo with them. Sergi had been sent to check out printers, Violante was trying the churches and monasteries, and Ascalchi was visiting jewellers, hoping to find the goldsmith who had made the cufflink and engraved the symbol. Ciuffi had distributed the photo to his men and told them to show it to their informers, and to junkies and dealers. Even Fanti had it, and had started searching for it on the internet.

Nor had Rizzo forgotten to inform Ferrara. He had made a colour copy of the photo with the scanner and had sent it to him as an email attachment.

In other words, the whole of the *Squadra Mobile* had been put to work, and Rizzo just had to wait for the results. For the first time, he felt confident there would be some. He himself, not wanting to leave any stone unturned, had sent specific and detailed requests to the Register of Companies and the Patent Office, since the symbol might not be a coat of arms after all, but a logo—although he doubted it, given the rather baroque, antiquated design. In fact he preferred to doubt it, since there were so many logos around these days—of companies, sports clubs, internet sites, and so on—that the search could well turn out to be virtually endless.

Now, as he waited for his men to return with their findings, he took a pen and paper and started playing with the symbol, isolating it, dividing it, decomposing it, enlarging parts of it, in search of something, anything that could unlock its secret.

The one thing that seemed constant was that there was a letter P in the middle. If you took that out, you were left with a baseless rectangle, and he had no idea what that meant at all. It might be a stylised M, or even an N, if the designer had been especially imaginative, or else it might not be a letter at all. But if not, what then?

Going back to the P, and removing it again, it occurred to him that what remained was the Greek letter Pi, and he wondered if it was worth consulting mathematicians: maybe they had a club in Florence. He made a note of it, then by a process of association it struck him that the letters might be Cyrillic, in which case the P would be an

215

R, but then he had no idea what the other letter might be . . .

Discouraged, he let that go, and tried to concentrate instead on the remaining elements of the symbol. The sun, the moon and the stars were obvious, which might have something to do with astronomy or astrology, but he realised that going down that road he'd be widening the investigation to take in the whole cosmos, and he dropped the idea. It was only worth checking out any of these theories when he had something else definite to go on. Otherwise, the whole thing would drive him mad.

The only conclusion he managed to reach was that they would do well to look for someone whose name or surname began with P.

*   *   *

'*Deri kur do na mbajnë këtu brënda?*' Nard asked.

'*Si her e tjera, pastaj bëjnë proçesin e na hedhin jashtë, pastaj rikthehemi,*' Alex replied.

'Will you shut up, or at least talk Italian?' Emilio Zancarotti protested. He didn't like the idea of the two brothers plotting behind his back, especially after the mutual threats of the previous night.

All morning the two of them had practically ignored him, and the afternoon was shaping up the same way. Zancarotti was irascible by nature, and had to hold himself back. If he exploded, he knew the consequences wouldn't be pleasant: as they had already remarked, there were two of them against one of him.

'*Heret e tjera ishin dozat e vogla,*' Nard

216

continued, purposely ignoring him.

'Çfar kerkon se di une? Kerkoja atij italianit!' Alex said irritably, uttering the word *'italianit'* with contempt. Zancarotti not only caught the word, he grasped the derisory tone of it as well.

'I'll kill both of you,' he almost spat, managing with difficulty to avoid lifting his hand to them. 'I'll kill you as soon as we get out of here!'

The Albanians laughed.

*　　　*　　　*

'Did you understand any of it?'

'Only when the Italian guy speaks,' Inspector Oliva said, taking off his headphones. 'How about you?'

'Quite a bit,' Inspector Aldo Guzzi said, also putting down his headphones. 'Nard is nervous because he doesn't know what's in store for him, and his brother thinks they'll be deported like they usually are. Frankly, with the kind of record they have, I think they'll be old men before they see Albania again . . . but you never know with the law.'

He was twenty-seven, of medium height, with a cavernous, almost ascetic face framed by long, smooth black hair and an untidy beard which made him look like the Count of Monte Cristo before he'd cleaned himself up. His right cheek was slightly disfigured by a piercing, and another two were visible whenever he nervously brushed the hair away from his left ear. His faded blue T-shirt hung loosely on his bony body. The chain dangling from a tab on his jeans jingled when he stood up.

Oliva chuckled. 'And Emilio doesn't understand

217

and is getting pissed off.'

'Yes, I think things are hotting up in there . . . And that's good for us. Time for me to go.'

'See you . . . Sorry, what did you say your name was?'

'Aldo. Aldo Guzzi, like the motorbike.'

* * *

The only food and drink Inspector Venturi had had all day was a sandwich and a Coke in a bar in the Via Borgo Allegri. He was in a bad mood because of the heat and the lack of results. Not that he'd been expecting any, to tell the truth. He had never had any faith in emblems and badges, apart from the police one.

At the Florentine Institute of Heraldry, they had given him a list of addresses of possible experts, among them the owner of an antiquarian bookshop called Belloni, in the Via delle Conce, which was one of the last he still had to visit, at least for today. This was a Saturday he wished was over.

The shop was small, on the left-hand side of a dingy courtyard. The sign was written on the frosted glass of the door, which had been left open to let the air in.

He was greeted by the owner, an elderly Jew who was probably also the only employee. He was short, with white hair and sharp, inquisitive blue eyes. The front room of the shop was bare apart from a wooden counter, behind which the old man was sitting on a high stool, and bookshelves full of folders along the walls. Through a door behind the man, another larger room was dimly visible, with a big table in the middle piled high with books, and wooden bookcases lined with the spines of other books, some of which might well be valuable.

'How can I help you?' the owner asked politely.

'I'm a police inspector,' Venturi said, immediately adding, so as not to disappoint him, 'I'm not here to buy anything, I only need some information.'

'Go on,' the man said, as politely as before.

Venturi placed the photocopy on the counter. 'Do you recognise this coat of arms?'

The man put on a pair of glasses with half-moon lenses and metal arms and studied the picture.

'It's not exactly a coat of arms, it's more a symbol, though of what I have no idea . . . No, I'm sure I've never seen it . . . but there is something . . . Do you mind waiting a moment?'

'Of course,' the inspector replied, even though he hadn't quite been following.

The old man went into the back room, where he bustled about among his books for what seemed to Venturi a very long time, and then came back shaking his head.

'No, I don't have anything. But I'd bet it has something to do with the Freemasons. I wouldn't swear to it, but something tells me . . .'

'What?'

'You see these three uprights under the sun? If you take away the round part in the middle—and I have to admit I have no idea what that is, it could be something to do with one of their rituals, I suppose—but if you take it away, then these three uprights could be columns. The two side ones may be the columns of the Temple. The one in the north is Boaz, and the one in the south is Jachin.

The Masons use this iconography a lot, and often add a third one, in the middle, like this shorter one here. The three columns symbolise Wisdom, Strength and Beauty. And then you've also got the sun, the moon and the stars, which they use a lot as well.'

Venturi did not ask any more questions. He thanked the man and left the shop. Probably just the ravings of an old eccentric, he thought.

$$* \qquad * \qquad *$$

The guard closed the heavy iron grating behind him, and Guzzi saw three pairs of eyes trained on him.

He responded with a hostile look.

He picked out the bunk which was meant for him, went to it and threw down the blanket he had been issued. Who needed a blanket in that heat? You could die in that cell.

'Aren't you going to say hello?' Emilio Zancarotti asked.

'Got any dope?' the newcomer retorted, with a scowl.

'In here?'

'Then don't piss me around,' Guzzi said, throwing himself on the bunk and turning his back on all of them.

'*Italian muti!*' Nard cried, none too happy with this intrusion.

'Leave him alone. Why the hell should you care about this arsehole?' his brother said, in Albanian. He wasn't too happy either, having this junkie in here with them. He despised junkies as much as he profited from them.

220

The cell was already small, and the enforced proximity to Emilio was creating a clash of wills which could be very dangerous. The Italian knew too much, and even though he was in it up to his neck he might be tempted to turn State's evidence and endanger the whole organisation. And he, Alex, had no way to warn Viktor. At least a couple of times in the last twenty-four hours he had toyed with the idea of killing the Italian to redeem himself in the boss's eyes.

Only Zancarotti had not been bothered by the newcomer's arrival. If he played his cards right, he'd balance out the forces.

*   *   *

It was getting late and none of the printers had recognised the symbol that Sergi, alias Serpico, was showing round.

A bell rang as he entered the Solari Brothers shop in the Via dei Serragli. For the umpteenth time that day, he was hit by the smell of lead, which many still used to print invitations and business cards.

He asked the usual questions and received the usual answers.

He was about to leave when he was struck by a coloured print showing two red marble columns with golden capitals, an open book full of Hebrew characters in the middle, a five-pointed star at the bottom and two stars at the top, a crescent moon on the left and a sun on the right which seemed to him identical to the one in the photograph. Around the outside were other, smaller objects, such as a skull and crossbones, an open compass

221

crossed with a ruler, stars and other things.

'What's this?' he asked, intrigued.

'That's just a proof,' the printer replied. 'An illustration for a book about Freemasonry.'

*   *   *

At the end of the day, Sergi reported disconsolately to Superintendent Rizzo that he had found nothing, absolutely nothing. But then, just as he was about to leave, he laughed and said that the sun might be a Masonic symbol. Rizzo would probably not have paid much heed to that, if it wasn't for the fact that when Venturi came to make *his* report, he mentioned the old bookseller's theory. Even though Venturi apologised and told him that the bookseller was probably senile, Rizzo started to give it some serious thought. It was true that two small clues like that didn't constitute evidence, but you couldn't rule them out. As Ferrara always said, there was no such thing as coincidence when you were investigating a crime.

Since he hadn't even got that much from any of the others, and since he also wanted to know how Ferrara was and if he needed any help, he decided to call him. That curious little clue was as good an excuse as any, and at least they could both have a laugh about it.

20

It was dark, and Ferrara was moving with difficulty along a narrow tunnel which was getting ever narrower. He felt as if he couldn't breathe, and he was sure he would die before he got to the end. He had to keep his arms out in front of him, lever himself with his elbows against the damp, viscous earth, and push himself forward. After an enormous effort, he had only moved a few inches. He should have used his legs, he thought, and it was then that he realised that his ankles were being held by icy hands which gripped like steel claws. They were what he was fighting against, what he was trying to escape.

Laughter—horrible, deafening, humiliating, macabre laughter—echoed inside his head, as if to point up the futility of his childish efforts. Childish, like everything he did. It wasn't Massimo Verga who hadn't grown up, it was him. He was the real Peter Pan, still playing cops and robbers at his age! And now the robbers had decided to get their own back.

But it wasn't the mockery in the laughter that made his heart miss a beat, it was its astonishing clarity. He would recognise it even surrounded by the laughter of thousands—only Francesco Leone laughed like that. And indeed there he was, bending over the immature, naked body of Claudia Pizzi: the undeveloped breasts with their small, pinkish nipples, the sparse black down on the mount of Venus, the frail, delicate limbs . . .

'Oh, it's you, Ferrara, come on, we were waiting for you,' Leone said to him, but he had the sneering face of Professor d'Incisa, and the same expensive

wristwatch.

'You were about to miss the best of it,' he continued, still in Leone's voice, picking up a small saw. 'You will stay this time, won't you?' Again, he laughed that infernal laugh.

'Let him go, it's better if he goes. He never takes a holiday, it'll do him good!' These words came from the corpse, which raised itself on its elbows and stared at him with the angry purple face of Commissioner Lepri.

'That's what I told him, chief, believe me,' the Deputy Prosecutor of Lucca, Armando Lupo, said obsequiously.

'He's a fool, a thickhead, a peasant, a loner, he should join us, brothers,' the Contessa Servi asserted loftily, and Anna Giulietti nodded in silent agreement.

The sprightly old woman was laden with jewels, and Ferrara felt guilty because she was wearing his Petra's rings. He ought to arrest her but he was powerless—even his best friend was accusing him. He could hear his voice, calling from the distance.

'Michele, where were you? . . . Where are you? . . . Michele . . . Michele . . .' The imploring voice came ever closer.

*　　　*　　　*

'Michele, Michele. Wake up, Michele!' Petra was calling him, shaking him gently, but it was hard to emerge from the nightmare.

He was in their hotel room, and sunlight was flooding in.

He couldn't remember anything about last night, just that he had flung himself onto a deckchair by the seashore. He hadn't been aware of anything when Petra, with the aid of the porter, had lifted him from the chair, helped him up to their room, and put him to bed.

He could clearly smell coffee. He put out his hand and took his wristwatch from the bedside table. It was 8.20.

'My God!' he exclaimed.

'I know, but I couldn't wake you earlier. You didn't sleep much, and when you did you slept badly. You were tossing and turning and moaning in your sleep all night. You didn't settle until about six in the morning. How could I have dared to . . . ?'

He jumped out of bed and made as if to go to the bathroom to have a wash, but Petra held him back.

'Let's have breakfast first, before it gets cold.'

The tray on the low table was laid the way they liked it. A tea pot, a coffee pot, a jug of milk, fresh orange juice, fruit, a basket of rolls and brioches, five little glass jars containing five different kinds of jam, and one jar of honey.

Ferrara realised that in spite of everything he was hungry.

As he devoured the food, he told her his nightmare.

'Brrr!' she said, smiling. It was the first time she had smiled since hearing about Massimo. 'That's good!'

'What do you mean?'

'Bad dreams help us to get rid of our feelings. You'll feel better today, you'll see.'

He found that hard to believe, remembering the way Massimo had called to him in the dream,

225

begging for help. But if he was calling him, he thought, somewhat illogically, that meant he was still alive. And strangely this thought did make him feel better.

'Any news?' he asked, seeing that Petra had already read the newspapers while he was asleep. She must have had them brought up with the breakfast.

'Unfortunately not. There's the news of Claudia Pizzi, but nothing we don't already know. Lojelo kept his word, your name isn't mentioned.'

'No news is good news,' he caught himself answering.

'You see? You're better already.'

As he washed, Ferrara made plans for the day.

He felt reenergised, and when he was ready the first thing he did was to call Lojelo.

'Thank you for Claudia Pizzi's article, Chief Superintendent. It's a bit worrying. She seemed to be suggesting some kind of Mafia involvement in the area, which I think is unlikely. There was a rumour going round to that effect a few years ago, about some businessman who was said to be money laundering, but then it all died down. But it's a line of inquiry we can't rule out. After all, she was killed—shot with a revolver, in fact.'

'A revolver? Not an automatic?'

'The bullet wounds came from a .38 calibre special, and we haven't found any cases . . . not that it's easy in the middle of a wood, of course.'

'It could well be a Mafia weapon. We'll have to check up on Sicilian businesses in the area. I know they don't have to be connected with the Mafia just because they're Sicilian, of course, I'd be the first to admit that. But Claudia Pizzi was on to

226

something, and we owe her that much, I think, don't you? In the meantime, have you managed to find out anything about the quarries?'

'Not yet. Today's Saturday, and the land registry officer is away for the weekend with his family. But he'll be back on Monday and I'm sure I'll get what I need from him then.'

'Good. Anything else new?'

'We're proceeding with the interviews. Her boyfriend, her relatives, friends, whoever can tell us anything about her. This afternoon we're expecting the local news editor of *Il Tirreno* and two colleagues who worked quite closely with her. Maybe they know something more about this Mafia story.'

'Let's hope so. Can I help you with anything?'

'Not for the moment, unless you want to sit in on the interviews,' Lojelo said, then paused almost imperceptibly before adding, 'We'd really like it if you could.'

'I don't know,' Ferrara temporised, not wanting to make Lojelo uncomfortable. 'I may drop by later, but I can't guarantee anything. Please keep me informed, though, if you find out anything. Even the smallest thing.'

'That goes without saying, Chief Superintendent!' Lojelo replied, with what seemed like a touch of relief. Or was it only Ferrara's imagination?

*   *   *

'There are at least three places we need to visit today,' he said to Petra as soon as he had put the phone down. 'Simonetta Palladiani's art gallery,

227

which is in Forte dei Marmi. Romano's restaurant, where she had dinner with Massimo on the night of the murder, which is in Viareggio. And the beach establishment he went to, wherever that is. Where should we start?'

'I'd start with the nearest place.'

'The bathing establishment, then . . . But there's a problem . . .'

'Which is?'

'If the Carabinieri find out I'm sticking my nose in, there'll be serious trouble this time. This really is their area.'

'So are Forte and Viareggio, if it comes to that. They're practically one town. We walked from one to the other yesterday, remember? Come on, let's be tourists and look for Massimo to start with. If they were such good friends'—Ferrara noticed that she had avoided using the word 'lovers'—'it's likely he rented a hut in whichever bathing establishment she was a member of, don't you think?'

'Good point. And in Forte and Viareggio?'

'We'll think of something,' Petra replied. She seemed to be taking the initiative, which made him smile. He wondered where she got the energy from. She was going through the same torments as him, like him she had hardly slept in the last few nights, and she'd been up all last night watching over him. She hadn't even had the chance to get rid of her tension and frustration in a nightmare, as far as he knew.

It did not occur to him that it might be his own renewed strength which had given her a new lease of life. Besides, before the blow of Massimo's disappearance, she had always been a practical, energetic and determined woman.

As they were about to leave, the phone rang. It was Rizzo, reporting the finding of the cufflink and announcing that he had emailed him a photo of it.

'Congratulations, Rizzo! Excellent. I'll look at it and call you back later, I'm just on my way out.'

'Any news?'

'No. Nothing good, anyway. Take a look at today's papers. A journalist on *Il Tirreno*, who may have known something about Simonetta Palladiani, has been murdered. I'll talk to you about it later.'

'All right, chief.'

'You're the chief now. Get cracking, you may be on to something.'

*   *   *

On Saturday morning the beaches, already full during the week, overflowed. A gaily-coloured, half-naked crowd kept flooding into the bathing establishments from the small streets that descended at right angles to the seafront, and in more than one the Ferraras had to queue at the cash desk or the bar before anyone would listen to them.

Starting with the bathing establishment directly opposite Simonetta's villa, they fortunately did not have to go too far to trace the one that had the name Massimo Verga on its list. It was the Blue Seagull, a bit further along the seafront and somewhat smarter than some of the others. Massimo was registered there as a permanent guest of Simonetta Palladiani, who had been a member for several years.

The manager, a bright and breezy woman of about fifty, friendly and talkative, said she was upset by what had happened at the villa and worried by the absence of Simonetta and her friend: he was 'a real gentleman, polite, well read,' she said, and she hoped she would see him again soon.

Had she been following the articles in *Il Tirreno*?

No, she was far too busy to read the newspapers. But they kept them for their members, and some of them had spoken to her about it. Besides, the villa was nearby, so obviously she knew absolutely everything there was to know.

And had she heard about the journalist that morning?

No, what journalist?

The one from *Il Tirreno*.

Why, had something happened to her?

The conversation was getting nowhere. Ferrara wanted to go, but Petra insisted, 'You know, we were supposed to be meeting Massimo here last Saturday, but we couldn't make it. He was so keen on having us meet Simonetta, I think he was in love with her . . .'

'I think you may be right! Her poor husband, the man who died . . . or did they kill him . . . well, he died anyway, may he rest in peace . . . anyway it was none of his business, he wasn't her real husband any more, everyone knows that. But if you'd come here last Saturday, you wouldn't have seen her. She wasn't here. He came on his own. I remember it well because at lunchtime he sat down at that table over there, the third one in the second row, you see? He only had an orange juice

230

and sat there smoking his pipe, looking a bit absent. He must have been feeling lost without her!'

'And how was he when they were together?'

'Always cheerful, chatty, very attentive . . . He talked a lot, you know? A walking encyclopaedia. Like I said, he was well read.'

'Did they have friends here?'

'No. She was always quite reserved. She knew a few people through her work, but she was always a bit . . . formal with them. They spoke sometimes to people, the way you do, but you know how it is. A chat sometimes with their neighbours or with someone on the beach, but in general they kept themselves to themselves. They seemed to have a lot to say to each other, as if they were plotting something!'

Ferrara did not appreciate her choice of words.

'Thank you, signora. I hope I get a chance to see her when she gets back. We're sure to come and visit him some time.'

They left and walked to their car. Forte dei Marmi was next on their list.

'You're very good!' Ferrara complimented Petra.

'But we didn't find out anything.'

'That's not quite true. If he was here on his own, that means Simonetta stayed at home, either quarrelling with her husband or making up with him. It would be nice to know which. If they did make up, she's less likely to have killed him, don't you think?'

'Right . . .'

'A pity there's no one they were friendly with in that place who could tell us more . . . Never mind!

231

At least we can cross the beach off our list. It's just a question of being methodical.'

'If you say so.'

*   *   *

They would have done better to walk, even in that heat, because finding somewhere to park in Forte dei Marmi on a Saturday, the day of the famous market which attracts crowds of tourists and locals from all along the Versilia coast, is practically impossible. After driving around in vain for more than half an hour, Ferrara left the Mercedes in the car park of a police station, displaying the red and white Ministry of the Interior signal paddle, which he usually kept in his car. God help them!

The Archivolto gallery was in the Via Roma, a small street that came out onto the Piazza Garibaldi near the small fortress built by Grand Duke Leopold I of Tuscany in the years 1782-1788 as a garrison and customs house, around which the town had developed.

The gallery consisted of two not very large white rooms. To get from one to the other, you went through a brick arch supported by white marble columns. There were paintings by contemporary artists on the walls, some incomprehensible, others interesting, and futuristic sculptures on various kinds of pedestal scattered through the two rooms.

A young woman in a white linen tailored suit and purple blouse was sitting at a tinted glass desk that did nothing to hide her long tanned legs— which may have been the intention. She was busy studying, or pretending to study, a catalogue, and did not look up.

Ferrara looked at one of the paintings, a large canvas, mostly light brown in colour, with a black stripe on the right. Against this brown background, various objects stood out, painted in black and grey with a technique that seemed quite unusual. They included a chair in the bottom left-hand corner and half a Pinocchio in the top right-hand corner. Against the black stripe was a white bird without wings. He decided he liked the painting, noted the name of the painter, and went up to the young woman with the catalogue.

'Um . . . Excuse me . . .'

'Yes?' she replied in a melodious voice, and at last looked up. Her eyes were violet, like her blouse.

'I was looking for Signora Palladiani.'

For a moment, she seemed uncertain what to say, then made up her mind. 'She's not here.'

'That's strange. This is Saturday the eleventh, isn't it?'

'Yes.'

'The thing is . . . we had an appointment. Didn't she say anything?'

'We've come all the way from Milan specially to see her,' Petra said.

The young woman sighed. 'I understand, but Signora Palladiani . . . Haven't you heard?'

'Heard what?' Petra asked, feigning surprise.

'She . . . she had to leave suddenly a week ago. Perhaps I could help you?'

'I don't know,' Ferrara said. 'We had an arrangement with her . . . she said she was going to show us some Baricchis, and a few other artists, too. When is she coming back?'

'I'm afraid I can't tell you. It was very sudden, as

233

I said.'

'But she has phoned you, hasn't she? Signora Palladiani must phone you to find out how things are going!'

'No, so far she hasn't called me.'

'And what about you? Don't you need to contact her?'

She was starting to become suspicious. 'I'm sorry, but why are you asking me all these questions?'

'Because I have to see her!' Ferrara said, raising his voice, pretending to be annoyed. 'I've come here specially from Milan to do a big deal. I have a gallery in Brera, one of the biggest, and I'm offering Signora Palladiani an incredible opportunity! And now she's nowhere to be found . . . Who does she think she's dealing with? Look, I'm not wasting any more time. I want you to tell me, right now, where and how I can find her. I haven't come a hundred and eighty miles just for the pleasure of seeing your pretty little face! I'm a businessman! Give me her mobile number, her home number, anything, and please be quick about it!'

'I can't,' the young woman murmured, a little scared.

'Why not?'

'Let's go, Fausto,' Petra said, acting her part to perfection. 'If she can't she can't.'

'Please don't interfere. I'm not going to be made a fool of by some provincial gallery assistant!'

'Please, signore, I assure you I can't. I would if I could, but—'

Ferrara looked her full in the face. 'I don't like

this at all. You're sure she hasn't phoned? You'd better not be lying because in my line of business my name means something, and I can make life very difficult for you! Why hasn't Signora Palladiani called me in all this time to cancel our appointment? Can you tell me that?'

'I don't know,' the young woman said, lowering her eyes. 'And I haven't lied to you.'

'I hope not! But if she gets in touch tell her Signor Benelli called, Fausto Benelli from Milan. Is that clear? Write it down!'

'Yes, Signor Benelli . . .'

*　　　*　　　*

On the autostrada to Viareggio they drew their conclusions. In the end, they had found out practically nothing. If Simonetta had run away, Ferrara thought, she would surely still have kept in contact with her business. But either the young woman with the violet eyes was very loyal to her— and a great actress, to boot—or Simonetta Palladiani really had disappeared, which was the likeliest hypothesis. It was the most reassuring too, because it meant she was innocent of the murder, but at the same time the least pleasant, because it meant that Massimo had disappeared along with her.

The journey took quite a while, because of the heavy traffic which slowed them down along the few miles separating the Versilia exit from the Viareggio exit, and then again at the entrance to the town.

Their visit to Romano's, one of the best restaurants in Viareggio, turned out to be more productive. The owner and the waiters were very kind, and understood how worried Signor Benelli—from Florence this time—must be by the absence of his associate who should have been back at work last Monday. But they couldn't tell him anything other than that the couple—who they remembered very well because he was a handsome man and she was a gorgeous woman— had spent a wonderful evening. They had seemed calm and happy, like two people who seemed to have just realised that they were madly in love. And the waiter who said this, who was gay, raised his eyes to heaven ecstatically.

If the Carabinieri had questioned them, too, they surely couldn't have gained the impression that the two 'accomplices' were hatching some deadly scheme that night!

But he knew that didn't matter. They were probably working on a different theory: that the two lovers had been surprised by the woman's husband, who had put up with a lot but couldn't get over the sight of them in bed together under his own roof—even though the roof wasn't really his, except in a figurative sense.

If that was the case, though, why was Ugo Palladiani found in the villa, at the foot of the stairs? Wouldn't he have been in the annex? Or had the Carabinieri found evidence that he had been dragged into the house? After all, the housekeeper had said that the house was absolutely tidy except for one bedroom. Was this the consistent evidence they were gathering?

No, it couldn't be. And the reason it couldn't be was that he knew perfectly well that Massimo had nothing to do with it, and if he hadn't, then neither had Simonetta . . . Or had she killed both of them?

He was distracted from these reflections by another waiter, the one who had made the reservation, explaining to Petra that Simonetta Palladiani was not known there, whereas her husband was a regular who came there to eat every time he went out in the boat.

'What boat?' Ferrara asked.

'His boat. His yacht.'

'Does he keep it here?'

'Yes.'

'What's it called? I'd like to see it. It may be up for sale.'

'I don't know, I've never seen it. But you can ask at the Port Authority, or the Yachting Centre, they're both in the Piazza Lorenzo Viani, down by the harbour.'

*   *   *

The Viareggio Yachting Centre was a steel and glass building, the steel painted blue, red and yellow. They pointed him in the direction of a 65-foot Princess 65 Fly moored at a nearby wharf.

The navigator was on board and the Ferraras approached him after pretending to admire the boat.

'She's beautiful!' Ferrara exclaimed.

The man, who was middle-aged and stocky, nodded.

'What kind of engine does she have?'

The navigator almost laughed. 'She has two. Two 1050-horsepower Man engines.'

'How many people can she take?'

'Four cabins, three bathrooms, plus mine.

237

Why?'

'I'm looking for one just like this. Do you know if the owner would be willing to sell?'

'It belongs to a PR company in Florence, UP Communications. The registered owner just died, though, so they may be willing to sell. You'll have to ask them.'

'Poor man . . . was he ill?'

'Not at all. In fact, we were supposed to be leaving last Saturday. Then I discovered a fault in the forward propeller, and he said he'd rather postpone. The stupid thing is, I'd already fixed the fault by Sunday, but he wasn't around any more . . . Just like that, from one day to the next.'

'Just like that? Suddenly?' Petra opened her eyes wide. *'Ach du lieber Gott!* How cruel life can be. And he was going on holiday, you said . . . A cruise?'

'We were supposed to be going to Nice. I don't know if it was for pleasure or business, he never told me.'

*   *   *

It was already nearly eight in the evening when Francesco Rizzo called Ferrara at the hotel.

On hearing his theory of the Masonic connection, Ferrara decided it was time to tell him everything he hadn't said when he'd entrusted the case to him, in order to avoid problems with the Prosecutor's Department and the Commissioner.

'Inform Anna Giulietti, but don't let her know I told you to. Find some excuse, tell her you need authorisation to get hold of the lists of all the Masonic lodges, some nonsense like that. She

238

won't give it to you of course, she'll just say these are the ravings of a crazy old man and a few witty remarks by a police officer who was fed up. But in the meantime, you'll have had a chance to tell her the whole story, and her interest will have been aroused because of the argument she already had with me.'

'Okay, I'll do that.'

'Do it straightaway. She works over the weekend. And there's something else you can do for me. Keep an eye on Professor d'Incisa. He's a Freemason—I know that for sure because I've seen the lists, I have them at home. And Stella ended up in his hospital! It may be a coincidence, but you know what I think. When you're investigating a crime, there's no such thing as coincidence.'

'I agree . . . but I don't see the connection. The cufflink was found before Stella was admitted to hospital, not after . . .'

It was like a flash of lightning.

He suddenly remembered the head nurse's words: *he got quite angry when he saw the girl . . .*

'What's to say he didn't already know her?'

'Who, d'Incisa? A highly-placed consultant and a young illegal immigrant?' Rizzo was incredulous.

'Why not? He could have been screwing her . . . But you're right, I may be getting ahead of myself. In fact, I'm sure I am. We don't even know if it's a Masonic symbol or not. Keep an eye on him anyway, trust me on this. In the meantime I'll have a look at the photo of the cufflink. I haven't had time yet. I'll also send it to the deputy prosecutor in Bologna who gave me the list. He knows all there is to know about the Freemasons and if he doesn't recognise it, you can be sure there's no connection.'

When the call had finished, he switched on his laptop, connected to the network, checked Rizzo's message, and opened the attachment.

For a long time he studied the photo of the cufflink.

A thought crossed his mind briefly, but he dismissed it, or rather filed it away in a recess of his brain: Ugo Palladiani was a Mason, too, and the photo showed the letter P, surrounded by the kind of classical columns associated with Palladio.

He was indeed getting ahead of himself. The case in Marina di Pietrasanta was already complicated enough, given the possible involvement of the Mafia. Putting the Freemasons into the mix seemed a bit too much, even to him.

He phoned the deputy prosecutor in Bologna, briefly explained what it was about, got him to give him his email address, and sent him the photo.

Once again, all he could do was wait.

Maybe Rizzo was on the right track after all. He certainly hoped so, however flimsy the lead was. His own flash of intuition during the phone conversation with Rizzo a little earlier might not mean anything: Profesor d'Incisa's anger at seeing the girl could well have been due to tiredness and the bother of having to intervene in a case which looked hopeless. Anyway, Rizzo was making progress, and he was pleased about that. Whereas Ferrara himself was either letting his imagination run away with him or getting nowhere fast.

Superintendent Lojelo had not been in touch, which meant there had been no new developments in the Claudia Pizzi investigation. But it hadn't been long since the body had been discovered, so they just had to wait.

Meanwhile, another day had passed, and there was still no news of Massimo. If the Carabinieri wanted him so badly, what were they doing to find him?

21

It was Ferrara who provided the solution to Rizzo's problem, and Rizzo who answered Ferrara's question.

Rizzo was the one who phoned Ferrara. Having temporarily taken Ferrara's place, he had also adopted his habits and had gone in to the office on Sunday morning. His wife and children were still in Sicily and he was bored at home.

As there was not much to be done, he had decided to spend the time examining the land registry results and the maps of the area where Stella had been found, which Venturi had left with him the day before. He wasn't expecting to find out anything useful—the cufflink was a much more promising lead—but it was best to leave no stone unturned.

The memo he had found waiting for him in the office had swept away all his good intentions, and made him regret he hadn't stayed in bed.

'I have something to tell you, chief,' he began.

'So have I, and it isn't good,' Ferrara said, not noticing the darker than usual tone in his deputy's voice: he had always been laconic.

'What is it?' Rizzo asked. He didn't mind

241

gaining time.

'You go first.'

'You're right, everything else can wait . . . There's some bad news . . .'

Ferrara immediately assumed it was something to do with Massimo and, imagining the worst, he felt his strength failing.

He said nothing, waiting for Rizzo to continue.

'Your friend Massimo Verga is now officially wanted, along with Simonetta Palladiani . . . A copy of a memo from the Carabineri in Lucca has arrived, signed by Captain Fulvi and sent to all police forces, especially those at ports, airports, railway stations and border posts. An order to detain on sight, issued by Deputy Prosecutor Lupo . . . It's already been put in the data bank at the Ministry of the Interior, chief.'

Ferrara did not feel up to asking for the name of the crime, but he could imagine what it was: accessory to murder. This was practically an arrest warrant! Which must mean they had evidence. If they found Massimo now, it wouldn't be easy to get him out of trouble. If he fell into the hands of the Carabinieri, and with a Prosecutor's Department so determined to charge him that Lupo hadn't even had the courtesy to inform Ferrara despite their previous connection—or probably *because* of it—Massimo's chances of getting away scot-free were slim indeed.

On the other hand, compared with the other, more terrible possibility that he had been found dead, this news was, if not acceptable, at least tolerable. While there's life, there's hope, Ferrara said to himself, and while there was even just a thread of hope he had no intention of giving up.

242

'All right, Rizzo. Thanks. I'll think about it . . . You think about Operation Stella. No good news on that front either, I'm afraid. The deputy prosecutor of Bologna didn't recognise the symbol. He doesn't think it has anything to do with the Freemasons, at least not the official ones. He admits there are Masonic elements in it, but they're all very common: the sun, the moon, the stars, the columns, if they really are columns . . .

'It might be best to drop that line of inquiry and consider some of the other theories that could help us to identify the symbol.'

'The trouble is we've gone through all of them, without any luck at all so far.'

'Sorry to hear that. But anyway, have you informed Anna Giulietti?'

'Of course, chief, last night, as you told me.'

'What was her reaction?'

'Pretty much as you predicted. She was too polite to tell me to go to hell, but she did ask me to come up with something a bit less woolly . . .'

'Of course. Given the way things are, she did the right thing. I'm afraid I didn't make you look good, Francesco.'

'I'm not worried about that at the moment.'

No. He was worried about something else. The same thing Ferrara was worried about.

They said goodbye, each determined to get back to his own work. Ferrara told Petra to get ready to go out, and Rizzo reluctantly started going through Venturi's file.

*   *   *

Deputy Prosecutor Anna Giulietti hadn't slept

243

well. Superintendent Rizzo's phone call, with that improbable allusion to the Freemasons, had disturbed her more than she had thought at the time. There was no doubt in her mind that Ferrara was behind it, and she felt guilty about Ferrara. Partly because he was in trouble and had been forced to take a holiday, but mostly because she had a lot of respect for him and knew he wasn't the kind of person to clutch at straws in order to solve a case.

If anything, Ferrara was quite the opposite: down-to-earth, rational, scrupulous, flexible, ready to change tack in an investigation if the evidence showed him he was going in the wrong direction.

As a prosecutor, her behaviour had been irreproachable, and yet in her heart of hearts she kept wondering if she wasn't doing him a disservice.

She had woken late and had a not very appetising breakfast—heating up last night's coffee out of laziness, which had left a bitter taste in her mouth—and now she was wandering around the large apartment where she lived alone, filled with a mounting anxiety.

At 10.20 she made up her mind to call him.

'Hello?' It was Petra who answered.

'Good morning, Signora Ferrara. This is Anna Giulietti. I was looking for your husband.'

'Good morning. He's driving at the moment, we're on the autostrada . . . Is it urgent?'

'No . . . no, it's nothing. Tell him I'll call him again.'

*   *   *

244

'It was Anna Giulietti. But it couldn't have been anything important. She said she'd call back.'

They had just got on to the A12, heading for Carrara. Petra was giving him a rundown of Claudia Pizzi's articles, which she had carefully read through the previous day, underlining the most important passages. Some of the articles had been published, some were drafts she'd saved on her computer. It was Lojelo who had passed them on to Ferrara.

'All right. Carry on.'

'Most of the articles, especially the recent ones, are about the marble quarries. She was clearly worried about the situation and was investigating it. Some articles are quite long and even a little boring, full of technicalities. But the gist of them is that the local heritage is in danger because of over-exploitation, some of it by outside entrepreneurs. Do you want me to outline the situation as I've understood it? It might help you to see things more clearly.'

'Go ahead. I'm listening.'

'Right. Well, to start with, it's important to know that the marble in this area is unique in the world. Without going into too many details, the key thing is that it's ninety-nine percent calcium carbonate— in other words, practically pure. A block of marble is nothing but compact calcium carbonate. They call it "white gold". The kind that's best for statues, the unveined kind, which is actually called statuary, is only extracted from a single quarry these days, which is known as "Michelangelo's Quarry" because that was where Michelangelo went to choose the blocks he needed. Although no one knows for sure whether it was actually that particular quarry.'

'You're not going to tell me the whole history, are you?'

'Only what might be useful to us to know, and I think this is.'

Ferrara didn't mind the use of the word 'us'.

'The marble is extracted in blocks, usually weighing about twenty tons each, and from the waste they obtain marble dust, which has many uses: it's used for some types of plaster, to restore old statues, even to make glossy paper for illustrated books. They even—and this you really won't believe—give it to hens mixed with their feed to make more eggs!'

'And we eat the eggs?'

'Well, we don't eat the shells. It's the shells that contain the calcium carbonate.'

'Okay . . . but do you want to tell me what all this has to do with anything? We'll be in Carrara soon.'

They had in fact left the autostrada and were now driving along the Viale XX Settembre towards Carrara. From there, Ferrara intended to continue to the spot where Claudia Pizzi's body had been found and even further, if necessary. He had decided to take advantage of the fact that it was Sunday to take a closer look, and that was why he had asked Petra to brief him on the articles, which might contain a clue to Claudia Pizzi's death and perhaps lead to Simonetta Palladiani.

'It does have something to do with it! The thing is, the trade in marble dust, although it doesn't have the prestige of the trade in marble blocks, is a lot easier to handle, and the profit margins are impressive. The manpower required is minimal

246

because most of the work is done by machines. Basically, it's an activity the—what shall we call them?—the purists look down on, and Claudia Pizzi was a real purist. In fact, she'd launched a virtual crusade against it. The way it works is, the market in marble is cyclical, depending on the state of the world economy. When things are going well, rich people in the richest countries build themselves villas, minarets, palaces, using our precious marble, but when things are going less well there's less demand for marble, and the economy of the area suffers. So they use the trade in marble dust as a stopgap, and keep the blocks in reserve until times are better. What Claudia Pizzi was trying to draw attention to was the fact that in the last few years the exploitation of the marble dust has been growing out of all proportion, even when the economy's fine. It's got to the point where sometimes even perfectly good blocks are sacrificed. And the thing is, a lot of this is being done not by the locals, but by companies that have come into the area from outside. Listen to this for instance . . .'

Petra put on her tortoiseshell glasses and leafed through the papers.

'It is impossible not to ask why a company based in Bellomonte di Mezzo, Sicily, should invest in the revitalisation of old quarries which have been unproductive, and then exploit them only for the manufacture of marble dust, using non-specialised, non-local workforces, and even getting fresh supplies from other quarries in order to increase production. Everyone knows that a ton of marble dust is not worth even a tenth of a block, and the old timers regard the newcomers as naïve fools. But is that

247

really the case? Or is there something behind it that no one sees or wants to see? Money laundering, for example, which would be a terrible stain on the whole of our community, or something even worse, something your reporter hopes to reveal when she has gathered sufficient evidence?'

'The woman certainly didn't use kid gloves,' Ferrara said. 'If the Mafia really is behind this, it's no surprise she ended up the way she did. When was this article written?'

'It's just a draft, Michele. The file was last opened on July twenty-sixth. And listen to what she wrote four days later in another file:

'Go on, go on reducing our mountain to dust. It's already shrinking! Come on, people of the islands, fill your pockets, and leave us with the crumbs! But be careful, there are predators in the mountains, and some have already smelled the stench of rottenness. They won't let you rest!'

'A brave woman, don't you think?'

'Reckless, I'd say,' he commented. 'Imagine if that had been published! But I suspect she'd already exposed herself quite a bit during her investigation. I'm certain she knew something about Simonetta's disappearance. Simonetta inherited the lease on the quarries from her father. She must have reinforced or even confirmed her theories. "I'm adding powder to the fire," she said to me . . . What did she mean? What fire? If there's any truth in what she wrote, she was sitting on something really big . . .'

They were driving through Carrara now, but their progress seemed to be blocked by an endless line of cars and coaches. Ferrara made a detour and found himself in the central square, where he

248

saw a stand belonging to the Provincial Tourist Authority and was struck by an idea.

He parked the car and asked Petra to wait for him.

He soon returned with a leaflet and a grim expression on his face.

'It isn't going to be easy to get up there today,' he said. 'They're holding the annual sledge celebration.'

'What's that?'

'You mean it wasn't written in Claudia Pizzi's notes?' It was meant to be a joke, but it fell flat. This wasn't the right moment.

'No, it wasn't, so what is it?'

'It was the method they used to use to bring the marble blocks down from the mountain. That's what the tourist information person told me. They slid them down on tree trunks laid over a bed of stones, like a sledge. Just think. They carried them all the way from up there right down to the sea! It was dangerous, too, people sometimes got killed . . . Fortunately it's all different now.'

'And they're doing it again today?'

'Every year, on the second Sunday in August, they have this celebration, where they slide a block down for about fifty yards. The event attracts about a thousand people who stand all along the roads for miles around. That's why the traffic's so slow today.'

'Would you rather give up and go back?'

'No,' Ferrara said. 'They gave me a map of the quarries, all numbered. We'll be able to check out the ones that belong to Simonetta Palladiani. Seeing as we've come this far . . .'

But it still took them almost two hours to get to

the spot where Claudia Pizzi's body had been found, and the area was so packed that it was impossible to park. They carried on and half an hour later reached quarry 206.

Ferrara got out of the car and, ignoring the sign that said PRIVATE PROPERTY, NO ENTRY walked around the barrier and continued along the stony path that led towards the excavation area. Everything seemed to be in order and completely devoid of life. He was struck by a strange smell, rather like rotten fish.

There was no sign of a watchman. A huge excavator stood near the terraced wall of the mountain, and close to a metal shack a tanker lorry was parked, whitened by marble dust. Ferrara walked up to it, wiped away the part of the window where he had caught a glimpse of writing, and read: MINING EXTRACTION LTD.

He wrote the name down in a notebook, went back to the car, and dialled Anna Giulietti's number on the mobile. But there was no reply.

Petra was coming towards him.

'I was worried,' she said.

He smiled and took her by the arm and they walked back to the Mercedes.

The other two quarries were similar to the first. In one of them there were no vehicles at all, in the other a lorry belonging to the same company.

By now they were near Colonnata, and they hadn't yet had lunch.

'How would you feel about having a bite to eat?'

'Why not?' She wasn't hungry, but she thought it would do him good.

'Maybe the traffic will ease off a bit while we're

eating and the road will be clearer on the way back.'

* * *

Finding a spot in the little car park in Colonnata wasn't easy. Then they climbed the steep stone staircase leading to the main square, with its plaque dedicated to the anarchists, the arch that gives access to the historic centre, and a few bar-restaurants.

They chose one at random, and sat down at a table next to a group celebrating something with plates of Colonnata paté and bottles of white wine. They weren't tourists, but locals.

The guest of honour was a man of advanced years who still seemed lively and quick-witted. Ferrara overheard that he had won a bet.

'What was it?' he asked the man closest to him at the other table, a sprightly, white-haired man, who was perhaps already a little merry.

The man explained that Franchi had beaten everyone at guessing the weight of a huge block of marble simply by hitting it with a hammer.

'We know these mountains,' he concluded proudly. 'We have to know them, otherwise we'd all be out of a job.'

'You're born a quarryman, you don't become one,' another man said.

At that point everyone turned to Ferrara and Petra. Franchi, who for reasons of honour was acting as the head of the group, invited the couple to join them. Ferrara declined, saying that they had to leave soon but he took the opportunity to say, 'I've read that not all the quarries are run by firms from Carrara. How do you feel about people coming in from outside?'

The old quarryman shrugged. 'Live and let live.'

'I read an article in *Il Tirreno* by a journalist from round here, saying they don't really know what they're doing and are ruining the mountain.'

The old man shrugged again. 'We all mind our own business. We do our work, they do their work . . .'

'So you don't mind them?'

'What they do doesn't concern us. If they want to buy our waste, that's fine with us. They can do whatever they like with it.'

'If they're stupid enough . . .' another man said, and chuckled.

'And do they make marble dust?'

'Some, yes.'

'Is that why they use tanker lorries? I think I saw one . . .'

'Yes, otherwise the dust blows away when they transport it.'

'Thank you. Sorry to interrupt you. We're just going to have a quick bite and then go. Enjoy the rest of your party!' Ferrara stood up to go and get a sandwich and a glass of beer for himself, and tea and a slice of cake for Petra, because no one had thought of coming to take their order.

*   *   *

On the way back, the road was indeed clearer, and Ferrara even managed to park close to the souvenir stand.

The mouth of the gully had not been cordoned off because the body had been found much lower

252

down, and the area had already been thoroughly searched by Lojelo's men.

He got out of the car and looked around, not sure what exactly he was looking for.

The mountain on the other side of the valley was partly covered by beeches and chestnut trees. Through them, he could see the white walls of marble all the way up to the summit. What had Claudia Pizzi been doing here at dawn, before the stand opened?

He walked along the wall of rock, which was separated from the rest of the mountain by the road. It was no longer than about ten yards. At the other end there was a stretch of meadow, strewn with wild bushes, and then the ground fell away sharply towards the bottom of the valley. A few of the branches were broken. Ferrara started climbing down, careful where he was putting his feet.

From here, it was possible to see the part of the mountain opposite which had previously been hidden by rocks and vegetation. The quarry was clearly visible, with a huge yellow excavator and a tanker lorry next to a metal shack.

He had a pretty good idea now of what had happened.

Claudia Pizzi must have taken up position here to photograph quarry 206 and whatever was going on there. From here, she had probably seen a vehicle coming up the road from Bedizzano. It must have scared her, and she had tried to get back to her own car, but her assailants had got to her while she was running along the edge of the gully. The impact of the bullets had sent her tumbling down the slope.

253

The killers had probably not climbed down to check on her, otherwise they would have found the handbag and the camera and, if they were Mafiosi, they might have shot her a few more times to make sure she was dead. The escarpment was very steep and she had fallen a long way: they must have assumed that even if the bullets hadn't finished her off, the fall had.

*   *   *

It was late afternoon by the time they got back to the hotel.

Petra was tired, Ferrara worried and nervous.

The porter came up to them. 'There's a lady to see you, Chief Superintendent.'

'To see me? Where is she?'

'Over there, in the lounge.'

'Has she been waiting long?'

'About half an hour.'

The woman was reading a magazine as she waited for him. Ferrara recognised her immediately.

'Anna?' he said in surprise as he and Petra walked towards her.

22

'So, was it you or wasn't it, who got Rizzo to make that phone call?'

'If you're asking me in your role as a deputy prosecutor, I won't say yes and I won't say no. I'll just say that Rizzo is in charge of the investigation

254

now and has full responsibility to take whatever measures he sees fit in order to reach a satisfactory outcome. If on the other hand you're asking me as a friend, I'll say that he's the one who mentioned the Freemasons, far-fetched as the idea is, but that I was the one who urged him to talk to you about it. And I'm sorry if I made him look an idiot.'

Anna Giulietti smiled. They were sitting in the lounge of the Principe and had ordered aperitifs. Ferrara had lit a cigar: he hadn't been able to smoke one in the car and really needed it now.

'Let's talk as friends,' Anna said. 'It may not have been such a bad move. To begin with, because it was obvious it came from you . . . it made me think. What if the hospital really did make a mistake? It may not have anything to do with the other part of the investigation, even though Rizzo—or rather, you—seem to think the opposite, dragging in the Freemasons at the very spot where they found the girl . . .'

'Stella.'

'You found out her name? You identified her? I didn't know that . . .'

The same reaction as Leone, with an added degree of touchiness, Ferrara thought.

'No, no. It's just the name we're using for her, so that we don't have to be constantly calling her "the girl" or whatever.'

'I see. Anyway, the point is, if the hospital did make a mistake, perhaps I shouldn't just drop it. There are other patients, it's not right that . . . Anyway, I came to say that tomorrow I'm giving the authorisation for you to look at the medical records.'

'Thanks Anna, I appreciate it. But you'll have to

talk to Rizzo about that. I'm away from there now, and I have other problems . . .'

And he told her everything. The only detail he left out was the curious presence of the letter P, which might link Palladiani, the Freemasons and the cufflink. But if he brought that up, it might risk muddying the whole doctors-Freemasons-d'Incisa connection, which Anna Giulietti had finally taken on board. Best to leave that be and just take a look at the clinical data, which might help both Leone and Fuschi.

As Ferrara spoke, Anna's mounting apprehension was indicated with mathematical precision by the gradual increase in the number of lines on her forehead. 'And you're sure Massimo had nothing to do with it?' she said when he had finished.

'If we can't be sure of our friends, who can we be sure of?' Ferrara said, although it was not clear whether this was an admission of certainty or of weakness.

'*Massimo ist kein Mörder,*' Petra said, categorically.

Anna Giulietti looked from one to the other and shook her head. 'Unfortunately, as far as that case is concerned, there's nothing I can do. It's in the hands of a different Prosecutor's Department, and I don't know this man Lupo . . . So tell me, Michele, how can I help you?'

'You can't,' Ferrara replied.

At that point his mobile started ringing. He looked at the screen. 'I'm sorry, I have to take this, it's Rizzo.'

* * *

256

'Hold on to your hat, chief!' his deputy began.

'What's up?'

'Isn't Ugo Palladiani the guy your friend Massimo is supposed to have killed, according to the Carabinieri?'

'Yes, why?'

'And didn't he have a factory making jeans and things like that?'

'No . . . he was in public relations . . . but he had one before.'

'So it is him.'

'What do you mean?'

'The owner of the factory.'

'What are you talking about, Francesco?'

'There's a factory half a mile or so from the place where they found Stella. A former jeans factory registered to Casual Clothing Ltd—director: Ugo Palladiani. It was abandoned after the company went into liquidation, but as far as we can tell from the maps and the land registry, it's still the property of the director, Ugo Palladiani. Curious coincidence, don't you think?'

It was a lot more than just curious, just as his idea about the P had turned out to be less absurd than it had seemed at first.

'Not so curious,' Ferrara replied, in not much more than a whisper. He was no longer thinking about the Stella case, but about the implications of that discovery. If Palladiani was now part of their investigation, then Florence might have official jurisdiction over his case. If that was so, he'd be able to investigate Massimo's disappearance openly.

'We need to take a look at the factory,' Rizzo

257

went on. 'Do you think Anna Giulietti will give us a search warrant?'

'Yes, I think she will,' Ferrara said, throwing a glance at the deputy prosecutor, who replied with a look of curiosity.

It was time to satisfy that curiosity as thoroughly as possible.

*　　　*　　　*

'Well, well!' Anna Giulietti said when Ferrara had finished updating her. 'Of course I'll issue a search warrant. By itself, owning a warehouse in the vicinity of the place where the girl was found isn't much, or we'd be searching every building in the area, but taken together with the letter P on the cufflink and the fact that the owner died in mysterious circumstances, there's more than enough there to justify it.'

'And don't forget the symbol on the cufflink, which may be Masonic.'

'Not that again! You have a one-track mind, Michele . . . First the doctor, now Palladiani . . .'

'Well, they're both Masons, aren't they? Though not from the same lodge.'

'Yes, and God knows how many other Masons there are in Florence . . . and in the whole of Italy, and France, and England, and America. I think we should drop that for the moment. We have more than enough to be getting on with without stepping on the toes of a lot of powerful people who may just respond by getting rid of the lot of us.'

As always, she was being sensible. She might even be right. But the whole Masonic aspect hung there like a shadow and it bothered him.

258

'But you're still going to give the authorisation for the medical records, right?'

'I promised, didn't I?' she replied, unconvinced.

23

The week of the August bank holiday looked all set to be chaotic, and not only because of the rush to the beaches. Rizzo's discovery had given Ferrara a shot of adrenalin which had kept him awake all night—though he was getting used to that—and had got him out of bed at dawn on Monday morning. He found himself pacing nervously up and down the deserted corridors of the hotel and then along the side of the swimming pool, smoking his cigar and waiting for a decent time to make his first phone call.

When finally the hands of the clock started to approach seven, he called Fanti.

'Good morning, chief. I haven't yet finished that research you asked me to do on Sicilian companies in Tuscany, but I'm working on it . . .'

'Don't worry about that for the moment. Right now I want you to find out all you can about a company called Mining Extractions, based in Bellomonte di Mezzo.'

'Yes, I think that's one of the names I already came across.'

'What did you find?'

'Nothing. Just that it's one of the Sicilian companies working up here.'

'Find out more.'

'Leave it to me, chief.'

'As soon as you know anything, call me, okay?'

'Of course.'

After the call, he had two more immediate goals he had set himself: to find out the results of the factory search, and to go further into the question of Simonetta Palladiani's quarries. For the first, he would have to wait at least until late morning. For the second, the best thing to do was to go back to Carrara.

He preferred not to wake Petra, who must have fallen asleep just as the sun was rising. He left a message on her bedside table, making sure it was conspicuous so that she would read it as soon as she woke up, and went out.

At eight on the dot, he entered Superintendent Lojelo's office.

'What time does the town hall open?'

'Ten o'clock.'

'Too late. I have to find out about those quarries as soon as possible. But I assume the staff start earlier than that?'

'That's no problem. As long as the land registry officer is there.'

'Can you get one of your men to go with me?'

'I'll go myself, Chief Superintendent, but I'll make sure first.' He ordered an officer to go and check and phone him as soon as the land registry officer had arrived.

'Thanks. Anything from the interviews?'

'We're still sifting through the answers, but I don't think anything important came out. Claudia Pizzi was respected because she didn't put on airs. You know, a woman in a small town who manages to get a job on a major paper, even if it's not a national one, counts for something. She was considered a bit of a "writer", an artist, even

260

though she dealt with fairly mundane things: local news, interviews . . . Everyone agrees she was very serious and conscientious. A tough cookie who didn't give up easily. She got excited about her various "crusades", but she didn't let her imagination run away with her, she always double-checked everything.'

'If only they were all that way,' Ferrara remarked, thinking of other journalists he knew who, in their search for a scoop, were ready to spread the first piece of local gossip they came across as gospel truth.

'Right . . . We spoke to her boyfriend. His name is Fabio Rubini, same age as her. He works as a sales rep for a company making building materials. He said she'd been very tense lately, but that was nothing new. They'd been together since university, and in those days whenever she had exams she usually became impossible. They always ended up quarrelling. He thinks she always did it deliberately, so she could be alone and concentrate on her studies. The same thing happened later, too, whenever she was involved in researching or investigating something difficult, only now they didn't quarrel. He'd learnt his lesson and left her alone . . . That's what happened during the last week, in fact.'

'So he can't fill us in on what she was doing?'

'Unfortunately not.'

'And you don't think they quarrelled and he . . .'

'Well, where couples are involved, anything's possible, we both know that. But I don't think so, in this case. Her father speaks well of him, and he has an alibi which we're checking: on Thursday ninth and Friday tenth he was working in the north

261

of his sales area: Ameglia, Sarzana, Aulla, Pontremoli. He spent the night at a hotel in Pontremoli. We should be able to eliminate him very soon.'

'I see. And you don't know of anyone who hated her enough to . . .'

'We haven't come across anyone so far.'

'Which brings us back to the whole Mafia idea . . . or whoever it was who was doing something dodgy in Simonetta Palladiani's quarries, and perhaps in others, too.'

'In the absence of any other lead . . .'

'Which means we must go to the town hall.'

'As soon as the land registry officer arrives.'

Ferrara looked at his watch. 'Why don't we get there before him? He should be arriving any minute now.'

* * *

The land registry officer arrived late and spent at least five minutes apologising. When Ferrara was at last able to ask him the question he needed to ask, he went off to consult his records. Most of these were handwritten. They only seemed to have discovered the typewriter here in the last half of the previous century: God alone knew how long it would be before they got round to computers!

The officer returned. 'They're the Tonelli quarries.'

'We already know who owns them,' Ferrara explained patiently. 'What we need to know is who's been working them.'

The officer gave him a puzzled look, glanced at Lojelo as if to say, 'Doesn't this fellow know anything?' then said to Ferrara, 'I'm not talking about the owner. The municipality owns them and leases them out. The Tonellis have had the lease since the days of Maria Teresa d'Este.'

'In other words, they're handed down from father to son? They're hereditary? But how long is the lease?'

'Until recently, ninety-nine years, renewable by the same leaseholder. It was actually Maria Teresa who started the practice, to boost marble production. The system was basically unchanged until two years ago, when they introduced a new rule, limiting the leases to a period of twenty-nine years, but it's a difficult business applying it. Some people challenge it, say the quarry was given by the princess to their family and doesn't belong to the municipality . . . you know how these things are. But they're gradually sorting it out. If a leaseholder doesn't renew within a certain period, which varies from case to case, then he loses the right to use the quarries.'

'I see. So in a way it is a kind of ownership . . . but does whoever has the right to use a quarry have to exploit it himself or can he lease it to others? In this particular case, who does Simonetta Tonelli lease hers to, since she doesn't seem to have anything to do with them directly?'

'That's also a complicated matter. Broadly speaking, the quarries can't be leased to third parties, which is another reason why the new rules were introduced. They establish that the mountain belongs to the municipality, which can lease the quarries to whoever exploits them, provided that person in fact does so. But there are private agreements whereby one person gets another

263

person to do the work, and the municipality isn't too bothered about that. As long as the quarries are kept going, no one loses his job, the rules are followed, and the taxes are paid, we're not going to stick our noses in.'

'Too bad. So you don't know who's running quarries 206, 219 and 225?'

'Wait a moment.'

He went away again and soon returned with a sheet of paper on which he had noted down a name. 'It seems that the taxes are paid on behalf of Simonetta Tonelli by a certain Ugo Palladiani of Florence. That's all we know.'

The two policemen looked at each other, discouraged, said, 'Thank you,' and left the office.

It was after midday.

'Don't worry, Chief Superintendent, I'll send one of my men to check it out properly.'

'You have enough on your plate,' Ferrara said. 'I'll deal with it.' He took out his mobile and dialled Headquarters in Florence.

'Ferrara here,' he said to the switchboard operator. 'Put me through to Superintendent Rizzo.'

'Hello, chief,' his deputy said when he came on the line.

'Did Anna Giulietti's warrant arrive?'

'Just got it. I'm on my way there now.'

'Good. Let me know how you get on. Did she also send you the authorisation to see Stella's medical records?'

'Yes, chief.'

'Perfect. Make sure Leone and Fuschi get copies.'

'Of course, chief.'

264

Outside Carrara Police Headquarters, he got back in his car and set off again for the mountains. He was starting to know the road as well as the route from the Via Zara to his apartment.

He didn't go straight to Simonetta's quarries, to avoid putting the supposed criminals on their guard, but stopped first to question workers in other quarries. He did not discover much. Perhaps there was a code of silence here, or perhaps it was just that people minded their own business, as the group he had met the day before in the bar in Colonnata had said.

In the third quarry he visited, he actually ran into old Franchi, the winner of the bet. He hadn't been one of the most talkative of the group, but it was worth a try.

Ferrara introduced himself as an academic who was writing an article on Carrara marble.

It didn't take long to get in his good books. The man wasn't hostile, just reserved. Gradually, Ferrara got him to talk about the presence of non-local operators in quarries 206, 219 and 225, where he had seen a lorry belonging to a Sicilian company.

'Yes, Mining Extractions. They're the people who work those quarries. At least, they're the ones we sometimes sell waste to. They make a little marble, but mostly dust.'

'But who are they?'

'I don't know. They're from Sicily, yes, but we don't know them and we don't know who their boss is. We usually just call him "the Sicilian". Some of us joke about it and call him "the saviour of the quarries".'

Just like Claudia Pizzi.

'Why's that?'

'Because those are the Tonelli quarries, which had been practically abandoned for ages. If it wasn't for those people, the municipality would have taken them over by now, because you can't keep quarries completely inactive when they could give work to lots of people. Not that there's much left to extract. Trust me, I know what I'm talking about.'

'Perhaps the main reason they took them over was the marble dust.'

The old man shrugged, as if he didn't understand an activity that seemed blasphemous to him and he preferred not to think about it.

'But what does this dust look like?' Ferrara asked.

The man looked around him, then down at Ferrara's shoes. Like everything else—the rubble-strewn path leading to the quarry, the machinery, the toolsheds—they were covered with a thin whitish layer like the one on the tanker lorry he had seen the day before.

'Can't you see?' the man said, with a smile. 'Come on, follow me.'

He led him towards the terraced flank of the mountain where a group of workers were extracting a block.

The operation was a fascinating one. The cutting machines sliced through the marble as if it were butter, raising clouds of white dust that looked like talcum powder.

The old man approached a heap of the dust, picked up a handful, and held it out to him. Ferrara took a pinch of it and let it run through his fingers. It could have been heroin, or pure cocaine.

266

'This is it, more or less,' Franchi said, raising his voice to make himself heard above the noise of the cutters. 'Except that this isn't the stuff they use. It's just residue, and it's dirty. The diamond used to cut the marble gets burnt in the process, which contaminates the dust. That's why the dust they use is specially ground from the residue.'

'I see,' Ferrara said, as they moved away to a spot where they could talk more easily. 'How long have these Sicilians been here?'

'Six or seven years.'

'Since the mid-Nineties?'

The man thought about it for a few seconds. '1994, to be precise.'

'And you've never noticed anything strange?'

'How do you mean?'

'I don't know. Unusual comings and goings, goods being moved at odd times, strangers visiting the quarries . . .'

'No, why? All I know is that the small amount of marble they produce they send to America. But the dust goes all over Italy: to paper mills in Garda, farms in Reggio Emilia, building companies in the north and in Rome, things like that.'

'And is that normal?'

'Perfectly normal, why?'

'Just trying to get an idea. I haven't quite got the commercial side of things clear. Marble I understand, it's a unique, centuries-old tradition, but dust . . .'

'I don't understand it myself . . . Sure, it sells. But there's no need really to come here for it, you can get it from any quarry anywhere. Our marble is special—to waste it like that . . . Well, what can you do? I'm old.'

'Which means you're wise. At least that's the way it used to be. Now things have changed and no one wants to get old. A mistake, in my opinion. You just have to look at the way the world's going.'

'Too true, Professor.'

*   *   *

He got back to the hotel in the afternoon and found Petra reading in the garden. He sat down beside her, kissed her, and told her what he had found out.

'I wouldn't be at all surprised if this Mining Extractions company turns out to be the centre of a drug trafficking operation. They could be using the marble dust to cut the drugs. It looks practically identical. But I don't understand . . .'

'What, Michele?'

'Why they had to take over three whole quarries. How much do they need? With what you can extract from just one quarry, I imagine you could cut half the heroin in the world for a year!'

'Yes,' Petra admitted. 'It doesn't make much sense.'

They were both silent for a while, then Ferrara, still puzzling over that question, called Police Headquarters in Florence. They told him Rizzo wasn't back yet and he asked to speak to Fanti.

'Well?' he began.

'Hi, chief! I spent all morning trying to get some information from the people in Bellomonte, but they're worse than the three wise monkeys. No one knows anything, they can't get to the files because of an earth tremor in '98 which made the place

268

unsafe and now they're somewhere temporary and are completely impossible to reach . . . plus, they say they've had it up to here with Rome and the mainland. I think I'll have to contact a colleague of mine down there.'

'Do it, Fanti. You have carte blanche. I need to know who's behind that company.'

24

Rizzo arrived at the abandoned factory just after two in the afternoon together with Sergi, Ascalchi and three constables. It was a white, one-storey, reinforced concrete building, some sixty-five feet wide and two hundred feet long. The only windows were long narrow ones high up on the walls, close to the roof.

Deputy Prosecutor Anna Giulietti's warrant authorised them to remove any obstacles they had to, and Sergi only took a few seconds with his wire cutters to get through the padlock on the heavy iron shutter. The shutter itself, although half rusted, was not hard to lift, as the runners were well oiled.

Nor was it difficult to force the lock on the iron door.

They found themselves in a large rectangular space, covered by the dust of years and cluttered with heaps of garments, piles of cardboard boxes, long trestle tables, some still standing, others thrown to the floor with all their contents, including sewing machines.

'We've come in on the workshop side,' Rizzo

said. 'Let's check the rest of the premises before we start to search.'

'With all this mess, that could take forever,' Ascalchi complained.

At the far end of this large room was a glass door. Beyond the door, a corridor, with two rooms on one side and three on the other. All of the rooms had walls of plasterboard and glass, apart from one which had plasterboard only. This was the toilet, which was filthy. The other four rooms had been the offices. The desks and cheap armchairs were still there. Papers, pattern books, binders and folders were strewn everywhere, telephone wires dangled, and there were masses of cables for computers which had long gone.

At the end of the corridor was another door, identical to the first.

It led to the reception area, shrouded in darkness because the windows, high up on the walls, had been blacked out.

Sergi found the light switch and turned it on.

The halogen lighting was very strong, almost harsh. Once their eyes had become accustomed to it, Rizzo and his men stood there, stunned.

It was a very large, elegantly furnished room, with modern sofas and armchairs—enough for about thirty people—low glass tables, wall to wall carpeting, modern paintings on the walls, and big loudspeakers cleverly placed in the corners. What must have been the reception desk had been pushed closer to the wall and was now used as a bar, to judge by the bottles of alcohol on it.

This room, too, was untidy, but it was a more recent untidiness: used glasses, ashtrays full of cigarette ends, cushions on the floor. It gave the impression of a place that had been abandoned in haste, which no one had bothered to come back and clear up.

But what really drew the police officers' attention was the huge plasma screen on the wall behind the desk, the focal point towards which the eyes of the guests must have converged from whichever part of the room they were in.

Once the first moments of astonishment were over, Rizzo walked behind the desk and found the remote control. He picked it up with his handkerchief, in order not to wipe off any fingerprints, and pressed the ON button.

The TV screen came to life. Simultaneously the lights dimmed and from the loudspeakers came the gentle, melancholy notes of a Chopin nocturne. A series of photographs began appearing on the screen.

At a pinch, the first ones could still have been defined as 'artistic'. They were of excellent quality and showed prepubescent children—boys and girls—of various races, completely naked but in innocent poses. It was a collection which would have gladdened any paedophile's heart. It was followed by a video. Here, the quality was less good and the poses less innocent: other children playing among themselves, exploring each other's private parts.

The rest was a crescendo of atrocities, all to the accompaniment of Beethoven's Ninth Symphony, in a repulsive contrast with the images.

More photographs and videos followed. The videos were merely of home movie quality, and showed children being manipulated by adult hands and made to perform all kinds of sexual acts.

271

Sometimes they seemed to consent, but at other times they were subjected to sadistic violence to force them to comply with their tormenters' wishes. The adults' faces had been obscured, while the camera lingered with undisguised pleasure on the suffering faces of the children.

Disgusted, even though he was used to seeing all kinds of things in his job, Rizzo switched off the TV. The lights came up and the music stopped.

Ascalchi, Sergi and the three constables were still standing in the doorway, transfixed.

Rizzo did not say anything. He simply shook his head, then called Headquarters to send for a forensics team.

'Careful how you move around,' he said to his men. 'This doesn't look like Signor Palladiani's private boudoir, more like the headquarters for a whole ring of perverts. So the more fingerprints and other things we can find the better. Okay, let's get to work.'

They started to search the factory inch by inch, inspecting the armchairs and sofas, examining the papers in the offices, turning over the piles of jeans and T-shirts. It was in the middle of one of these piles that Ascalchi found a pair of knickers with the label 'Steaua Rosie' and a pair of shoes with the label 'Orhei'.

The forensics team soon arrived, and spent more than two hours collecting samples. As they were working, one of the team, equipped with a luminol lamp, called Rizzo over.

'Superintendent, come and have a look at this.'

He aimed the beam of purplish-blue light at one of the sofas. The hurriedly washed bloodstains on the upholstery were clearly highlighted. There were other stains on the carpet near the same sofa.

It was nearly seven in the evening.

Superintendent Rizzo dialled Ferrara's number.

*   *   *

'Let's pack our bags, we're going home,' Ferrara, filled with renewed energy, announced to his wife as soon as he had finished on the phone. 'Ugo Palladiani could be the person responsible for Stella's death . . .' He told her everything, concluding, 'Whatever happens, the investigation into his death will have to become part of the Stella inquiry, which means I'd be involved officially. I'm going back to work.'

'That's good, Michele!' Petra said, feeling her mood lifting, but almost immediately the shadow of a doubt seemed to temper her enthusiasm.

'What's the matter?'

She smiled. 'Nothing, Michele, nothing . . . But don't you think it's strange that the killer was then himself killed?'

'Why? If he wasn't alone, and from what Rizzo tells me he definitely wasn't, we're probably dealing with those infamous paedophile parties involving several people. One of the others might well have been afraid he'd talk.'

'It's possible, I suppose . . .'

He looked at her closely. 'But you're not convinced, is that it?'

'Well . . . we know he was planning to go to Nice, and in the light of what you've just told me it probably wasn't a holiday, he was running away. Wouldn't it have been simpler to just let him go?'

Once again, Ferrara had to admire his wife's

perceptiveness. She would have made an excellent detective if she had ever set her mind to it!

'You may be right—I admit I hadn't thought of that. Or perhaps I didn't want to think of it. I want to get back to work right now. You've raised a perfectly reasonable objection, and if we looked closely at the evidence we have so far, which isn't much, we'd probably think of a thousand others.' He smiled. 'But we're the only ones who know he was planning to leave, aren't we? So?'

'*Lass' uns zurückkehren!* Let's go!' Petra exclaimed, going to the wardrobe to get their bags.

25

Setting foot back in the office that Tuesday morning at seven was like being reborn.

Not that his anxiety over Massimo's disappearance had lessened. On the contrary, it was increasing with every hour that passed. But sitting at his desk, surrounded by the objects he had become used to over the years, with his feet on that floor which had been trodden by other, greater heads of the Florence *Squadra Mobile*—he had almost been moved to tears when he had first crossed that threshold—pleased even by the slight smell of stale smoke with which the furniture and walls were impregnated, Ferrara felt his strength returning. He would need it, and all his organisational abilities and clear-headedness, to make sense of this complex tangle of drugs, paedophiles and Mafiosi. What had been uncovered in the abandoned factory, he well knew, was only the tip of the iceberg.

He had even had a relatively quiet night, going over the various theories and working out strategies which he could not wait to put into practice.

Only one thing was missing: Fanti. As usual, the sergeant had arrived before his chief, but he wasn't in his office at that moment.

He summoned Rizzo, who soon appeared.

'Have you sent the report to the Prosecutor's Department?' he asked after they had exchanged greetings. His deputy seemed relieved by his return, which somehow put things back on track.

'Yes, chief. And I've also asked for a warrant to search Palladiani's apartment, office and car.'

'Add his yacht. He has one in the harbour in Viareggio.' He leafed through his own notebook, and tore off the half-page with the relevant details. 'Here.'

'Okay, chief.'

'And another thing, Francesco,' he added, thinking of that planned escape to Nice, which Petra had brought up. 'It might be a good idea to have a look at his bank account and his phone records.'

'Sure . . . It would certainly be a strange coincidence if the man who was killed in Pietrasanta also turns out to be Stella's killer . . .'

'And in our business, there is no such thing as coincidence, is there?'

'That's right, chief . . .'

In the meantime Fanti had returned, but had not dared to interrupt their talking.

'Fanti!' Ferrara called. 'Come in here!'

But the sergeant did not appear immediately. In

fact, he did not appear even after several minutes.

'Fanti, did you hear me?' Ferrara yelled, surprised and a little annoyed.

He heard the chair being shifted in the next room, followed by slow, shuffling footsteps.

When Fanti at last came in, he was pale and his eyes were watery.

'What's the matter? Are you all right?'

The sergeant nodded and lowered his eyes.

'What is it? You look worn to a frazzle. You haven't even brought me in the mail. What's the matter, isn't anything happening in this city?'

Fanti gave him a hangdog look. 'Right away, chief. I'll bring it in right away.' He went out again.

Not even 'Good morning' or 'Welcome back'! What was going on?

He threw a questioning look at Rizzo, who did not know how to respond.

The only item of mail that Fanti brought in was a one-page document.

Ferrara felt the ground give way. All his renewed energy abandoned him suddenly. It was a scene he had already lived through and he had no desire to live through it again, in what looked like being its worst ever version.

The hand he held out to take the document was shaking slightly.

He realised immediately that it was not what he had feared, but the relief was short-lived.

The document bore at the top the letterhead of the Head of the State Police and Director General of Public Safety.

It was an official order.

His hands were still shaking as he read it.

The Head of the State Police ordered he be

relieved of his duties for one month, without pay except for a living allowance equal to half his salary.

The reason: *Behaviour towards representatives of the Carabinieri in no way befitting the standards expected from the Head of the Squadra Mobile, and likely to damage the reputation of the State Police.*

'No way!' he cried, flying into an uncontrollable rage, and passing the document to his deputy. 'There's no way I'm going now! I don't give a damn about the Head of the Police, the Carabinieri, the Commissioner, the Public Prosecutor . . . Even if they send the Carabinieri to arrest me, I'm not moving from here!'

'Calm down, sir,' Rizzo begged. 'You'll only make things worse.'

'Worse than this? My best friend may be dead for all I know, and this jumped-up young captain who can't see any further than his own nose is looking for a couple on the run while the Mafia are playing fast and loose in his territory! No, Francesco, it's really not on! You don't defeat organised crime by being polite! The idiot thinks this is some kind of crime of passion, but while he's been wasting time reporting me instead of looking for Massimo, we've opened up something bigger than Pandora's box! And you think I should just step aside?'

Ferrara's private mobile started ringing.

'Of course not, but maybe if you talk to the Commissioner—'

'Oh, sure, he's bound to be a lot of use!'

It was odds on that Riccardo Lepri had been one of those pressing for this action to be taken— he'd virtually threatened as much.

'But it's the only way.'

The phone was still ringing and Ferrara took it out of his pocket, irritably.

'Who's that?' he yelled.

'This is Anna, Michele. I'm on my way to Siena, but I heard all about Rizzo's operation yesterday and I just wanted to congratulate you. You were right. This could be the breakthrough you were looking for, don't you think? Now we'll really have to look into this Palladiani and coordinate our investigation with the one in Lucca. I think the best thing you can do is go back to Florence and take over the investigation again—'

'I'm already in Florence, but I can't do anything.'

'What do you mean?'

'That right now I'm not the head of the *Squadra Mobile*, and maybe I never will be again. In fact I'm nothing!' And he told her the whole story, from the exchange of threats with Captain Fulvi to the order he had just received, which must also have been sent to the Commissioner and the Public Prosecutor. 'Didn't you know anything about it?'

'I haven't been into the office, I've got things to do in Siena first . . . How do you plan to handle it?'

'I don't know. I think I should talk to Lepri.'

'I don't know if that's such a good idea . . . Let me think about it.' It was obvious her brain was already working overtime. 'No, Michele, don't do it. Who's seen you at Headquarters?'

'Apart from the sentry, only Rizzo and Fanti.'

'Do you trust them?'

'Are you kidding? I trust them more than I trust myself.'

'Cover yourself. Go home and make sure no one can reach you. You haven't seen that order, okay? You mustn't receive it. I'll call you later.'

'Okay, bye.'

'Bye.'

'Fanti!' he called after he'd hung up.

The sergeant came back in. 'Yes, chief?'

'Listen to me carefully,' Ferrara said, addressing both of them. 'You haven't seen me. I haven't been here, okay? And you can't get in touch with me. You have no idea where I am.'

Fanti and Rizzo nodded.

'But what are you planning to do?' Rizzo asked.

'Stay head of the Squad as long as I can. Right now I'm going home. You know where to find me, if you need me.'

'I've finished my report on the Sicilian companies,' Fanti said. 'Do you want it now?'

'Yes, I'll take it with me, at least I'll have something to pass the time. Did you find out anything from Bellomonte?'

'I talked to a colleague in Trapani who was at police academy with me. He'll try to give us a hand, but he says we shouldn't be under any illusions. The town is practically a Mafia stronghold. It's just like the Wild West, he says.'

'Bring Superintendent Rizzo up to date on this,' Ferrara said, seeing that Rizzo wasn't following them. 'Try the Chamber of Commerce if you have to, or the Ministry, or God Almighty. Whatever happens, we need to know who's in charge of Mining Extractions. I mean who's really in charge, I don't want the directors, they're sure to just be figureheads.'

'All right, chief.'

He went out and walked across the courtyard. As he did so, a prison van came to a halt, and two guards brought out a young man in handcuffs. He was in his mid-twenties, of medium height, with a hollow face and a piercing in his left cheek.

Ferrara recognised Inspector Guzzi, one of Ciuffi's undercover men. It was only in this disguise that he could set foot in Headquarters. Ferrara remembered that he'd been planning to ask Ciuffi what he thought of his theory that the quarries were being used for drug trafficking. But now he couldn't, because his own office and his own men were off limits to him.

*   *   *

Out of handcuffs now, Guzzi made his report to Superintendent Ciuffi.

'The Albanians' boss is called Viktor. The drugs were meant for him. The suppliers are definitely Mafia. Apparently the drugs are brought in from Asia, especially Afghanistan. The Mafia use Zancarotti to launder the money in Albania, but he either doesn't know or won't say who the important Mafiosi are. He says he's always contacted by different people. He's a kind of middle man between the two gangs. He knows the Albanians and works on commission for the Sicilians. Usually he isn't directly involved in the traffic, not even in small quantities, but in this case they were forced to use him because he had to get the fee directly from Viktor's hideout. That's because Viktor didn't trust the Sicilians, but he knew Zancarotti wouldn't fuck around with him, given the way he's got things set up in Albania.'

280

'But why directly from Viktor's hideout? Couldn't they have met on neutral ground?'

'Even he doesn't know that. Those were his orders and he had to follow them.'

'At least you managed to get something out of him. Congratulations.'

'Pure luck. He needs me. He's really scared the other two are going to kill him. Now they're inside, they hate each other. The brothers think it's Zancarotti's fault they were arrested, because the car was his and he was driving, and Zancarotti's convinced the traffic cops stopped them because Nard wasn't wearing a seat belt.' He smiled ironically. 'The Albanians are another matter. They don't really talk to me. It's not surprising, they think I'm on Zancarotti's side. But they don't know I can understand their language and sometimes I catch a few words, like their boss's name. Every now and again they mention this guy Zitturi, the one Zancarotti also mentioned, and when they do they look at him. It could be the name of the man in charge of the Sicilians. I tried to ask Zancarotti, as casually as I could, but he said he had no idea what I was talking about.'

'Which would seem to confirm it. He was the one who said they'd fucked it up for Zitturi.'

'Precisely. Have you found out who this guy is?'

'No. We've tried the name Zitturi and several variations, but so far we haven't come up with anything. Let's hope we get something from the mobile phones we confiscated, but I doubt the boss used his own phone!'

'Well, good luck. I think my interview with the examining magistrate must have ended by now, and it's time for me to be taken back to my cell.'

'I'll call the guards.'

*   *   *

Being a prisoner in his own home, Ferrara decided to get down to studying Fanti's report. But first he had one phone call to make. To Carrara, to find out what was happening with the investigation into Claudia's murder.

But there was no news. When Superintendent Lojelo asked him how things had gone the previous day in the quarries, he was almost tempted to mention the Bellomonte connection but something held him back. He told himself it must have been because the lead was quite a weak one, but in his heart of hearts he was afraid that it needed a lot more experience than Lojelo had to avoid compromising everything and alerting the criminals.

By the time he had finished examining Fanti's report, he was sure he was on the right track.

He had just put the report down when Anna Giulietti called him.

'I'm on my way back from Lucca,' she began.

'I thought you went to Siena.'

'That was this morning. Then I went to Lucca, because I can't set foot in my office, if I did I'd find out you'd been suspended. And besides, I wanted to meet this Armando Lupo, who's a Sicilian like you. He has a lot of respect for you. You didn't tell me that.'

'He may respect me, but he wasn't very cooperative the last time we met.'

'Strange, I got the opposite impression. He had nothing but good to say about you, and anyway the

282

most important thing is that he agrees we should link the two investigations. We've arranged a meeting tomorrow morning, in Lucca, with you and Captain Fulvi.'

'Tomorrow? August bank holiday?'

'Why? Have you ever taken it off?'

Ferrara thought about it. 'Yes, twenty-seven times . . . then I joined the police.'

'Lucky you, I didn't even get that many!'

'Anyway, I don't know if I should . . . given the way things are . . .'

'Why? How are things? I know you're on holiday, but in the light of recent developments in a case involving murder, paedophilia and possible criminal conspiracy, I need you, and I'm forced to call you back on duty urgently.'

26

Captain Fulvi was nervous.

After his first, relatively cursory but accurate assessment of the results obtained from both the crime scene investigation and the autopsy on the victim, he had not found it difficult to formulate a plausible hypothesis about the events leading up to Ugo Palladiani's murder. The housekeeper's testimony and the fact that the two lovers had absconded had reinforced it, and there was more than enough evidence to lead him to expect a result very shortly.

But that result was taking rather longer than he had thought.

The detention order on Simonetta Palladiani

and Massimo Verga had produced no results so far. The two of them seemed to have vanished into thin air. Without them, the investigation had stalled, and the summons from Deputy Prosecutor Armando Lupo, on a public holiday, didn't bode at all well.

Lupo had told him to expect an important piece of news, but the fact that this news was coming from another source and not from himself merely increased his unease. His birth sign was Virgo and he didn't like surprises.

When he entered Lupo's office and saw, as well as Lupo, a woman he didn't know, with vaguely aristocratic and authoritarian features, and the chief superintendent from the Florence *Squadra Mobile*, whom he'd already met in circumstances he'd have preferred to forget, he knew this would be an August bank holiday to remember.

'Please sit down, Captain, we were waiting for you,' Lupo said cordially, offering him a seat next to him, facing the other two across the desk.

The woman was smiling, and seemed at her ease. Ferrara was smoking a cigar, which did not seem to bother the others.

The captain did not sit down immediately. He stood by the chair, waiting for the introductions.

'Deputy Prosecutor Anna Giulietti, of the Prosecutor's Department of Florence,' Lupo said. 'Chief Superintendent Michele Ferrara you already know.'

'Pleased to meet you,' he replied, addressing Anna, as he sat down.

In those few seconds he tried to prepare himself. This unexpected tableau was eloquent enough: the two Prosecutor's Departments had got together to try to settle the dispute between the police and the Carabinieri, in an attempt to save Ferrara from an unpleasant procedure: a procedure he, Fulvi, had requested. Was he ready to negotiate? He wasn't sure. After all, Ferrara had been the first to threaten to go to the Director of Public Prosecutions, and he had simply got in ahead of him in order to safeguard himself and his own investigation. If Ferrara was eating humble pie now, he would have to sweat to obtain his 'forgiveness'.

Ready to savour Ferrara's unconditional surrender, he was caught off guard by Lupo's introduction, which was about something else entirely.

'Captain, allow me to bring you up to date on a number of developments which cast a new and unexpected light on Ugo Palladiani. Thanks to these developments, we have decided that the investigation into his death can only benefit from a collaboration between this department and the one in Florence, represented by Deputy Prosecutor Giulietti, who is in charge of the investigation into the murder of an unknown girl in Florence. Once we have pooled our knowledge, it will be easier to decide on the strategies to follow in pursuing our respective investigations.'

'I'm listening,' Captain Fulvi said.

Lupo, appealing only twice for confirmation, once to Ferrara, once to Anna Giulietti, effectively summarised the events which had led to the discovery of paedophile activities in Palladiani's abandoned factory, culminating in the death of a young girl, still unnamed, beside whose body a cufflink had been found bearing the letter P. He

285

showed Captain Fulvi the photograph.

'At this stage of the investigations,' he concluded, 'we don't know if Palladiani's death is related to his paedophile activities, but Deputy Prosecutor Giulietti and I have agreed that it would be negligent on our part not to consider the possibility that there may indeed be a connection. That's why we think it's desirable for there to be an exchange of information between the forces dealing with both cases and, if necessary, active collaboration on the investigation into Palladiani's murder. I know that you and the chief superintendent haven't seen eye to eye over the involvement of Signor Massimo Verga, but I hope your differences can be put aside, in the interests of justice. Is everyone agreed?'

Giulietti and Ferrara nodded. Fulvi, unable to find an immediate counter-argument, did the same.

He was, however, thinking hard. Even though the paedophile angle did not necessarily contradict his own theory of a crime of passion, it did weaken it. It was hard to imagine a man with such perverse sexual interests harbouring resentment towards the boyfriend of a mature woman from whom he had been virtually separated for years and who had certainly had many other lovers. But if he was on the right track—and he didn't doubt for a moment that he was—then the conclusions which Chief Superintendent Ferrara and Deputy Prosecutor Giulietti were trying to reach must be wrong.

'From your reconstruction, Signor Lupo, there would appear to be a strong possibility that Ugo Palladiani was involved in circumstances which led to the death of this unknown girl—'

'Call her Stella,' Anna Giulietti interrupted. 'That's what we've been calling her for the sake of convenience.'

'All right,' the captain resumed. 'What I'd like to understand, though, is how strong this possibility really is. In other words, has Palladiani's guilt been proved or demonstrated, or is the evidence just circumstantial?'

'We know that paedophile activities took place in his factory,' Anna Giulietti said. 'We also found items of clothing that very probably belonged to the victim there.'

'But Ugo Palladiani abandoned the factory years ago,' Fulvi insisted, 'and he was involved in another business entirely. How can we be sure he didn't rent it to someone—or even lend it, which would be even more difficult to demonstrate because there wouldn't be any paperwork?'

'What about the cufflink with the letter P?' Lupo asked.

'I admit it may be a significant coincidence, but for it to be considered proof that Palladiani was present at the spot where the girl was found, we'd need to demonstrate it was his . . . There are a lot of surnames that begin with the letter P. We'd have to find the other one of the pair among his things, or something else that indicates that he used that symbol, but we haven't found anything like that. On the contrary, the idea we've built up of him suggests he preferred a totally different style, to be honest . . . A more modern, casual, youthful style. Nothing baroque like that . . .'

Noticing that Lupo seemed quite impressed with this argument, Ferrara hastened to refute it.

'We're checking everything we can. My men

287

have a warrant from Deputy Prosecutor Giulietti to search Palladiani's apartment, office, car and yacht. We'll see what emerges from that. Obviously, by itself the cufflink isn't much of a lead. I brushed it aside myself at first, but when you put it together with what we discovered in the factory . . . Though I have to admit, Captain, your idea that he might have lent the factory to someone else is a good one. We certainly can't rule it out, if we want the investigation to be consistent and exhaustive, as all investigations should be. Fortunately the warehouse was abandoned in a great hurry and Forensics have found a large number of fingerprints. In fact, I'd like to take advantage of this opportunity to ask Deputy Prosecutor Lupo for a copy of the fingerprints taken during the autopsy on Palladiani. That should help us to prove whether or not he was in the factory that night.'

'No problem,' Lupo said. 'Any other questions?' he asked the captain.

'Not for the moment. But I'd just like to make one thing clear, because I don't want you to misunderstand my position. I'm not trying to say that what you discovered in the factory is unimportant, or that your theory about the cufflink isn't an attractive one. But to be absolutely honest, as evidence they do seem to me a lot weaker than the evidence we've already gathered, which points us in a different direction entirely. Not to mention the fact that, in the last analysis, the two crimes could be completely unrelated. The man might have killed the girl that night and then himself been killed for other reasons, without there necessarily being a connection. That's why I consider it my duty to continue along the same track as I have been. Naturally, if you find any actual evidence in the course of your investigation which you think might help mine, I'd welcome any suggestions, but for now I can't see that any such evidence exists.'

Lupo took note of the captain's clearly expressed position and turned to Ferrara. 'Chief Superintendent?'

'If I can go back to the beginning,' Ferrara responded, 'Captain Fulvi told me that Ugo Palladiani was definitely murdered, and the newspapers confirmed it. May I know why he was so sure?'

'Would you like to answer that, Captain?'

'Do I have to?'

Lupo kept his patience. 'Listen, Captain,' he said good-naturedly. 'I've known Chief Superintendent Ferrara in other professional situations, and I can guarantee that he is a first-class detective. I have no hesitation in saying it in front of him. I realise that he is emotionally involved in this case, and I respect his distress and his strong sense of friendship, but I'm absolutely certain that this hasn't had, isn't having, and won't have the slightest influence on his work. I don't even have to ask him first when I say that if Massimo Verga turns out to be guilty he himself would be the first to want to bring him to justice.

'I started this meeting hoping that you could collaborate, but I have no intention of forcing you to do so. It's up to you to decide.'

Captain Fulvi said nothing. The character testimony may not have meant anything to him, but the reference to friendship seemed to have struck the right note.

'I'm sorry,' he said at last. 'Believe me, Chief Superintendent, I'm sorry about your friend. But he is a prime suspect. Ugo Palladiani didn't die by falling down the stairs. According to the autopsy, there were two previous factors which contributed to his death: internal lesions not consistent with those of a fall, and the consumption of narcotics in a quantity much higher than the average limit of tolerability.'

'An overdose?' Ferrara said, glancing at Anna.

'Yes,' the captain confirmed.

'Like Stella . . .' Anna said, slightly regretfully. 'It could be a mere coincidence, but I must point out how damaging the consequences of a conflict between the police and the Carabinieri would be . . .'

Convinced that he was on the side of reason, Captain Fulvi ignored her remark and gave Ferrara an openly reproachful look.

'So Palladiani was hit before he fell, or was pushed, down the stairs?' Ferrara asked, lightly, as if downplaying it.

'Exactly,' Lupo confirmed.

'The state of the room where Palladiani had been sleeping suggested that a fight may have taken place there,' the captain added.

'Any fingerprints?' Anna Giulietti asked.

'Lots. Unfortunately we can't attribute them with certainty to Massimo Verga because we don't have any prints to compare them with. They weren't taken when he was arrested in 1970. But they will certainly be a determining factor when we find him and Simonetta Palladiani . . . if we ever find them.'

290

'Of course,' Ferrara admitted with a pang in his heart. 'Although seeing that Massimo was Simonetta Palladiani's guest, it can't be ruled out that he might have left his prints at some other time, can it?'

'Signor Verga had his room in the guest apartment. But it's possible that before renting it he may have slept in that bedroom, you're right about that. The totality of the evidence will be what decides . . . and his confession, of course, when he makes it—as I'm sure he will.'

'That's as maybe,' Ferrara said. 'One thing, though. You're surmising that the motive was jealousy. In that case, wouldn't it be more logical for the murder to have happened in the guest apartment, perhaps after the two lovers were surprised by the husband?'

'That can't be ruled out either. The guest apartment was also in a state of disorder. According to the housekeeper's statement, Massimo Verga is a meticulously tidy man.'

'I can vouch for that,' Ferrara said, now with a new source of worry: what had happened in that apartment? 'But aren't two untidy rooms a bit too much? The fight should have happened in one or the other.'

'As far as the captain and his men have been able to reconstruct it,' Lupo said, 'this might have been the sequence of events. Ugo Palladiani, perhaps in a drugged state, surprises the lovers in the guest apartment and a quarrel ensues, in the course of which he is killed. The body is carried into the house to simulate a fall down the stairs and explain away the bruises, and his room is turned upside down to give the impression that his behaviour had become uncontrollable because of the drugs leading to some kind of fainting fit, hence the fatal accident. Alternatively, he wasn't dead, but only fainted during the fight, and the drugs were injected afterwards. It doesn't make much difference.'

'It's plausible,' Anna Giulietti admitted.

Yes, it was, Ferrara thought. Except that it was impossible because Massimo couldn't have done it. And Ugo Palladiani's possible paedophile activities and the Mafia connection to Simonetta's quarries were further factors which muddied the clarity of this simple domestic theory.

He was tempted to bring up the Mafia connection, but he held back. It would have been an admission that he had been taking an active interest in the investigation, and the captain certainly wouldn't have liked that. And besides, if even Lupo, who knew about it, hadn't seen fit to mention it, it wasn't up to him to take the initiative. For the same reason, since Anna Giulietti had not mentioned the Masonic connection, he kept quiet about that, too.

'I agree,' he conceded finally. 'Of course if we can confirm that Palladiani was a paedophile, that might significantly alter the picture, but for the moment this is probably the most sensible lead to follow. We'll try to speed up the checks we have in progress, and we'll also lend a hand in searching for the two people who've gone missing, if that's all right with you.'

The captain shrugged. 'The more the merrier. Though by now . . .'

'What do you mean?'

'They've had plenty of time to escape abroad.

We put out the detention order all over Italy days ago, and so far we've had no luck. We've checked departures from every port and airport in the period since August fifth and their names haven't come up. But if they crossed the border by car and then took a plane from some other European country, it won't be easy to trace them. Anyway, we've already alerted Interpol.'

'Are their cars missing?'

'Her car. A black BMW X5.'

Another point in favour of the captain's theory, Ferrara thought sadly, and it was clear from Anna Giulietti's face that she was thinking the same thing.

'Well, if there are no other questions or suggestions, I think we can bring this meeting to a close. We'll continue to concentrate on the line of inquiry that Captain Fulvi has been following. The captain will continue and if possible increase his efforts. But we also have to take a closer look at other aspects of the case. One of them is the coincidence of the factory and the cufflink with the letter P. Another is the fact that both murders involved drug overdoses. My experience tells me there are no coincidences in criminal cases. We also need to confirm whether or not Ugo Palladiani was a paedophile. I'll leave that to Chief Superintendent Ferrara and his men.

'We've also agreed that the Carabinieri in Lucca and the Florence *Squadra Mobile* should combine forces in searching for the killer or killers of Ugo Palladiani. Thank you, everyone, for coming. Deputy Prosecutor Giulietti, if you don't mind staying behind for a moment, we have a few technicalities to sort out. It won't take long.'

'Of course. Will you wait for me, Chief Superintendent?'

'No problem. I'll be outside in the car park.'

'Make sure you stay in the shade,' Lupo said. The heat, that August, was still relentless.

*　　　*　　　*

Ferrara and Captain Fulvi left the Prosecutor's Department together, and said goodbye once they were outside. It might only have been an impression, but it seemed to Ferrara that the captain shook his hand with a small degree of warmth.

27

Florence—Lucca 15 August 2001

To: Head of the State Police
Ministry of the Interior
Via del Viminale
Rome

Re: combined investigations according to article 317, code of criminal procedure, concerning case no. 1307/01 of the Public Prosecutor of Florence, the homicide of a young immigrant girl, identity currently unknown, and case no. 589/01 of the Public Prosecutor of Lucca, the homicide of Ugo Palladiani.

(By mail)

With regard to the above investigations, certain evidence has come to light which in order to be developed further requires active cooperation between the Carabinieri and the State Police in Florence. Of particular importance is the collaboration of Chief Superintendent Michele Ferrara, who because of his widely recognised abilities and experience must be considered an indispensable element of the investigation.

In addition, these public prosecutors have conferred on Chief Superintendent Ferrara specific duties in the investigation which need to be urgently fulfilled.

As you have ordered the suspension from duty of the above-mentioned officer for a period of a month, which could fatally compromise the outcome of the investigations in progress, we request that this decision be reconsidered, or at least that its execution be suspended until the conclusion of the investigations.

With gratitude and best regards
Deputy Prosecutor Armando Lupo
Deputy Prosecutor Anna Giulietti

'I don't know how you did it, but thank you,' Ferrara said, handing the draft back to Anna.

'I didn't do anything. Lupo did it all. I wasn't sure if it was out of sympathy for you or because of some code of honour among Sicilians . . . Anyway, as early as possible tomorrow morning, this letter will be delivered to the Head of the State Police in Rome.'

'Code of honour isn't the right expression.'

'Whatever. But, if it's of any interest, he told me he wasn't so convinced by Fulvi's theory any more, even though he considers him a good detective, and that he'd feel much happier knowing you were on board.'

They were sitting at a table in a bar in the Piazza Napoleone in Lucca. Ferrara had suggested they have lunch together but neither of them had much appetite, so they just ordered raisin cakes and cappuccinos.

'But you're not convinced?'

'I don't know. You have to admit that objectively the captain's theory is a reasonable one, and has the advantages of economy and simplicity, which many theorists of science consider the basic requisites in assessing the validity of a theory.'

'Life isn't scientific and it certainly isn't simple.'

'I agree, Michele, I was joking . . . but only up to a point. If you put to one side the fact that it's convenient for us to think that the two crimes are related, the idea that Palladiani may have been killed because he was a paedophile is pretty random, you have to admit. If we then discover he has nothing to do with all of that, and that other people were using his factory, we're in an even worse mess.'

'So our captain convinced you, did he?'

'He made a pertinent observation, Michele. You said so yourself. But that's not the point. The point is that we still don't know why he was killed!'

'But we do know—or at least *I* know—that Massimo Verga didn't kill him! That's where the Carabinieri's case falls down, don't you realise that?'

Anna Giulietti looked at him with sympathy. 'Tell me something sincerely. If Massimo wasn't your friend, would you accept that Fulvi's line of inquiry was the right one?'

'Yes, you know perfectly well I would,' Ferrara admitted, with an almost imperceptible rush of anger. He didn't like having to admit, even to himself, that anyone was getting special treatment. If Chief Superintendent Michele Ferrara hadn't had complete faith in him, everyone would have considered Massimo Verga a common criminal. Including him . . .

'Of course. You would accept it, I would accept it . . . So can you explain to me why the man in charge of the investigation shouldn't accept it? If that's not a code of honour, I don't know what is. And while we're about it, can you also explain to me why no one mentioned the Mafia connection, and yet when we said goodbye he told me to remind you not to neglect that lead?'

Ferrara thought it over for a while. 'I wondered that too, and I thought maybe he didn't want to annoy Fulvi by admitting that I'd been working on the case when I shouldn't. But now I think there was another reason . . .'

'What?'

'I think Lupo's sending me a message. He probably doesn't care much about the factory and whatever went on there, and may not even believe it can help the investigation. But he really wants to look into this Mafia thing and he's right. Except that he doesn't want to involve Fulvi, for two reasons. One, because he's too young and inexperienced, and might compromise the investigation. And two, because he doesn't know

297

the Mafia the way we know it. We've fought it, we know it's a dangerous animal. A young officer from the north could easily underestimate it. This is a serious business, Anna!

'I've had some research done and I've found out some pretty incredible things. Since 1993 there's been a sharp rise in the number of Sicilian companies operating in Tuscany. By 1999, there were six hundred and seventy-three, most of them with head offices in the province of Palermo. Do you know how many there were before 1993?'

'How many?'

'Sixty-two.'

These were impressive figures, and Anna Giulietti took the leather-bound diary she carried everywhere from her briefcase and started making notes. 'How do you explain it?'

'Let's be clear about one thing. Sicily doesn't automatically mean Mafia, and some of these companies may well be clean. But it's a fact that the Nineties were when the State hit organised crime in Sicily the hardest, making the area a lot less safe for them . . . I remember this businessman in Sicily at the beginning of the Nineties, no criminal record but obvious Mafia connections, his name escapes me. He decided to turn State's evidence, and it emerged that he was a kind of 'Minister of Public Works' for the Mafia. He was always there in the shadows, making sure the Mafia got all the best contracts, especially for public works. That may have been when businesses with Mafia connections started to feel the heat and gradually emigrated to other parts of the country, including Tuscany.'

Anna Giulietti finished writing and closed her

298

diary. She looked pensive but determined. 'Thanks, Michele. I think we need to get the Organised Crime Division in on this to get a better idea of what's going on. Perhaps they could start by seeing if there's been anything suspicious about the adjudication of competitive tenders for public works in Tuscany. But is the Sicilian company that's running the quarries part of all this?'

'I have no idea. We know marble dust is used in the building industry, but I suspect their real activity is drugs. And I think I know what to do while I'm waiting for your request to the Head of the State Police to go through.'

'What?'

'Carry out the orders in Lupo's coded message,' he replied cryptically.

'Would you care to be more specific?'

'When the time is right.'

'All right. But don't get into trouble.'

'In my profession?'

Anna merely smiled cheerlessly.

'Are you going back to Florence?' he asked her.

'Why, aren't you?'

28

There were only three Franchis in the Carrara phone book and Ferrara found the one he was looking for at the second attempt. His name was Emilio.

Emilio remembered the academic who had visited the quarry and was happy to help. Marble was his life, and he was flattered and excited at the

299

thought that he could contribute to a book about it. Since he had to go to Marina di Carrara in the afternoon, he suggested they meet in the Bar Imperiale in the church square, near the harbour, which had small rooms where they would be able to talk without being disturbed.

Then Ferrara called Lojelo. He told him his plan and asked him to join him outside the Imperiale. Finally, he phoned Petra to tell her he wouldn't be coming back to Florence that night.

He got to the Piazza Gino Monconi and waited in the blazing sun, smoking his cigar. By the time he saw Lojelo walking towards him, he was bathed in sweat.

They went inside the bar and waited for Franchi. He was not long in coming.

Once they were seated, Ferrara introduced Superintendent Lojelo. Franchi was clearly taken aback, and shut up like a clam.

'I'm also a police officer. Chief Superintendent Michele Ferrara, head of the Florence *Squadra Mobile*. I'm sorry I misled you, but it was necessary. We're involved in an operation which requires the utmost secrecy. We need you, Signor Franchi, and your expertise. Are you willing to help us?'

Still confused, the old man did not reply.

'We have reason to believe that the company running the Tonelli quarries is involved in illegal activities. If that's the case, I think you honest quarrymen should be more interested than anyone else in having them brought to justice. They may be tarnishing the reputation of your profession. We need to investigate, but without the company being aware of it, otherwise we may never get to

300

the people who are really responsible.'

'And what's it got to do with me?' Franchi asked finally.

'You know marble like the back of your hand, am I right?'

'Well, yes,' the old man replied proudly.

'So listen.'

And Ferrara again expounded his plan.

*   *   *

At 10 p.m. on the night of 15 August, Chief Superintendent Ferrara, Superintendent Lojelo, three police constables and Emilio Franchi were in the Falcone e Borsellino Park, opposite the commercial port where the marble blocks intended for export were stored, waiting to be loaded onto freighters. The old man had a heavy bag of tools with him.

There was traffic on the road that ran alongside the harbour, but the pavements were deserted. For the festivities most people were further north, where the pubs, ice cream parlours and funfairs were concentrated.

They reached the entrance to the port, which was blocked by a long sliding metal door. To the left was the Port Authority building, to the right a low yellow building that housed the Border Police and the Coast Guard.

Lojelo, using his authority over the Border Police for the first time, had no difficulty in obtaining entry and, much more importantly, the total complicity of the guards.

The depot was illuminated by floodlights mounted on three tall steel posts, six floodlights on

301

each post, and by the lights on board an imposing Japanese freighter which occupied almost the entire length of the quay.

The officer on duty led them into the office where they kept the registers of the goods left in the depot. In them, the place in which they were stored, their final destination, and the date of loading were all noted.

'Do you know where the goods going to America are?' Ferrara asked.

'I'm sorry, I wouldn't know that. The customs people deal with that. We just do a brief check of the contents. But it should be in the registers.'

They heard three explosions in rapid succession.

'Fireworks,' Lojelo said. The August bank holiday festivities were starting.

It took almost ten minutes to find out where the marble blocks belonging to Mining Extractions were located and how many of them there were.

'This way,' Ferrara said to the men, leaving the office with Lojelo. 'There are five blocks in all,' he said to Franchi as they walked.

'Not many. I told you they don't produce much.'

'I don't think production is what interests them.'

They moved with some difficulty through the labyrinth of aisles, between piles of crudely cut stones.

From the direction of the sea came the sound of a ship's siren.

The five blocks of white marble were all numbered. The numbers were stamped on the stone, along with the words MINING EXTRACTIONS and, separately, PHILADELPHIA USA.

One of the constables, who had a video camera

with him, started filming them.

'Can you manage?' Ferrara asked.

'There's enough artificial lighting. It won't come out perfectly but it'll do.'

'Good.' He turned to Franchi. 'Now it's up to you.'

Franchi approached the first block and started to examine it.

It wasn't an easy task, because the beams from the floodlights only allowed him to see parts of the surface, while the rest remained in shadow. After a cursory examination, he took a mallet from his bag and started hitting the block, without marking it. The knocks made a slightly hollow sound.

He repeated the same experiment on all five blocks, then stopped and rubbed his cheek pensively. Finally he went up to the third block, which had been hoisted onto two of the others, and hit it again, harder this time. A chip flew off. At the same time, a green rocket rose into the sky and exploded into a large ball of golden sparks which fell slowly towards the sea, bathing the scene for a moment in a ghostly light.

Ferrara saw the old man shaking his head with displeasure.

'I hope we don't have to lift it, or we'll be here all night,' he muttered. 'Is there a ladder anywhere?'

'Find him one,' Lojelo ordered his men.

When they had brought it, he propped it against the block and climbed it, dragging the heavy bag behind him. He seemed frail, but he moved precisely and confidently.

He disappeared over the top of the block.

A few minutes went by, then they heard a cry of

satisfaction and Franchi's face appeared over the edge.

'It's here, I found it!'

Ferrara and Lojelo scrambled up the ladder and joined him. Two more fireworks exploded.

'Here,' the old man said, aiming his torch.

They couldn't see anything. Only the surface of the marble.

'There's a piece patched up with cultured marble, can't you see?' Franchi said, and neither Ferrara nor Lojelo had the heart to disappoint him by admitting that they hadn't the faintest idea what he was talking about. So they said nothing.

Franchi dipped into his bag again and took out a battery drill with a long, thick bit.

'No, hold on!' Ferrara said in alarm, holding him back. 'If you make a hole, they'll notice.'

'They won't notice. I told you, this is cultured marble. It's like a putty made of limestone and marble dust. I'll put it back as good as new, don't worry.'

He bent, chose the best spot, and was about to start drilling the hole when Ferrara stopped him again.

'Get the constable with the camera over here,' he said to Lojelo.

Only when the constable was ready to film the scene did Ferrara give the order to start.

The bit went in quite quickly for about four inches, then sank through.

'You see?' Franchi said, looking pleased with himself. 'It's empty underneath.' He pulled out the drill and used the mallet to widen the hole. When it was wide enough, he slid his arm in, then took it out again, holding a small bag of white powder.

'This certainly isn't marble dust,' he said, almost laughing, and his lined face took on the iridescent colours of the fireworks which were lighting up the sky all the way along the coast.

The event was greeted from the big freighter with cries of joy in Japanese and a popping of champagne corks.

Even Ferrara and Lojelo were smiling. This was a good way to celebrate the August bank holiday.

29

Ferrara had spent what little remained of that night in Lojelo's apartment.

With one thing and another, they had stayed at the depot until almost three in the morning. They had extracted all the bags of drugs from their hiding place. Including those that the drill had made a hole in, mixing the heroin with the marble dust, they had calculated that there must be around fifty kilos. If you multiplied that by five, which was the number of blocks, you got an almost unheard-of quantity. Two hundred and fifty kilos. Roughly speaking the equivalent of five or six billion lire. On the market, suitably cut, that might even give a figure seven times higher.

Lojelo was all for seizing the drugs there and then, but Ferrara, who knew from the register that the blocks were due to be sent out on 23 August, preferred to have them put back before Franchi filled in the hole and reconstructed the surface of the marble. Lojelo had given in, reluctantly, and when they were in his apartment he had reopened the discussion.

'I'm sorry, Chief Superintendent, but I think it's my duty to make a report first thing tomorrow morning. This is an extremely serious crime, and I can't just pretend nothing happened. As you know, in these cases there's a legal requirement to confiscate the evidence. Of course I'll mention that it was your initiative, I don't intend to steal the credit, but I'll also have to say that I didn't proceed with the confiscation at your express request.'

'Listen, Lojelo, if this gets out, and it will if you write your report, the real bosses are sure to get away.'

He didn't say that if they got away, then his hopes—so steadfastly nourished—of finding Massimo vanished.

'I realise that, and I'll point it out in my report. My chiefs will have to assume that responsibility, but I have to do my duty according to the regulations. I have to inform my Commissioner, my Public Prosecutor and even the National Narcotics Division.'

'The law also allows the Prosecutor to issue an order delaying the confiscation depending on the needs of the investigation, if more time is required to gather evidence, or to identify and arrest the members of a criminal conspiracy.'

'All right. If you like, tomorrow morning I'll inform the deputy prosecutor coordinating the investigation into the murder of Claudia Pizzi and get his opinion before making my report.'

'There's no need. The Prosecutor's Department of Florence is dealing with the case. I'll make sure you get your order.'

'I don't understand. As you know, for some offences, including those relative to drug trafficking, we don't come under the jurisdiction of Florence, but of Genoa. The murder of Claudia Pizzi took place here, the drugs were found here . . . so how could Florence . . . ?'

'Trust me. How do you think the drugs got to the depot? What we did tonight was part of a much wider investigation into organised crime in the whole of Tuscany, including Massa-Carrara.'

This wider investigation had barely got under way, but Ferrara thought it was worthwhile exaggerating a little, in order to convince Lojelo. For the same reason, he also decided to tell him all he knew about the expansion of Sicilian companies in Tuscany.

'The operation is being coordinated by Deputy Prosecutor Anna Giulietti. She'll make sure you get your order. Then everything will be above board.'

'All right . . . but we'll have to inform the National Narcotics Division in case we need international cooperation. The drugs seemed intended for the United States, specifically Philadelphia . . .'

'No problem. We'll do everything we need to do. We're also interested in who the drugs were going to, which means the DEA will have to be involved.'

*   *   *

On the morning of Thursday 16th, as soon as decency allowed, Ferrara phoned Anna Giulietti.

'Good morning. I searched the depot in the port of Carrara with the help of Superintendent Lojelo and some of his trusted men. We did it during the night, to minimise the risk of being discovered. The results exceeded all our expectations. We found at least fifty kilos of heroin ready to be shipped to America. Perhaps five times that . . . two hundred and fifty kilos!'

'Have you gone crazy, Michele? What have you been up to?'

'It's all completely certified and documented. Now I need you to issue Superintendent Lojelo with an urgent order to delay confiscation. As I'm sure you'll appreciate, the secrecy of the whole operation depends on it.'

It was a good thing that Anna Giulietti was a smart woman—a prosecutor with balls, as he had once called her. She understood immediately. She asked him if Lojelo was there, and he put him on to give her the address where the order should be sent. Then she spoke to Ferrara again.

'I can't mention your name on the order, Michele. You're still officially suspended. I'll stick to generalities.'

'It doesn't matter. Don't worry.'

'I want you in my office as soon as possible. You need to tell me the whole thing in detail. I get the impression this is all much bigger than we thought.'

'That's my impression, too.'

Now that he had set Lojelo's mind at rest, Ferrara was able to leave for Florence, secure in the knowledge that for a few days there was no risk that the gang would be alerted. Not too many, though: the operation would take its course and sooner or later their sins would find them out.

Back in Florence, Ferrara did not go straight to see Anna Giulietti. He went to his apartment first, filled Petra in on what had been happening, and then called Rizzo. He did not tell him about the heroin, but did mention that the request for his reinstatement had been sent off and that he expected to be back at Headquarters soon. He asked him if there was any news, but there wasn't. Then he asked to speak to Fanti.

'Anything new on Bellomonte di Mezzo?'

'I'm in contact with my colleague in Trapani, chief. He's doing the best he can, but he told me again that I shouldn't be under any illusions. The town is practically all in the hands of the Mafia, from the mayor to the local councillors to the court ushers.'

'We're in a mess, in other words. Tell your colleague to keep at it, but not to expose himself. Life is cheap in a place like that. Listen, is Ciuffi there by any chance?'

'I'll check, chief.'

Ciuffi was the most suitable person to talk to about the developments in Carrara, and Ferrara, preferring not to go to the office, arranged to meet him at the Belvedere. He would go to see Anna Giulietti after that: he'd probably have more to tell her after talking to Ciuffi, who was his expert in the field.

They met an hour later, in Ferrara's parked Mercedes. Ferrara had kept the engine running, so that the air conditioning could still function.

Ferrara told Ciuffi everything, right from the beginning. When he mentioned the amount of heroin they had found in one block of marble, Ciuffi, mentally multiplying by five, let out a prolonged whistle of admiration.

'It's the haul of the century, chief! They're bound to reinstate you now, unless they transfer you to Rome to be Head of the State Police!'

'I don't know about that, Florence is more than enough for me. But I didn't call you so you could flatter me. There's something about all this that doesn't feel right. If these people are using the blocks of marble to ship the drugs to America, what in your opinion do they do with the marble dust, which is supposedly their main activity? They can't use it all to cut the heroin, surely?'

Ciuffi thought about it for a while, then said, 'It's certainly ingenious. I'd never have thought of using the marble quarries, and I've been in lots of seminars, including international ones, where we've come up with all kinds of scenarios . . . Supplying the American market with drugs from Asia is one of the most lucrative businesses in the whole of the underworld. This has to be a very powerful organisation, chief, which means they're also extremely dangerous . . .' He seemed to be thinking aloud. 'But even the national market isn't bad, and if these people have quantities like that at their disposal, you can bet they're exploiting the stuff for all it's worth . . . The marble dust could be a good excuse for transporting it freely around Italy, don't you think? It's used in the building industry, isn't that right?'

'Not just that. Paper mills, farms, everything . . .'

'In the whole of Italy. What more could you want? You drive around in a lorry full of marble dust and in the back you carry sachets of

310

samples . . .'

'Tanker lorries, actually,' Ferrara corrected him.

'Works out the same, doesn't it?' Ciuffi said, frowning.

'Yes, works out the same.'

'You did say tanker lorries?'

'Yes, why?'

'Nothing. Just something I remembered, I'll have to check up on it in the office . . . but I'd wager those Albanians we took in last week were using the same suppliers.'

'Are you sure?'

'More or less. It's all starting to fit . . . The Mafia, the Versilia coast . . . maybe the tanker lorries, too, but as I said, I'll have to check in the office.'

'Let's go, then!'

'You too?'

'Yes, but in your car. It's better if they don't see mine.'

'What if we run into Lepri?'

'I don't care. I can make a social call on my colleagues if I want to, can't I?'

On the way, Ciuffi filled him in on the gradual progress they were making with the Albanians thanks to Guzzi. Then Anna Giulietti called him on his mobile to tell him the results of Gianni Fuschi's report on the sample of the fabric of Stella's jeans, which confirmed that on the night of 28 to 29 July, the girl had been gang-raped.

*　　　*　　　*

'Here it is,' Ciuffi exclaimed, showing him one of the photos showing the two Albanians and

311

Zancarotti loading the spare tyre into the boot of their car. They were half hidden between two heavy goods vehicles—one of which was a tanker lorry.

Ferrara felt a slight shudder at the sight of the inscription MINING EXTRACTIONS.

'Now it's your turn to tell me everything,' he said. 'And don't leave anything out, even if it takes all afternoon. This is big, and anything could be useful.'

It didn't take all afternoon, but a large part of it, interrupted by a call from Rizzo to Ferrara's mobile.

'I have some news about the Stella case, chief.'

'Go ahead.'

'Doctor Leone has been looking at the medical records, and there's something he says doesn't quite fit. Apparently, two blood tests were done on Stella after she was admitted. The first one didn't show the presence of drugs, but the second one, which was done a few hours later, did. Leone thinks that as the first test didn't confirm what seemed evident after they'd administered Narcan, Profesor d'Incisa wanted to double check. Are you following me?'

'Yes, go on, I'm in a bit of hurry and the battery's running low on my mobile.' It was a lie.

'I'm sorry. Where are you? Do you want me to call you on a landline?'

'I'm on the same floor as you are. I'm with Ciuffi, but pretend you don't know. Go on before my battery runs out completely.'

'Well, Dr Leone says that the second blood sample was taken at 9.45. According to him, that's the limit of the time period during which the

312

heroin stays in the bloodstream. After that, the morphine is metabolised and doesn't leave any more traces. Which is a bit strange because it would mean that when Stella was found that morning she had only just taken the drugs. He'd like to talk to Professor D'Insisa to get him to clarify it, but no one's seen him at the hospital today and there's no reply on his home number. We managed to trace his wife in Viareggio, but she doesn't know where he is. In fact, she's quite worried because she says it's not like him to vanish like that. We're on our way to his apartment. I wanted to tell you.'

Ferrara had a split-second reaction, related to that shadow that seemed to hang over everything, the one thing that linked Palladiani and d'Incisa: Freemasonry.

'Run, Francesco! Knock the door down if you have to, even if you don't have Anna Giulietti's permission. First, though, send out an alert. Anyone who sees him should stop him on sight. It's obvious Stella wasn't drugged just before she was found. There weren't any syringes there, and anyway she was drugged in the factory, and it would have taken time to get her dressed. True, they were in a hurry and forgot half her clothes, but even so. Then it would have taken time to drive her out to the place she was found and dump her there, don't you think? In my opinion, the man's making a run for it!'

*   *   *

'So ultimately, chief,' Ciuffi concluded, 'everything seems to point to this Zitturi, but we still have no idea who he is.'

After Rizzo's phone call, it had taken a while to resume the conversation where they had left off. But in the end Ferrara had managed to set aside the problem of d'Incisa and they had returned to the Carrara case. For both of them it was the priority, although for different reasons: for Ferrara because he still had to find his friend, for Ciuffi because it was clearly a narcotics operation of major significance.

That name, Zitturi, had rung a bell with Ferrara right from the moment Luigi Ciuffi had first mentioned it in connection with the transcript of the recording from the bugged cell.

It recalled something: something that was struggling to emerge from his fevered subconscious.

He went over and over the transcript, but couldn't find anything.

'Do you still have the tape?' he asked in the end.

Ciuffi had it. They put it on the tape recorder and listened. The bits of dialogue in Albanian irritated and distracted him, but when Emilio Zancarotti spoke he paid careful attention.

When they reached the phrase, 'Nor will Zitturi—we've fucked it up for him, too . . .' he cried, 'Stop! Go back a little, let me hear that bit again,' he said.

The sound was not good and the pronunciation not very clear. There seemed to be a slight stress on the first syllable, and a doubling of the final 'r' as if the man were saying 'Zitturri'. Suddenly, it all became clear. It was as if a chain reaction had been set off in his mind.

Zì Turri . . . *Zì Turi* . . . Sicilian for Uncle

314

Salvatore . . . Salvatore meant saviour . . . *The Saviour of the quarries* . . .

Without saying a word he leapt to his feet, raced along the corridors of Police Headquarters, leaving everyone he passed open-mouthed, and ran into his office.

'Fanti!' he called, going directly into his secretary's room. Fanti went white, seeing him materialise like that in an unsettling role-reversal. 'Get on the phone and call your friend in Trapani right now! I need to know which Mafia family controls Bellomonte di Mezzo.'

The sergeant dialled the number.

'Hello? Could I speak to Inspector Cavallari, this is Police Headquarters in Florence . . . Yes, thanks, I'll wait.'

'Pass him to me as soon as they put him on.'

'Giuseppe? This is Nestore, I'm passing you Chief Superintendent Ferrara.'

'I need a great favour, Inspector. Which family runs Bellomonte di Mezzo?'

'The Lapruas, Chief Superintendent.'

'Never heard of them . . . who are they?'

'Three brothers. The father's not around any more.'

'What are their names?'

'Tonio, Vito and Alfio.'

'No Salvatore?'

'That's the father's name. Salvatore Laprua, known as Zì Turi.'

Ferrara could feel his heart beating faster. 'What happened to him? Is he dead?'

'No one knows. He vanished.'

'When?'

'At the beginning of the Nineties.'

'Was he ever charged with anything? Is he wanted?'

'No, they weren't a leading family. They've only really emerged in the last ten years—in fact, since the sons took over. We've had our eye on them for four or five years, but we've never been able to pin anything on them.'

'Thanks very much, Inspector. That's all I need for the moment. Forget about Mining Extractions, I know who's behind it now. And don't expose yourself, okay?'

He hung up and turned to Fanti.

'I have another little bit of research for you. I want you to find out if there's a Salvatore Laprua anywhere in Tuscany and what he does. Concentrate particularly on the coast. I think this time we're almost there!'

Now at last he was ready to go and see Anna, but before he could leave there was another phone call from Rizzo.

'We found d'Incisa, chief. He's at home. Dead. The woman who's standing in for the caretaker let us in, though she had to phone the professor's wife first to ask permission.'

'How did he die?'

'To judge by the syringe next to the body, I'd say drugs this time, too. Dr Leone and Forensics are on their way. I've already informed Anna Giulietti, she's on her way there too.'

He was the only one missing, but he realised he couldn't go. There would be too many professionals there in their institutional roles, all of whom knew by now that he had been suspended. His presence would have been an embarrassment to them. Especially to Anna.

'Okay. Keep me updated. I'll be at home.'

30

Since Ferrara had not yet been reinstated, Anna Giulietti decided to summon everyone to her home instead of to the Prosecutor's Department.

Her apartment occupied the entire first floor of a fifteenth-century building in the Via de' Sassetti, and had high frescoed ceilings that inspired respect and admiration rather than awe. The study, a brightly lit room large enough for receptions, contained furniture from various periods, all strictly Florentine. Apart from the seventeenth-century walnut desk, there were enough sofas and armchairs to easily accommodate about ten people.

Ferrara, Rizzo and Leone arrived separately but punctually at nine in the morning, and she welcomed them with a silver pot full of steaming coffee.

To start the meeting off, Ferrara had them tell him about the discovery of the body.

Apparently, once they had gone in, Rizzo and his men had immediately noticed that there was only one light still on in the whole apartment: in Ludovico d'Inisa's bedroom. They had found the professor lying on his back on the bed, fully dressed, his left shirtsleeve rolled up and a syringe not far from his open right hand. Pending the autopsy, Leone was inclined to think that the death was due to an overdose and had probably occurred late in the evening of 15 August,

317

probably between seven and midnight.

The professor's bedroom was relatively tidy, as was the rest of the apartment. The body bore no apparent signs of violence. In a cabinet in the bathroom, not very well hidden, they had found a few grams of heroin and cocaine, no more than five in all, sufficient for a few doses.

'I'd rule out an accident,' Rizzo said in conclusion. 'The man was no beginner, and he was a doctor, too. And the drugs were normal, not badly cut. At the present stage, suicide looks the most likely hypothesis.'

Leone and Anna Giulietti nodded in confirmation.

'A suspicious suicide, to say the least,' Ferrara observed, 'given what we've found out about the two blood tests.'

'Which would confirm your initial suspicion of malpractice, wouldn't it?' Anna Giulietti remarked, with an admiring smile for both Ferrara and Rizzo.

Ferrara, however, did not seem pleased. 'But what if there was something else?' he said, and it was clear it had cost him some effort to ask the question.

They all looked at him uncomfortably, waiting for him to continue.

Again Ferrara remembered the head nurse's words: *he got quite angry when he saw the girl.* They put d'Incisa in a very sinister light if read as evidence that he already knew the girl before she was brought in to the Nuovo that morning, which in turn might mean that it would have been convenient to him if she died without talking. But if d'Incisa was the killer, and the Stella case was

318

solved, where did the cufflink fit in—or was Captain Fulvi right after all?—and, above all, what became of their jurisdiction over the Palladiani case?

Of course, it was possible that Palladiani and d'Incisa, both Masons, were accomplices. D'Incisa might have finished off what Palladiani had started: Palladiani had dumped her at the edge of the clearing thinking she was dead, and the consultant had found her in hospital still alive . . . But this was conjecture within conjecture. So far, there was no evidence of any connection between Palladiani and d'Incisa. It was a point he would have to insist on, but later.

'Doctor Leone's discovery,' he resumed, 'suggests something more than an error, don't you think?'

'What do you think, Doctor?' Anna Giulietti asked Leone.

Taken by surprise, Leone hesitated. 'Frankly, I don't know. I wasn't intending to arouse any suspicions. The way I see it, there's no doubt that Stella was taken to hospital in a critical condition due to an overdose. Her reaction to the Narcan, which is documented in her medical record, confirms that absolutely. No, the fact that the first blood test revealed nothing is probably due to laboratory error, which is what I would have liked Professor d'Incisa to clarify. Unfortunately that won't be possible now . . .'

'But don't the traces of heroin in the second test place the taking of the heroin too close to the time when her body was found?' Ferrara objected.

'Yes, half an hour before, at the most. Possibly a little more, it depends on how each organism

319

reacts, but not much.'

'That isn't proof of anything,' Anna Giulietti retorted. 'Theoretically there was time to take her there from the factory . . .'

'Very theoretically,' Ferrara commented sarcastically, thinking of the distance from the warehouse, the time it would have taken for the drug to take effect, then the time to dress her again, load her in the car . . .

Anna Giulietti silenced him with a cutting look. 'Let's stick to the facts, if possible. We've asked for you to be reinstated, Chief Superintendent, since there is a well-founded suspicion, on the basis of his ownership of the factory and the letter P on the cufflink, that it was Ugo Palladiani who killed Stella . . .'

'And Palladiani was about to run away,' Rizzo said, unexpectedly.

'What do you mean?' Anna Giulietti asked.

'We've checked his bank account, as you asked, chief, and you authorised, Prosecutor. Palladiani's account is practically empty. Almost everything has been transferred to an account in his name in a bank in Nice, France.'

'If he was afraid his paedophile ring was about to be discovered, I'm not surprised,' Anna Giulietti said with satisfaction. 'One more clue, if we like. D'Incisa is another matter. It's true he also had dealings with Stella, but there could be several reasons for his suicide . . . Let's investigate and then we'll decide. But they're separate investigations, there's nothing specifically connecting d'Incisa and Palladiani.'

'Did you search the apartment thoroughly?' Ferrara asked Rizzo. 'Weren't there any documents, diaries, anything suggesting a connection between the two of them?'

'It wasn't a thorough search,' Rizzo admitted. 'We followed standard practice, and only collected things relevant to d'Incisa 's death for later analysis. Since there was no suggestion of a crime, at least as far as we knew, we weren't authorised to confiscate documents or any personal material belonging to the dead man.'

'For the moment that's certainly the case,' Anna Giulietti confirmed. 'Unless his wife gives her consent, which I doubt she will. Don't forget that Professor d'Incisa was a high-profile figure with powerful connections: you know what I'm talking about. His wife has been informed and is coming back to Florence today. She's not in a condition to drive and there was no one to bring her back last night. I'm sure she'll ask us to handle the affair as discreetly as possible. She certainly won't want a scandal to blemish her husband's memory and his family's reputation. I'll go and see her today. Superintendent Rizzo, I'd like you to go with me. I somehow don't think she'll ever agree to a search like the one you suggest, Chief Superintendent Ferrara. That's why I say we should concentrate on what we have and draw conclusions from that as to how to proceed with the investigation.'

'I'll come, of course,' Rizzo said.

'I've authorised the autopsy. I'd like you to do it as soon as possible, Doctor Leone, and get the results to me immediately. You can call me any time on my mobile.

'Let's keep any idea that d'Incisa was murdered out of the equation for the moment. We'll only consider that as a last resort, if our other inquiries don't yield anything. Assuming that we're dealing with suicide, it was either motivated by a sense of guilt, or by something else we don't know about. If we manage to establish that it was guilt, we'll be able to proceed as Chief Superintendent Ferrara would like, but only if we're certain that d'Incisa really has something to do with the death of Stella. At this stage there's not much to suggest that, do we all agree?'

They all nodded.

'If he killed himself out of a sense of guilt, we'll have to reconstruct his movements and his network of acquaintances, and try to demonstrate that he had connections with Palladiani. I trust you and your men, Superintendent Rizzo.'

'Of course.'

'Finally, and this is the most important thing, we need to trace any other possible accomplices of Palladiani—in other words, the people who were present at the party where Stella the victim may have been drugged.'

'I agree,' Rizzo said.

'Good. I think we've covered everything and now we can get down to work. We all have a lot to do. You can go, but if Chief Superintendent Ferrara would be so kind as to stay, I still have something to discuss with him. Superintendent Rizzo, I'll call you as soon as I know when we can go to see Signora d'Incisa. Thank you, everyone.'

*   *   *

When they were alone, Anna Giulietti retained her formal tone: they still had official matters to discuss, and a rule was a rule.

'First of all, I'd like to confirm that the request for your reinstatement was presented to the Head of the State Police this morning. As soon as they tell me it's approved, I'll be able to put you back on the case.'

'Thank you, Deputy Prosecutor.'

'But now I want you to tell me in detail this story about the drugs in the port of Carrara.'

Ferrara did so.

Anna expressed her anxiety over the size of the find, which made this a particularly serious, difficult and dangerous case and placed an extra burden on all of them. 'How do you intend to proceed now?' she asked.

'First of all I have to locate this Salvatore Laprua. Then I have to figure out how Simonetta Palladiani fits in to all this, if they killed her and why.'

Even though he had avoided mentioning the name of Massimo Verga, Anna Giulietti knew perfectly well what such a discovery would mean for him. She hesitated before replying.

'Why would they beat up and almost torture her husband?' she asked at last. 'You do realise, don't you, that this latest turn in the Palladiani case makes it all the more unlikely that it has anything to do with the Stella case? I can't imagine two things more different than a criminal organisation of that size and a bunch of perverts. If it then emerged that it was d'Incisa and not Palladiani who killed Stella, as you seem to believe and were stubbornly trying to get the others to believe as well, then you can forget about our jurisdiction over the Palladiani case!' Her tone had become less formal now.

'Of course I realise that. But right now the Palladiani case is the only one I'm interested in. Operation Stella is close to being solved, it's just a question of work and luck in tracking down the whole ring. You and I both know, and so do the others, that technicalities aside, the girl was killed by d'Incisa, with or without help from Palladiani . . . Stella was drugged quite some time before she was found, that much is clear, and when they did the first blood test, the drugs had already metabolised. Only she didn't die, and to make sure d'Incisa drugged her again. Do you agree?'

'Absolutely,' she said.

'So, good as you are, why didn't you find a legal ploy to go straight ahead and seize d'Incisa's papers?'

'Because I don't consider it convenient for you, for us, for the investigations on the coast, which have priority right now. To me, it seems obvious. As you yourself say, the culprit is almost certainly d'Incisa. What if we found something among his papers . . . for example, something that showed he'd rented the factory? And what if that let Palladiani off the hook, apart from the cufflink— and as Captain Fulvi kindly pointed out, we still haven't proved it even belonged to him? How would I then justify to Lupo your direct involvement in the investigations in Pietrasanta? If I'm not mistaken, you don't want this drug business to come out yet, and without the drugs and the possible involvement of Palladiani in the Stella case, Lupo would ask me, quite rightly, to take you off the case, don't you see? You don't want that because you'd like to find your friend, and I don't want it because right now I'm up to my ears in this whole drug operation—all thanks to you.'

'There's still the fact that Palladiani was about to make a run for it,' Ferrara suggested, weakly.

Anna Giulietti gave a rueful smile. 'If you were the wife of a man who was trying to get away with the family fortune, wouldn't you try to stop him?'

Ferrara smiled too, defeated. That argument was grist to Captain Fulvi's mill.

'Let's not forget,' Anna went on, the tension inside her obvious in her tone of voice, 'that time is running out. We can't put off seizing the drugs forever, and they mustn't leave the port of Carrara. By the twenty-third of August, the National Narcotics Division will have to be informed of everything, so that the drugs can be seized and the people waiting for them in America can be identified and actively pursued. It's a huge quantity and we're playing with fire . . .' She gave him a severe look, swallowed, and concluded with a sentence that clearly made her uncomfortable. 'Slowing things down just to find your friend may cost us more than our careers.'

'We're not slowing things down,' he immediately retorted. 'We're tracing them to their source.'

'I really hope so,' Anna Giulietti said finally. Her words echoed like a warning in that solemn, austere room, and Ferrara took note of them.

'I'm ready to hand in my resignation,' he said, 'if you feel I've let you down.'

31

In the afternoon, while Rizzo was tied up visiting Signora d'Incisa along with Anna Giulietti, Ferrara asked Fanti, Ascalchi and Sergi to come over to his apartment.

He filled them in on the latest developments in Operation Stella, and then, binding them all to secrecy, he got on to the question of Salvatore Laprua.

'There are only two Salvatore Lapruas in Tuscany,' Fanti stated, having diligently completed the task his chief had assigned him. 'A twenty-seven-year-old technician who works for a company in Pistoia making household appliances, and a seventy-five-year-old man who's been living in Viareggio since 1993.'

'That's him!' Ferrara cried without hesitation. 'Ascalchi, Sergi, get cracking! Go to Viareggio and keep an eye on him! Find out how he spends his time, what links he has with Mining Extractions, everything . . .'

'Erm . . .'

'Yes, Fanti?'

'His business isn't marble, but fishing. He owns a small fishing fleet, La Prua Fisheries, which operates out of the port of Viareggio. He's not as involved with it as he used to be, he seems to have retired, but the fleet is still active.'

'Strange . . . Well, find out all you can about the fishing business, too. But without him noticing, please!'

'No problem, chief,' Ascalchi replied, and

Serpico smiled at him sideways as if to say, *Don't worry, I'll keep an eye on him*.

Petra brought cold drinks out to the terrace, where they were sitting under the arbour. The sun was still beating down, and they were all grateful.

*   *   *

Later, when Ferrara's men had gone, Petra asked him if he was really making progress, as the few snatches of conversation she had caught seemed to suggest.

'I think we are,' he replied, and for the first time she saw him looking confident.

'Do you think you'll manage to find Massimo?'

'Yes,' he said ruefully, thinking about his conversation with Anna Giulietti, about all the time that had passed, and about the strong likelihood, given the ferocity of the organisation he was dealing with and the chain of murders which had bloodied the soil of Tuscany in these past few weeks, that what they found would be the bodies of Simonetta and Massimo. 'Alive or dead, as they used to say on those Wild West posters,' he could not help adding.

'No, Michele, *bitte*, don't even think it!' Petra almost shouted. Then she said, in a firm voice, 'Massimo's alive, I can feel it.'

'Thank you, my love,' was all he said.

*   *   *

Marisa d'Incisa was so horrified by Anna Giulietti's account of the circumstances of her husband's death that she tried to cover her eyes

327

and ears with her slender, tremulous fingers. They were not enough to protect her from the horrors of a world which until the previous day had been untroubled and comfortable and was now suddenly revealed to be absurd, distasteful, intolerable.

Not even the presence of one of her sons, Piero, could help. He was a lawyer who worked in Paris in the European office of an American law practice with offshoots all over the world. Her other two children, a son and a daughter, were on holiday with their families, the son in Bali and the daughter in Argentina, and they had not yet had time to join their mother.

'I'm sorry to have to ask you this, signora, but did you know that your husband used drugs?'

Distressed as she was at the woman's pain, Anna Giulietti was still a public official who had to do her duty.

The woman shook her head repeatedly. 'Of course not,' she said at last, in a low but firm voice.

'And you, Signor d'Incisa?'

He was a man of about forty, tall and well built, with an aristocratic nose and clear, calm eyes. He must have been living abroad for a long time, because he had lost all trace of a Florentine inflection. He spoke with a slight French accent and even used the odd French word when he spoke.

'No. But are you sure about that? I realise the way things must appear, but before making such a . . . *eh bien,* such a serious allegation, you'd need proof, wouldn't you?'

'We found the drugs. They were hidden, not even particularly well hidden, in a bathroom cabinet.'

'It was his bathroom,' the wife explained. She was tiny and thin, her face was ravaged by exhaustion, and yet she was still full of dignity. Dignified was the word both Giulietti and Rizzo would have used to describe her: not arrogant, but dignified. 'I almost never went in there . . . only the maid did, and even she never cleaned it very much,' she added, in a disapproving tone. 'I can't believe it . . .'

'In fact, it's quite incredible,' the son said. 'My father was a good man, a highly respected man, as you know. Perhaps someone put the drugs there to make it look like suicide when in fact it was murder.'

'Do either of you know anyone who hated him enough to do that?' Rizzo asked.

'No, quite the contrary . . . Am I right, *maman*?'

'Absolutely. My husband was respected as a professional and loved as a person.' There was pride in her voice as she said this.

'Naturally, in his position, it's always possible that some madman, perhaps in revenge for the death of a relative . . . Don't you think?'

'That's possible, Signor d'Incisa. But there were no signs of a struggle when we arrived, no indication that a third party had been here. The front door was locked and there was no sign of a forced entry. The pattern was typical of a death by overdose, and since the professor knew what he was doing, we have to assume it was suicide. The autopsy will be able to confirm if he was a habitual drug user . . .'

The woman collapsed in tears.

'Is an autopsy really necessary?' her son asked.

'Yes. I'm sorry.'

'There, there, *maman* . . .'

'It's not possible, it's not possible . . .' the woman said, making a visible effort to get a grip on herself. She made the sign of the cross. 'Not suicide . . . it's a mortal sin . . .'

Anna Giulietti felt uncomfortable. If they managed to establish that the man was not only a drug addict but also a paedophile and a murderer, the poor woman could very well die of grief.

'Erm . . .' Piero d'Incisa said.

'Go on.'

He assumed a more professional tone. 'Look, this is all very unpleasant. *Je comprends* . . . I understand that you have to do your duty, but I'd like to ask you if there's any way to make sure none of this gets out, I mean if it could just remain between ourselves . . . You see, the d'Incisas are an old family, a highly respected family. I'm thinking of my brother and sister, my nieces and nephews . . . My sister's children are still small, it would be terrible if they ever found out. A scandal would be a disaster for all of us, believe me. Whatever mistakes my father may have made, if indeed he made them, his heirs don't deserve . . .'

Here we go, Anna Giulietti thought.

'Don't worry,' she said. 'I shan't speak to the press until we know something for certain, and when I do I'll try to tone things down as far as possible. I'm sure Superintendent Rizzo agrees with me. We'll have to mention suicide, otherwise there'll only be lots of harmful speculation, but we won't reveal the details.'

She did not feel up to asking Piero d'Incisa in return for permission to examine his father's documents. She doubted that he would give his consent, given the circumstances. He was a lawyer after all, and he was sure to find some kind of objection. Besides, even if he did agree, she was afraid that among the papers might well be a contract to lease the factory, and she preferred not to find something like that, at least for the moment.

Signora d'Incisa, who had been struggling to understand, said, 'The suicide could have been due to the stress of work. He was impossible that way. He could never keep away from that blasted—from that hospital. It was his whole life. He was there day and night, even when we could have been enjoying our old age together in Viareggio.'

Or perhaps he preferred to enjoy youth—young girls, in fact: the thought occurred almost simultaneously to both Giulietti and Rizzo.

'It's very possible,' Anna admitted. 'Can you think of any reasons? Money worries, for example, or health problems . . . did he seem unusually anxious recently?'

'Oh, no. We've never had money worries, thank heavens! He was as well as you can be at our age, and with the children all settled, we didn't really have anything to be anxious about. As I said, we should have been enjoying his retirement, instead of which . . .'

'Yes, of course. Apart from his medical colleagues, did your husband see a lot of people?'

'Oh, yes, a lot. He loved company. He often visited friends in the evenings. Sometimes he was invited out for dinner, sometimes he dropped in on them after dinner. But I almost never went with him. I'm bored by social occasions.'

'Could you possibly make a list of his closest

331

friends?'

'What's the point of that?' the son asked, suspiciously.

'Don't worry, Signor d'Incisa. I've given you my word that I'll be discreet. But in cases of suicide I like to have a complete picture of the . . . victim's personality, to try and understand the psychological reasons for his act.' She was lying but Piero d'Incisa seemed reassured.

'I don't know all their names,' his mother said, 'but I can try.'

Rizzo gave her a pen and paper.

Marisa d'Incisa started to write, with a shaking hand, but the effort was too much for her and she fainted.

A Filipino butler, who probably doubled as the signora's nurse and driver, came running, and he and her son carried her into the bedroom.

Piero d'Incisa soon came back in. 'Sorry about that, but at her age . . .'

'I can imagine. She's been really remarkable. We're the ones who should be apologising. Unfortunately, our duty . . .'

'Of course, of course. And I'm grateful to you for the consideration you've been showing our family.'

'Don't mention it. In return, though, I'd like to ask you a favour. If you find any diaries, engagement books, personal objects belonging to your father that you think may help us to understand his frame of mind in his last hours, could you make sure they get to Superintendent Rizzo at Police Headquarters?'

It was a way of putting the ball in his court. She was showing him that she trusted him, practically

332

inviting him to check his father's things before handing them over. But he seemed honest and sincere, and Anna was sure she could count on him to do the right thing.

'I'll do that.'

'One last thing, Signor d'Incisa. Did you know that your father was a Freemason?'

The man smiled indulgently, as if she had mentioned an innocent pastime or an old man's whim. 'Yes, of course. He told me as soon as I turned eighteen. He wanted me to become one, too . . .'

'And did you?'

'Good Lord, no! I mean, not that there's anything wrong with it. Lots of famous people have been Masons. George Washington, Winston Churchill . . . But they're all in the past. I think Freemasonry is now just a rather nostalgic relic of a bygone age. These days, with globalisation as unstoppable as a speeding train, there are far more effective support networks.'

Coming from him, with his international connections, it sounded like a convincing view of the subject.

But Anna Giulietti was no longer so sure.

*   *   *

Late that evening, Ferrara received the telephone call he had been expecting.

'You can come in to the office tomorrow. They called me from Rome to tell me the request has been granted. If anyone says anything about it, they can talk to me. I'll say I asked you personally to come back without waiting for confirmation in

333

writing because Lupo and I need you back on the case urgently.'

'Thanks, Anna.'

'Don't thank me. Just break up that drug ring.'

32

It was nearly midday, and for the past couple of hours Elisa Rocca had been slumped on the old sofa in her apartment in the Santa Croce area.

It was a small apartment, in which dirt and disorder took up more space than the few cheap pieces of furniture. Clothes were strewn everywhere, dirty glasses and cups. On the floor near the sofa lay a four-day-old newspaper showing a photo of the girl, almost a child, who had died in the Ospedale Nuovo.

Elisa was holding a bottle of Chianti with some difficulty in one hand, a glass in the other. She had lost count of how many glasses she'd had.

This was her way of getting through the moments of pain and suffering. Not that there'd been very much else in her life.

When there was not even a single drop left in the bottle, she left the apartment.

She crossed the Piazza Santa Croce and set off in the direction of the Arno. Before reaching the river, she went into a wine shop and ordered a glass of red wine, then another. She went out and walked slowly, with just enough self-control not to collapse on the ground. It was very hot, but she didn't feel the heat.

With small steps, she crossed the bridge.

When she got to the other bank, she headed for the Ponte Vecchio, which seemed to sway in front of her like a big barge on the waters of the river.

She went into another wine shop.

She ordered another glass and drank it, then left because they told her they wouldn't serve her another. The owner knew her and felt sorry for her.

She carried on towards the Pitti Palace. As she crossed the road, a young motorcyclist swerved to avoid her, a manoeuvre which sent him hurtling to the ground. He lay on the asphalt for a few minutes, dazed. Then he grabbed his mobile.

Elisa Rocca was taken to Police Headquarters.

*   *   *

Ferrara was waiting impatiently for Rizzo to get back from Viareggio. He had sent him there first thing in the morning, as soon as he arrived, to check on the progress of the operation. No one had raised any objections.

He hadn't run into Commissioner Lepri, but given that Lepri always kept his ears open, he must know by now that Ferrara was back at his post. But he hadn't sent for him.

He had spent the rest of the morning putting his papers in order and making and receiving phone calls, which kept him out of trouble. He had called Anna Giulietti and asked for authorisation to bug all telephones registered to Salvatore Laprua, and she, in her turn, had filled him in on the encounter with d'Incisa's wife and son. She had reminded him again that time was pressing, as if time were not already Ferrara's prime anxiety. Then he had called Lojelo, who had nothing new to report on the Claudia Pizzi case. Armando Lupo had called from Lucca to congratulate him on his reinstatement and tell him that Captain Fulvi seemed to have reached a dead end, which was why he was really hoping Ferrara would be able to lend a hand.

The last phone call came from the inspector on duty in the operations room at Headquarters.

'Chief, a woman named Elisa Rocca has just been brought in drunk. She claims she knows you.'

This was true.

Elisa Rocca was thirty-five years old, but looked more than fifty. She was short and plump, with a light complexion, dark eyes, and black shoulder-length hair. She had been a prostitute since she was young and some years earlier had told him a few things in confidence which had helped him to track down a ring of pimps who were running high-class call girls from various apartments in the historical centre.

'That's right. Treat her nicely, she's down on her luck.'

'She's drunk, chief, and she wants to talk to you.'

'Oh, no, for Heaven's sake!' he said, but there was no malice in his words: it was just another way of making himself feel at home again.

'She's going on and on about the girl from the Ospedale Nuovo.'

'Don't let her go!' he ordered. 'I'll send someone straightaway.'

Obviously there was no point in going himself. The Stella case was practically solved now, and whatever that poor, prematurely-aged prostitute could tell them was unlikely to add much they didn't already know. He had other things to think about, and above all to do.

He called Fanti and told him to ask Ascalchi to deal with it. Then, as Fanti was walking away, he had second thoughts and added, 'And tell him to take Inspector Venturi with him. He knows her well.'

*   *   *

'He lives in the Via Sant'Andrea, near the harbour. Nothing especially luxurious—an apartment on the second floor of an ordinary-looking building, early twentieth century.'

Rizzo, back from Viareggio, was delivering his report on Salvatore Laprua.

'He didn't come out during the time I was there. In the neighbourhood he's known as a polite, softly spoken person. He's been living there for several years with his wife, they don't have any particular friends, they're old and don't get out much. Just to do the shopping, or sometimes they take a stroll down to the sea.'

'Do they ever go to the harbour?'

'He does sometimes, but not often. And he always goes alone, never with his wife. He has a manager who runs the fishing fleet for him. He doesn't deal with it himself.'

'Not surprising, if it's just a cover. Let's keep him under surveillance, shall we?'

'Sergi and two constables are at the harbour, another two are keeping watch on the house.'

'Good. Deputy Prosecutor Giulietti has given us authorisation to tap his phones. I'll leave you to

337

see to that. Thanks.'

*　　*　　*

Serpico was sitting under the awning of the Piccolo Tito on the Lungomolo Corrado del Greco, savouring a *granita*.

With his long hair, unkempt beard, ripped jeans and Iron Maiden T-shirt, he looked like a tourist mingling with the regulars in the bar, enjoying the merry, colourful spectacle of the small fish market, where the fishermen who had returned from fishing all night were displaying their wares, as they did every morning.

They moored alongside the canal, set up low metal stalls in front of their boats, and arranged the crates of fish on them. Many of the fish were still alive.

The quayside was packed with people looking around in fascination and buying contentedly.

'Haven't you ordered anything for me?' Officer Scugni asked, sitting down next to Sergi. He was also wearing jeans and a T-shirt, and had a Nikon digital camera slung across his shoulder.

'Yes, a coffee, but it was getting cold so I drank it myself. What do you want?'

'I'll have a *granita*, too.'

'It's better if you go inside and order it, they take forever here.'

When he came back, Sergi gave him a questioning look.

'They're not back yet,' Scugni said. 'I checked with the others and they told me that sometimes they're late back because they go a long way out to sea, and when they do come back they're heavily

338

loaded. They're easy to recognise, because they have three large boats, the biggest ones around, and they always travel together. They're called *Alfio*, *Vito* and *Tonio*.'

'That's them,' Sergi said, seeing two of the three trawlers approaching the mouth of the canal. The third soon appeared. 'Let's go.'

They watched as the three forty-foot fibreglass Merlin Craft with their two 350-horsepower engines docked. The boats attracted a clientele of connoisseurs, who had been waiting patiently for them. They did not put out stalls, but sold straight from the boats to the most insistent customers, a few crates going directly to restaurant owners. But most of the fish were quickly loaded onto a white van bearing the words *La Prua Fisheries* on the side.

Sergi made a note of the licence number. He and Scugni walked to the anonymous silver Fiat Punto, got in, and drove to the harbour exit. When they saw the van come out, they started following it, making sure there were a few cars between them.

The van took the autostrada leading north.

It exited at the Carrara tollbooth and set off in the direction of Carrara itself, but bypassed the town and instead took the mountain road. Afraid he would lose sight of it, Sergi put on speed, and managed to keep it in view without being spotted.

Before Colonnata, the van turned left towards Torano and Fantiscritti. There were only the two vehicles on the road now, and Sergi slowed down, as if undecided on the road to follow, then also turned left.

The van was gone.

He put on speed.

He drove round in a long curve, but the van was nowhere to be seen.

After driving another four hundred yards or so, Sergi and Scugni spotted it parked inside a quarry. They made a note of the quarry number: 206.

*　　　*　　　*

Elisa Rocca was sitting on a chair in one of the waiting rooms on the ground floor, shivering despite the heat, and nursing a plastic cup of coffee which a constable had offered her.

She looked up when Ascalchi and Venturi came in.

'Look who's here!' Venturi said, sitting down on the chair next to her. 'They say you drank a few glasses too many.'

Elisa tried to smile, then, turning to Ascalchi, said, 'I don't know you . . . We've never met, have we?'

'This is Superintendent Ascalchi,' Venturi said.

'But I wanted to talk to Ferrara.'

'He's not here, but we spoke to him on the phone and he told us to come and hear what you have to say. Then we'll report back to him.' Being near her, Venturi could smell her: the unpleasant odour of someone who hasn't washed for several days.

Elisa said nothing.

'I haven't seen you for a while,' Venturi went on.

She looked down at the floor and smiled slightly, but did not reply.

'Elisa,' Venturi said, 'the chief said you can talk to us . . . Is something the matter? Is someone

340

giving you trouble?'

Still she said nothing.

She seemed lost in thought.

Ascalchi was starting to get impatient.

It was Venturi who spoke again, almost as if to forestall him. 'If you won't talk, Elisa, we can't help you.'

She looked up. Her eyes were watery and quite wary, as if she had suddenly returned to the real world. 'Inspector,' she started to murmur in a thin voice and a calm tone, 'I'd stopped drinking . . . I was on medication . . . but then . . .'

She broke off.

A pause.

'Then what? Tell us, Elisa, the chief wants to know what you have to say.'

She glanced at Ascalchi, then looked Venturi right in the eyes and said, 'I don't want to talk to you . . .'

She broke off again.

'What is it?' Venturi insisted. 'What's worrying you?'

'I don't know if I can tell you,' she said.

'If there's something you need to say, Elisa, you can tell us.'

'I know something about the girl.'

Silence.

'The one who was found drugged . . . the one they wrote about in *La Nazione*.'

Ascalchi remained impassive, but Venturi nodded. 'What do you know about her?' he asked.

'You won't believe me,' she replied, 'because I'm a drunk and a schizophrenic.'

'I know you, Elisa,' Venturi said softly, 'and I know the chief thinks a lot of you.'

'I know that, and that's why I want to talk to him.'

'He's not here. I told you.'

'Then tell him I knew the girl. I know who she is and where she comes from, and I even know who killed her . . .'

Another pause.

Ascalchi intervened for the first time. 'Who? You have to tell us, signora. You can't keep quiet now!'

'But you have to protect me . . . I'm scared. Let me talk to Ferrara . . .'

'Don't worry,' Venturi said. 'You mustn't be scared, the chief will take care of you, you'll see.'

'Come on, now, who was she?' Ascalchi insisted.

But Elisa did not reply.

Ascalchi exchanged glances with Venturi, who immediately left the room. They had understood each other. Ferrara had to be involved.

*   *   *

At that moment, Ferrara was filling Luigi Ciuffi in on what Serpico had told him over the phone on his way back from Carrara.

'I'd say it all fits,' Ciuffi said when Ferrara had finished. 'And I'm ready to bet on two things. That if we stopped the van, we'd find something interesting in the stomachs of those fish.'

Ferrara nodded. 'And the other thing?'

'That if we asked the Port Authority in Viareggio to monitor the three trawlers when they go out, we'd find they sometimes go well beyond territorial waters, to meet up with a ship from somewhere in Asia which supplies them with these

342

fish that have something interesting in their stomachs.'

'You've got me,' Ferrara said. 'I'd lose both bets. I think the itinerary is pretty clear now. They get the drugs out at sea, take it to the quarries where they cut it, and then send it to America in blocks of marble and around Italy mixed with powder . . . And Laprua's in charge of everything.'

'No doubt about it. In my opinion we should simply nab them the next time they come back with a consignment. I assume they don't get supplies every time they go out, but with the cooperation of the Port Authority we can easily discover when they go out of territorial waters and we'll be able to stop them when they come back.'

'I agree. Will you see about contacting them? In the meantime I'll inform the deputy prosecutor and get the authorisations.'

'Perfect.'

Ciuffi left the room and Ferrara phoned Anna Giulietti. After the call, he sat back in his armchair and lit a cigar.

'Chief,' Fanti said, putting his head round the door, 'Venturi says the drunk woman has some important information, but she'll only speak to you. She says she knows who killed Stella.'

We know that, too, Ferrara thought with a smile, but it was worth hearing her version, and anyway he had a bit of time on his hands. 'Tell him to bring her here.'

33

Elisa was opposite Ferrara.

He had watched her curiously as she entered the room. She had seemed quite unsteady on her feet, was a good few pounds heavier than when he had first met her, and her eyes, which had always been sad, now also seemed scared.

'I wanted to talk to you,' she said as soon as she had sat down on the visitor's chair.

'I just arrived and they told me . . . But why have you started drinking again?'

'I haven't started again, I mean, it isn't that . . . I mean, I was taking the medication . . . but I've been so worried lately. I had to have it . . .' She burst into tears.

'Cheer up, Elisa, don't do that.'

He stood up from his chair, went around the desk, sat down next to her, and handed her a paper handkerchief. Then he called Fanti and told him to bring in a bottle of water and two coffees.

Elisa wiped her eyes. She seemed even sadder.

He tried to comfort her, and made her promise she wouldn't drink again. 'So tell me what happened,' he said gently.

'I don't even know . . . Poor Anila . . . She wasn't a junkie, you know.'

'The girl who died in the Ospedale Nuovo?'

'That's her . . . but she didn't just die, they killed her, it was her brother, I know it was, it was bound to end like that sooner or later.'

'Tell it from the beginning,' Ferrara said. He was intrigued: what she had just said introduced a whole new element into the story. Alcohol-induced hallucinations, maybe, but best to get to the bottom of it.

'I don't know where to start.'

'Did you know her?'

'A bit. I felt sorry for her.'

'How did you meet her?'

Elisa did not reply. She looked around warily.

'Well?'

'It wasn't that I saw a lot of her, like I said . . .'

'I understand, but where did you meet her?'

'In my apartment,' she replied, clearly uncomfortable.

'How come?'

'I don't want this to get out. It's just that sometimes I . . . how else am I supposed to live?'

'Sometimes what, Elisa?'

'Lend my apartment to an old client, who brings a friend there, you know what I mean?'

'Yes, and don't worry . . . But you mustn't do it again, okay?'

'Okay,' she lied.

'So one of your clients brought Anila?'

Elisa nodded.

'When?'

'The first time was more than a year ago.'

'Wasn't she just a child?'

'Yes, that's why I felt sorry for her.'

'And who was the client?'

'I can't tell you that.'

Ferrara let it go for the moment. He would come back to it later.

'But he wasn't the one who brought her,' Elisa continued. 'She came with her brother, an Albanian named Viktor, who came back later to pick her up.'

The name made Ferrara prick up his ears. Guzzi
had said in his report to Ciuffi that the Albanians'
boss was named Viktor.

'What kind of man was he?'

'He's a violent man. He's the one who killed
her, I'm sure of it. But if he finds out I told you,
he'll kill me, too.'

'Can you describe him?'

'Not really . . . tall, fair hair, ugly face, a
squashed nose . . .'

'All right. How many times did they come?'

She thought it over. 'Three in all, I think.'

'So you didn't exactly meet her. You just saw
her. I assume you didn't stay there?'

'Oh, no,' she replied, almost indignantly. 'I had
to leave, but twice the brother came back late to
pick her up and I got back just as the client was
leaving and he asked me to keep her company . . . I
was waiting downstairs, you know?'

'And what did she say to you?'

'That she was scared . . . She didn't speak much
Italian, and she cried all the time, poor girl . . .
She'd come from Albania with her brother, who'd
been fucking her—pardon my language—since she
was six. He also beat her, and sold her . . . He
always told her he loved her, but then he made her
do things . . . She told me this the last time, then I
never saw her again—until I saw her picture in the
paper.'

'When was this last time?'

'A month ago, more or less . . .'

'And what about Viktor? Did you see him
again?'

'No, thank God,' she said with a shudder.

'What makes you think he killed her?'

'Because I know she wasn't a junkie . . . She was just a poor kid with a bastard for a brother, but she was clean. If only you'd seen her. He was the one who drugged her, the animal! And it killed her.'

'I see . . . But couldn't it have been your client who killed her?'

'No, no—he's a respectable guy, in public relations, a rich man, he wouldn't give her that shit.'

P for public relations, P for Palladiani, Ferrara thought, remembering the cufflink and feeling almost dazed by this tangle of new connections.

'What did you say his name was?' he asked.

'Ugo, Ugo Palladiani, you know, the guy . . .' Elisa replied, before realising she had fallen into the trap. 'Oh, no! I don't want him to find out . . .'

'Don't worry, I already knew. And anyway, you don't need to protect his name any more. He's also dead.'

She looked puzzled. 'What do you mean?'

'It happens, unfortunately,' was all he said.

She shook her head and her eyes again filled with tears.

*   *   *

'Let's recap,' Ferrara said, more for his own benefit than for Rizzo's. Rizzo was sitting where Elisa had sat, now that Elisa, reassured for the umpteenth time, was with the technicians trying to put together an identikit of Viktor.

'Stella's real name is Anila,' Ferrara went on. 'She's the sister of an Albanian named Viktor, who treats her like a slave. On the morning of July

347

twenty-ninth, she's found not far from a factory we know used to belong to Ugo Palladiani. Palladiani, who has already had contact with Anila, is killed on the night of the fourth to the fifth of August, a few days after the girl's death. Ugo is married to Simonetta Tonelli, the leaseholder of three quarries in the Carrara area. The quarries are run by a company which uses them as part of a drug trafficking racket. Among those involved in the racket are a Florentine and two Albanians whose boss, as it happens, is named Viktor. Simonetta Palladiani disappears on the day of her husband's murder together with my friend Massimo Verga . . . What does it all mean?'

Rizzo would have given half his salary to have the answer, and the other half to be able to light a cigarette, but he knew his chief wouldn't let him because, according to him, it ruined the smell of his cigar.

He had to be content with breathing in that foul stench.

'On the one hand, there's the drugs racket,' he said, 'on the other a sex crime. They're probably not related, but they've got mixed up because the people involved knew each other in one way or another.'

'That's possible,' Ferrara agreed reluctantly, turning the cufflink over in his fingers: he had asked his deputy to bring it in.

'Anyway,' Rizzo went on, 'we'll know the truth when we get our hands on Laprua. When are you thinking of making a move on him?'

'The same thing Anna Giulietti asked me when I told her about Elisa's statement a few minutes ago. She's breathing down my neck but—I don't know. Time's running out, but I can't risk making the wrong move. I still don't know what's happened to Massimo, or how he fits in to this whole story.'

'The old man should know that, too,' Rizzo said.

'But we don't have any real evidence, Francesco. This is the trickiest moment. If we're too hasty, we could screw it all up . . . He could easily claim he doesn't know anything about the drugs, that other people are using his company for the traffic.'

'The fishing fleet, too?' Rizzo asked. He knew the enormous tension his boss was experiencing at that moment. On the one hand there was the pressure to act quickly, on the other he was afraid of making a mistake, because a mistake could prove fatal for his friend.

'We still have to catch them red-handed,' Ferrara said. 'Have you alerted the Port Authority?'

'Yes, and they've agreed to keep a discreet eye on them.'

'That's good—or is it? We're not there yet, something's missing, I don't have all the pieces . . . Maybe after I've spoken to Zancarotti and the two Albanians . . .'

'You're thinking of interviewing them?'

'At this point I have to. Anna Giulietti has given the authorisation and I've arranged it with the warden of the prison, who I already know. I'm going there tomorrow afternoon.'

'Do you want me to come, too?'

'No, thanks, better not.'

Fanti interrupted them. 'Chief, Piero d'Incisa is here, he's brought in something for Superintendent Rizzo.'

Ferrara gave his deputy a questioning look.

'D'Incisa's son,' Rizzo explained. 'Anna Giulietti asked him to bring in his father's papers.'

'Send him in,' Ferrara said.

*   *   *

'I did what I could but there's not much, I'm afraid,' Piero d'Incisa said after the introductions, handing Rizzo a not very bulky envelope. 'His diary, a notebook—but I think all the notes are medical—an invitation to a conference in Cagliari last month with the list of delegates, it may be useful to you to question some of them . . . I also put in his mobile phone. There are lots of numbers in the memory.'

'Thank you, Signor d'Incisa, you've been very thorough,' Rizzo said, while Ferrara started to leaf through the diary.

'I did it myself to avoid upsetting *maman*, if I could. She's still in shock, I don't want to alarm her any further, and unfortunately I have to leave tomorrow. They're expecting me back at work on Monday. I have a flight this evening, but from Fiumicino, so I have to go to Rome . . .'

'Leave us your contact details, in case we need to get hold of you,' Ferrara said, distractedly, his mind still on Massimo, Simonetta, Laprua . . .

'Of course,' d'Incisa replied. He took out a business card, placed it on Ferrara's desk, and wrote down his private numbers. As he did so, he moved a few of the papers on the desk, causing the cufflink to roll over onto its broken pin.

'Ah, you found it?' Piero d'Incisa asked in surprise.

350

'What?'

'Dad's cufflink. But where did you get it? He wasn't wearing them when he was found, was he?'

Ferrara made no attempt to answer his question, but quickly asked, 'Are you sure it's your father's?'

'*Mais oui*, those are his initials!' he exclaimed, picking up the cufflink and showing it to the two men in turn.

They had both been conditioned by the photograph Rizzo had taken originally, in which the sun was at the top so that there appeared to be a P in the middle, and the way Piero d'Incisa was holding the cufflink they would have considered upside-down only a few moments earlier.

'You see? L d I, Ludovico d'Incisa . . . I know these cufflinks well, he had them made many years ago by a jeweller in Geneva when he came to see me there once. He was very fond of them.'

Ferrara and Rizzo exchanged knowing glances.

'Listen, Signor d'Incisa . . .' Ferrara began.

*   *   *

Piero d'Incisa had turned whiter and whiter as Ferrara told him about the death of Anila and the development of the investigation up until the discovery of the cufflink in the place where the dying girl had been dumped. He did not mention the factory or the paedophile activities that had apparently taken place there, because he did not want to overwhelm the man too much all at once, but even so Piero d'Incisa seemed totally devastated when Ferrara stopped speaking.

'*Ce n'est pas possible, pas possible . . .*'

351

They waited in silence for him to absorb the information.

'Unfortunately, those are the facts,' Ferrara said finally, 'and as I'm sure you'll appreciate . . .'

'Of course, you have to . . . Oh, *mon Dieu . . .*'

'Yes, I have to ask the deputy prosecutor for a search warrant. It's absolutely essential that we search your father's apartment.'

'And what if I give you permission?' D'Incisa suggested after a long and clearly difficult pause for reflection.

'You?'

'I know, it seems impossible. I'm his son, and a lawyer . . . But apart from the fact that I have no wish to stop the truth coming out—though I hope the truth is not what you think—I'd prefer to keep my mother out of this. She'll be in church tomorrow morning, for the nine o'clock mass. She'll be leaving home at about eight thirty, and I can arrange for her to be taken to the park for some fresh air after the service . . .'

'The search might take a while.'

'I'll take that risk. If necessary I'll make something up to keep her away from the apartment. It would be much worse if you turned up with a search warrant, don't you see?'

'Yes, of course. So, tomorrow morning before nine?'

Piero d'Incisa nodded, thanked them, said goodbye and walked out, as unsteady on his feet as Elisa Rocca had been, crossing that same threshold only a few hours earlier.

Ferrara shuddered.

34

Ferrara got to the d'Incisa apartment at eight fifty, accompanied by Rizzo, Venturi and a three-man team from Forensics, one of them a computer expert. Piero d'Incisa was alone and waiting for them.

'We'll try not to make too much of a mess,' Ferrara reassured him.

The man was obviously sceptical, but shrugged. Nevertheless he kept his eyes on what they were doing, checking that everything was put back in place, in order to avoid having to explain things to his mother later.

He had to hop from one room to another, though, because they had split up in order to cover the largest number of rooms in the shortest time possible.

Venturi concentrated on the sitting room, two of the forensics men on the servants' rooms, kitchen and bathrooms, and Ferrara, Rizzo and the computer expert on the bedrooms and the professor's study. The study, in particular, was subjected to a thorough search. They emptied the drawers and sifted through notes, receipts, cheque stubs and photographs. The technician switched on the computer on the professor's desk and connected it to his own laptop. After a few fruitless attempts to gain access, he asked Piero d'Incisa for the dates of birth of all the members of the family. The fifth one, Ludovico's daughter's date of birth, did the trick. Then he copied the entire contents of the computer onto his own laptop.

Rizzo, who had gone into Professor d'Incisa's bedroom, called Ferrara.

'There's a safe,' he said, pointing at the wall. A large painting had been removed, and was now on the floor propped against the wall. The removal had revealed the door of a safe, measuring some three feet by three feet. The lock had an electronic code.

'Do you know the combination?' Ferrara asked Piero d'Incisa, who had joined them when he heard Rizzo calling.

'No, I didn't even know he had a safe.'

'If we can't open it I'm afraid we'll have to call a technician to force it open,' Ferrara said.

'Why don't you try the dates of birth again, as your officer did?'

He called the computer expert and had Piero d'Incisa give him the dates again. He started with the one that had given access to the computer and the lock worked immediately. With a click the door of the safe half-opened. Ferrara opened it wide.

There were three shelves inside, filled with objects and documents: a large leather box containing five expensive-looking watches, a blue velvet case with nineteen pairs of cufflinks identical to the one found by Pietro Franceschini —which surprised the son but not Ferrara—a Sony digital video camera, various CDs marked with letters and numbers, and a lot of document folders.

Ferrara passed the CDs to the expert. 'Go and see what's on them.'

Then he opened the video camera and saw that

354

there was a tape inside. He closed it again, took another look in the safe, and found the leads for connecting the camera directly to the TV set.

'Will you come with us?' he asked Piero d'Incisa as he walked back towards the study. Rizzo remained in the bedroom, examining the documents.

'I'd say it's my duty,' d'Incisa replied.

They connected the video camera to the TV set but before they could start the video the technician called them over to the desk. Images had started appearing on the computer screen: images of naked children.

Piero d'Incisa turned white.

'Turn it off, please,' Ferrara ordered.

Then they started the video.

*   *   *

The girl, perhaps only a child, was looking around, frightened by the men surrounding her. They could hardly be made out, but they seemed to be distinguished-looking, commanding, rich.

And old. Terribly old compared with her, but that wasn't supposed to matter. She was not supposed to be bothered by the greedy looks they gave her, the hands that fondled her, the patches of saliva they left in turn on her cheeks and neck. On the contrary, she was supposed to stimulate them herself, if they had needed stimulating. But the girl was too pretty, and the men too old, for her to require any subtle skills which she had not yet learnt.

She was the prettiest of them all, prettier than the other children—all younger than her—at whom the camera pointed every now and again. The camera was shaky, as if held by an amateur. The children were naked, and were being forced to manipulate the old men's private parts with their hands and mouths, and to play with each other while their tormentors watched avidly. But the camera did not linger on these scenes. It returned as soon as it could to her, the queen of this obscene party.

Intimidated by that surreal atmosphere, with its multi-coloured lights and deafening music and the laughter and salacious, contemptuous comments of the hosts, Alina, who had been taught to be docile and obedient, let herself be touched, caressed, stripped, passed from one man to the next. The champagne and the ecstasy pills circulated freely, as did the lecherous words they murmured to her, which she did not understand. She humoured them without really participating, and that was enough for these men who just wanted to savour the pleasure of young flesh.

All of them except Ugo Palladiani, who wasn't satisfied with Alina's passivity and complained angrily, 'She's too stiff, someone loosen her up!'

An order, not an invitation.

They tied a rubber strap round her arm and when the vein swelled, they inserted the needle. She made no objection, did not protest.

She soon slipped into a limbo which must have been populated by wild obscene images escaping from the thin plasma screen, invading her brain and echoing deafeningly in her mind. She slid to the floor and tried to cover her ears with her hands but her limbs did not respond. It was clear she was nauseous. And she was shivering with cold despite the sweat glistening on the bodies of the participants.

'Shit, now she's really stiff,' remarked an off-

screen voice which made Ferrara go pale. The remark was answered with sinister murmurs of assent.

It was at this point that the image suddenly juddered, and the screen went completely brown. But the camera continued to record sounds.

'Let me have a look.'

A different voice, which sounded like Ludovico d'Incisa's, although he had not been visible in the video.

'What did you give her?'

'Heroin, Professor.'

'How much, damn it? The girl's dying!'

The sudden silence was broken by a hysterical yell.

'Get her out of here! Right now! Everybody get out of here!'

*   *   *

Piero d'Incisa had covered his eyes, and was shaking with anger and pain. To say he was devastated would have been an understatement this time. He was a man whose world had come crashing around his ears.

Ferrara felt sorry for him.

'Did you recognise the voice?'

The man nodded.

'Chief, can you come here a minute?' Rizzo said. He had come back in with two sheets of paper in his hand and had stood there in silence, hypnotised by the images unfolding on the screen.

Ferrara followed him, but Piero d'Incisa stayed where he was, sitting on the sofa in an almost catatonic state.

They moved only as far as they needed to in order to be out of earshot, and then Rizzo showed Ferrara the sheets of paper.

In the middle at the top was the same emblem that appeared on d'Incisa's cufflinks, and just beneath it an inscription in elaborate baroque characters.

Loggia degli Innocenti
Lodge of the Innocents

The text read:

Oath
I the undersigned, Ugo Palladiani, in the presence of the brothers here assembled, do hereby unite sincerely and solemnly with them. Of my own free will I promise not to reveal to anyone the secrets of this Grade.
I swear to observe all the Statutes, Regulations and Instructions inherent in the grade of Secret Master unless they are contrary to the sincere impulses of my reason. I promise to conform to the internal Laws and decisions of this Lodge until I have reached this Grade. Finally, I promise and swear to be faithful unto death to the protection of every secret that is imparted to

me, to every task which is imposed upon me, to every duty which is requested of me for the good of my Country, my family, my brothers and friends and never to abandon them in times of need, danger or persecution.

I promise to destroy every prejudice and superstition in myself and to try to constantly improve my Initiatory and profane knowledge.

Florence, 24 March 1999

Ugo Palladiani

There followed the signatures of the regional inspector, the speaker and the secretary. All were illegible.

The other document was, if possible, even more unsettling. It was the recommendation for Palladiani to be accepted into the new grade. Among the names of the brothers sponsoring this, all of them from the thirtieth, thirty-first and thirty-third grades, was that of Alberto Gallo, Public Prosecutor of Florence.

The voice Ferrara had heard off-screen.

35

'Incredible,' Anna Giulietti said, handing him back the two sheets of paper.

She was not only incredulous, she was worried. Extremely worried.

Not only did she have the drug racket to deal with—and she couldn't forget that time was

359

passing and a decision would have to be made soon—but now she had been presented with a discovery that could shake the whole edifice of the judiciary to its foundations!

It was evening, and they were sitting in the shade of the arbour on Ferrara's terrace. The sultriness had eased off, and Petra had prepared aperitifs and sat down next to her husband. Each time she discovered the depths of depravity to which the human heart could descend—and given her husband's profession, that happened all too often—she would open her eyes wide and exclaim, '*Ach du lieber Gott!* Is that really true, Michele?'

Ferrara was not in a very good mood.

He had only just got back from interviewing the three men in Sollicciano prison. The journey had proved pointless. The Albanians, Nard and Alex, had remained silent, had pretended not to know Zancarotti, and had not responded to threats or promises. Zancarotti had been apparently more malleable, but whether it was true or not, he had claimed to be just a small fish in a large pond, who had only ever heard other people talking about Zì Turi and knew nothing about how his gang and his clan worked.

The only time he had looked a little afraid was towards the end of the interview, when Ferrara, in exasperation, had first threatened to accuse him of complicity in the murder of Claudia Pizzi, and then offered to get him into the witness protection programme if he decided to cooperate seriously, giving him no more than twelve hours to make up his mind.

'Now we know why Gallo was so determined to

block any investigation of the Freemasons,' Anna Giulietti resumed. 'And I fell for it hook, line and sinker! And it's also clear now why he supported the request for you to be suspended . . . Not to mention what I had to go through to get authorisation to see the medical records from the Ospedale Nuovo and then, worse still, when he found out that the request for you to be reinstated came from me. The only thing that saved me was the fact that the Prosecutor's Department of Lucca was involved as well, otherwise I don't think I'd be here to tell the tale.'

'Thank you.'

Ferrara was genuinely grateful to her. Few deputy prosecutors have the courage to oppose their boss, even when they know he is wrong.

Petra, who was listening to them attentively, was still astonished by the ease with which Michele and Anna went from being formal with each other to talking like old friends.

'I thought he still had it in for you personally for all those things in the past . . .'

'Which aren't over yet,' Ferrara said.

'. . . and it turned out to be something else entirely. Well, he won't have anything to crow about now. He'll have to tell us who the other people at the party in the factory were, and help us to find them . . .'

'Some won't be difficult. We have the complete list of the members of the Lodge of the Innocents . . . What nerve to think up a name like that! It's almost blasphemous. What kind of mentality do these degenerates have?'

'Do you want to bet they'll all swear they love children?'

Ferrara and his wife exchanged looks of disgust mixed with sorrow.

'The poor children will be harder to identify,' he said.

'That's what I was thinking,' Anna Giulietti replied.

'We have the video, but if they're all immigrants like Anila, God knows where they are now.'

'Precisely,' Anna said, sadly. 'Anyway, thanks to what you found out we can widen the investigation three hundred and sixty degrees, involving all national and international police forces. It may take months, even years, but I promise you this, Ferrara: someone's going to pay. In the meantime, though . . .'

'Yes, I know. I'm certainly not neglecting the other case. I have much more to lose than you, I think . . . But first I have to nail Laprua definitively. And I still don't understand the link between the parties in the factory and the drugs racket. The only connection seems to be Viktor, who was Anila's brother and master and also the person who was waiting for the drugs that were seized on the autostrada.'

'Do you think you'll be able to track him down? As you say, he could be the crux of the whole thing.'

'We have an identikit of him, and just today Superintendent Ciuffi of Narcotics told me there's talk on the streets about a ruthless gang leader called Viktor Makregi, who's been operating for quite a while in Tuscany—which is quite unusual in itself because the Albanians never usually stay in one place for very long. But no one seems to know much about him. Either they're scared, which is quite likely given the kind of person he is, or he's good at melting into the background.'

'I see,' Anna Giulietti said.

'Anyway, as far as Laprua is concerned, don't worry,' Petra said calmly. 'Michele will get him, because he's the one who has Massimo.'

She had broken her tacit rule not to interfere in her husband's work, especially in the presence of a third party—a prosecutor, to boot! But it had been stronger than her, and she hadn't been able to restrain herself.

'Either him or Viktor,' Ferrara corrected her.

The two women exchanged questioning glances.

Ferrara's eyes narrowed like a cat's and after a very brief pause, he continued, 'I've been thinking about it a lot. We know now for certain who killed Anila. It was an accident, but all the adults at the party were responsible. Especially the two men who subsequently died. Ugo Palladiani, who owned the factory and probably organised the evening, and Ludovico d'Incisa, the head of the Lodge, *de facto* the person who got rid of the body by dumping it at the side of the road, and who later injected the fatal dose.

'By coincidence, the two main culprits both die, too . . . I thought first of all that d'Incisa killed Palladiani for fear that he might talk, then killed himself . . . It's possible. Or at least it would be, for a normal person. But for the head of a powerful Masonic group, with connections to the judiciary and God knows what else . . .'

Anna Giulietti nodded pensively. She was following the thread of Ferrara's argument and starting to anticipate it. 'Whereas Viktor . . .'

'Precisely. What's one of the most frequent

motives for murder? Revenge. The Albanian loved his sister . . . in a perverted way, I agree, but he loved her. And anyway, he got a good profit out of her. Clients don't pay peanuts to have sex with minors. That night something unforeseen happened. The members of the Lodge of the Innocents killed Anila. How did Viktor react when he went to pick her up and probably found no one there? The factory had been abandoned in a hurry, remember?'

The two women nodded, fascinated despite themselves by this reconstruction, which seemed to put every piece of the horrifying jigsaw in its place.

'Viktor is a violent man. He knows Palladiani, but probably not the others. Palladiani is scared, and plans to get out of the country. But Viktor tracks him down to his wife's villa, and kills him with a drug overdose, the way they killed Anila. But first he tortures him. Why?'

'To find out the names of the others,' Petra said immediately.

'After which we find another corpse,' Anna Giulietti said, looking increasingly worried. 'And he also died of an overdose . . .'

'It's just a theory, mind you,' Ferrara said.

'But a bloody convincing one,' Anna said. 'Much more so than any of the others. Only, if it's true . . .' She broke off, perhaps fearing what she had been about to say.

Ferrara finished the sentence for her. 'If it's true, then all the others are in danger, too— including Gallo.'

'We'll have to warn him, provided it's not too late.' She rummaged in her bag for her mobile.

'No!' he stopped her. 'You can't. First of all, it's

just a theory, it might not even be true. And if it is, you'll only alert him and may never find him again . . . or any of the others!'

'Are you joking, Michele?' she replied, angrily. 'What are you trying to do, force me to make a moral choice? A man's life on the one hand, letting justice take its course on the other? Well, it may surprise you to hear this coming from me, but I don't give a damn about justice!'

Ferrara smiled. It was the first time he had ever heard her express herself in that way, about something to which she had devoted her life. Obviously, the woman not only had balls, she had a heart, too.

'Call him then, but only to make sure he's still alive and to say hello. Find some excuse. In the meantime I'll tell my men to send a patrol to keep an eye on his apartment. From now on we'll protect him as if he were the President of the Republic himself, and he won't even know, don't worry. But you know what I think?'

'What?'

'I'm willing to bet that when we put the handcuffs on him, he'll breathe a sigh of relief.'

*   *   *

Once they had made their respective phone calls, they carried on discussing Ferrara's theory.

It was getting dark. Petra asked Anna if she'd like to stay for dinner. After a slight hesitation, she accepted.

'There's one weak point in the theory,' Ferrara said as his wife walked away.

'Which is?'

'Simonetta and Massimo. If Viktor killed Palladiani, why didn't he kill them, too? Why should he take them with him?'

Anna Giulietti lowered her voice in order not to be overheard by Petra. 'I'm sorry, Michele, I know what you're thinking . . . He could have done it later . . .'

'Yes,' he replied simply, and Anna was surprised by the cool, clear-headed way he made that statement, as if the mere thought of it were not unbearable in itself. 'But once again why? And why not straightaway? Why not there?'

'Perhaps to create a false lead. It certainly deceived the Carabinieri. This is assuming your theory is correct.'

'I've thought of that, Anna, and I don't buy it. Do you really think someone like him, blinded by rage, and leading an underground existence anyway, would bother to work out a clever plan to throw people off the scent? No, we're not dealing with some sophisticated mastermind in a film, the man's a brute, a wild animal, someone who raped his own sister, someone who exploits women and traffics in drugs . . . an Eastern Mafioso.'

'So what, then?' Anna asked, not knowing the answer.

'I don't know. That's what worries me . . . I don't know.'

36

From early in the morning on Monday 20 August, the offices of the Florence *Squadra Mobile* were a hive of activity. Keeping in constant telephone contact with Anna Giulietti, Ferrara and his men prepared arrest warrants, to be signed by the deputy prosecutor, for all the men identified on the video. The charge: accessory to murder and possession and use of narcotic substances.

For all the names on the membership list of the Lodge of the Innocents, whether or not they had been identified on the video, search warrants were also prepared, together with information indicating that the men would also be charged with the offence of criminal conspiracy.

Anna Giulietti signed the warrants, and the operation was under way.

And so the search began. It was made more difficult by the summer exodus which had scattered the men all over Italy and abroad. More than sixty police officers—superintendents, inspectors and constables—were suddenly handed the task of carrying out the deputy prosecutor's orders in the shortest time possible.

The sound of screeching tyres as police cars drove out of the Headquarters car park could be heard almost constantly from the courtyard.

Ferrara gave his men their instructions with cold efficiency, but his mind was elsewhere: he was thinking of Massimo Verga, which meant he was also thinking of Salvatore Laprua and Viktor Makregi.

He had Viktor's identikit in front of him, and from time to time he went back to studying it, powerless with anger, in a vain attempt to find in it some secret it stubbornly refused to divulge. It seemed impossible that this face with its vulgar features, its clear eyes, blond crew-cut hair, flat nose and prominent cheekbones, could have the power of life and death over his closest friend. But wasn't it that power, absolute and yet easy—because nothing is easier than to snap the thin thread that connects us to life—which made murderers contemptible, all of them, without exception?

By late morning, everyone had been phoned and all the orders had been given. Ferrara sent for Ciuffi, hoping for news, but there was none.

'What kind of informers do you have, Luigi?' he protested.

'It's not that, chief. It's just that this guy is tough, and he's smart. If it really is Viktor Makregi we're dealing with, Interpol lost all trace of him in 1999. They believe he's still in Moldova, which is where he was last seen, just think about that . . . Anyway, they have him classified as a leading light of the Albanian underworld, highly dangerous and extremely violent. We know for certain that he slaughtered a whole rival gang once in Tirana. He's not some two-bit pusher, chief.'

'Track him down, Luigi. He's the key to finding Massimo Verga, I know it, I can feel it . . . Flush him out, and I promise . . .'

'No need to promise anything, chief. Just finding him will be enough to make me happy for the next ten years!'

Ferrara knew he meant it.

The breakthrough came early in the afternoon, with a phone call from Mazzorelli, the warden of Sollicciano prison, whom he had met during the investigation into the series of homosexual murders the previous year.

'I may have good news for you, Chief Superintendent,' Mazzorelli said.

'Is it Emilio Zancarotti? Has he decided to cooperate?'

'That's what he says. And he also says he has some important things to tell you.'

'Can you have him brought here? I have to stay here, we've got a major operation in progress, and I need to monitor it constantly. But I need to hear what Zancarotti has to say urgently.'

Mazzorelli thought it over. 'It won't be easy, just like that . . . but for you I think it can be done.'

'Thanks—you don't know what a favour you're doing me!'

'Well, I owe you one, Chief Superintendent.'

*　　　*　　　*

'I'm ready to talk because you promised to put me into the witness protection programme and because I don't want to go back inside. You have to tell the warden those two are going to kill me . . .'

'Calm down, Zancarotti.'

He was sitting in handcuffs opposite Ferrara, Rizzo and Ciuffi. Two of the prison guards who had come with him were standing guard outside

369

the door of Ferrara's office. Fanti had asked them if they wanted coffee, but they had refused. So had Zancarotti, but he had asked for a glass of water.

'Do you want me to have your handcuffs removed?' Ferrara asked, watching him take the glass with both hands.

'What difference would that make? I want you to do what I said.'

'Hold your horses. If what you have to tell me is important, and there's something to back it up, I'll get you into the programme, you have my word on that. Especially if what you tell me puts your life in danger.'

The man grimaced. 'You don't know Zì Turi. He's a tough old guy. He'll have you killed just like that, if he wants to. If he knows I've talked, he'll have me killed in prison. Look what happened to that journalist. I'll tell you everything, but you've got to protect me, get me away from here, out of the country . . .'

'Start talking, and we'll see. So, you know Salvatore Laprua, also known as Zì Turi, quite well, even though the other day you told us you didn't. Start from there. Where did you meet him for the first time?'

'In Viareggio, seven years ago. I was desperate, I owed money left, right and centre. I thought I'd find work more easily in a holiday resort, any kind of work, a barman, whatever . . . Someone told me there was this guy, the harbour people called him the Sicilian, who was looking for people for his trawlers. I don't know anything about fishing, I'm even a bit scared of the sea, but you know how it is, beggars can't be choosers . . . He took me on, but he didn't always make me go out to sea with the others. They were all Sicilians like him, not exactly talkative . . . oh, I'm sorry . . .'

'It doesn't matter. Yes, I'm Sicilian, too, and it's true, I don't talk much. I prefer to listen. Go on.'

'The times he didn't send me out to sea, he took me with him to different places. He said he had enemies, and I was his bodyguard. After a while, he let me have a gun. He started to trust me. Then after about a year . . . yes, it was in 1995, he promised he'd set me up in a bar in Florence if I helped him with some important business he had. Then he made me go out in the boat, sometimes on long trips. We'd go a long way out, where the three trawlers would meet up with a freighter. They'd unload a lot of crates. They looked like fresh fish, but inside they were full of bags of drugs.'

Ciuffi threw Ferrara a triumphant look: he'd been right. This part of the story sounded substantially true. It still had to be confirmed, of course, but it seemed highly unlikely that he would be making it up.

'And where did these drugs end up?'

'Zì Turi didn't even see them. They carried them up to Carrara, where he runs some marble quarries. I never saw them with my own eyes, but I heard about them. That's where the guys who gave us the drugs on the autostrada came from—the quarries.'

'You can tell me about that later. What I want to know now is why he should have helped you to open a bar in Florence.'

'Because I was useful to him. I didn't have a criminal record. I was on the inside now, and Florence is a good place to make contacts with the underworld, especially from Eastern Europe. I'm a Florentine, no criminal record, it was normal for me to have my own little business . . . and with their help I soon built up the right clientele. I helped the money to circulate, sent it on to buy more drugs. It was a nice scene. With my contacts, I sent out five hundred million, even a billion once, which then came back to Zì Turi multiplied— what? Ten times? A hundred times?—as heroin. Put that on the market, and you multiply it again . . .'

Ciuffi mentally totted up the figures and, as he thought about the number of years this racket had gone on undisturbed, his eyes widened in astonishment. Zì Turi must have been richer than a lot of Third World countries!

'I see. Now tell us about the foreigners you came in contact with.'

Emilio Zancarotti started to list names of people in various Eastern European countries, supplying details of bank accounts and the ways the money was carried across borders. It was valuable stuff, and Luigi Ciuffi noted it all down religiously. But Zancarotti did not mention Viktor, or the two Albanians he had ended up in prison with.

Finally, before losing his patience, Ferrara decided to go on the offensive. 'Does the name Viktor mean anything to you?'

Emilio Zancarotti raised his hands awkwardly to his forehead, and wiped off the film of sweat which had formed despite the air conditioning. 'Of course it does,' he replied in a disgusted tone. 'It's his fault we ended up inside.'

'Where does he live?'

'Who, Viktor?' he said, close to laughter. 'How should I know? In my opinion not even those two bast— that Alex and Nard—know where he lives.'

'Where did you see him?'

'I've never seen him. I don't even know what he looks like. All I know is that those two are scared shitless—pardon my language—of even mentioning his name. They're terrified of him. Me too, if you must know. He has a bad reputation even among the Albanians.'

'Why do you say it was his fault you ended up inside?'

'Because he was the one who organised the whole thing. We were supposed to give the drugs to him. He had something on Zì Turi, can you imagine?'

'What do you mean?'

'Those ten kilos of heroin were a payment.'

Ferrara's heart missed a beat. 'Mind explaining that?'

'Sure, I know everything! I'm the one who got caught in the middle. I knew those two before. Alex and Nard. They used to come to the bar, they were part of the scene. They knew I was one of Zì Turi's men, I'd told them that myself, to impress them. One day they tell me their boss, Viktor, has an important message for my boss, and I have to give it to him. Viktor is holding a hostage, a woman who's very important to Zì Turi, her name is Simonetta, and he's willing to let her go in exchange for ten kilos. For Zì Turi, that's peanuts. He doesn't think twice about it. He tells me to do everything they ask. So they organise an exchange.'

'But when you had the drugs, they didn't give

373

you anyone in exchange,' Ciuffi objected.

'That wasn't how it was supposed to work. Viktor didn't trust the Mafia. The understanding was that I was supposed to go with the two Albanians to get the drugs, then they would take me to the place where the woman would be handed over.'

'Only the woman?' Ferrara asked, unable to restrain himself. 'Wasn't there a man as well?' His voice came out sounding hoarse and thick.

Zancarotti looked at him blankly. 'A man as well? No, they didn't tell me anything about that . . .'

'Do you know why Salvatore Laprua was so interested in this woman?' Rizzo asked, knowing what Ferrara was going through and thinking it best to take his place at this point.

'No, they didn't tell me, and neither did he. I was supposed to do what I was told and that was it.'

'So you have no idea where she was being kept prisoner?'

'No. They were supposed to take me there . . . but then you police butted in.'

'Does Viktor still have the woman?'

'I hope so, if they haven't done another exchange in the meantime. I'm sure Viktor wouldn't have handed her over without getting the drugs.'

'We're going to check all this out now, Zancarotti,' Ferrara cut in, before the other two men could say anything, 'and if what you say turns out to be true, you're guaranteed a place on the witness protection programme. I'm sending you back to prison now but I'll tell the warden to put

374

you in a different cell. From now on, it'll be better if you don't have any more contact with the two Albanians.'

'Thanks,' Zancarotti replied, relieved.

It struck Ciuffi that he ought to phone Mazzorelli. It was time to get Inspector Guzzi out of there. There was no point any more in having him share a cell with Alex and Nard, and it could actually be dangerous.

*   *   *

Petra knew as soon as he came in.

It wasn't so much the tired look on his face or the sad expression in his eyes, as his stance, the position of his body, which seemed all at once to droop. He looked like someone who had fought too many battles and lost the latest one.

She said nothing.

Later, as Ferrara was forcing down his third forkful of spaghetti—which also turned out to be the last—she looked affectionately at him and said softly, 'Talk to me, Michele.'

Perhaps it was all the time that had passed, perhaps it was the anxiety which had been with him for too long and was now consuming him, or perhaps it was the tension reaching breaking point—or perhaps all three things together— which resulted in two large, agonised tears streaking his cheeks.

'It's over now,' Petra sighed in such a heartfelt way that Ferrara felt obliged to tell her everything.

When he had finished, he realised that Petra was struggling to find words that were not platitudes, and she did so in her own way, drawing

375

from that well of practicality which had always been her husband's anchor.

'Michele, you mustn't give up now. *Das darfst du nicht*. The man didn't tell you anything about Massimo. *Nichts*. Until you know for certain you have to keep thinking he's alive and waiting for you. Do you remember your nightmare? You don't know where he is, but he's still calling you. I can hear him, Michele. I can hear his voice, you can't not hear it yourself.'

The nightmare did not recur that night, but he did not need it to release the tension.

His wife had seen to that, and the following morning he woke up very early, more determined than ever.

37

Before ringing the entryphone, Ferrara checked his watch. It was exactly ten in the morning.

It had taken him more than an hour to get here. He had had a bit of difficulty in finding the Via Sant'Andrea, which went from the canal to the heart of Viareggio without any street signs on the corners. In the end he had had to ask directions from one of the two plain-clothes men who were keeping an eye on the area around the building.

It was a four-storey building, with a balcony in front of the central window on the first floor. The façade was of grey-green concrete, made to look as if it were stone.

'Who is it?'

The voice was rather hoarse, the voice of an old

man who had just woken up.

'Police! Open up, please.'

He heard a click, and the wooden door half-opened.

He climbed to the second floor.

Salvatore Laprua was waiting for him in the doorway.

He was tall, thin and dark-skinned, with white hair combed back. He was still wearing silk pyjamas beneath a burgundy dressing gown, also of silk. On his feet he wore a pair of very elegant slippers. His small, inquisitive eyes studied Ferrara as he completed the climb.

'I'm Chief Superintendent Ferrara, head of the Florence *Squadra Mobile*,' he said as soon as he stood facing him.

'Are you alone?' the man asked in surprise.

If he had come to arrest him, as he was perhaps expecting him to, he wouldn't have come without his men.

'This time, yes,' Ferrara replied, sustaining his gaze. 'For what we have to say to each other, we don't need anyone else.'

Both men's eyes had started saying more than their words, conveying messages no tongue could express.

'Please come in, Chief Superintendent.'

He led Ferrara along a short, pleasantly appointed corridor to the living room, where he invited him to sit down on a green velvet sofa and took a seat in the armchair next to it.

It was an ordinary middle-class living room, with a few nice pieces of furniture and a large, ugly TV set.

The apartment smelt pleasantly clean.

'Tell me,' the old man said, 'why has an officer of your rank come all the way from Florence to see me?'

'Because I need you.'

The man nodded. He was used to giving and receiving favours.

A short, plump, elderly woman with completely white hair entered the room at that moment and stared at Ferrara wide-eyed.

'Rinuzza . . . don't worry . . . You know, this man is in charge of the police in Florence, he's an important person. Make us some coffee.' His Sicilian accent was stronger when he spoke to her.

The woman went out.

'Chief Superintendent, it's an honour for me that you've come to my house . . . We're just two old people, two poor old people with not many years left, as you can see. What little we have I've worked for. All my life I've worked. Now I'm retired, I have little money and not many friends. I don't know if I . . .' He trailed off.

'I'm not asking for anything difficult. You just have to help me find someone.'

'Who?' the man asked, apparently surprised. 'A friend of mine . . . or someone I know?'

'Not a friend of yours. A friend of mine. His name is Massimo Verga and he went missing at the same time as a woman named Simonetta Palladiani.'

Laprua did not bat an eyelid. 'Verga . . . That's a Sicilian surname . . . and I think you're Sicilian, too, there's a hint of it in your accent.'

'Yes.'

'I think that'll make it easier for us to understand each other. But I've never heard of the

378

man you mentioned. I've never heard his name.'

'You have heard of the woman, though,' Ferrara said, with such conviction in his voice that Laprua made no attempt to deny it. They were entering a territory where caution was essential, because it was easy to make the wrong move.

'If you say so. May I smoke a cigar? It helps to refresh my mind. At my age . . .'

'Of course, this is your home. In fact, let me offer you one of mine . . . here.' He took two cigars from a leather case.

Laprua lit his cigar with a gold Cartier lighter which he picked up from a low table. It was one of the few discreet signs of opulence in the room. Everything else had been cleverly chosen to give the impression of a man of modest means. Ferrara stuck with his usual disposable plastic lighter.

The woman returned with the coffee.

'Rinuzza, if you could leave us alone, we have important things to talk about,' he ordered as soon as his wife had finished serving him.

'So maybe you could refresh my memory,' he said to Ferrara. 'Who is this woman and why should I know her?'

'She's the owner, or rather the leaseholder, of the marble quarries contracted out to a company called Mining Extractions Ltd, which is based in Bellomonte di Mezzo. I think that's your home town, isn't it? And you know where the woman is because she was abducted by an Albanian who either still has her or has already given her back.'

Laprua did not move a muscle. He had his hands together and continued to look fixedly at Ferrara.

'It sounds like something from a TV movie,' he

379

said at last. 'You must excuse me . . .'

He was only trying to gain time—it was clear that this policeman knew too much.

'But you know perfectly well that's not the case.'

Another long silence followed.

'Let's say it's the way you say it is . . . why should I help you?'

'Because I know everything . . .'—he looked him straight in the eyes—'. . . Zì Turi.'

The use of that nickname had abruptly moved the game onto another level.

'Or rather, not everything. I don't know where Simonetta is, or if the man who was with her is still alive or not.'

He said this, knowing he was giving his adversary an advantage. In negotiations, you always had to have something to bargain with. The man ought to have had the impression that they were playing on equal terms.

'And what if I told you that I don't know anything about any of this?' Laprua said, though he must have been aware that this was just another pointless delaying tactic.

'Then I'd tell you about some kilos of heroin hidden in blocks of marble currently in storage at the port of Carrara, ready to be sent to the United States. I'd tell you that I'm sorry for you, but those blocks will never get to their destination. And I'd also tell you about three trawlers named after your sons which sometimes fish way out at sea, a long way out, and come back with a large quantity of fish—fish which have already been filled . . . Do you want me to go on?'

But the man had already made a gesture with his hand for Ferrara to stop. 'Chief

380

Superintendent, we're both Sicilians—both men of honour . . . If you think you know all these things, why don't you arrest me?'

'Because I can't.'

'So what do you want from me? Money?'

'You'd make me a millionaire if I wanted, right? No, Zì Turi, that's not why I need your help. I told you: I need you to find someone, that's all.'

'Why are you so interested?'

Ferrara thought before answering. 'Have you ever had a friend?'

Salvatore Laprua looked at him, and it seemed to Ferrara that his eyes clouded over for a moment. 'If I help you, what do I get in return?'

'I can keep you out of this drugs investigation.'

'Am I supposed to believe the police, at my age?' he sneered.

'I'm not asking you to believe the police, Zì Turi. I'm asking you to believe Michele Ferrara.'

Laprua weighed this up for a few moments. 'Ferrara the man may be able to do it, I see it in your eyes. You're a man of respect. But not Ferrara the policeman! You can't betray the State that you serve . . . I could do what I can to find your friend, but after you find him, you won't need me any more.'

'In life there always comes a moment when we have to compromise. I am and will always be a policeman, I'm not pretending I want to go over to your side to buy your help, and you wouldn't believe me anyway. What I will do is break up your racket, and you can't do anything about that. And then what will Zì Turi be? Just an old man living with his wife, as far as I can see. Why should I put an old man in prison?'

381

Could he believe him? Laprua must have been thinking. But above all, did he have any choice?

'If what you're telling me is true, putting the handcuffs on me would make you a hero,' he said after a while. 'Is this friendship worth sacrificing that for?'

'It's worth a lot more.'

In a roundabout way, the old man started putting his cards on the table. 'Chief Superintendent, I was born in Bellomonte di Mezzo. Do you know it? A poor place, a really poor place. No work, not even unpaid work. I grew up poor . . . I had two choices: stay poor or take an oath that bound me for the rest of my life . . . Am I making myself clear?'

'You're making yourself very clear.'

'I chose the second option. I was only young. Over the years, I took other oaths and made other promises . . . Do you understand what I'm saying?'

'Yes.'

'I started to work at an honest job, but then after a while I had to keep the promises I'd made. Those are the kind of promises you keep!'

Or else you're a dead man, Ferrara thought.

'Now you're the one making a promise to me,' Laprua said.

'And it'll be kept. But you have to be honest with me.'

They looked at each other for an unusually long time.

'So be it,' Laprua said, seeming satisfied at last.

'Where is Simonetta Palladiani?'

'The Albanian still has her.'

'Viktor Makregi?'

'You did your work well,' Laprua replied, with

382

genuine admiration.

'Does he still have the man who was with her?' Ferrara asked, somewhat apprehensively.

'Yes, he took the two of them.'

'And are they both . . . still alive?'

'The woman for sure.'

'What about the man?'

'I don't know.'

Ferrara preferred to dismiss that answer. 'Why do you care so much about the woman?'

'Because she has to renew the lease on the marble quarries. More than that, she has to go in person to the town hall to negotiate the renewal of the lease. You probably know that with the new laws the leaseholders don't have the leases forever, and if the woman loses that lease we're screwed! She's already two years late. Her husband managed to put it off, but now the time's up.'

'How did you know about her?'

'Through her husband. I met him when his business was in trouble and I gave him a hand in return for the lease on the quarries. I tell you, it was the best deal of my life. The woman doesn't know anything about it. She signed and that was it, she's not interested in the quarries.'

'And what about Viktor, how did he know?'

'About Simonetta, you mean?' Laprua smiled ruefully. 'By chance. He went to kill Ugo Palladiani over some woman, from what I gathered . . . The guy was always a good for nothing, a wastrel—Palladiani, I mean. To try to save himself, he told the Albanian he could make him rich, gave him the whole story about our agreement and what we're doing in the quarries. The Albanian realised the woman was a good bargaining counter and

383

took her, along with the man who was with her . . . Then he started to make demands.'

'Why didn't he give her back to you, since you'd already agreed to give him ten kilos of heroin?'

'You already know why. Because he didn't get the heroin, and he says it's our fault because the man who was driving the car was one of ours.'

'So he wants more?'

'Lots more . . . he's increased his demands. He wants three times more. And if it goes wrong again this time he says he'll increase it ten times.'

'So now he wants thirty kilos?' Ferrara said, astonished. 'And are you prepared to give it to him?'

'What can I do? If I don't pay he kills the woman and we're out of the quarries. The municipality doesn't want "foreigners". We'd never get the quarries back.'

'But someone like you surely doesn't have to give in to blackmail? Why didn't you take the initiative and go and track down the Albanian?'

'We tried. But he's good at hiding himself.'

'He must have a mobile phone or something?'

Laprua shook his head. 'He's always the one who calls me. I can't call him.'

'How come?'

'He sends me a text message on my mobile. A number from one to five. The numbers correspond to five public telephones in this area, and when I see the number I have to go to that particular phone. He calls me from another public phone, after half an hour, and then every half-hour until he reaches me.'

It was a simple and ingenious system. They would never be able to intercept a conversation between the two men. Ferrara asked Laprua for the locations of the five phones and also his own mobile number. The number corresponded to the one they were already tapping along with his house phone.

'If you want to pay, why haven't you done it?' he asked. 'It's now nearly two weeks since the first attempt misfired.'

The old man looked surprised. 'Do you think I can get hold of thirty kilos of heroin just like that?'

'You have it now, though, don't you?' Ferrara said, thinking of the fish van.

'Yes, I have it now.'

'And does he know?'

'Yes. I told him the new consignment was arriving on Saturday.'

'So he'll get in touch.'

'Oh, yes!'

'Good. How will the swap be done this time?'

'I don't know. He has to give me instructions.'

Ferrara reacted instinctively. 'No. Get him to bring the prisoners to the quarries. Tell him number 225.'

It was the most difficult of the quarries to reach, with only one access road, and so the easiest to keep under surveillance.

'It's not as simple as that.'

'Tell him this time you don't want to take any risks. He has to come and get the drugs himself. Once he has them it's up to him. Don't leave him any choice. Either that or the deal's off. You're good at convincing people, aren't you?'

'It's a big risk. He may think we're setting a trap for him and that we're going to take the drugs back off him as he's leaving. That's our territory after all. What happens if he won't come?'

'Let's deal with that later. But he'll be there, Zì Turi. He doesn't care about those two people, but he's not going to give up on thirty kilos of heroin that easily. He'll take precautions, but he'll come, I'd be prepared to bet on it.'

Later, he would often ask himself why he'd been prepared to gamble like a poker player with the life of the best friend he'd ever had. He was never able to answer his question. It taught him that poker was good training for the police force. And vice versa.

'You may be right . . . And what happens then?'

'We'll be there, waiting for him.'

'If he comes! He could just as easily send someone else, don't you think?'

'That's not the most important thing. The important thing is to get Massimo and Simonetta back . . .'

'But at this point it's better if you get him.'

The words, spoken in a low voice, struck him. 'Are you afraid?'

The old man smiled ironically. 'Afraid? Me? Salvatore Laprua has never been afraid of anyone! I've lived with fear since I was born, now I don't even know what it is any more . . . No, it's not that . . . it's just that we don't like these foreign criminals. They don't have any rules, they don't respect women, they don't keep their word, they kill people for no reason . . . they're turning Italy upside down.'

It might have seemed strange, coming from him, but it wasn't. The fact that he referred to rules that were fast disappearing from the underworld marked Zì Turi out as a boss of the old generation.

A generation that had considered Italy, or at least a part of it, as their own property, and therefore opposed change.

Ferrara smiled at the irony of the bizarre alliance between police and Mafia which he had set up. The forces of order and the underworld united against the foreign invader!

'What now?' Laprua asked.

'Now we wait for his text message.'

The old man nodded and looked at his watch. 'Rina!' he called.

The woman soon appeared.

'Chief Superintendent Ferrara is honouring us with his presence at our table. Get out a bottle of Firriato, please!'

Ferrara hadn't counted on this, but he realised that he couldn't say no.

Before his wife walked out of the room, Laprua added, 'Rinuzza, another thing . . . if anyone asks for me, I'm not feeling well. I don't want to see anyone. The chief superintendent and I still have a lot of things to talk about. He's a Sicilian, did you know that?'

*   *   *

The lunch was all based around authentic Sicilian products, like the wine which Laprua kept praising.

'They make it in our area, in Firriato, near Trapani, a place rich in wines. They make as much wine as Piedmont and Tuscany put together . . . What a taste, eh?'

Ferrara would have preferred not to touch alcohol, but he knew it would be rude of him not

387

to humour his host. As he drank, he realised it would have been unforgivably rude twice over.

'Do you know why it's called that?'

'The wine?'

'The village, too. It's a very old name. To increase the population, the prince who founded the village gave the peasants pieces of land for growing vines, and these pieces of land, which were under his protection, were known as *firriati*.'

'Nice to know.'

When it was time for Ferrara to go, the two men said goodbye with a firm handshake and the understanding that as soon as Laprua received the text message, he would let him know with three rings on his private mobile, Ferrara having left him the number.

'To you, my home is always open!'

These were the words with which Zì Turi bade him goodbye.

38

The following morning, while they were taking stock at Headquarters of the first phase of Operation Stella, assessing the outcome of the house searches, and waiting to interview the men under investigation for criminal conspiracy, an important interview was getting under way in the Prosecutor's Department.

It was exactly nine o'clock when Emilio Zancarotti, escorted by two prison guards, entered the room used for interviewing witnesses who might turn State's evidence. Waiting for him, along with Superintendent Ciuffi, were Deputy Prosecutors Erminia Cosenza and Anna Giulietti.

From the start, Zancarotti demonstrated the clear intention of cooperating with the law in order to be included, together with his family, in a witness protection programme which would guarantee his physical safety.

He started by explaining the drug trafficking and money laundering operation in which he was involved, supplying details both of those members of the Albanian criminal organisation whom he knew, and of how the money had been invested. Then he talked about the abduction of Simonetta Palladiani and was just telling them what he knew about the murder of Claudia Pizzi, which had been ordered by Salvatore Laprua, when Ciuffi felt his mobile vibrate in the inside pocket of his jacket. He left the room to answer it.

It was Serpico.

'A message from the chief. Can you tell Deputy Prosecutor Giulietti that the contact we were waiting for has been made.'

'What does it say?'

'Four.'

'What?'

'Four!' Serpico repeated, and continued, 'Just that. The chief knows what it means and he's gone to see the person . . .'

'Got that, Sergi,' Ciuffi said. 'I'll tell her.'

*   *   *

'Good morning, Zì Turi,' Ferrara said, shaking his hand firmly. 'I came as soon as I heard the three rings.'

'I got the message,' Laprua replied, dressed in his best clothes and ready to go out.

'What does it say?'

'Four.'

Ferrara nodded, pleased that Laprua was keeping to his word: the number corresponded to the text message his men had intercepted. The public phone had been placed under surveillance along with the others.

'Shall we go?' he said.

'There's no rush . . . we still have time and the bar's right near here.'

'But I'd prefer it if we left now,' Ferrara insisted.

'As you wish,' Laprua replied, with a slight smile on his lips. 'Rina, I won't be long,' he said to his wife.

The woman, who had not spoken a word the day before, didn't say anything this time either.

*   *   *

The two plain-clothes officers on guard, one of them pretending to read a newspaper on a bench in the square not far from the apartment, the other lounging in the doorway of a building across the street, smoking a cigarette, were surprised to see Chief Superintendent Ferrara come out with the old Mafia boss.

When they were near the officer in the square, Ferrara apologised to Laprua, asked him to wait, and walked over to the bench.

The officer stood up.

Turning his back on Laprua, Ferrara quickly gave him his instructions and then told him to follow him.

He led him over to Laprua.

'This is one of my men,' he said. 'I trust him. It'll be up to him to protect you when I'm not there.'

The old man made no comment. He realised he was under a kind of house arrest, and could only hope it was just a temporary measure until the Chief Superintendent's friend was recovered. Then, if Ferrara kept his word, it would all be over.

If Ferrara kept his word.

For Ferrara, all that mattered right now was that the old man knew he could not leave home freely.

They continued walking towards the canal.

Laprua walked slowly, stopping from time to time.

His breathing was somewhat laboured, a sign that he was not in very good health.

They walked along the quayside. The place was packed. Locals, holidaymakers and fishermen mingled in a carefree, brightly coloured crowd, and Ferrara wondered if they would be equally carefree knowing that a powerful Mafia boss walked among them, a man who dealt in drugs and death. Was it a good or a bad thing that they didn't know?

They entered a café called the New York and Laprua looked at his watch. There were still ten minutes to go.

'Let's have a coffee,' he suggested, and chose a table.

'It's on me.'

'No. It'll be a pleasure for me to buy you a coffee. You offered me a cigar yesterday . . . and this is where I live, it's up to me.'

When he ordered, he told the young waiter that he'd taken the liberty of giving the telephone number of this café to a friend, and was waiting for him to call, could he please let him know when the call came.

'No problem,' the waiter replied. He did not seem to know Laprua, nor did anyone else in the place.

The call came exactly on time.

Laprua stood up, and when Ferrara did the same he reacted slightly irritably but made no objection. Ferrara followed him at a short distance. The bar was packed and noisy and he couldn't hear much of the conversation, but if necessary he'd be able to hear the recording later.

'Viktor?' Laprua said as soon as he picked up the receiver. Then, a few moments later, 'I have it.'

After that, Ferrara caught only snatches over the din of voices and dishes and orders hurled from the room to the barman.

'. . . you have to come here this time . . .' 'there's no danger . . .' 'that's your problem, once I've handed it over . . .'

The negotiation took a while, and Ferrara felt a pang in his heart when he caught the words '. . . do you still have the man . . .?' but he couldn't read the answer in the old man's glacial expression.

Nor in the way he stared at Ferrara after he had put the phone down and was coming towards him.

'Well?' Ferrara asked.

'Ten o'clock tonight, quarry 225.'

'Does he still have Massimo Verga?'

The man let a few seconds go by, still looking in Ferrara's eyes, enigmatically. 'Yes,' he said at last.

The lump in his throat—and in his soul—

dissolved all at once in an expression that surprised him more than Laprua, but would have moved Petra.

'*Gott sei Dank!*' he exclaimed and closed his eyes.

*   *   *

They had gone back to Laprua's apartment, where they had gone over the preparations. Ferrara did not want to go before making sure there would be no other contacts, even though all the telephones were being tapped and he felt quite calm because everything that Laprua had done so far had showed that he was keeping to his side of the bargain. In any case, he preferred to wait there for Rizzo's call.

Laprua said he was feeling tired and asked permission to go to his bedroom and take a nap. He left his mobile in the living room. Ferrara could only hope he didn't have another one.

Rizzo's call came just after two. 'Chief, it's all arranged. They're ready to move in. Everything's going well at the Prosecutor's Department, too.'

'What happened there?'

'Zancarotti has come clean about everything . . . even the murder of Claudia Pizzi.'

'Excellent, Francesco.'

'They only finished a few minutes ago and Ciuffi is joining me at Headquarters with a copy of the statement and the request from the Prosecutor's Department to the Head of the State Police to provide immediate protection for Zancarotti and his family.'

'Good. We'll talk about that . . . In the

meantime get the men together as agreed. We'll meet at the police station in Carrara at six.'

'Okay, chief.'

Laprua, having finished his nap or perhaps having been disturbed by this conversation, came back into the living room and they went over the strategy.

They fine-tuned the last details and Ferrara said goodbye.

'We'll pick you up about five, is that okay?'

'I'll be waiting.'

39

'A black Ford Fiesta with four people on board, a red lorry with a green tarpaulin, no passengers, just the driver, and behind it a silver Alfa 156 with another four people.'

Superintendent Ascalchi was hidden in the vegetation just after the last bend in the dirt road leading to quarry 225, talking on his two-way radio to Chief Superintendent Ferrara and the two strategically placed patrols, one just above and one just below the Fantiscritti fork, which the Albanians would have to pass on their way back.

'I'll give you the licence numbers . . .'

It was 9.45 p.m.

Ferrara was in the quarry, waiting for the convoy, along with Salvatore Laprua, Superintendent Rizzo, Inspector Sergi, Sergeant Fanti, two constables and one of the workers. The other workers, almost all unskilled labour put in by the Mafia, had been sent home in the afternoon by

Laprua, who had kept just that one worker because he trusted him blindly.

Ferrara and Fanti ran to hide behind the tanker lorry. Laprua stayed where he was, next to the sheet metal prefab which served as an office. Rizzo and the others spread out, although they all remained well within sight, close to Laprua, as if they were his men.

Ferrara would have preferred to be closer to the thick of the action, so that he could control it, but he was too well known and he did not want to take the risk of being recognised by the Albanians.

At last the vehicles appeared: first the Ford Fiesta, then the lorry, and finally the Alfa Romeo. They stopped at the entrance to the clearing.

The scene was illuminated by the moonlight reflected off the white wall of the mountain, as well as the weak lighting from the prefab and the car headlights.

The Albanians got out of their vehicles.

Nine of them in all, armed with pistols and submachine guns. Two of them stayed close to the lorry, ready to open fire at the least sign of danger.

From his position, Ferrara squinted with the effort to make out Massimo's silhouette in one of the vehicles, but they all looked empty. The hostages must be in the lorry, hidden under the tarpaulin. He tried to figure out which of the men was Viktor Makregi, but as far as he could see none of them bore any resemblance to the identikit that had been put together from Elisa Rocca's description.

As Laprua had predicted, the Albanians' boss had been too cautious and mistrustful to show up.

For a few minutes, they were all still, sizing each

other up. Then the Albanians, satisfied that no one on the other side seemed to be carrying a weapon, talked briefly among themselves, and one of them, either the man in charge of the operation or the one who spoke Italian best, started walking towards them.

Laprua did not go to meet him. He stayed where he was and waited for the man to come closer, as if to underline his superior rank in the hierarchy.

'Where are they?' he asked, when the man, who was short and sturdy, with black hair and sky-blue eyes, was near him.

'And heroin?' the Albanian retorted. 'Where is?'

'It's here. We've got it hidden. But first you have to show me the woman at least . . . You're all armed. What's to say you won't take the drugs without keeping your side of the bargain?'

The man made a face. 'Armed, yes . . . we make conditions, not you.'

'You're wrong. If you kill us, you'll never find the drugs. More than that, you'll never get out of here alive. You can only see a few of us. We have other men in hiding,' he bluffed. 'They're on the mountain and on the road, and they're watching you. They have their orders. If all goes well, they won't do anything to you, they won't harm a hair on your heads, but if anything goes wrong . . .'

The Albanian's left eye twitched. 'Wait here,' he said and turned back to confer with his people.

They talked in Albanian for a few minutes which seemed to last forever, then the man came back followed by two others. In the meantime Rizzo and the others started to gather around Laprua.

396

'Not good. If your men wait for us, we do swap then you kill us . . . not good.'

'You have to trust us,' Zì Turi said.

The man translated and the other two burst into a scornful laugh. Then one of them gave him a few curt, almost shouted instructions.

'We do swap, then you come with us.'

Ferrara stiffened. He hadn't foreseen this possibility and he didn't like it.

Rizzo clearly didn't like it either. 'Leave him be,' he said. 'He's an old man. I'll come with you.'

Christ! Ferrara thought. *Has he gone mad?* He knew perfectly well what Rizzo was doing, but he couldn't allow one of his men to sacrifice himself, not even to save Massimo's life. Why wasn't he there instead of Rizzo, as he should have been?

He was about to make the irreparable mistake of coming out into the open when the Albanian's contemptuous reply prevented him.

'You no good. They kill us and also you, who cares? But they not kill him.' He nodded towards Laprua.

Now everything depended on Laprua.

'I'll come with you,' he said.

But Ferrara didn't like this either. He couldn't allow the situation to get out of control, even in the smallest way. He was almost tempted to radio Ascalchi and tell him to come immediately with the teams who were waiting just a few miles down the road, but in all probability that would lead to a bloodbath. For the second time, he just had to resign himself to the situation.

'On one condition,' Rizzo said, freezing the smiles of satisfaction on the Albanians' faces.

'What?'

'We follow him and bring him back when you let him go.'

The man translated. Then the man who was giving instructions exchanged a few words with the others. Finally the one who was translating said, 'You follow us, we kill him.'

Rizzo didn't have time to reply. In a tired but determined voice, Laprua said, 'I guarantee, no one will follow you. Now let's go.' He gave Rizzo a cold look and started walking slowly to the Albanians' cars.

He was made to sit in the back seat of the Alfa, and one of the Albanians sat down next to him.

They lifted the back of the tarpaulin and took out two flat metal boards. The hostages must have been under a false bottom on the bed of the lorry.

Ferrara kept his eyes peeled on the lorry. It was hard to see clearly because of the glare of the headlights, but he had the impression they were bringing a man out first. Yes, it was a man, and Ferrara had to make an effort to hold back a sudden wave of emotion. The man had his hands tied behind his back and a hood over his head. He seemed in a poor physical state, perhaps in pain, at least judging by the way he moved. Unsteady on his legs, he groped for the side of the lorry as if for support.

Then it was the turn of a woman. She, too, had her hands tied behind her back and a hood over her head. She was steadier on her feet than the man, as if she had been treated more gently during her captivity.

Rizzo, Sergi and the two constables approached

them. 'How do we know these are the real hostages?' Rizzo asked the man who had been translating.

'Him,' the Albanian replied, pointing to Laprua, who was made to get out of the car.

Laprua lifted the hood just enough to recognise Simonetta Palladiani. He nodded and returned to the car.

'Your turn,' the Albanian said to Rizzo, who, because he had taken the initiative, must have been considered some kind of big shot, or at least a man the boss trusted.

Rizzo threw a last glance at the hostages, turned round and walked to a point not far from there, where a block of marble had already been separated from the side of the mountain. It had two vertical cuts on the sides and one horizontal cut in the base. Thin metal sheets had been inserted into the cut in the base.

He shouted at the worker to start the hydraulic pumps.

The metal sheets, growing thicker until they were like cushions swollen by the force of the water, slowly lifted the enormous block.

The Albanians were following the operation without understanding what was happening.

When the crack was about a foot wide, the worker shut off the pumps and slid two wooden beams in to support the raised block. Rizzo then put his hand in and started to pull out the small bags which had been hidden in a niche gouged into the base on which the block rested.

Serpico joined them, and they arranged these small bags in two overnight bags, which they then handed over to the Albanians. One of them opened one of the overnight bags, took out a small bag at random, tasted and sniffed the contents, and nodded in approval.

'*Ikim!*' their chief said, after the two overnight bags had been placed in the bed of the lorry.

The cars and the lorry reversed to the edge of the clearing, turned and sped away.

Finally able to come out into the open, feeling doubly liberated, Ferrara ran towards the group, screaming into the microphone of the two-way radio, 'Don't stop them! Let them pass! Alert Superintendent Ciuffi!'

Rizzo almost snatched the radio from his hand when he reached him and said, 'I'll deal with it, chief. You have something else to do.'

*   *   *

Massimo Verga and Simonetta Palladiani stood petrified between the two constables who had untied them and removed their hoods. Massimo had thought he recognised the voice of Superintendent Rizzo, his friend Michele's deputy, and he had felt a glimmer of understanding, but he had feared it was a hallucination, and he'd had a lot of those during this absurd captivity. He had been close to death many times, and had even reached the point where he had longed for it. The one thing that may have saved him was that his tormentors had to keep Simonetta safe. For some reason they needed her. But they certainly hadn't used kid gloves with him.

Now that he could see as well as hear, he managed to get Michele's dear face in focus just for a fraction of a second, before his eyes filled with uncontrollable tears.

Ferrara, too, had come to a halt. Seeing the wounded, suffering face of the man he had feared he would never see again, looking almost ghostly in the moonlight, he had frozen, as if spellbound, as if he wanted to savour the magic of the moment. But it was only for a matter of seconds, then he broke into a run.

They embraced for a long time, in silence. And Ferrara finally realised that he had emerged from the nightmare and come back to real life.

'It's all over . . . you'll soon be good as new,' he said, separating from him at last.

'I knew you wouldn't abandon me, Michele . . . I always knew it. That's why I'm alive.'

'Take them to emergency in Carrara,' Ferrara ordered the two constables, with a glance at the woman. Despite all she had suffered, she still looked beautiful. Then he ran to the car, where Rizzo, Sergi and Fanti were waiting for him.

*   *   *

'Ciuffi is getting the signal loud and clear,' Rizzo said, as Sergi put on speed. They were driving in the direction of Bedizzano.

Tracking devices had been hidden in both overnight bags, which would allow them to follow the path of the target on the screen of a laptop. The Florence *Squadra Mobile* had a van equipped for the purpose, which in the past had allowed them to follow the cars of people suspected of being the accomplices of dangerous fugitives and had eventually led them to the fugitives' hiding places.

The van, with Ciuffi and two technicians on board, had been parked in a clearing about a mile and a half from the quarry, ready for the eventuality that Viktor wouldn't come, which would have made it pointless to arrest the Albanians on the return journey. Now it was following the convoy at a safe distance, and the police cars which had been waiting near the Fantiscritti fork were following Ferrara's car.

'They've checked those licence numbers,' Rizzo said to Ferrara. 'There's no record of the vehicles being stolen. They're registered to various owners in the provinces of Prato and Pistoia. They're checking them out now.'

Ferrara had just dialled his home number, but it was engaged. 'Good, Francesco,' he said. 'But they'll probably turn out to have been stolen anyway . . . If the thefts were recent they may not yet register in the data bank.'

Rizzo nodded.

Ferrara was starting to relax.

If everything went according to plan, the tracking devices would lead them to the lair of the elusive Viktor Makregi.

He still had one thing to do.

He redialled his home number.

*   *   *

Petra answered at the third ring. 'Michele? I was trying to call you . . . well?'

The words—those words he had been hoping to say to her for nearly twenty interminable days—would not come. There was a lump in his throat which held them back.

402

'Hello? Michele? What's happening? *Mein Gott!* Michele, are you still there? *Sag' doch etwas*, I beg you, Michele, say something!!!'

Ferrara made an effort and overcame the emotion of the moment, but his voice sounded rough and tired. 'He's safe and well . . .'

'And what about you?' she asked, and burst into tears that were a mixture of unrestrained joy at the fact that their friend was safe and continued anxiety about her husband.

'I'm okay, don't worry, but I haven't finished yet . . . Take care of Massimo now. They're taking him to hospital in Carrara.'

There was a pause.

Then, almost in a whisper, 'Michele. I love you, Michele . . . Be careful . . . You know you're everything in the world to me!'

'And you to me.'

*　　　*　　　*

Suspicious by nature, the Albanians did not release Salvatore Laprua in Carrara, or even at the entrance to the autostrada.

It was not until they were about a mile past the Montecatini junction that Rizzo's mobile rang. He recognised Ciuffi's number on the screen and answered immediately.

'Yes, Luigi!'

'The signal stopped—in a service area . . . Ah, now they're starting again . . . I'm carrying on . . . I'll leave it to you . . .'

'Okay,' Rizzo said and passed the message onto Ferrara, who ordered Sergi to enter the service area, which could not be far, and then immediately gave instructions to one of the cars following them to do the same, while the others would carry on and join Ciuffi.

They reached the service area a few minutes later.

Salvatore Laprua was standing in the car park of the motorway restaurant.

Ferrara and his men got out of their car and joined him.

He seemed calm.

Pointing towards the officers in the other car, Ferrara said, 'Signor Laprua, you have to go with my men.'

'Are they taking me home?' Laprua asked dubiously, catching something different in Ferrara's tone.

'No, Laprua. Unfortunately, things aren't over for you yet.'

'Shall I handcuff him, chief?' Fanti, who had never before been involved in a field operation, asked diligently.

Surprised, Ferrara nodded, and his secretary performed the task with a rapidity and professionalism which left them all speechless. Simple as the action was, it suggested he had been training for it. The faithful sergeant must have unsuspected ambitions!

Ferrara didn't have time to decide if he was amused or worried by this, because at that moment the old man gave him, Ferrara, a look of such hatred, it was as if he had spat in his face.

He had betrayed his word; he was nothing but a common, despicable police officer.

In his old age, Salvatore Laprua had helped Ferrara to find his friend, who mattered more than

404

all the police operations in the world, and the *Squadra Mobile* to track down a dangerous gang of drug traffickers and bring them to justice. He had not done it out of generosity, altruism or civic duty, that went without saying, but partly because he had been forced to, partly in obedience to an old code of honour and respect. But he was still a criminal. A powerful Mafia boss, a drug trafficker and a murderer.

Ferrara did not consider that he owed him any explanation but, before leaving him, he could not help saying, 'It's not what you think, Zì Turi. I'm not arresting you over the drugs, I gave you my word on that. I'm arresting you for the murder of Claudia Pizzi.'

40

'They left the autostrada at the Pistoia tollbooth, but then got straight back on it,' Ciuffi said. 'Now they're heading back in the same direction they came from.'

It was a few minutes since Ferrara's car had left the service area, preceded by the one with Salvatore Laprua on board, which had set off back to Headquarters at top speed, with the flashing light attached to the roof.

'We'll be there!' Rizzo replied, then passed Ciuffi's message on to Ferrara, adding, 'They may be smarter than we thought. They wouldn't even tell Laprua where they were going.'

While Rizzo had been talking to Ciuffi, Ferrara had received a communication from the operations room at Headquarters, telling him that the three vehicles the Albanians were using had been stolen from their rightful owners in the last twelve hours.

'That's why there was no record in the data bank. It was all calculated. They're professionals . . . Get on to the helicopter pilots. I want them up in the air now. Tell them to stay over the Pistoia area and keep in contact with Ciuffi.'

There were two helicopters, Augusta Bell 212 troop carriers, authorised for night flying. On each of them, apart from the two crew members, were six officers from NOCS, the special forces unit brought in to deal with high-risk situations. Ferrara had sent for them from Rome when he and Rizzo had worked out their plan of action and the possible variations.

They joined the tracker van and the other cars just after the Montecatini Terme tollbooth. Here, the Albanians left the autostrada, and the police vehicles did the same.

'From now on we'd better keep more of a distance. We don't want to risk being spotted at a traffic light or if there's an unexpected traffic jam.'

Rizzo passed Ferrara's instructions on to the other vehicles—especially Ciuffi's van.

'No problem, Francesco,' Ciuffi replied. 'The signal is still loud and clear.'

Montecatini, one of the best known spa resorts in Europe, celebrated for its wonderful thermal park which covers a million and a half square feet in the heart of the town, had in the past few years become a magnet for leading Mafiosi, especially from Catania. Drugs and drug money flowed freely in the local bars and at the famous race course, Il Sesana.

It also attracted organised crime figures from outside Italy. It was a place where it was easy for them to merge into the background amid the fluctuating population of visitors and patients taking the waters. It was also a place where there were many nightclubs employing young girls from Eastern Europe as strippers and hostesses— useful for luring wealthy businessmen, local or otherwise.

So that's where Viktor Makregi hangs out, undisturbed, Ferrara thought with a touch of irony. If you wanted to hide, best to hide in the most obvious place—just like in Edgar Allan Poe's story *The Purloined Letter*, which his friend Massimo had made him read in one of his endless attempts to elevate him culturally!

The messages between Ciuffi and the other cars were coming thick and fast now. The road system was getting denser, and prompt, precise directions were needed. The helicopter pilots were ordered to fly as close as possible to the built-up area of Montecatini, but not over the town itself, until further orders.

*   *   *

Once past the centre of town, the Albanians went in the direction of the village of Montecatini Alta. They drove a few more miles and then turned onto a dirt road which led to a small, isolated two-storey brick house, with a renovated old barn and other outbuildings adjoining it.

Hiding their vehicles in the barn, next to

Simonetta Palladiani's black BMW, the men took out the overnight bags and started towards the house.

Viktor Makregi was waiting for them together with four more men and two beautiful young women, clearly prostitutes. He was tall and fair-haired, with a squashed nose—as ugly as Elisa Rocca had described him.

The Albanian who had made the decisions in the quarry put the two overnight bags on a table. '*Në rrëgull, Viktor, këtu është malli,*' he said, indicating that he had the heroin.

Viktor embraced him. One of the men who had been waiting with him poured the contents of a bottle with the word *Konjak* on it into crystal glasses already laid out on the table.

'*Gëzuar!*' they cried, laughing and toasting their boss.

The only one who did not laugh was Viktor. He never laughed.

*   *   *

Ferrara took a pair of night vision goggles from the boot of the car and put them on. They had approached with their headlights off, shielded by the vegetation, and had stopped at a safe distance from the house. The windows on the ground floor were all lit up despite the hour.

There were no cars parked outside, and no sign of people or animals. But this had to be the place: this was where the signal had stopped, and there were no other houses in the vicinity.

'Let's get ready,' Ferrara ordered. 'Francesco, give the helicopter pilots the coordinates. Tell them to come down over the target in exactly ten minutes. They'll have to light up the area and land their crews. You'll be in charge of them. Split them between the main target and the other buildings.'

The countdown had begun. This wasn't the first time he had directed an operation like this. It required split-second timing, especially in coordinating movement on the ground with that of the helicopters. In order not to alert the occupants of the house, the helicopters would have to arrive only when the target and the surrounding area were completely covered.

In the seven, or at most eight, minutes remaining, the men under his command—twenty in all—put on bulletproof vests, got ready the weapons they had been issued—some had M12 machine pistols, others 92/SB Berettas—and listened to Ferrara's curt, precise orders. They would have to surround the target so that all possible escape routes were closed off, and almost simultaneously break in, counting on the element of surprise.

When everything was clear and they had radio confirmation that the helicopters would be directly overhead in exactly two minutes, Ferrara gave the signal for the final phase of Operation Stella to get under way.

*   *   *

The young women had been sent to bed. The men were still euphoric. They sat around the long rectangular dining table strewn with empty glasses and bottles, the two open overnight bags on one side and on the other the bags of drugs. The drugs

409

were the centre of attention, and the men stared adoringly and drunkenly at them.

But not Viktor Makregi, the only one who never lowered his guard and the only one who had time to raise his rifle—which he had propped against the table beside him—when all hell broke loose, the doors and windows were smashed open, the police yelled at them to surrender, and helicopter blades whirred deafeningly outside.

Without even shouldering his rifle, Viktor fired a first shot just as the door was broken down and a group of policemen appeared in the doorway with Ferrara at their head. The bullet missed Ferrara but hit the left arm of one of the officers behind him. Serpico, once again giving proof of his quick reflexes—the origin, along with his appearance, of the nickname—shoved Ferrara to the floor with his shoulder. There was a burst of fire from one of the M12s, which hit Viktor full in the chest, throwing him to the floor. He died in a vain attempt to get back on his feet.

When they saw that, the members of the gang decided not to offer any resistance. Some tried running into the other rooms, but were soon caught and rounded up.

Ferrara walked up to Viktor and knelt beside him.

He couldn't even count the number of bullets which had hit him. Probably the entire round. He searched in his pockets until he found his wallet.

There were no papers, which was only to be expected, and nothing else that gave the slightest clue to his identity. Only a few hundred-thousand-lire notes and a photograph of Stella beside a rustic hearth with a blazing fire. She was smiling at the camera. On the ring finger of her right hand, he noticed the ring with the fake amethyst. Then he stood up, went to Serpico and, without a word, hugged him tight. He had saved his life.

AUTHOR'S NOTE

Like A Florentine Death, *this is a work of imagination, but with a basis in fact: that of my own professional experience. The methods and procedures depicted are those of the Italian police, with one exception: it would not be permitted to send an undercover police officer into prison in order to gain information. I could have changed the particular episode by again resorting to the device of a bugged cell, which in fact I use elsewhere. I preferred to use the idea of an undercover officer because it made for a more effective narrative, and also to demonstrate that in such cases, the law could be made more flexible, giving wider possibilities to the investigators while still respecting the rights of those under investigation. I have also introduced into this novel certain episodes which I actually experienced, although I have transposed them in time and otherwise changed them for the purposes of the narrative. Apart from these, any reference to real people or events is purely coincidental.*

ACKNOWLEDGEMENTS

I would like to thank all those who have encouraged me with their support and advice, especially those who had already supported me during the writing of *A Florentine Death* and to whom I am now doubly grateful.

I would also like to thank, among others, Rosaria Carpinelli, Paolo Zaninoni, Franco Grassi, Daniele Folli, Sandro Alfieri, Iris Gehrmann, Tony Cartano, Roberta Tana and Romano Paolini, an incomparable guide to the quarries of Carrara and the fascinating secrets of marble.